Praise for RUTH RENDELL And KISSING THE GUNNER'S DAUGHTER

"Fans can breathe again. Wexford is back."
—Julian Symons, *The Sunday Times* (London)

"An intricate story . . . charged with meaning and malice."
—*New York Times Book Review*

"One of the best mystery writers in the world . . . the Wexford series has achieved a depth and a feeling of impending doom seldom seen in the run-of-the-mill procedural."
—*Los Angeles Daily News*

"Rendell is a tirelessly inventive plotter, an unabashed trickster . . . an evocative stylist, a deft character portraitist. . . . No other living mystery writer gives me as much pleasure."
—Dennis Drabelle, *Washington Post Book World*

"Ruth Rendell is regarded by many mystery/detective readers as the best of the best. . . . She weaves a tight, nearly seamless plot, and has created a wonderfully authentic portrait of contemporary English life."
—*Dallas Morning News*

"Starts with a bang. . . . You don't guzzle *Kissing the Gunner's Daughter*. You sip it, savoring the subtle, sophisticated flavor, as rich as a cup of Earl Grey."
—*People*

"Every page is worth reading . . . there are few writers with the skill of Ruth Rendell—or the compassion."
—*Book Page*

more . . .

RUTH RENDELL

KISSING THE GUNNER'S DAUGHTER

THE MYSTERIOUS PRESS

Published by Warner Books

A Time Warner Company

In memory of Eleanor Sullivan,
1928–1991
A great friend.

MYSTERIOUS PRESS EDITION

Copyright © 1992 by Kingsmarkham Enterprises Ltd.
All rights reserved.

Cover Illustration by Mel Odom
Cover Design by Jackie Merri Meyer/Michele Brinson-Dyson

The Mysterious Press name and logo are trademarks of Warner Books, Inc.

Mysterious Press Books are published by
Warner Books, Inc.
1271 Avenue of the Americas
New York, NY 10020

Visit our Web site at
http://pathfinder.com/twep

A Time Warner Company
Printed in the United States of America

Originally published in hardcover by The Mysterious Press.
First Printed in Paperback: May, 1993
10 9 8 7 6

CHAPTER ONE

The thirteenth of May is the unluckiest day of the year. Things will be infinitely worse if it happens to fall on a Friday. That year, however, it was a Monday and quite bad enough, though Martin was scornful of superstition and would have engaged in any important enterprise on May 13 or gone up in a plane without a qualm.

In the morning he found a gun in the case his son took to school. They called it a satchel in his day but it was a briefcase now. The gun was among a jumble of textbooks, dog-eared exercise books, crumpled paper and a pair of football socks, and for a single frightening moment Martin thought it was real. For about fifteen seconds he thought Kevin was actually in possession of the largest revolver he had ever seen, though of a type quite beyond his ability to identify.

Recognizing it as a replica didn't stop him confiscating it.

"You can say goodbye to this weapon, and that's a promise," he said to his son.

The discovery was made in Martin's car just before nine on

the morning of Monday, the thirteenth of May, on the way to Kingsmarkham Comprehensive. Kevin's briefcase, insecurely fastened, had fallen off the back seat and some of its contents had come out onto the floor. Kevin watched in silence and ruefully as the replica gun found its way into the pocket of his father's raincoat. At the school gates he left the car with a muttered goodbye and did not look back.

This was the first link in a chain of events that was to lead to six deaths. If Martin had found the gun before he and Kevin left the house, none of it would have happened. Unless you believe in predestination and fate. Unless you believe our days are numbered. If you can imagine it, if you can perceive them numbered in reverse, from death to birth, Martin had reached Day One.

Monday, May 13.

It was also his day off, this Day One of his life, Detective Sergeant Martin of Kingsmarkham CID. He had come out early, not only to take his son to school—that was incidental, a by-product of leaving the house at ten to nine—but to have a new pair of windscreen wipers fitted to his car. It was a fine morning, the sun shining from a clear sky, and the forecast was good, but still he wouldn't risk taking his wife to Eastbourne for the day with wipers that failed to function.

The people at the garage behaved in typical fashion. Martin had made this arrangement by phone two days before, but that did not prevent the receptionist reacting as if she had never heard of him or the only available mechanic shaking his head and saying it was just possible it could be done, but Les had been called out unexpectedly in an emergency and Martin had better let them phone him. At last Martin got a promise of sorts out of him that the job would be done by ten-thirty.

He walked back along Queen Street. Most of the shops were not yet open. The people he passed were commuters on their way to the British Rail station. Martin could feel the gun in his pocket, its weight and its shape, the heaviness of it weighing him down on the right side. It was a big, heavy gun with a four-inch barrel. If the British police were eventually armed, this was how it would feel. Every day, all day. Martin thought this might have its drawbacks as well as its advantages, but anyway he couldn't imagine such a measure getting through Parliament.

He wondered whether he should tell his wife about the gun, he seriously wondered if he should tell Chief Inspector Wexford. What does a boy of thirteen want with a replica of what was probably a Los Angeles policeman's weapon? He was too old for a toy gun, certainly, but what could be the purpose of a replica except to threaten, to make others believe it was real? And could this be for anything but criminal intent?

There was nothing Martin could do about it at present. Tonight, of course, whatever else he decided on, he must have a serious talk with Kevin. He turned into the High Street, from where he could see the blue-and-gold clock on the tower of St. Peter's Church. It was coming up to half past nine. He was heading for the bank, intending to draw out enough to cover the garage charges as well as pay for petrol, lunch for two, incidental expenses in Eastbourne, and have a bit left over for the next couple of days. Martin distrusted credit cards, and though he possessed one, seldom used it.

His attitude was the same in respect of the cash-point dispenser. The bank was still closed, its solid-oak front door firmly shut, but there was the automatic bank, installed in the granite facade for his convenience. The card was in his wallet and he went so far as to get it out and look at it. Somewhere he had written down the vital number. He tried to recall it—fifty–fifty-three? Fifty-three–oh–five? He heard the bolts being shifted, the hammers in the lock fall. The front door swung inwards to reveal the inner door of glass. The huddle of bank customers who had been waiting when he arrived went in before him.

Martin made his way to one of the counters that were provided with a blotter and a ball-point chained to a false ink-well. He took out his cheque-book. His credit card would not be needed here to back the cheque, for everyone knew him, this was where he had his account, he had already caught the eye of one of the cashiers and said good morning.

Few, however, knew his Christian name. Everyone called him Martin and always had. Even his wife called him Martin. Wexford must know what he was called, and the accounts department must, and whoever attended to such things in this bank. When he was married he had uttered it and his wife had repeated it. Quite a lot of people thought Martin was his first name. The truth of it was a secret he kept locked within himself so far as he could, and now as he made out the cheque he signed it as always, "C. Martin."

Two cashiers dispensed cash or received deposits behind their glass screens: Sharon Fraser and Ram Gopal, each with name tag on the glass and overhead light to flash to indicate they were free. A queue had formed in the area newly designated for waiting in with chrome uprights and turquoise-blue ropes.

"As if we were cattle in a market," said the woman in front of him indignantly.

"Well, it's fairer," said Martin, who was deeply committed to justice and order. "It makes sure no one goes out of turn."

It was then, just after he had spoken, that he was aware of disturbance. There is something very calm in the atmosphere of a bank interior. Money is serious, money is quiet. Frivolity, amusement, swift movement, haste can have no place in this seat of custom, of pecuniary exchange. So the slightest change of mood is felt at once. A raised voice is remarked on, a pin dropped becomes a clatter. Any minor disturbance makes waiting customers start. Martin felt a draught as the glass door was opened too suddenly, he sensed the falling of a shadow as the front door, which was never shut in the daytime, which remained permanently fastened back during opening hours, was carefully and almost silently closed.

He turned round.

Everything happened very fast after that. The man who had closed the door, who had bolted the door, said sharply,

"All get back against the wall. Quickly, please."

Martin noticed his accent, which was unmistakably Birmingham. He would have called it Brum. When the man spoke someone screamed. There is always someone who screams. The man, who had a gun in his hand, said in his flat nasal tones,

"Nothing will happen to you if you do as you're told."

His companion, a boy really, who also had a gun, advanced up the passage of turquoise rope and chrome uprights towards the two cashiers. There was a cashier behind a window to the left of him and another behind a window to the right of him, Sharon Fraser and Ram Gopal. Martin got back against the left-hand wall with all the others from the queue, they were all on that side, covered by the man's gun.

He was pretty sure the gun in the boy's gloved hand was a toy. Not a replica like the one in his own pocket, but a toy. The boy looked very young, seventeen or eighteen, but Martin knew that though not himself old, he was old enough not to be able to tell if someone was eighteen or twenty-four.

Martin made himself memorize every detail of the boy's appearance, not knowing, not dreaming then, that any memorizing he might succeed in doing would be in vain. He noted the man's appearance with similar care. The boy had a curious rash on his face, or spots perhaps. Martin had never seen anything like them before. The man was dark with tattooed hands. He had no gloves on.

The gun in the man's hand might not be real either. It was impossible to tell. Watching the boy, he thought of his own son, not so many years younger. Had Kevin contemplated something of this sort? Martin felt the replica in his pocket, met the eyes of the man fixed on him. He removed his hand and brought it up to clasp the other.

The boy had said something to the woman cashier, to Sharon Fraser, but Martin hadn't caught what it was. They must have some alarm system in the bank. He confessed to himself that he didn't know what kind. A button that responded to foot pressure? Was an alarm going off even now in the police station?

It did not occur to him to commit to memory any details of

the appearance of his companions, those people who cowered with him against the wall. In the event it would have made no difference if he had. All he could have said of them was that none of them was old and they were all but one adults. The exception was the baby in a sling on its mother's chest. They were shadows to him, a nameless, faceless public.

Inside him was rising an urge to do something, take some action. He felt an enormous indignation. It was what he always felt in the face of crime or attempted crime. How dare they? Who did they think they were? By what imagined right did they come in here to take what was not their own? It was the same feeling that he had when he heard or saw that one country had invaded another. How dared they commit this outrage?

The woman cashier was handing over money. Martin didn't think Ram Gopal had set off an alarm. He was staring, petrified with terror or merely inscrutably calm. He was watching Sharon Fraser pressing those keys on the cash dispenser at her side which would tumble out banknotes already packed into fifties and hundreds. The steady eyes watched pack after pack pushed under the glass barrier, through the metal valley, into the greedy gloved hand.

The boy took the money in his left hand, scooping it up, shovelling it into a canvas bag strapped round his hips. He kept the gun, the toy gun, trained on Sharon Fraser. The man was covering the rest of them, including Ram Gopal. It was easy from where he stood. The bank interior was small and they were all huddled together. Martin was aware of the sound of a woman crying, quiet sobs, soft whimpers.

His indignation threatened to spill over. But not yet, not quite yet. It came to him that if the police had been authorized to bear arms he might now be so used to them that he would be able to tell a real gun from a false.

The boy had moved to stand in front of Ram Gopal. Sharon Fraser, a young plump girl whose family Martin slightly knew, whose mother had been at school with his wife, sat with her hands in fists and her long red nails digging into the palms. Ram Gopal had begun passing packs of notes under the glass barrier. It was nearly over. In a moment it would all be over and he, Martin, would have done nothing.

He watched the dark stocky man retreat towards the doors. It made very little difference, they were still all covered by his gun. Martin slid his hand down to his pocket and felt there Kevin's huge weapon. The man saw but did nothing. He had to get that door open, the bolts drawn, for them to make a get-away.

Martin had known at once that Kevin's gun wasn't real. By the same process of recognition and reasoning, if not from experience, he knew this boy's gun wasn't real either. The clock on the wall above the cashier's, behind the boy's head, pointed to nine forty-two. How swiftly it had all happened! Only half an hour before he had been in that garage. Only forty minutes ago he had found the replica in the satchel and confiscated it. He put his hand into his pocket, snatched Kevin's gun and shouted,

"Drop your guns!"

The man had turned for a split second to unbolt the door. He backed against it, holding the gun in both hands like a gangster in a film. The boy took the last pack, swept it into his canvas bag. Martin said it again.

"Drop your guns!"

The boy turned his head slowly and looked at him. A woman made a strangled whimpering sound. The feeble little gun in the boy's hand seemed to tremble. Martin heard the front door crash back against the wall. He didn't hear the man go, the man with the real gun, but he knew he had gone. A gust of wind blew through the bank. The glass door slammed. The boy stood staring at Martin with strange impenetrable, perhaps drugged, eyes, holding his gun as if he might at any moment let it fall, as if he were carrying out a test to see how loosely he could suspend it from a finger before it dropped.

Someone came into the bank. The glass door swung inwards. Martin shouted, "Get back! Call the police! Now! There's been a robbery."

He took a step forwards, towards the boy. It was going to

be easy, it *was* easy, the real danger was gone. His gun was trained on the boy and the boy was trembling. Martin thought, I will have done it, I alone, my God!

The boy pressed the trigger and shot him through the heart.

Martin fell. He did not double up but sank to the floor as his knees buckled under him. Blood came from his mouth. He made no sound beyond a little cough. His body crumpled, as in some slow-motion film, his hands grasped at the air, but with weak graceful movements, and gradually he collapsed into utter stillness, his eyes cast up to stare unseeing at the bank's vaulted ceiling.

For a moment there had been silence, then the people burst into noise, into screams and shouts. They crowded round the dying man. Brian Prince, the bank manager, came out from the office behind and members of his staff came with him. Ram Gopal was already on the phone. The baby began to utter heart-rending desperate cries as its mother screamed and gibbered and flung her arms round the sling and the small body. Sharon Fraser, who had known Martin, came out into the bank and knelt beside him, weeping and twisting her hands, crying out for justice, for retribution.

"Oh, God, oh, God, what have they done to him? What's happened to him? Help me, someone, don't let him die . . ."

But by then Martin was dead.

CHAPTER TWO

Martin's Christian name appeared in the newspapers. It was spoken aloud that evening on the BBC's early-evening news and again at nine o'clock. Detective Sergeant Caleb Martin, aged thirty-nine, married and the father of one son.

"It's a funny thing," said Inspector Burden, "you won't credit it but I never knew he was called that. Always thought he was John or Bill or something. We always called him Martin like a first name. I wonder why he had a go? What got into him?"

"Courage," said Wexford. "Poor devil."

"Foolhardiness." Burden said it ruefully, not unkindly.

"I suppose courage never has much to do with intelligence, does it? Not much to do with reasoning or logic. He didn't give the pale cast of thought a chance to work."

He had been one of them, one of their own. Besides, to a policeman there is something peculiarly horrible in the murder of a policeman. It is as if the culpability is doubled and the

9

worst of all crimes compounded because the policeman's life, ideally, is dedicated to the prevention of such acts.

Chief Inspector Wexford did not expend more effort in seeking Martin's killer than he would have in the hunt for any other murderer, but he felt more than usually emotionally involved. He hadn't even particularly liked Martin, had been irritated by his earnest, humourless endeavours. "Plodding" is an adjective, pejorative and scornful, often applied to policemen, and it was the first which came to mind in Martin's case. *"The Plod"* is even a slang term for the police force. But all this was forgotten now Martin was dead.

"I've often thought," Wexford said to Burden, "what a poor piece of psychology that was on Shakespeare's part when he said that the evil that men do lives after them, the good is oft interred with their bones. Not that poor Martin was evil, but you know what I mean. It's the good things about people that we remember, not the bad. I remember how punctilious he was and how thorough and—well, dogged. I feel quite sentimental about him when I'm not bloody angry. But God, I'm so bloody angry I can hardly see out of my eyes when I think of that kid with the spots shooting him in cold blood."

They had begun by the most careful in-depth interviewing of Brian Prince the manager, and Sharon Fraser and Ram Gopal the cashiers. The customers who had been in the bank—that is, those customers who had come forward or they had been able to find—were seen next. No one was able to say exactly how many people had been in the bank at the time.

"Poor old Martin would have been able to tell us," Burden said. "I'm sure of that. He knew, but he's dead and if he wasn't, none of it would matter."

Brian Prince had seen nothing. The first he knew of it was when he heard the boy fire the shot that killed Martin. Ram Gopal, one of Kingsmarkham's very small Indian immigrant population, of the Brahmin caste from the Punjab, gave Wexford the best and fullest description of both men. With descriptions like that, Wexford said afterwards, it would be a crime not to catch them.

"I watched them very carefully. I sat quite still, conserving my energy, and I concentrated on every detail of their appearance. I knew, you know, that there was nothing I could do, but that I could do and I did it."

Michelle Weaver, on her way at the time to work in the travel agency two doors away, described the boy as between twenty-two and twenty-five, fair, not very tall, with bad acne. The mother of the baby, Mrs. Wendy Gould, also said the boy was fair but a tall man, at least six feet. Sharon Fraser thought he was tall and fair but she had particularly noticed his eyes, which were a bright pale-blue. All three of the men said the boy was short or of medium height, thin, perhaps twenty-two or twenty-three. Wendy Gould said he looked ill. The remaining woman, Mrs. Barbara Watkin, said the boy was dark and short with dark eyes. All agreed he had a spotty face, but Barbara Watkin was doubtful about the cause being acne. More like a lot of small birthmarks, she said.

The boy's companion was described invariably as much older than he, ten years older or, according to Mrs. Watkin, twenty years older. He was dark, some said swarthy, and with hairy hands. Only Miche le Weaver said he had a mole on his left cheek. Sharon Fraser thoug ᵗ he was very tall, but one of the men described him as "tiny" and another as "no taller than a teenager."

Ram Gopal's confidenc. and concentration inspired belief in Wexford. He described the boy as about five feet eight, very thin, blue-eyed, fair-haired and with acnaceous spots. The boy wore blue-denim jeans, a dark T-shirt or sweater and a black leather jacket. He had gloves on, a point no other witness thought to mention.

The man wore no gloves. His hands were covered in dark hairs. The hair of his head was dark, nearly black, but receding severely, giving the effect of a superlatively high forehead. He was at least thirty-five and dressed similarly to the boy except that his jeans were of some dark colour, dark grey or dark brown, and he wore some sort of brown pullover.

The boy had only spoken once, to tell Sharon Fraser to hand

over the money. Sharon Fraser was unable to describe his voice. Ram Gopal gave his opinion that the accent was not cockney but not an educated voice either, probably from south London. Could it be the local accent, "Londonized" as it was by the spread of the capital and by television? Ram Gopal admitted that it could be. He was unsure about English accents, which Wexford discovered by putting him to the test and finding he defined a Devon accent as Yorkshire.

So how many people were in the bank? Ram Gopal said fifteen including the staff and Sharon Fraser said sixteen. Brian Prince didn't know. Of the customers, one said twelve and another said eighteen.

It was clear that, however many or however few there had been in the bank, not all had come forward in response to police appeals. During the time between the raiders' departure and the arrival of the police, perhaps as many as five people had quietly left the bank while the rest concerned themselves with Martin.

As soon as they saw their opportunity, they made their escape. Who could blame them, especially if they had seen nothing relevant? Who wants to be drawn into a police investigation if there is nothing to contribute? Even if someone does have something to contribute, but something small and trivial which other, more observant eyewitnesses can supply?

For peace of mind and a quiet life, how much simpler to slip away and continue on your way to work or the shops or home. Kingsmarkham Police faced the fact that four or five people had kept mum, knew something or nothing but kept silent and hidden. All the police knew was that not one of these people, four or five or perhaps only three, were known by sight to the bank staff. So far as they could remember. Neither Ram Gopal nor Sharon Fraser could remember a face in that queue in the roped-off area that they recognized. Apart, that is, from those regular customers who had all remained inside the bank after Martin's death.

Martin himself had of course been known to them, and Michelle Weaver and Wendy Gould among others. Sharon

Fraser could say only this: she had an impression that the missing bank customers were all men.

The most sensational piece of evidence given by any of the witnesses was that of Michelle Weaver. She said she had seen the boy with acne drop his gun just before he escaped from the bank. He had thrown it onto the floor and run away.

At first, Burden hardly believed she expected him to take this statement seriously. It seemed bizarre. The act which Mrs. Weaver described he had read of somewhere, or been taught, or gleaned from some lecture. It was a classic Mafia technique. He even said to her that they must have read the same book.

Michelle Weaver insisted. She had seen the gun skid across the floor. The others had crowded round Martin, but she had been the last in the line of people the gunman had directed to stand against the wall, so therefore the farthest from Martin, who had been at the head of it.

Caleb Martin had dropped the gun with which he made his brave attempt. His son Kevin later identified it as his personal property, taken from him by his father in the car that morning. It was a toy, a crude copy with several design inaccuracies, of a Smith & Wesson Model 10 Military and Police Revolver with four-inch barrel.

Several witnesses had seen Martin's gun fall. A building contractor called Peter Kemp had been standing next to him and he said Martin dropped the gun at the moment the bullet struck him.

"Could it have been Detective Sergeant Martin's gun that you saw, Mrs. Weaver?"

"Pardon?"

"Detective Sergeant Martin dropped the gun he was holding. It skidded across the floor among people's feet. Could you be mistaken? Could it have been that gun which you saw?"

"I saw the boy throw it down."

"You said you saw it skid across the floor. Martin's gun skidded across the floor. There were two guns skidding across the floor?"

"I don't know. I only saw one."

"You saw it in the boy's hand and then you saw it skid across the floor. Did you actually see it leave the boy's hand?"

She was no longer sure. She thought she had seen it. Certainly she had seen it in the boy's hand and then seen a gun on the floor, skating across the shiny marble floor among the people's feet. An idea came to her that silenced her for a moment. She looked hard at Burden.

"I wouldn't go into court and swear I saw it," she said.

In the months that followed, the hunt for the men who had carried out the Kingsmarkham bank robbery became nationwide. Gradually, all the stolen banknotes turned up. One of the men bought a car for cash before the numbers of the missing notes were circulated and paid out six thousand pounds to an unsuspecting second-hand car dealer. This was the older, darker man. The car dealer furnished a detailed description of him and gave, of course, his name. Or the name the man had given him—George Brown. After that, Kingsmarkham Police referred to him as George Brown.

Of the remaining money, just under two thousand pounds came to light wrapped in newspapers in a town waste-disposal dump. The missing six thousand was never found. It had probably been spent in dribs and drabs. There was not much risk in doing that. As Wexford said, if you give the girl on the checkout two tenners for your groceries she doesn't do a spot-check on the numbers. All you need do is be prudent and not go there again.

Just before Christmas, Wexford went north to interview a man on remand in prison in Lancashire. It was the usual thing. If he co-operated and offered helpful information, things might go rather better for him at his trial. As it was, he was likely to go down for seven years.

His name was James Walley and he told Wexford he had done a job with George Brown, a man whose real name was George Brown. It was one of his past offences he intended to ask to be taken into consideration. Wexford saw the real George Brown at his home in Warrington. He was quite an elderly man, though probably younger than he looked, and he walked with a limp, the result of falling off a scaffold some years before when attempting to break into a block of flats.

After that Kingsmarkham Police started talking of their wanted man as o.k.a. (otherwise known as) George Brown. Of the boy with acne there was never any sign, not a whisper. In the underworld he was unknown, he might have died for all that was heard of him.

O.k.a. George Brown surfaced again in January. He was George Thomas Lee, arrested in the course of a robbery in Leeds. This time it was Burden who went up to see him in the remand prison. He was a small, squinting man with cropped carrotty hair. The tale he spun Burden was of a spotty boy he had met in a pub in Bradford who had boasted of killing a policeman somewhere in the south. He named one pub, then forgot it and named another, but he knew the boy's full name and address. Already sure that the motive behind all this was revenge for some petty offence, Burden found the boy. He was tall and dark, an unemployed lab technician with a record as spotless as his face. The boy had no memory of meeting o.k.a. George Brown in any pub, but he did remember calling the police when he found an intruder in the last place he worked at.

Martin had been killed by a shot from a Colt Magnum .357 or .38 revolver. It was impossible to tell which because although the cartridge was a .38, the .357 takes both .357 and .38 cartridges. Sometimes Wexford worried about that gun, and once he dreamt he was in the bank watching two revolvers skating round the marble floor while the bank customers stared like spectators at some arena event. Magnums on Ice.

He went to talk to Michelle Weaver himself. She was very obliging, always willing to talk, showing no signs of impatience. But many months had gone by and the memory of what she had seen that morning when Caleb Martin died was necessarily growing dim.

"I can't have seen him throw it down, can I? I mean, I must have imagined that. If he'd thrown it down it would have been there and it wasn't, only the one the policeman dropped."

"There was certainly only one gun when the police arrived."

15

Wexford talked to her conversationally, as if they were equals in knowledge and sharers of inside information. She warmed to this, she grew confident and eager. "All that we found was the toy gun D.S. Martin took away from his son that morning. Not a copy, not a replica, a child's toy."

"And was that really a toy I saw?" She marvelled at it. "They make them look so real."

Another conversational interview, this time with Barbara Watkin, revealed not much more than her obstinacy. She was tenacious about her description of the boy's appearance.

"I know acne when I see it. My eldest son had terrible acne. That wasn't what the boy had. I told you, it was more like birthmarks."

"The scars of acne, perhaps?"

"It wasn't anything like that. You have to picture those strawberry marks people have, only these were the purple kind, and all blotched, dozens of them."

Wexford asked Dr. Crocker and Crocker said no one had birthmarks of that description, so that was the end of that.

There was not much more to say, nothing left to ask. It was the end of February when he talked to Michelle Weaver and the beginning of March when Sharon Fraser came up with something she had remembered about one of the missing men among the bank customers. He had been holding a bunch of banknotes in his hand and they were green notes. No English banknotes were green since the pound note had been replaced by a coin several years before. She could remember nothing else about this man—did it help?

Wexford couldn't say it did much. But you don't discourage this kind of public-spiritedness.

Nothing much else happened until the 999 call came on March 11.

CHAPTER THREE

"They're all dead." The voice was a woman's and young, very young. She said it again. "They're all dead," and then, "I'm going to bleed to death!"

The operator who had taken the call, though not new to the job, said afterwards she turned cold at those words. She had already uttered the formula of asking if the caller wanted police, the fire service or an ambulance.

"Where are you?" she said.

"Help me. I'm going to bleed to death."

"Tell me where you are, the address . . ."

The voice started giving a phone number.

"The address, please . . ."

"Tancred House, Cheriton. Help me, please help me . . . Make them come quickly . . ."

The time was eight twenty-two.

The forest covers an area of something like sixty square miles. Much of it is coniferous, man-made woods of Scots pine and larch, Norway spruce and occasionally a towering Douglas fir. But to the south of this plantation a vestige of the ancient forest of Cheriton remains, one of seven that existed in the County of Sussex in the Middle Ages, the others being Arundel, St. Leonard's, Worth, Ashdown, Waterdown and Dallington. Arundel excepted, they once all formed part of a single great forest of thirty-five hundred square miles which, according to the Anglo-Saxon Chronicle, stretched from Kent to Hampshire. Deer roamed it and in the depths, wild swine.

The small area of this which remains is woodland of oak, ash, horse chestnut and sweet chestnut, birch, and the wayfaring-tree, which clothes the southern slopes and borders on a private estate. Here, where all was parkland until the early thirties, green turf on which grew Douglas firs, cedars and the rarer wellingtonia, an occasional half-acre of mature woodland, a new forest was planted by the new owner. The roads up to the house, one of them no more than a narrow track, wind through the woods, in places between steep banks, in others through groves of rhododendron, past trees in the prime of life and here and there overshadowed by an ancient giant.

Sometimes fallow deer can be seen among the trees. Red squirrels have been sighted. The blackcock is a rarity, the Dartford warbler common, and hen-harriers are winter visitors. In late spring, when the rhododendrons come out, the long vistas are rosy pink under a green mist of unfolding beech leaves. The nightingale sings. Earlier, in March, the woods are dark yet glowing with the coming life, and underfoot the ground is a rich ginger-gold from beech mast. The beech trunks shine as if their bark were laced with silver. But at night there is darkness and silence, a deep quiet fills the woods, a forbidding hush.

The land is not fenced but there are gates in the boundary hedge. All are of red cedar and five-barred. Most give access only to paths, impassable except on foot, but the main gate closes off the woods from the road that turns northwards from the B 2428, linking Kingsmarkham with Cambery Ashes. There is a sign, a plain board attached to a post and bearing the words, TANCRED HOUSE, PRIVATE ROAD, PLEASE CLOSE THE GATE, which stands to the left of it. The gate is required to be kept closed, though no key, code or device is needed to open it.

On that Tuesday evening, eight fifty-one on March 11, the gate was shut. Detective Sergeant Vine got out of the first car and opened it, though he was senior to most of the officers in the two cars. He had come to Kingsmarkham to replace Martin. There were three vehicles in the convoy, the last being the ambulance. Vine let them all through and then he closed the gate once more. It was not possible to drive very fast, but once they were inside, on this private land, Pemberton went as fast as he could.

Later they were to learn, using it daily, that this road was always known as the main drive.

It was dark, sunset two hours past. The last street lamp was a hundred yards down the B 2428 before the gate. They relied on their headlights alone, lights which showed up the mist that drifted through the woods as streamers of greenish fog. If eyes looked out of the forest, the lights did not show them up. The tree trunks were colonnades of grey pillars, swathed in scarves of mist. In the depths between was impenetrable dark.

No one spoke. The last person to speak had been Barry Vine when he said he would get out and open the gate. Detective Inspector Burden said nothing. He was thinking about what they would find at Tancred House and telling himself not to anticipate, for speculation was useless. Pemberton had nothing to say and would not have considered it his place to initiate a conversation.

In the van behind were the driver, Gerry Hinde, a scene-of-crimes officer called Archbold with a photographer called Milsom, and a woman officer, Detective Constable Karen Malahyde. The paramedics in the ambulance were a woman and a man and the woman was driving. A decision had been taken at an early stage to display no blue lamps and sound no sirens.

The convoy made no sound but for that produced by the engines of the three vehicles. It wound through the avenues of trees where the banks were high and where the road passed across sandy plateaux. Why the road should wind like this was a mystery, for the hillside was shallow and there were no features to avoid except perhaps the isolated giant trees, invisible in the dark.

The whim of a forest planter, thought Burden. He tried to remember if he had seen these woods in their younger days but he did not know the region well. Naturally, he knew who owned them now, everyone in Kingsmarkham knew that. He wondered if the message left for Wexford had reached him yet, if the Chief Inspector was even now on his way, in a car a mile or two behind them.

Vine was staring out of the window, pressing his nose against the glass, as if there were something to be seen out there besides darkness and mist and the verges ahead, yellowish and shining and wet-looking in the headlights. No eyes looked out from the depths, no twin points of green or gold, and there was no movement of bird or animal. Even the sky was not to be discerned here. The tree trunks stood separated like columns, but their top branches seemed to form an unbroken ceiling.

Burden had heard there were cottages on the estate, houses to accommodate whatever staff Davina Flory kept. These would be near Tancred House, no more than five minutes' walk away, but they passed no gates, no paths leading into the woods, saw no distant lights, dim or bright, on either side. This was fifty miles from London but it might have been northern Canada, it might have been Siberia. The woods seemed endless, rank upon rank of trees, some of them forty feet in height, others half-grown but tall enough. As each bend was turned and you knew that round this corner must be an opening, must be a break, a sight of the house must at last be granted, there were only more trees, another platoon in this army of trees, still, silent, waiting.

He leaned forward and said to Pemberton, his voice sounding loud in the silence, "How far have we come from the gate?"

Pemberton checked. "Two miles and three-tenths, sir."

"It's a hell of a way, isn't it?"

"Three miles according to the map," said Vine. He had a whitish squash mark on his nose where it had pressed against the window.

"It seems to be taking hours."

Burden was grumbling like this, peering out at the endless groves, the infinite reaches of cathedral-like columns, when the house came into view, reared suddenly into sight with an effect of shock.

The woods parted as if a curtain were drawn aside, and there it was, brilliantly lit as for some stage set, bathed in a flood of artificial moonlight, greenish and cold. It was strangely dramatic. The house gleamed, shimmered in a bay of light, thrown into relief against a misty dark well. The facade itself was punctured with lights, but orange-coloured, the squares and rectangles of lighted windows.

Burden had not expected light, but dark desolation. This scene before him was like the opening shot of a film about characters in a fairy story living in a remote palace, a film about Sleeping Beauty. There should have been music, a soft but sinister melody, with horns and drums. The silence made you feel an essential was missing, something had gone disastrously wrong. The sound was lost without fusing the lights. He saw the woods close in again as the road wound into another loop. Impatience seized him. He wanted to get out and run to the house, penetrate it, break in there to find the worst, what the worst was, and he kept his seat petulantly.

That first glimpse had been a brief foretaste, a trailer. This time the woods fell away for good, the headlights showed the road crossing a grassy plain on which a few great trees stood. The occupants of the cars felt very exposed as they began to cross this plain, as if they were the outriders of an invading force with an ambush ahead of them. The house on the other side of it was now illuminated with absolute clarity, a fine country manor that looked Georgian but for its pitched roof and candlestick chimneys. It looked very large and grand and also menacing.

A low wall divided its immediate surroundings from the rest

of the estate. This ran at right angles to the road they were on, bisecting the treeless open land. A left-hand turn branched off just before the gap in the wall. It was possible to go straight on or turn left by this road, which looked as if it would take you to the side and back of the house. The wall itself concealed the floodlights.

"Go straight ahead," said Burden.

They passed through the gap, between stone posts with ogee tops. Here the flagstones began, a vast space paved in Portland stone. The stone was golden-grey, pleasingly uneven, too close-set for even moss to spring between. Plumb in the centre of this courtyard was a large circular pool, coped in stone, and standing in the midst of it, on a stone island laden with flowers and broad-leaved plants in varied marbles, green and pinkish and bronze-grey, was a group of statuary—a man, a tree, a girl—in grey marble, that might or might not have been a fountain. If it was, it was not at present playing. The water lay stagnant, unruffled.

Shaped like an E without the central crosspiece or like a rectangle missing one long side, the house stood unadorned beyond this great plain of stone. Not a creeper softened its smooth plasterwork or shrub grew nearby to compromise its bands of rusticated stone. The arc lamps on this side of the wall showed up every fine line and every tiny pit on its surface.

The lights were on everywhere, in the two side wings, in the central range and the gallery above. They glowed behind drawn curtains, pink or orange or green according to the colours of the curtains, and they shone, too, out of uncurtained panes. Light from the arc lamps competed with these softer-glowing colours but was not able entirely to quell them. Everything was quite motionless, windless, giving the impression that not only the air but time itself had been stilled.

Though, as Burden asked himself afterwards, what was there that could have moved? If a gale-force wind had been blowing, there was nothing here for it to move. Even the trees were behind them now and thousands more beyond the house, lost in that cavern of darkness.

The convoy drove up to the front door, passing to the left of the pool and the statuary. Burden and Vine threw open their doors and Vine made it first to the front door. This was approached by two wide shallow stone steps. If there had ever been a porch it was gone now, and all that remained on either side of the door were a couple of unfluted recessed columns. The front door itself was gleaming white, shining in this light as if the paint on it were still wet. The bell was the kind you pull, a sugar-stick rod of wrought iron. Vine pulled it. The sound it made when he tugged at the spiral rod must have clanged through the house, for it was clearly audible to the paramedics getting out of their ambulance twenty yards away.

He pulled at the bell a second and a third time and then he banged on the brass knocker. The door furniture gleamed like gold in the bright light. Remembering the voice on the phone, the woman who had cried for help, they listened for a sound. There was nothing. Not a whimper, not a whisper. Silence. Burden banged on the knocker and flapped the letter box. Nobody thought of a back door, of what numerous rear doors there might be. No one considered that one might be open.

"We're going to have to break in," Burden said.

Where? Four broad windows flanked the front door, two on each side of it. Inside could be seen a kind of outer hall, an orangery with bay trees and lilies in tubs on the mottled white marble floor. The lily leaves glistened under the light from two chandeliers. What was beyond, behind an arch, could not be seen. It looked warm and still in there, it looked civilized, a well-appointed gentle place, the home of rich people fond of luxury. In the orangery, against the wall, was a mahogany-and-gilt console table with a chair placed negligently beside it, a spindly chair with a red velvet seat. From a Chinese jar on the table spilled out the long tendrils of a trailing plant.

Burden turned away from the front door and began to walk across the stone-flagged plain of this vast courtyard. The light was like moonlight much magnified, as if the moon had doubled or reflected itself in some celestial mirror. Afterwards, he said to Wexford that the light made it worse. Darkness would have been natural, he could have handled darkness more comfortably.

He approached the west wing, where the window at the end, a shallow bow, had its base only a foot above the ground. The lights were on inside, reduced from where he was to a soft green glow. The curtains were drawn, their pale lining towards the glass, but he guessed that on the other side they must be of green velvet. Later he was to wonder what instinct had led him to this window, to reject those nearer and come to this one.

A premonition had come to him that this was it. In there was what there was to see, to find. He tried to look through the knife-blade sliver of bright light that was the gap between the edges of those curtains. He could see nothing but a dazzlement. The others were behind him, silent but close behind him. To Pemberton he said, "Break the window."

Pemberton, cool and calm, prepared for this, broke the glass in one of the largish rectangular panes with a car spanner. He broke one of the flat panes in the centre of the window, put his hand through the space, lifted the curtain aside, unlocked the lower sash and raised it. Ducking under the bar, Burden went in first, then Vine. Heavy thick material enveloped them and they pushed it away from their faces, drawing the curtain back with a swish, its rings making a gentle clicking sound along the pole.

They stood a few feet into the room, on thick carpet, and saw what they had come to see. From Vine came a strong indrawing of breath. No one else made a sound. Pemberton came through the window and Karen Malahyde with him. Burden stepped aside to allow them space, aside but not for the moment forwards. He did not exclaim. He looked. Fifteen seconds passed while he looked. His eyes met Vine's blank stare, he even turned his head and noted, as if on another plane somewhere, that the curtains were indeed of green velvet. Then he looked again at the dining table.

It was a large table, some nine feet long, laid with a cloth and with glass and silver. There was food on it, and the table-cloth was red. It looked as if it were meant to be red, the material scarlet damask, except that the area nearest the window was white. The tide of red had not reached so far.

Across the deepest-scarlet part someone lay slumped forward, a woman who had been sitting or standing at that table. Opposite, flung back in a chair, another woman's body was slung, the head hanging and the long dark hair streaming, her dress as red as that table-cloth, as if it had been worn to match.

These two women had been sitting facing one another across the precise middle of the table. From the plates and the place settings, it was apparent someone else had sat at the head and someone else at the foot, but no one was there now, dead or alive. Just the two bodies and the scarlet spread between them.

There was no question but that the two women were dead. The elder, she whose blood had dyed the cloth red, had a bullet wound in the side of her head. You could see that without touching her and no one touched her. Half her head and the side of her face were destroyed.

The other had been shot in the neck. Her face, curiously undamaged, was as white as wax. Her eyes were wide open, fixed on the ceiling, where a sprinkling of dark spots might have been bloodstains. Blood had splashed the dark-green-papered walls, the green-and-gold lampshades in which the bulbs remained alight, stained the dark-green carpet in black blotches. A drop of blood had struck a picture on the wall, trickled down the pale thick oil paint and dried there.

On the table were three plates with food on them. On two of them the food remained there, cold and congealing, but recognizably food. The third was drenched with blood, as if sauce had been poured liberally over it, as if a bottle of sauce had been emptied onto it for some horror meal.

There was doubtless a fourth plate. The woman whose body had fallen forward, whose blood had fountained and seeped everywhere, had plunged her mutilated head into it, her dark hair, grey-streaked, had been loosened from a knot on the nape and spread out among dining litter, a salt cellar, an overturned glass, a crumpled napkin. Another napkin, soaked in blood, lay on the carpet.

A trolley with food on it was drawn up close to where the

younger woman was, she whose hair streamed over the back of her chair. Her blood had splashed the white cloths on it and the white dishes and sprayed across a basket of bread. The drops of blood sprinkled the slices of French bread in speckles like currants. There was some sort of pudding in a large glass dish, but Burden, who had looked at everything without his gorge rising, could not look at what the blood had done to that.

It was a long time, an age, since he had felt actual physical nausea at such sights. On the other hand, had he ever before seen such a sight as this? He felt a blankness, a sensation of being stricken dumb, of all words being useless. And, although the house was warm, of sudden bitter cold. He took the fingers of his left hand in the fingers of his right and felt their iciness.

He imagined the noise there must have been, the huge noise of a gun barrel emptying itself—a shotgun, a rifle, something more powerful? The noise roaring through the silence, the peace, the warmth. And those people sitting there, talking, halfway through their meal, disturbed in this terrible untimely way . . . But there had been *four* people. One on either side and one at the head and one at the foot. He turned and exchanged another blank glance with Barry Vine. Each was aware that the look he gave the other was of despair, of sickness. They were dazed by what they saw.

Burden found himself moving stiffly. It was as if he had lead weights on his feet and hands. The dining-room door was open and he passed slowly through it into the house, a constriction in his throat. Afterwards, several hours later, he reminded himself that then, during those minutes, he had forgotten about the woman who had phoned. The sight of the dead had made him forget the living, the possibly still living . . .

He found himself not in the orangery but a majestic hall, a large room whose ceiling, lanterned high up in the centre of the roof of the house, was also lit by a number of lamps but less brightly. There were lamps with silver bases and lamps with glass and ceramic bases, their shades in colours of apricot and a deep ivory. The floor was of polished wood, scattered with rugs that Burden perceived as oriental, rugs patterned in lilac and red and brown and gold. A staircase ascended out of this hall, branching into two at first-floor level, where the double set of stairs mounted out of a gallery balustered with Ionic columns. At the foot of the staircase, spread-eagled across the lowest treads, lay the body of a man.

He too had been shot. In the chest. The stair carpet was red and his shed blood showed like dark wine stains. Burden breathed in and, finding that he had put up his hand to cover his mouth, resolutely brought it down again. He looked round him with a slow deliberate gaze and then he saw a movement in the far corner.

The jangling crashing sound that came suddenly had the effect of unlocking his voice. This time he did exclaim.

"My God!" His voice struggled out as if someone held a hand across his throat.

It was a telephone which had fallen onto the floor, had been pulled to the floor by some sudden involuntary movement which jerked its lead. Something was crawling towards him out of the darkest part, where there was no lamp. It made a moaning sound. The phone lead was caught round it and the phone dragged behind, bouncing and sliding on polished oak. It bounced and jiggled like a toy on a string pulled by a child.

She was not a child, though she revealed herself as not much more, a young girl who crept towards him on all fours and collapsed at his feet, making the bewildered gibbering moans of a wounded animal. There was blood all over her, matting her long hair, sodden in her clothes, streaking her bare arms. She lifted her face and it was blotched with blood, as if she had dabbled in it and finger-painted the skin.

He could see, to his horror, blood welling out of a wound in her upper chest on the left side. He fell on his knees in front of her.

She spoke. It came in a clotted whisper. "Help me, help me . . ."

CHAPTER FOUR

Within two minutes the ambulance was off, on its way to the Infirmary at Stowerton. This time its lamp was on, and its siren, blaring its two-tone shriek through the dark woods, the still groves.

It was going so fast that the driver had to brake for dear life and pull over sharply to avoid Wexford's car, which entered the main gateway from the B 2428 at five minutes past nine.

The message had reached him where he was dining with his wife, his daughter and her friend. This was at a new Italian restaurant in Kingsmarkham called La Primavera. They were halfway through their main course when his phone started bleeping and saved him in a peculiarly drastic way, as he thought afterwards, from doing something he might be sorry for. With a quick word to Dora and a rather perfunctory good-bye to the others, he left the restaurant immediately, abandoning his veal Marsala.

Three times he had tried calling Tancred House and each time got the engaged signal. As the car, driven by Donaldson, negotiated the first bend in the narrow woodland road, he tried again and this time it rang and Burden answered.

"The receiver was off. It fell on the floor. There are three people dead here, shot dead. You must have passed the ambulance with the girl in it."

"How bad is she?"

"I don't know. She was conscious, but she's pretty bad."

"Did you talk to her?"

Burden said, "Of course. I had to. There were two of them got into the house but she only saw one. She said it was eight when it happened, or just after, a minute or two after eight. She couldn't talk any more."

Wexford put the phone back in his pocket. The clock on the car's dashboard told him it was twelve minutes past nine. When the message came he had been not so much in a bad temper as disturbed and increasingly unhappy. Already, sitting at that table in La Primavera, he had begun struggling with these feelings of antipathy, of positive revulsion. And then as he checked, for the third or fourth time, the sharp comment which rose to his lips, controlling himself for Sheila's sake, his phone had rung. Now he pushed aside the memory of a painful meeting. There would be no time for dwelling on it, everything must now give place to the killings at Tancred House.

The illuminated house showed through the trees, was swallowed in darkness, reappeared as Donaldson drove up the drive and across a wide empty plain. He hesitated at the gap in the low wall, then accelerated and went ahead, swinging onto the forecourt. A statue that probably represented the pursuit of Daphne by Apollo was reflected in the dark waters of a shallow pool. Donaldson drove to the left of it and in among the cars.

The front door stood open. He saw that someone had broken one of the panes in a bow window on the left-hand, or west, wing of the house. Inside the front door, from an orangery full of lilies, a pillared screen at each end of it in what he thought was called the Adam style, an arch opened onto the big hall where there was blood on the floor and the rugs. Blood made a map of islands on the pale oak. As Barry Vine came out to him, he saw the man's body at the foot of the staircase.

Wexford approached the body and looked at it. It was a man of about sixty, tall, slim, with a handsome face, the features finely cut and of the kind usually called sensitive.

His face was now waxen and yellowish. The mouth hung open. The blue eyes were open and staring. Blood had dyed scarlet his white shirt and stained blacker his dark jacket. He had been formally dressed in a suit and tie, had been shot twice from the front at close range, in the chest and in the head. His head was a mess of blood, a brownish stickiness matting the thick white hair.

"Do you know who this is?"

Vine shook his head. "Should I, sir? Presumably the guy who owned the place."

"It's Harvey Copeland, former MP for the Southern Boroughs and husband of Davina Flory. Of course you haven't been here long, but you'll have heard of Davina Flory?"

"Yes, sir. Of course."

You could never tell with Vine whether he had or not. That dead-pan face, that unruffled manner, stolid calm.

He went into the dining-room, preparing himself, but just the same what he saw made him catch his breath. No one, ever, becomes entirely hardened. He would never reach a stage of looking at such scenes with indifference.

Burden was in the room with the photographer. Archbold as scene-of-crimes officer was measuring, making notes, and two technicians had arrived from forensics. Archbold stood up when Wexford came in and Wexford motioned to him to carry on. When he had allowed his gaze to rest for a few moments on the bodies of the two women, he said to Burden, "The girl, tell me everything she said."

"That there were two of them. It was about eight. They came in a car."

"How else would you get up here?"

"There were sounds from upstairs. The man who's dead on the stairs went to investigate."

Wexford walked round the table and stood beside the dead woman whose head and streaming hair hung over the back of her chair. From there he was able to get a different view of the woman opposite. He looked at the remains of a face laid, left cheek downwards, in a blood-filled dinner plate, on the red cloth.

"That's Davina Flory."

"I guessed it must be," Burden said quietly. "And no doubt the man on the stairs is her husband."

Wexford nodded. He felt something unusual for him, a kind of awe. "Who's this? Wasn't there a daughter?"

The other woman might have been about forty-five. Her eyes and hair were dark. Her skin, white and drained in death, had probably been very pale in life. She was thin, dressed in gypsyish clothes, trailing patterned cottons with beads and chains. The colours had been predominantly red but not so red as they now were.

"It would have made a hell of a din, all this."

"Someone may have heard," Wexford said. "There must be other people on the estate. Someone looked after Davina Flory and her husband and daughter. I'm sure I've heard there's a housekeeper and maybe a gardener live in houses up here, tied cottages on the estate."

"I've seen to that. Karen and Gerry have gone out to try and locate them. You'll have noticed we didn't pass a house on the way in."

Wexford moved round the table, hesitated, came closer than he had hitherto been to the body of Davina Flory. Her copious dark hair, threaded with white, escaping from a loose knot on the back of her head, lay spread in blood-dabbled tendrils. The shoulder of her dress, a red silk which clung closely to her thin shape, bore a huge blackish stain. Her hands lay on the blood-dyed table-cloth in the position of someone at a seance. They were the kind of preternaturally long thin hands such as are seldom seen except on oriental women. Age had done little to damage them, or else death had already shrunk the veins. The hands were unadorned but for a plain gold wedding ring on the left one. The other had half-closed in death as the fingers contracted to clutch a handful of bloody damask.

His sense of awe increasing, Wexford had stepped back to

take in more fully this scene of horror and destruction when the door crashed open and in walked the pathologist. Some moments before he had heard a car draw up outside but had assumed it was only the return of Gerry Hinde and Karen Malahyde. It had in fact brought Dr. Basil Sumner-Quist, a man who was anathema to Wexford. He would have much preferred Sir Hilary Tremlett.

"Dear, oh dear," said Sumner-Quist, "how are the mighty fallen!"

Bad taste, no, worse than that, outrageous, revolting lack of any taste at all, characterized the pathologist. He had once referred to a garrotting as "a tasty little titbit."

"I suppose that's her?" He prodded at the red silk, blood-stained back. The prohibition on touching dead bodies applied to all but himself.

"We think so," Wexford said, keeping the note of disapproval in his tone to a minimum. He had no doubt shown enough disapproval for one night. "This is most probably Davina Flory, the man on the stairs is her husband Harvey Copeland, and we guess that's her daughter. I don't know what she's called."

"You finished?" Sumner-Quist said to Archbold.

"I can come back, sir."

The photographer took another last shot and followed Archbold and the forensics men from the room. Sumner-Quist did not delay. He lifted up the head by grasping the mass of grey-threaded dark hair. The pathologist's body hid the ruined half of this face and a noble profile was revealed, majestically high forehead, straight nose, a wide curved mouth, the whole scored with a thousand fine lines and deeper indentations.

"Cradle-snatching when she picked him, wasn't she? She must have been at least fifteen years older."

Wexford dipped his head.

"I've just been reading her book, Part One of the autobiography. A life packed with incident, you might say. Part Two must remain forever unwritten. Still, there are too many books in the world, in my humble opinion." Sumner-Quist let out his shrill braying laugh. "I've heard it said that all women when they get old turn into goats or monkeys. She was a monkey, I'd say, wouldn't you? Not a sagging muscle to be seen."

Wexford walked out of the room. He was aware that Burden was following him but he didn't look round. The anger which had been brewing in the restaurant, fermenting now from another cause, threatened to explode.

He said in a cold dull voice, "When I kill him, at least it'll be old Tremlett doing the post-mortem."

"Jenny's a great admirer of her books," said Burden, "the anthropology ones or whatever you call it. Well, I suppose they're political too. A remarkable woman, she was. I gave Jenny the autobiography for her birthday last week."

Karen Malahyde came into the hall. She said, "I wasn't certain what to do, sir. I knew you'd want to talk to the Harrisons and Gabbitas before it got too late, so I told them the bare facts. It seems to have come as a complete shock."

"You did quite right," said Wexford.

"I said it was likely you'd be along within the half-hour, sir. The houses, they're a pair, semi-detached, are about two minutes away down the lane that runs from the back garden."

"Show me."

She led him to the side of the west wing, past the broken bow window, and pointed to where the road skirted the garden and disappeared into the dark.

"Two minutes in a car or two minutes on foot?"

"I'd say ten minutes on foot, but I'll tell Donaldson where they are, shall I?"

"You can tell me, I'll walk."

Donaldson was to follow with Barry Vine. Wexford set out along the lane that was separated from the garden by a high hedge. On the other side of it the forest encroached. There was very little mist here and the moon had risen. Out of the reach of the arc lamps, the moonlight washed the path ahead with a greenish phosphorescence on which conifers laid smooth or feathery black shadows. Also black against the clear shining sky were the silhouettes of marvellous trees, specimen trees planted decades before, and even by night discernible as fantastic or strange by their immense height or curious leaf formations or contorted branches. The shadows they cast were like letters in Hebrew on an old stained parchment.

He thought of death and of contrast. He thought of the ugliest of all things happening in this most beautiful place. Of ''right perfection wrongfully disgraced.'' The memory of that blood splashing the room and the table like spilt paint made him shudder.

Here, so nearby, was another world. The path had a magical quality. The wood was an enchanted place, not real, a backdrop perhaps to *The Magic Flute* or a setting for a fairy tale, an illustration, not a living landscape. It was totally silent. Underfoot he trod on pine needles and his shoes made no sound. On and on, as the path wound, opened new moonlit vistas of leafless larches, araucarias with monkey-puzzle branches like anchored reptiles, cypresses pointing spires into the sky, Scotch pines whose crowns were concertinas, macrocarpas dense as tapestries, junipers slender and frondy, firs with last year's cones knobbing their tufted boughs. Moonlight, gaining strength, flooded the pinetum, glimmered through its alleys, was here and there excluded by a dense barrier of needled branches or trunks like twisted hanks of rope.

Nature, which should have risen up and howled, sent a gale roaring through these woods, driven the wild things to protest, the branches of trees to toss and lament, was quiet and sweet and placid. The stillness was almost unnatural. Not a twig moved. Wexford rounded a bend in the path, saw it peter out, the woods thin before him and a clearing emerge. A narrower path opened out of it, penetrating a screen of the more common sort of conifers.

The lights of houses showed gleaming at the end of the path.

Barry Vine and Karen Malahyde had been upstairs to the first and second floors to check that there were no more bodies.

Curious to know what might be up there, Burden was nevertheless chary of passing Harvey Copeland until Archbold had logged the body's position, it had been photographed from all angles and the pathologist had given it his preliminary examination. To pass it he would have had to step over the dead man's outflung right arm and hand. Vine and Karen had done so, but an inhibition, squeamishness and a sense of what was fitting, stopped Burden. He made his way instead across the hall and looked into what turned out to be the drawing-room.

Beautifully furnished, exquisitely tidy, a museum of pretty things and *objets d'art*. Somehow, he would not have imagined Davina Flory living like this, but in a more slapdash or Bohemian fashion. He would have pictured her, robed or trousered, seated with like-minded spirits at some ancient and battered refectory table in a big warm untidy place, drinking wine and talking long into the night. A kind of banqueting hall it was that his imagination had conjured up. Davina Flory inhabited it dressed like a matriarch in a Greek tragedy. He smiled to himself shamefacedly, looked again at the festooned windows, portraits in gilded frames, the *jardinière* of kalanchoe and ferns, the spindle-legged eighteenth-century furniture, and closed the door on it.

At the back of this east wing and behind the hall were two rooms that seemed his and her studies, another that opened into a large glazed room full of plants. One or more of the dead had been an enthusiastic gardener. The place was sweet-scented from bulb plants in bloom, narcissi and hyacinths, and with that damp green feel, humid and mild, peculiar to conservatories.

He found a library behind the dining room. All these rooms were as orderly, as sleek and tended as the first one he had looked into. They might have been in some National Trust mansion where certain rooms are open to the public. In the library all the books were contained behind screen doors of trellis-work, dark-red wood, fine gleaming glass. A single book only lay open on a lectern. From where he stood Burden could see that the print was old and he guessed at long *s*'s. A passage led away to kitchen regions.

The kitchen was big but in no way cavernous. It had been newly fitted in the pseudo-farm-dairy style, but he thought the cabinet doors were oak, not pine. Here was the refectory table he had been imagining, glowingly polished and with fruit on a polished wooden platter in the centre of it.

A cough behind him made him look round. Archbold had come in with Chepstow, the fingerprint man.

"Excuse me, sir. Prints."

Burden held up his right hand to show the glove on it. Chepstow nodded, got to work on the door handle on the kitchen side. The house was too grand to have that kitchen exit known as the "back door." Burden gingerly approached the open doors, one which led to a laundry room with washing machine, dryer and ironing things, the other to a kind of lobby with shelves, cupboards and a rack where coats hung. Yet another room had to be passed through before an exit to the outside was reached.

He looked round as Archbold came through. Archbold gave a half-nod. The door had bolts but they were not secured. A key was in the lock. Burden wouldn't touch the doorknob, glove or no glove.

"You're thinking they came in this way?"

"It's a possibility, isn't it, sir? How else? All the other outside doors are locked."

"Unless they were admitted. Unless they came to the front door and someone opened it and invited them in."

Chepstow came through and did his test on the doorknob, the finger-plate, the jamb. A cotton glove on his right hand, he carefully turned the knob. It gave and the door came open. Outside was cool greenish darkness with a remote wash of moonlight. Burden could make out a high hedge enclosing a paved court.

"Someone left the door unlocked. The housekeeper when she went home, maybe. Maybe she always left it unlocked and they only locked it before they went to bed."

"Could be," said Burden.

"Terrible thing to have to lock yourselves in when you're in an isolated place like this."

"They evidently didn't," Burden said, irritated.

He made his way through the laundry room which led, by a doorway where the door stood open, into a kind of back hall lined with cupboards. An enclosed staircase, much narrower than the principal one, mounted between walls. These then were the "back stairs," a feature of big old houses Burden had often heard of but seldom if ever seen. He went up, found himself in a passage with open doors on both sides.

The bedrooms seemed innumerable. If you lived in a house this size you might lose count of how many bedrooms you had. He turned lights on and then off as he proceeded. The passage turned to the left and he knew he must be in the west wing, above the dining-room. The only door here was closed. He opened it, pressed the switch his fingers felt on the left-hand wall.

Light flooded onto the sort of disorder he had imagined Davina Flory living in. It took him an instant only to realize that this was where the gunman or two gunmen had been. The disturbance had been caused by them. What was it Karen Malahyde had said?

"They took her bedroom apart, looking for something."

The bed had not been stripped but the covers thrown back and the pillows tossed aside. The drawers in the two bedside tables were pulled out and so were two of those in the dressing-table. One of the wardrobe doors was open and a shoe from inside lay on the carpet. The lid of the ottoman at the foot of the bed had been raised and a length of silken fabric, a rose-and-gold floral pattern, trailed over the side of it.

It was odd, this feeling Burden had. His image of the kind of life he had expected Davina Flory to lead, the kind of person he would have thought she was, kept returning to him. This was how he would have envisaged her bedroom, beautifully appointed, cleaned and tidied daily, but subjected by its owner to a continual untidying process. Not through wanton disregard of a servant's labours but because she simply did not know or notice, was indifferent to the neatness of her surroundings. It had not been so. An intruder had done this.

Why then did he find something incongruous about it? The

jewel box, a red leather case, empty and upturned on the carpet, expressed the truth plainly enough.

Burden shook his head ruefully, for he would not have expected Davina Flory to have possessed jewels or a case to put them in.

Five people in the Harrisons' small front room turned it into a crowded place. John Gabbitas, the woodsman, had been fetched from next door. There were not enough chairs and an extra had to be brought from upstairs. Brenda Harrison had insisted on making tea, which no one had seemed to want, but of which Wexford thought now they all needed the relief and comfort.

She was cool about it. She had had, of course, some half-hour in which to adjust to the shock before he got there. Nevertheless, he found her briskness disconcerting. It might have been some minor disaster befalling her employers that Vine and Malahyde had told her about, a bit of the roof blowing off, for instance, or water through a ceiling. She bustled about with the teacups and a tin of biscuits while her husband sat stunned, his head occasionally moving from side to side as if in disbelief, his eyes staring.

Before running outside to boil a kettle and lay a tray—she seemed a hyperactive, restless woman—she had confirmed his own identification. The dead man on the stairs was Harvey Copeland, the elder of the dead women at the table Davina Flory. The other woman she identified as certainly Davina Flory's daughter Naomi. In spite of the exalted status, in anyone's estimation, of her employers, it appeared that they had all been on Christian-name terms here, Davina and Harvey and Naomi and Brenda. She even had to think for a moment before recalling Naomi's surname. Oh, yes, Jones, she was Mrs. Jones, but the girl called herself Flory.

"The girl?"

"Daisy was Naomi's daughter and Davina's granddaughter. Her name was Davina too, she was sort of Davina Flory the Younger, if you see what I mean, but they called her Daisy."

"Not 'was,'" said Wexford. "She's not dead."

She lifted her shoulders a little. Her tone seemed to him indignant, perhaps only because she had been proved wrong, "Oh. I thought the policewoman said they all were."

It was after this that she made the tea.

He could already tell that of the three she was to be his principal informant. Her apparent callousness, an indifference that was almost repulsive, was of no particular account. Because of it, she might make the better witness. In any case, John Gabbitas, a man in his twenties, though living in one of the Tancred Wood houses and managing the woodland, worked for himself as well as a woodsman and tree expert and said he had only returned an hour before from a job on the other side of the county. Ken Harrison had scarcely uttered a word since Wexford and Vine arrived. "When did you last see them?" Wexford asked.

She answered quickly. She was not the kind of woman to take thought. "Seven-thirty. I always did, regular as clockwork. Unless she had a dinner party. When it was just them, the four of them, I'd cook whatever it was and dish it up and put it on the heated trolley and wheel it in the dining-room. Naomi always served it, or so I presume. I was never there to see. Davina liked to be at the table by seven forty-five sharp, same every night when she was home. It was always the same."

"And it was the same tonight?"

"It was always the same. I wheeled the trolley in at seven-thirty. It was soup and sole and apricots with yoghurt. I put my head round the sare door, they were all in there . . ."

"Round the what?"

"The sare. That's the name they had for it. The conservatory. I said I was off and I went out the back way like I always do."

"Did you lock the back door?"

"No, of course I didn't. I never do that. Besides, Bib was still there."

"Bib?"

"She helps out. Comes up on her bike. She's got a morning

job some mornings, so she mostly comes here in the afternoons. I left her there finishing off the freezer and she said she'd be off in five minutes.'' A thought suddenly struck her. Her colour changed—for the first time. ''The cat,'' she said, ''is the cat all right? Oh, they didn't kill the cat!''

''Not so far as I know,'' Wexford said. ''Well, no, certainly not.''

Before he could add, as he had begun to, suppressing a tone of irony, ''Only the people,'' she exclaimed, ''Thank God for that!''

Wexford gave her a moment. ''Around eight, did you hear anything? A car? Shots?''

He knew the shots would not have been heard from here. Not shots fired inside the house. She shook her head.

''A car wouldn't go past here. The road ends here. There's only the main road in and the by-road.''

''The by-road?''

She answered him impatiently. She was one of those people who expect everyone to know, as well as they themselves do, the workings and rules and geography of their little private world. ''It's the one comes up from Pomfret Monachorum, isn't it?''

Gabbitas said, ''That's the way I came home.''

''What time was that?''

''Twenty past eight, half past. I didn't see anyone, if that's what you're asking. I didn't meet a car or pass one or anything like that.''

Wexford thought that came out rather too pat. Then Ken Harrison spoke. The words came slowly, as if he had suffered an injury to his throat and was still learning how to project his voice. ''We didn't hear a thing. There wasn't a sound.'' He added, wonderingly—and incomprehensibly, ''There never was.'' He explained. ''You can never hear anything at the house from here.''

The others seemed long to have registered and accepted what had happened. Mrs. Harrison had adjusted to it almost at once. Her world had altered but she would contend with it. Her husband reacted as if the news had just that moment been broken to him. "All dead? Did you say they were all dead?"

It sounded to Wexford like something out of *Macbeth*, though he wasn't sure it was. A lot of tonight was like something out of *Macbeth*.

"The young girl, Miss Flory, Daisy, she's alive."

But, he thought, is she? Is she still alive? Harrison shocked him. He thought that was impossible but Harrison did it.

"Funny they didn't finish her off, wasn't it?"

Barry Vine coughed.

"Have another cup of tea, will you?" said Brenda Harrison.

"No, thank you. It's getting late and we'll be off. You'll want to get to bed."

"You've finished with us, then, have you?"

Perhaps it was a favourite word with him. Ken Harrison was looking with a kind of glazed wistfulness at Wexford.

"Finished? No, by no means. We shall want to talk to you all again. Perhaps you'll let me have Bib's address. What's her other name?"

No one seemed to know. They had the address but no surname. She was just Bib.

"Thanks for the tea," said Vine.

Wexford went back to the house by car. Sumner-Quist had gone. Archbold and Milsom were working away upstairs. Burden said to him, "I forgot to mention it but I had road-blocks put on all the roads out of here when the message came through."

"What, before you knew what it was about?"

"Well, I knew it was in the nature of a—a massacre. She said, 'They're all dead' when she made her 999 call. You think I over-reacted, do you?"

"No," said Wexford slowly, "no, not at all. I think you were right, insofar as it's possible to block all roads. I mean, there must be dozens of ways out."

"Not really. What they call the by-road goes to Pomfret Monachorum and Cheriton. The main drive goes directly to the B 2428 into town and there happened to be a squad car on that about half a mile along. In the other direction the road goes to Cambery Ashes, as you know. It was a piece of luck for us or it looked that way. The pair in the squad car knew about it within three minutes of her call. But they didn't go that way, they must have gone by the by-road, and then there wasn't much of a chance. No description, no index number or approximation to it, no idea what to look for. We haven't now. I couldn't have asked her anything more, could I, Reg? I reckoned she was dying.''

"Of course you couldn't. Of course not.''

"I hope to God she doesn't die.''

"So do I,'' said Wexford. "She's only seventeen.''

"Well, naturally one hopes for her sake she'll live but I was thinking of what she can tell us. Pretty well everything, don't you think?''

Wexford just looked at him.

CHAPTER FIVE

The girl could tell them everything. Davina Jones called Daisy Flory could tell them when the men came and how they came, what they looked like, even perhaps what they wanted and took. She had seen them and perhaps spoken to them. She might have seen their car. Wexford thought it likely she was intelligent and hoped she was observant. He hoped very much she would live.

Entering his own house at midnight, he thought of phoning the hospital to check on her. What good would it do, his knowing whether she lived or died?

If they told him she was dead he wouldn't sleep, because she had been young and with all of her life before her. And for Burden's reason too; he had better be honest. Because if she was dead the case would be all that much harder. But if they told him she was all right, she was doing well, he would be too hyped up at the prospect of talking to her to sleep.

Anyway, they wouldn't tell him that, but either that she was dead or "holding her own" or "comfortable." In any case,

Woman Police Constable Rosemary Mountjoy was with her, would sit outside the ward door till morning and be relieved at eight by WPC Anne Lennox.

He went quietly upstairs to see if Dora was still awake. The light from the open door fell, not on her face but in a wide band across the arm that lay outside the covers, the sleeve of her night-dress, the rather small neat hand with round pink fingernails. Deep sleep held her and her breathing was steady and slow. She could sleep easily then, in spite of what had happened earlier that evening, in spite of Sheila and the fourth member of their party he was already calling "that wretched man." He felt unreasonably exasperated by her. Retreating, he pulled the door to behind him, went down again, and in the living-room hunted through the paper rack for the *Independent on Sunday* of two days before.

The review section was still there, pushed between *The Radio Times* and some freebie magazine. It was the Win Carver interview he was looking for and the big portrait photograph he remembered as a double-page spread. Page eleven. He sat down in an armchair, found the page. The face was before him, the face he had seen an hour before in death when Sumner-Quist had lifted it from the table by a handful of hair like an executioner holding aloft a severed head.

The text began as a single column on the left-hand side. Wexford looked at the picture. The portrait was of a kind a woman would only tolerate seeing of herself if she had succeeded overwhelmingly in fields distant from the triumph of youth and beauty. These were not lines on the face but the deep scoring of time and the pleating of old age. From a bird's nest of wrinkles the nose stood out beaklike and the lips curved in a half-smile that was both ironic and kindly. The eyes were still young, dark, burning irises and clear unveined whites in the tangle of gathered folds.

The caption read: "Davina Flory, the first volume of whose autobiography *The Youngest Wren of Nine* is published by St. Giles Press at £16.00." He turned the page and there she was when young: a little girl in a velvet dress with lace collar, ten years later a grown-up girl with a swan neck, mysterious smile, shingled hair and one of those dresses with no waist and a belt round the hips.

The print swam before his eyes. Wexford gave a huge yawn. He was too tired to read the piece tonight and, leaving the paper open on the table, he went back upstairs. The evening past seemed immensely long, a corridor of events with at the opening of the tunnel, distant but very much *there*, Sheila and that wretched man.

While the reader had recourse to a magazine, the non-reader went to a book for help.

Burden let himself into his house to the sound of his son yelling. By the time he was upstairs the noise had stopped and Mark was being comforted in his mother's arms. Burden could hear her telling him, in that rather didactic confident way of hers which was immediately reassuring, that diplodocus the two-ridged reptile had not walked the earth for two million years and in any case had never been known to inhabit toy cupboards.

By the time Jenny came into their bedroom Burden was in bed, sitting up with her birthday copy of *The Youngest Wren of Nine* resting against his knees.

She kissed him, went into a detailed description of Mark's dream, which for a little while distracted him from the biographical note he had been reading on the back flap of the book jacket. In that moment he decided to say nothing to her of what had happened. Not till the morning. She had deeply admired the dead woman, followed her travels and collected her works. Their pillow talk of the previous night had been about this book, Davina Flory's childhood and the early influences that helped to form the character of this distinguished anthropologist and "geo-sociologist."

"You can't have my book till I've finished it," she said sleepily, turning over and burying her head in the pillows. "Anyway, can't we have the light out?"

"Two minutes. Just to let me unwind. Good night, love."

Unlike many writers past a certain age, Davina Flory had had no reservations about her birth date appearing in print. She had been seventy-eight, born in Oxford, the youngest of the nine children of a professor of Greek. Educated at Lady Margaret Hall, with later a Ph.D. from London, she had married in 1935 a fellow-undergraduate at Oxford, Desmond Cathcart Flory. Together they had set about the redemption of the gardens of his home, Tancred House, Kingsmarkham, and had begun the planting of the famous woods.

Burden read the rest, put the light out, lay looking into the dark, thinking of what he had read. Desmond Flory had been killed in France in 1944, eight months before his daughter Naomi was born. Two years later Davina Flory began her travels in Europe and the Middle East, remarrying in 1951. He had forgotten the rest of it, the new husband's name, the titles of all the works.

None of this would matter. That Davina Flory had been who she was would turn out to be no more important than if she had been what Burden called "an ordinary person." It was possible that the men who had killed her had no idea of her identity. A good many of the kind of people Burden came across in his work were, in any case, unable to read. To the gunman or gunmen at Tancred House she had been only a woman who possessed jewellery and lived in an isolated place. She and her husband and daughter and granddaughter were vulnerable and unprotected and that was enough for them.

The first thing Wexford saw when he woke up was the phone. Usually the first thing he saw was the little black Marks and Spencers alarm clock, the arch-shaped clock that was either braying away or about to go off. He couldn't remember the phone number of Stowerton Royal Infirmary. WPC Mountjoy would have phoned if anything had happened.

In the post, on the doormat, was a card from Sheila. It had been posted in Venice four days before, while she was there with that man. The picture was of a gloomy baroque interior, a pulpit and drapery over it, marble probably but cunningly contrived to look like cloth. Sheila had written, "We have just been to see the Gesuiti, which is Gus's favourite joke-church in all the world and not to be confused, he says, with the Gesuati. Stone Wilton is a bit cold on the feet and it is freezing here. Much love, S.''

He would make her as pretentious as himself. Wexford wondered what on earth the card meant. What was a joke-church, and come to that, what was Stone Wilton? It sounded like a village in the Cotswolds.

The *Independent on Sunday* review section in his pocket, he drove himself to work. The removal of furnishings and equipment had already begun for the setting up of an incident room at Tancred House. The investigation would be conducted from there. DC Hinde told him as he came in that a Kingsmarkham systems manufacturer on the industrial estate was offering them, free of charge as a gesture of goodwill, computers, word processors with laser printers, printer ancillaries, workstations, software and fax.

"The managing director's chairman of the local Tories," Hinde said. "Chap called Pagett, Graham Pagett. He's been on the blower. He says this is his way of implementing the Government's policy that fighting crime is up to the private individual."

Wexford grunted.

"We can do with that kind of support, sir."

"Yes, it's very good of him," Wexford said absently. He wouldn't go up there yet but waste no time, take Barry Vine with him and find the woman called Bib.

It had to be straightforward, this business. It had to be murder for robbery or murder in the course of robbery. Two villains in a stolen car after Davina Flory's jewellery. Maybe they'd been reading the *Independent on Sunday*, except that this newspaper hadn't mentioned jewellery except for Win Carver's comment that Davina wore a wedding ring, and they'd be more likely anyway to read the *Sunday People*. If they could read. Two villains certainly, but not strangers to the place. One who knew all about it, one who didn't, his mate, his pal, met perhaps in prison . . .

Someone connected with those servants, the Harrisons? With

this Bib? She lived at Pomfret Monachorum, which probably meant she had gone home by the by-road. Wexford fancied the by-road as an exit for the gunman and his companion. That was their most likely way out, especially as one of them must have known the place. He could almost hear one saying to the other that this was the way to avoid the Plod coming in.

The forest separated Pomfret Monachorum from Tancred and Kingsmarkham and almost from the rest of the world. Behind it the road ran to Cheriton and to Pomfret. The ruined walls of an abbey still stood, the church was pretty outside, wrecked inside by Henry VIII and later Cromwell, and the rest of the place consisted of the vicarage, a cluster of cottages and a small council estate. Out on the Pomfret road was a row of three shingle-and-slate cottages.

It was in one of these that Bib lived, though neither Wexford nor Vine knew which one. All the Harrisons and Gabbitas knew was that it was in the row called Edith Cottages.

A plaque bearing this name and the date 1882 was embedded in the shingles above the upper windows of the middle one. All the cottages needed painting, none looked prosperous. Each one had a television aerial on its roof and the one on the left a dish sticking out from the side of a bedroom window. A bicycle leaned up against the wall by the front door of the cottage on the right and a Ford Transit van was parked half on the grass verge outside its gate. A wheelie-bin stood in the garden of the middle cottage, on a piece of concrete with a manhole cover in it. There were daffodils in bloom in this garden but no flowers in either of the others and the one with the bicycle was overgrown with weeds.

Because Brenda Harrison had told him Bib rode a bicycle, Wexford decided to try the house on the right. A young man came to the door. He was rather tall but very slight, dressed in blue jeans and an American college sweat-shirt, so worn and washed and faded that only the "U" of University and a capital "S" and "T" were discernible on the greyish background. His was a girlish face, the face of a pretty tomboy. The youths who played heroines in sixteenth-century drama must have looked like him.

He said, "Hi," but in a dazed way and rather slowly. Seeming considerably taken aback, he looked past Wexford at the car outside, then back warily at his face.

"Kingsmarkham CID. We're looking for someone called Bib. Does she live here?"

The young man was studying Wexford's warrant card with great interest. Or even anxiety. A lazy grin transformed his face, suddenly making him appear more masculine. He shook back the long lock of black hair that fell over his forehead.

"Bib? No. No, she doesn't. Next door. The one in the middle." He hesitated, said, "Is this about the Davina Flory killings?"

"How do you know about that?"

"Breakfast TV," he said and added, as if Wexford were likely to be interested, "We studied one of her books at college. I minored in English Literature."

"I see. Well, thank you very much, sir." Kingsmarkham police called everyone "sir" or "madam" or by their name and style until they were actually charged. It was for politeness' sake and one of Wexford's rules. "We won't trouble you any further," he said.

If the young American had the look of a girl cross-dressing, Bib might have been a man, so few concessions had she or nature made to her gender. Her age was equally an enigma. She might have been thirty-five or fifty-five. Her dark hair was cropped short, her face was reddish and shiny as if scrubbed with soap, her fingernails square-cut. In one ear-lobe she wore a small gold ring.

When Vine had explained what they had come for, she nodded and said, "I saw it on telly. Couldn't believe it." Her voice was gruff, flat, curiously expressionless.

"May we come in?"

In her estimation the question was no mere formality. She seemed to be considering it from several possible angles before giving a slow nod.

Her bicycle she kept in the hall, resting against a wall papered in sweet peas faded to beige. The living-room was furnished like the abode of a very old lady and it had that sort of smell, a combination of camphor and carefully preserved not very clean clothes, closed windows and boiled sweets. Wexford expected to encounter an ancient mother in an armchair but the room was empty.

"For a start, could we have your full name, please," Vine said.

If she had been in court on a murder charge, brought there peremptorily and without counsel to defend her, Bib could not have behaved with greater caution. Every word must be weighed. She brought out her name with slow reluctance and a hesitation before each word.

"Er, Beryl—er, Agnes—er, Mew."

"Beryl Agnes Mew. I believe you work on a part-time basis at Tancred House and were there yesterday afternoon, Miss Mew?"

"Missus." She looked from Vine to Wexford and said it again, very deliberately. "Mrs. Mew."

"I'm sorry. You were there yesterday afternoon?"

"Yes."

"Doing what?"

It might be shock that affected her like this. Or a general distrust and suspicion of humanity. She seemed stunned by Vine's question and looked at him stonily before lifting her heavy shoulders in a shrug.

"What do you do there, Mrs. Mew?"

Again she considered. She was still but her eyes moved rather more than most people's. Now they moved quite wildly. She said, incomprehensibly to Vine, "They call it the rough."

"You do the rough work, Mrs. Mew," Wexford said. "Yes, I see. Scrubbing floors, washing paint and so on?" He got a ponderous nod. "You were cleaning the freezer, I think?"

"The freezers. They've got three." Her head swayed slowly from side to side. "I saw it on telly. Couldn't believe it. They was all right yesterday."

As if, Wexford thought, the inhabitants of Tancred House had succumbed to a visitation of plague. He said, "What time did you leave for home?"

If the imparting of her own name had caused such inner searching, a question such as this might be expected to give rise to whole minutes of pondering, but Bib answered fairly quickly. "They'd started on their meal."

"Mr. and Mrs. Copeland and Mrs. Jones and Miss Jones had gone into the dining-room, do you mean?"

"I heard them talking and the door shut. I put me bits back in the freezer and switched it on. Me hands was froze, so I put them under the hot tap for a bit." The effort of saying so much silenced her for a moment. She seemed to be recouping unseen forces. "I got me coat and then I went to fetch me bike as was in that bit round the back with hedges like round."

Wexford wondered if she ever talked to the man next door, the American, and if she talked like this, would he understand a word? "Did you lock the back door after you?"

"Me? No. It's not my job to lock doors."

"So this would have been—what? Ten to eight?"

A long hesitation. "I reckon."

"How did you get home?" said Vine.

"On my bike." She was made indignant by his stupidity. He should have known. Everyone knew.

"Which route did you take, Mrs. Mew? Which road?"

"The by-road."

"I want you to think very carefully before you answer." But she always did. That was why this was taking so long. "Did you see a car on your way home? Did you meet one or did one overtake you? On the by-road." More explanation was doubtless called for. "A car or a van or a—a vehicle like the one next door."

For a moment Wexford feared he had made her think her American neighbour might be involved in this crime. She got up and looked out of the window in the direction of the Ford Transit. Her expression was confused and she bit her lip. At last she said, "That one?"

"No, no. Any one. Any vehicle at all. Did you meet any vehicle on your way home last evening?"

She thought. She nodded, shook her head, finally said, "No."

"You're sure of that."

"Yes."

"How long does it take to get home?"

"It's downhill going home."

"Yes. So how long did it take you last evening?"

"About twenty minutes."

"And you met no one? Not even John Gabbitas in the Land Rover?"

The first flash of any sort of animation showed. It came in her restless eyes. "Does he say I did?"

"No, no. It's unlikely you would have if you were home here by, say, eight fifteen. Thank you very much, Mrs. Mew. Would you like to show us the road you take from here to the by-road?"

A long pause and then, "I don't mind."

The road where the cottages were fell steeply down the side of the little river valley. Bib Mew pointed their way down this road and gave some vague instructions, her eyes straying to the Ford Transit. Wexford thought he must have ineradicably planted in her mind the notion that she should have met this van last night. As they drove off down the hill, she could be seen leaning over her gate, following their progress with those darting eyes.

At the foot of the hill the stream was not bridged but forded. A wooden foot-bridge spanned it for the use of foot passengers and cyclists. Vine drove through the water, which was perhaps six inches deep and flowing very fast over flat brown stones. On the other side they came to what he insisted on calling a T-junction, though the extreme rusticity of the place, steep hedge banks, overhanging trees, deep meadows with cattle glimpsed beyond, made this a misnomer. Bib's instructions, if such they could be called, were to turn left here and then take the first right. This was the Pomfret Monachorum way into the by-road.

There came a sudden sight of forest. The hedge trees parted and there it was, a dark, bluish canopy hanging high above them. Half a mile up the road it appeared again, was quickly all round them, as the deep tunnel of lane running between high banks plunged into the start of the by-road where a sign said: "Tancred House only. Two miles. No through road."

Wexford said, "When we think it's only one mile I'm going to get out and walk the rest of the way."

"Right. They'd have had to know the place if they came this way, sir."

"They knew it. Or one of them did."

He left the car at an auspicious moment, when he saw the sun come out. The woods would not begin to grow green for another month. There was not even a green haze to mist the trees that flanked this sandy path. All was a bright brown, a sparkling vigorous colour that gilded the branches and turned the leaf buds to a glowing shade of copper. It was cold and dry. Late on the previous night, when the sky had cleared, a frost had come. The frost was gone now, not a silver streak of it remaining, but a chill hung in the clear still air. Above the dense or feathery tree-tops, through spaces in the groves, the sky was a light delicate blue, so pale as to be almost white.

The Win Carver interview told him about these woods, when they had been planted, which parts dated from the thirties and which were older but augmented with planting from that time. Ancient oaks and here and there a horse chestnut with looped boughs and glutinous leaf buds towered above ranks of smaller, neater trees, vase-shaped as if by a natural process of topiary. Wexford thought they might be hornbeams. Then he noticed a metal label secured to the trunk of one of them. Yes, common hornbeam, *Carpinus betulus*. The taller graceful specimens a little way along the path were the mountain ash, he read, *Sorbus aucuparia*. Identifying trees when bare of leaves must be a test for the expert.

The groves gave place to a plantation of Norway maples *(Acer platanoides)* with trunks like crocodile skin. No conifers were here, not a single pine or fir to provide a dark-green shape among the shining leafless branches. This was the finest part of the deciduous woodland, man-made but a copy of nature, pristinely ordered but with nature's own neatness. Fallen logs had been left when they fell and were overgrown with bright fungus, frills and ruffs and knobbed stalks in yellow or bronze. Dead trees still stood, their rotting trunks weathered to silver, a habitation for owls or a feeding ground for woodpeckers.

Wexford walked on, expecting each twist in the narrow road to bring him out to face the east wing of the house. But every new curve only afforded another vista of standing trees and fallen trees, saplings and underbrush. A squirrel, blue and silvery brown, snaked up the trunk of an oak, sprang from twig to twig, took a flying leap to the branch of a nearby beech. The road made a final ellipse, broadened and cleared, and there was the house before him, dreamlike in the veils of mist.

The east wing rose majestically. From here the terrace could be seen and the gardens at the rear. Instead of the daffodils, which filled the public gardens in Kingsmarkham and the council flower-beds, tiny scillas sparkling like blue jewels clustered under the trees. But the gardens of Tancred House had not yet wakened from their winter sleep. Herbaceous borders, rose-beds, paths, hedges, pleached walks, lawns, all still had the look of having been trimmed and manicured, coiffed and in some cases packaged, and put away for hibernation. High hedges of yew and cypress made walls to conceal all outbuildings from sight of the house, dark screens cunningly planted for a privileged privacy.

He stood looking for a moment or two, then made his way to where he could see the parked police vehicles. The incident room had been set up in what was apparently a stable block, though a stables that no horse had lived in for half a century. It was too smart for that and there were blinds at the windows. A blue-faced gilt-handed clock under a central pediment told him the time was twenty to eleven.

His car was parked on the flagstones, so were Burden's and two vans. Inside the stable block a technician was setting up the computers and Karen Malahyde was arranging a dais, lectern, microphone and half-circle of chairs for his press conference. They had scheduled it for eleven.

Wexford sat down behind the desk provided for him. He was rather touched by the care Karen had taken—he was sure it must be Karen's work. There were three new ball-point pens, a brass paper-knife he couldn't imagine he would ever use, two phones—as if he hadn't got his Vodaphone—a computer and printer he had no idea how to work and, in a blue-and-brown-glazed pot, a cactus. The cactus, large, spherical, grey, covered in fur, was more like an animal than a plant, a *cuddly* animal, except that when he poked it a sharp thorn went into his finger.

Wexford shook his finger, cursing mildly. He could see he was honoured. These things seemingly went by rank, and though there was another cactus on the desk evidently designated Burden's, it had nowhere near the dimensions of his nor was it so hirsute. All Barry Vine got was an African violet, not even in bloom.

WPC Lennox had phoned in soon after she took over hospital duty. There was nothing to report. All was well. What did that mean? What was it to him if the girl lived or died? Young girls were dying all over the world, from starvation, in wars and insurrections, from cruel practices and clinical neglect. Why should this one matter?

He punched out Anne Lennox's number on his phone.

"She seems fine, sir."

He must have misheard. "She *what*?"

"She seems fine—well, heaps better. Would you like to talk to Dr. Leigh, sir?"

There was silence at the other end. That is, there was no voice. He could hear hospital noise, footsteps and metallic sounds and swishing sounds. A woman came on.

"I believe that's Kingsmarkham Police?"

"Chief Inspector Wexford."

"Dr. Leigh. How can I help you?"

The voice sounded lugubrious to him. He detected in it the gravity which these people were perhaps taught to assume for some while after a tragedy had taken place. Such a death would affect the whole hospital. He simply gave the name, knowing that would be enough without inquiry.

"Miss Flory. Daisy Flory."

Suddenly all the gloom was gone. Perhaps he had imagined it. "Daisy? Yes, she's fine, she's doing very well."

"What? What did you say?"

"I said she's doing well, she's fine."

"She's *fine*? We are talking about the same person? The young woman who was brought in last night with gunshot wounds?"

"Her condition is quite satisfactory, Chief Inspector. She will be coming out of intensive care sometime today. I expect you'll want to see her, won't you? There's no reason why you shouldn't talk to her this afternoon. For a short while only, of course. We'll say ten minutes."

"Would four o'clock be a good time?"

"Four P.M., yes. Ask to see me first, will you? It's Dr. Leigh."

The press came early. Wexford supposed he should really call them the "media" as, approaching the dais, he saw from the window a television van arriving with a camera crew.

CHAPTER SIX

Estate'' sounded like a hundred semi-detached houses crowded into a few acres. "Grounds" expressed land only, not the buildings on it. Burden, unusually fanciful for him, thought "demesne" might be the only word. This was the demesne of Tancred, a little world or, more realistically, a hamlet: the great house, its stables, coach-houses, outbuildings, dwellings for servants past and present. Its gardens, lawns, hedges, pinetum, plantations and woods.

All of it—perhaps not the woods themselves—would have to be searched. They needed to know what they were dealing with, what this place was. The stables where the centre had been set up were only a small part of it. From where he stood, on the terrace which ran the length of the back of the house, scarcely anything of these outbuildings could be seen. Cunning hedge-planting, the careful provision of trees to hide the humble or the utilitarian, concealed everything from view but the top of a slate roof, the point of a weather vane. After all, it was winter still. The leaves of summertime would shield these gardens, this view, in serried screens of green.

As it was, the long formal lawn stretched away between herbaceous borders, broke into a rose garden, a clockface of beds, opened again to dip over a ha-ha into the meadow beyond. Perhaps. It was a possibility, though too far away to see from here. Things had been so arranged as to have the gardens blend gently into the vista beyond, the parkland with its occasional giant tree, the bluish lip of woods. All the woods looked blue in the soft misty late-winter light. Except the pinetum to the west with its mingled colours of yellow and smoky black, marble green and reptile green, slate and pearl and a bright copper.

Even in daylight, even from here, the pair of houses where the Harrisons and Gabbitas lived were invisible. Burden walked down the stone steps and along the path and through a gate in the hedge to the stables and coach-houses area where the search had begun. He came upon a row of cottages, dilapidated and shabby but not derelict, that had once no doubt housed some of the many servants the Victorians needed to maintain outdoor comfort and order.

The front door of one of them stood open. Two constables from the uniformed branch were inside, opening cupboards, investigating a hole of a scullery. Burden thought about housing and how there were never supposed to be enough houses, and he thought about all the homeless people, even on the streets of Kingsmarkham these days. His wife, who had a social conscience, had taught him to think this way. He never would have done before he married her. As it was, he could see that a surplus of accommodation at Tancred, at the hundreds and hundreds of houses like this there must be all over England, solved no problems. Not really. He couldn't see how you could make the Florys and Copelands of this world give up their unused servants' cottage to the bag lady who slept in St. Peter's porch, even if the bag lady would want it, so he stopped this line of thought and walked once more round the back of the house to the kitchen regions where he was due to meet Brenda Harrison for a tour.

Archbold and Milsom were examining the flagged areas here, looking no doubt for tyre marks. They had been working on the broad space at the front when he first arrived that morning. It had been a dry spring, the last heavy rain weeks ago. A car could come up here and leave no trace of its passage behind.

In the still waters of the pool, when he bent over to look, he had seen a pair of large goldfish, white with scarlet heads, swimming serenely in slow circles.

White and scarlet . . . The blood was still there, though the table-cloth, along with a host of other items, had gone off in bags to the forensics laboratory at Myringham. Later on in the night the room had been filled with sealed plastic bags containing lamps and ornaments, cushions and table napkins, plates and cutlery.

With no qualms about what she might see in the hall, for sheets covered the foot of the stairs and the corner where the phone was, he had been steering Brenda clear of the dining-room, when she side-stepped and opened the door. She was such a quick mover, it was a risk taking his eyes off her for an instant.

She was a small thin woman with the skinny figure of a young girl. Her trousers scarcely showed the outline of buttock and thigh. But her face was as deeply lined as if by knife cuts, her lips sucked in by a constant nervous pursing. Dry reddish hair was already thin enough to make it likely Mrs. Harrison would need a wig in ten years' time. She was never still. All night long she probably fidgeted in fretful sleep.

Outside the bow window, gaping in, stood her husband. The night before they had sealed up the broken pane but not drawn the curtains. Brenda gave him a swift look, then surveyed the room, swivelling her head. Her eyes rested briefly on the worst-spattered area of wall, for a longer time on a patch of carpet beside the chair where Naomi Jones had been sitting. Archbold had scraped off a blood-stained section of the pile here and it had gone to the lab with the other items and the four cartridges which had been recovered. Burden thought she was going to comment, to make some remark on the lines of police destroying a good carpet which cleaning would have restored to pristine condition, but she said nothing.

It was Ken Harrison, who made—or mouthed, for inside the room it was nearly inaudible—the expected censure. Burden opened the window.

"I didn't quite catch that, Mr. Harrison."

"I said that was eight-ounce glass, that was."

"No doubt it can be replaced."

"At a cost."

Burden shrugged.

"And the back door wasn't even locked!" exclaimed Harrison in the tone a respectable householder uses to refer to an act of vandalism.

Brenda, left to herself to examine this room for the first time, had turned very pale. That frozen look, that increasing pallor, might be the prelude to a faint. Her glazed eyes met his.

"Come along, Mrs. Harrison, there's no point in remaining here. Are you all right?"

"I'm not going to pass out, if that's what you mean."

But there had been a danger of it, he was sure of that, for she sat down on a chair in the hall and hung her head forwards, trembling. Burden could smell blood. He was hoping she wouldn't know what the stench was, a mixture of fishiness and iron filings, when she jumped up, said she was quite all right and should they go upstairs. She bounded quite jauntily over the sheet that covered the steps where Harvey Copeland had lain.

Upstairs, she showed him the top floor, a place of attics that were perhaps never used. On the first floor were the rooms he had already seen, the two tidy rooms, the untouched rooms, those of Daisy and Naomi Jones. Three-quarters of the way along the passage to the west wing, she opened a door and announced that this was where Copeland had slept.

Burden was surprised. He had assumed that Davina Flory and her husband shared a bedroom. Though he didn't say this, Brenda followed his thought. She gave him a look in which prudery was curiously mixed with lubriciousness.

"She was sixteen years older than him, you know. She was a very old woman. Of course you wouldn't have said that of her, if you know what I mean, she sort of didn't seem to have much to do with age. She was just herself."

Burden knew what she meant. Her sensitivity was unexpected. He gave the room a quick glance. No one had been in there, nothing was disturbed. Copeland had slept in a single bed. The furniture was dark mahogany, but in spite of its warm rich colour, the room had an austere look with plain cream curtains, a cream carpet and the only pictures prints of old county maps.

The state of Davina Flory's bedroom seemed to upset Brenda more than the dining-room had. At least it stimulated her to an outburst of feeling.

"What a mess! Look at the bed! Look at all that stuff out of the drawers!"

She ran about picking things up. Burden made no attempt to stop her. Photographs would provide a permanent record of how the room had been.

"I want you to tell me what's missing, Mrs. Harrison."

"Look at her jewel box!"

"Can you remember what things she had?"

Brenda, as agile as a teenager and as thin, sat on the floor, reaching out all round her for scattered objects—a brooch, a pair of eyebrow tweezers, a suitcase key, an empty perfume bottle.

"That brooch, for instance, why would they leave that?" Her short laugh was like a snort. "It wasn't worth anything. I gave it to her."

"You did?"

"For a Christmas present. We all gave each other presents, so I had to get something. What d'you give the woman who has everything? She used to wear it, maybe she liked it, but it was only worth three quid."

"What's missing, Mrs. Harrison?"

"She didn't have much, you know. I say 'the woman who has everything' but there are things you can afford you don't always want, aren't there? I mean fur, even if you could afford it. Well, it's cruel, isn't it? She could have had diamonds galore, but it wasn't her style.'' She had got up and was rummaging through drawers. ''I'd say the lot was gone, what there was. She had some good pearls. There was rings her first husband gave her, she never wore them, but they were here. Her gold bracelet's gone. One of the rings had enormous diamonds in it, God knows what it was worth. You'd have thought she'd have kept it in the bank, wouldn't you? She told me she thought of giving it to Daisy when she was eighteen.''

''When would that be?''

''Soon. Next week or the week after.''

''Only 'thought of'?''

''I'm telling you what she said and that's what she said.''

''Do you think you could make me a list of the jewellery you think is missing, Mrs. Harrison?''

She nodded, slammed the drawer shut. ''Fancy, this time yesterday I was in here doing the room, I always did the bedrooms on a Tuesday, and she came in, Davina that is, and was talking ever so happily about going off to France with Harvey to do some programme on French TV, some very important book programme for her new book. Of course she spoke French like a native.''

''What do you think happened here last night?''

She was walking ahead of him down the back stairs. ''Me? How should I know?''

''You must have had ideas. You know the house and you knew the people. I'd be interested to know what you think.''

At the foot of the stairs they met a large cat of a colour known to Burden as ''Air Force blue,'' which had come out of the opposite door and was crossing the back hall. When it saw them it stopped in its tracks, opened its eyes very wide, laid back its ears and began to swell until its dense fluffy smoky fur stood on end. Its attitude was of a brave animal menaced by hunters or some dangerous predator.

''Don't be silly, Queenie,'' said Brenda fondly. ''Don't be such a silly old girl. You know he won't hurt you while I'm here.'' Burden felt a little affronted. ''There's some chicken livers for you on the back step.''

The cat turned tail and fled the way it had come. Brenda Harrison followed it through a door Burden had not entered on the previous evening and along a passage that opened into the morning-room. The sun-filled conservatory was as warm as summer. He had been in here briefly the night before. It looked different by day and he saw that this was the glazed building, of classical shape and curved roof, which protruded into the centre of the terrace where he had stood surveying the lawns and the distant woods.

The scent of hyacinths was stronger, sweet and cloying. Sunlight had opened the narcissi to show their orange corollas. In here it was humid and warm and perfumed, the way you thought a rain forest might be, the air damply tangible.

"She wouldn't let me have a pet," Brenda Harrison said suddenly.

"I'm sorry?"

"Davina. Like I say, there was no side to her, all of us was equal—I mean, that's what she *said*—but I wasn't allowed to have a pet. I'd have liked a dog. 'Have a hamster, Brenda,' she said, 'or a budgie.' But I never liked the idea of that. It's cruel keeping birds in cages, don't you reckon?"

"I shouldn't fancy one myself," said Burden.

"God knows what'll become of us now, me and Ken. We've got no other home. The way property prices are, we don't have a chance—well, it's a joke, isn't it? Davina said this was our home forever, but when all's said and done it's a tied cottage, isn't it?" She bent down and picked up a dead leaf from the floor. Her expression became coy, a little wistful. "It's not easy starting afresh. I know I don't look my age, everyone says so, but when all's said and done we're not getting any younger, either of us."

"You were going to tell me what you think happened here last night."

She sighed. "What do I think happened? Well, what does happen in these awful cases, I mean it's not the first, is it? They got in and went upstairs, they'd heard about the pearls and maybe the rings. There's always bits in the papers about Davina. I mean, anyone'd know there was money here. Harvey heard them, went to go upstairs after them and they came down and shot him. Then they had to shoot the others to stop them talking—I mean, telling people what they looked like.''

''It's a possibility.''

''What else?'' she said, as if there were no room for doubt. Then, briskly, astonishing him, ''I'll be able to have a dog now. Whatever becomes of us, no one can stop me having a dog now, can they?''

Burden returned to the hall and contemplated the staircase. The more he thought of it, the less he could match up the mechanics with the evidence.

Jewellery was missing. It might be very valuable jewellery, worth as much as a hundred thousand pounds, but kill three people for it and intend to kill a fourth? Burden shrugged. He knew that men and women have been murdered for fifty pence, for the price of a drink.

The memory of his television appearance rankling a little, Wexford was still able to congratulate himself on the discretion he had maintained in the matter of Daisy Flory. Television was no longer a mysterious and frightening medium. He was getting used to it. This was his third or fourth appearance in front of the camera, and if he was not blasé, he was at least assured.

One question only had ruffled him. It had seemed to have little or nothing to do with the Tancred House murders. Were they any more likely to find the men responsible for this than those guilty of the bank shooting? He had replied that he was certain both crimes would be solved and Sergeant Martin's killer caught, as the Tancred House killers would be. A small smile had appeared on the face of his interrogator, which he tried to ignore, keeping calm.

The question had not been asked by the ''stringer'' for the national papers, nor by either of the national papers' representatives who were there, but by a reporter from the *Kingsmarkham Courier*. This was a very young man, dark-haired, rather handsome, cocky-looking. His was a public-school voice without trace of London accent or the local burr.

"It's getting on for a year since the bank killing, Chief Inspector."

"Ten months," said Wexford.

"Isn't it a fact that statistics show the longer time goes by, the less likely—"

Wexford pointed to another questioner with her hand up and the *Courier* reporter's words were drowned by her inquiry. How was the young Miss Flory? Davina or Daisy, didn't they call her?

Wexford meant to be discreet about that at this stage. He replied that she was in intensive care—possibly, at this hour, still true—that she was stable but seriously ill. She had lost a lot of blood. No one had told him this but it was bound to be true. The girl stringer asked him if she was on "the danger list" and Wexford had been able to tell her that no hospital kept such a list and so far as he knew never had.

He would go alone to see her. He wanted no one accompanying him at this first questioning. DC Gerry Hinde, in his element, was feeding into his computer masses of collated information from which, he had mysteriously announced, he would produce a data base to be distributed to every system in the stable block. Sandwiches had been brought in, fetched from the Cheriton High Road supermarket. Opening his own package with the paper-knife, understanding how useful it would after all prove to be, Wexford wondered what the world had done before the arrival of the wedge-shaped plastic sandwich container. Worthy to be ranked in the scale of blessed inventions, he thought with a glance of distaste at Gerry Hinde, at least on a level with facsimile machines.

Just as he was leaving, Brenda Harrison arrived with a list of Davina Flory's missing jewellery. He only had time to give it a quick scan before passing it on to Hinde. That was a real snip for the data base, that would give him something to mouse through his systems.

To his annoyance, the *Courier* reporter was waiting for him as he came out of the stables. He was sitting on a low wall, swinging his legs. Wexford made it a rule never to talk "cases" to the press except at the arranged conferences. This man must have been hanging about for an hour, on the chance he must emerge sooner or later.

"No. Nothing more to say today."

"That's very unfair. You ought to give priority to us. Support your local sheriff."

"That means you supporting *me*," Wexford said, amused in spite of himself, "not me feeding facts to you. What's your name?"

"Jason Sherwin Coram Sebright."

"A bit of a mouthful, isn't it? Too long for a by-line."

"I've not decided what to call myself for professional purposes yet. I only started at the *Courier* last week. The point is I've got a distinct advantage over the rest of them. I know Daisy, you see. She's at my school, or where I *was*. I know her very well."

All this was delivered with a confident brashness that was uncommon, even these days. Jason Sebright seemed entirely at ease.

"If you're going to see her I hope you'll take me with you," he said. "I'm hoping for an exclusive interview."

"Then your hopes are doomed to be dashed, Mr. Sebright." He shepherded Sebright out, waited there watching until the reporter had got into his own car. Donaldson drove him down the main drive, the way they had come on the previous night. Sebright's tiny Fiat followed close behind. A quarter of a mile on, in an area where there were many fallen trees, they passed Gabbitas operating something Wexford thought might be a planking machine. The hurricane of three years before had done damage here. Wexford noticed cleared areas where there had been recent planting, the two-foot-high saplings tied to posts and sheathed in animal guards. Here, too, seasoning sheds had been built to protect the planked wood, and under tarpaulins were stacked boards of oak and sycamore and ash.

They came to the main gate and Donaldson got out to open it. Hanging from the left-hand gatepost was a bouquet of flowers. Wexford wound down the window to get a better look. This was no ordinary florist's confection but a flower-filled basket with one side deeply curved over to afford the maximum display. Golden freesias, sky-blue scillas and waxen-white stephanotis spilled over the gilded lip of the basket. Attached to the handle was a card.

"What does it say?"

Donaldson stumbled over the words, cleared his throat and began again. " 'Now, boast thee, death, in thy possession lies, A lass unparallel'd.' "

He left the gate open for Jason Sebright, who Wexford saw had also got out to read the words on the card. Donaldson turned on to the B 2428 for Cambery Ashes and Stowerton. They were there in ten minutes.

Dr. Leigh, a tired-looking woman in her mid-twenties, met Wexford in the corridor outside MacAllister Ward.

"I can understand it's urgent to talk to her, but could you keep it down to ten minutes today? I mean, as far as I'm concerned and if it's all right with her, you can come back tomorrow, but just at first I think it should be limited to ten minutes. That will be enough to get the essentials, won't it?"

"If you say so," said Wexford.

"She has lost a lot of blood," she said, confirming what he had told the press. "But the bullet didn't break the collar-bone. More important, it didn't touch the lung. A bit of a miracle, that. It's not so much that she's physically ill as that she's very distressed. She's still very very distressed."

"I'm not surprised."

"Would you come into the office a moment?"

Wexford followed her into a small room which had "Charge Nurse" on the door. It was empty and full of smoke. Why did hospital staff, who must hear more than most people of the evils and dangers of cigarettes, smoke more than anyone else? It was a mystery that often intrigued him. Dr. Leigh clicked her tongue and opened the window.

"A bullet was extracted from Daisy's upper chest. Her shoulder blade prevented it from exiting. Do you want it?"

"Certainly we do. She was shot only once?"

"Only once. In the upper chest on the left side."

"Yes." He wrapped the lead cylinder in his handkerchief and put it in his pocket. The fact that it had been in this girl's body brought him a slight unexpected flutter of nausea.

"You can go in now. She's in a side room; we're keeping her on her own because she's a very unhappy girl. She doesn't need company at the moment."

Dr. Leigh took him into MacAllister Ward. The corridor walls of the single rooms were panelled in frosted glass and each door had an insertion of clear glass. Outside the room with "2" printed on the glass Anne Lennox sat on an uncomfortable-looking stool, reading a paperback Danielle Steel. She jumped up when Wexford appeared.

"Do you need me, sir?"

"No, thanks, Anne. You stay where you are."

A nurse came out of the room and held the door open. Dr. Leigh said she would be waiting for him when he had finished and repeated her injunction about a time limit. Wexford went in and the door was closed behind him.

CHAPTER SEVEN

She was sitting up in a high white bed, propped by a mass of pillows. Her left arm was in a sling and her left shoulder thickly bandaged. It was so warm in the ward that, instead of an enveloping hospital gown, she wore a little white sleeveless shift that exposed her right shoulder and upper arm. An intravenous line was attached to her bare right arm.

The photograph from the *Independent on Sunday* came to mind. This was Davina Flory all over again, this was Davina Flory as *she* had been at seventeen.

Instead of shingled hair, she wore hers long. It was copious straight hair of a very fine very dark brown, which fell down to and half-covered the wounded shoulder and the bare, whole shoulder. Her forehead was high like her grandmother's, her eyes large and deep-set, not brown but a bright clear hazel with a black ring round the pupils. The skin was white for such a dark woman and the rather thin lips very pale. A prettier nose than her grandmother's eagle's beak tilted a little at the tip.

Wexford recalled Davina Flory's dead hands, narrow and long-fingered, and saw that Daisy's were the same but the skin still soft and childish. She wore no rings. On the pale pink lobes of her ears the pierce marks showed as tiny pink wounds.

When she saw him she did not speak but began to cry. The tears rolled silently down her face.

He pulled out a handful of tissues from the box on her bedside cabinet and handed them to her. She wiped her face, then dropped her head, screwing up her eyes. Her body heaved with suppressed sobs.

"I'm sorry," he said. "I'm very sorry."

She nodded, clutching the damp tissues in her left hand. It was something he hadn't given much thought to, that she had lost her mother in the violence of the previous night. She had lost a grandmother too, who might have been as much beloved, and a man who had been like a grandfather since she was five years old.

"Miss Flory . . ."

Her voice came out muffled as she held the tissues up against her face. "Call me Daisy." He could tell she was making an effort as she swallowed hard and lifted her head. "Call me Daisy, please. I can't be doing with 'Miss Flory,' I'm called Jones really anyway. Oh, I must stop crying!"

Wexford waited a moment or two, though mindful of how few moments he had. He saw she was trying to expel pictures from her mind, to wipe them away, expunge the videotape, come to the here and now. She drew a long breath.

He waited awhile but he couldn't afford to wait too long. A minute only for her to breathe steadily in, smooth the tears away with her fingers. "Daisy," he began, "you know who I am, don't you? I'm a policeman, Chief Inspector Wexford."

She was nodding quickly.

"They're only allowing me ten minutes with you today, but I'm going to come back tomorrow if you'll let me. I want you to answer one or two questions now and I'll try not to make them painful questions. Will that be all right?"

A slow nod and another gasp.

"We have to go back to last night. I'm not going to ask you

exactly what happened, not yet; just when you first heard them in the house and where.''

The hesitation was so long he couldn't help looking down at his watch.

''If you could just tell me what time you heard them and where it was . . .''

She spoke suddenly and in a rush. ''They were upstairs. We were eating our dinner, we'd got to the main course. My mother heard them first. She said, 'What's that? It sounds like someone upstairs.' ''

''Yes. What next?''

''Davina, my grandmother, said it was the cat.''

''The *cat*?''

''She's a big cat called Queenie, a Blue Persian. Sometimes, in the evenings, she sort of rampages about the house. It's amazing what a racket she can make.''

Daisy Flory smiled. It was a wonderful wide smile, a young girl's smile, and she held it steady for a moment before it trembled on her lips. Wexford would have liked to take her hand but of course he couldn't do that.

''Did you hear a car?''

She shook her head. ''I didn't hear anything but the noise upstairs. A bumping noise and footsteps. Harvey, that's my grandmother's husband, he went out of the room. We heard the shot and then another. It made a terrible noise, it was really terrible. My mother screamed. We all jumped up. No, I jumped up and my mother did and I—I sort of started to go out and my mother shouted, 'No, don't,' and then he came in. He came into the room.''

''*He*? There was only one?''

''I only saw one. I heard the other one, I didn't see him.''

The recollection of it silenced her again. He saw the tears come back into her eyes. She rubbed her eyes with her right hand.

''I only saw one,'' she said in a choked voice. ''He had a gun, he came in.''

''Take it easy,'' Wexford said. ''I have to ask you. It'll soon be over. Think of it like that, it's something that must be. All right?''

"All right. He came in . . ." Her voice went dead, automatic machine tones. "Davina was still sitting there. She never got up, she just sat there but with her head turned towards the door. He shot her in the head, I think. He shot my mother. I don't know what I did. It was so terrible, it was like nothing you could imagine, madness, horror, it wasn't real, only it was—oh, I don't know . . . I tried to get onto the floor. I heard the other one getting a car started outside. Then the one in there, the one with the gun, he shot me and I don't know, I don't remember . . ."

"Daisy, you're doing very well. Very well indeed. I don't suppose you can remember what happened after you were shot. But can you remember what he looked like? Can you describe him?"

She shook her head, put her right hand up to her face. He had the impression it wasn't that she couldn't describe the man with the gun but was unable for the present to bring herself to do so. She murmured, "I didn't hear him speak, he didn't speak." Though he hadn't asked, she whispered, "It was just after eight when we heard them and ten past when they went. Ten minutes, that was all . . ."

The door opened and a nurse came in. "Your ten minutes is up. I'm afraid that's all for today."

Wexford got up. Even if they had not been interrupted he would hardly have ventured to go on. The girl's abilities to answer him were almost exhausted.

In a voice just above a whisper, she said, "I don't mind you coming back tomorrow. I know I have to talk about it. I'll talk some more tomorrow."

She took her eyes from his and stared hard at the window, slowly lifting her shoulders, the one that was wounded and the one that was whole, and brought her right hand up to cover her mouth.

The piece in the *Independent on Sunday* was imbued with a kind of clever bitchiness. Wherever it was possible to be snide, Win Carver was snide. No opportunity for a sneer was neglected. Yet it was a good essay. Such was human nature, Wexford confessed to himself, that it was *better* for its ironic and slightly malicious tone than a blander article would have been.

A journalist on the *Kingsmarkham Courier* would have adopted a sycophantic style when describing Davina Flory's reafforestation, her dendrology studies, her gardening and her collecting of rare specimen trees. Ms. Carver treated the whole subject as if it were slightly funny and an instance of mild hypocrisy. "Planting" a wood, she implied, was a not quite accurate way of referring to an exercise others did for you while all you forked out was the money. Gardening might be a very pleasant way of passing the time if you were only obliged to do it when at a loose end and on fine days. Strong young men did the digging.

Davina Flory, she went on to say in much the same vein, had been a stupendously successful and acclaimed woman, but she hadn't exactly had to struggle, had she? Going to Oxford had been an obvious step, given her intelligence and with her father a professor and there being no shortage of money. A great landscape gardener she might be, but the acreage and the wherewithal fell into her lap when she married Desmond Flory. Being widowed in the last stages of the war had been sad but surely mitigated by inheriting on her first husband's death an enormous country house and a huge fortune.

She was a little scathing too about the short-lived second marriage. However, when she came to the travels and the books, the uniqueness of Davina Flory's penetration of Eastern Europe and her political and sociological investigations of it, this at the most difficult and dangerous of times, Win Carver had nothing but praise to offer. She wrote of the "anthropological" books to which these travels had given rise. She harked back with a charming adulatory nostalgia to her own student days some twenty years before, and to her reading of Davina Flory's only two novels, *The Hosts of Midian* and *A Private Man in Athens*. Her appreciation she compared to Keats's feeling for Chapman's *Homer*, she even said she had been silenced "upon a peak in Darien."

Finally, but not briefly, she came to the first volume of the autobiography: *The Youngest Wren of Nine*. Wexford, who had supposed this title a quotation from *Twelfth Night*, was pleased to have his guess confirmed. A résumé of Davina Flory's childhood and youth, as described in these memoirs, came next, a passing reference to her meeting with Harvey Copeland, and Ms. Carver ended with a few words—a very few—about Miss Flory's daughter Naomi Jones, who had a part-share in a Kingsmarkham craft gallery, and Miss Flory's granddaughter and namesake.

In the last lines of the article Win Carver speculated as to the chances of a DBE in a future honours' list and judged them pretty high. A year or two only must pass, she implied, before Miss Flory became Dame Davina. Mostly (wrote Ms. Carver) "they wait till you've passed your eightieth birthday so that you won't live too long."

Davina Flory's life had not been sufficiently protracted. Death had come unnaturally to her and with the maximum violence. Wexford, who was still in the incident room, laid the newspaper aside and studied the print-out Gerry Hinde had produced for him of the missing items of jewellery. There were not many, but what there was sounded valuable. Then he walked across the courtyard to the house.

The hall had been cleaned. It reeked of the kind of disinfectant that smells like a combination of Lysol and lime juice. Brenda Harrison was rearranging ornaments that had been put back in the wrong places. Her prematurely lined face wore an expression of intense concentration, the cause no doubt of the lines. On the staircase, three stairs up, where the carpet, perhaps ineradicably stained, was covered in a sheet of canvas, sat the Blue Persian called Queenie.

"You'll be glad to hear Daisy is making a good recovery," Wexford said.

She already knew. "One of the policemen told me," she said without enthusiasm.

"How long had you and your husband worked here, Mrs. Harrison?"

"Getting on for ten years."

He was surprised. Ten years is a long time. He would have expected more emotional involvement with the family after so long an association, more *feeling*.

"Mr. and Mrs. Copeland were good employers then?"

She shrugged. She was dusting a red-and-blue Crown Derby owl and she replaced it on the polished surface before she spoke. Then she said in a thoughtful way, as if considerable cogitation had been going on before she came up with it, "There was no side to them." She hesitated, then added proudly, "Not with us, at any rate."

The cat got up, stretched itself and walked slowly in Wexford's direction. It stopped in front of him, bristled up, glowered and quite suddenly fled up the stairs. After a moment or two the noises began. Sounds like a miniature horse galloping along the passage, bumps, crashes, reverberations.

Brenda Harrison switched a light on, then another. "Queenie always carries on like that about this time," she said.

"Does she do any damage?"

A small smile moved her features, spread her cheeks an inch or so. It told him she was one of those who find their amusement in the antics of animals. Their sense of humour is confined almost exclusively to tea-partying chimpanzees, anthropomorphic dogs, kittens in bonnets. They are the sort that keep circuses going.

"You could go up in half an hour," she said, "and you wouldn't know she'd been there."

"And it's always at this time?" He looked at his watch: ten to six.

"Give or take a bit, yes." She gave him a sidelong glance, grinning a very little. "She's as bright as a button, but she can't tell the time, can she?"

"I want to ask you just one more thing, Mrs. Harrison. Have you seen any strangers about in the past days or even weeks? Unfamiliar people? Anyone you wouldn't expect to see near the house or on the estate?"

She thought. She shook her head. "You want to ask Johnny. Johnny Gabbitas, that is. He gets about the woods, he's always outside."

"How long has he been here?"

Her answer slightly surprised him. "Maybe a year. Not more. Wait a minute, I reckon it'll be a year in May."

"If you think of anything, anything odd or unusual that may have happened, you'll be sure to tell us, won't you?"

By now it was growing dark. As he walked round the side of the west wing, the lights in the lee of the wall came on, controlled by a time switch. He paused and looked back towards the woods and the road that led out of them. Last night the two men must have come that way or else along the by-road, there was no other possible route.

Why had none of the four people in the house heard a car? Perhaps they had. Three of them were no longer alive to tell him. Daisy had not, that was all he could know or would know. But if one of them had heard a car, he or she had not remarked on it in Daisy's hearing. Of course he was to hear much more from Daisy tomorrow.

The two men in the car would have seen the lighted house ahead of them. By eight the wall lights had been on for two hours and lights indoors on for much longer. The road ran up to the courtyard, passed between a stone-pillared opening in the wall. But suppose the car had not come up to the house but turned to the left *before* the wall was reached. Turned left and right onto the road where he now was, the road that led past the west wing, twenty yards from it, curved past the kitchen regions and the back door, skirted the garden and its high hedge, and penetrated the pinetum, which led to the Harrisons' house and that of John Gabbitas.

Taking this route would presuppose knowledge of Tancred House and its grounds. It might presuppose knowledge that the back door was not locked during the evenings. If the car in which they came was driven that way and parked near the kitchen door, it was possible, even likely, that no one in the dining room would have heard it.

But Daisy had heard the man she had not seen start a car she had not seen after the man she *had* seen had shot her and her family.

Probably he had left the house by the back door and brought the car round to the front. He had escaped when he heard noises overhead. The man who shot Daisy also heard noises overhead, which was why he had not fired another shot, the shot that would have killed her. The noises were, of course, made by the cat Queenie, but the two men were not to know that. Very likely, neither of them had been to the top floor, but they knew there *was* a top floor. They knew someone else might be up there.

This was an entirely satisfying explanation in all respects but one. Wexford was standing by the side of the road, looking behind him, pondering on this single exception, when car lights came up out of the wood on the main road. They turned off to the left just before the wall was reached and in the light from the house Wexford saw that this was Gabbitas's Land Rover.

Gabbitas stopped when he saw who it was. He wound down the window. "Were you looking for me?"

"I'd like a word, Mr. Gabbitas. Can you spare me half an hour?"

For answer, Gabbitas leaned across and opened the passenger door. Wexford hauled himself in. "Would you come over to the stables, please?"

"It's a bit late for that, isn't it?"

"Late for what, Mr. Gabbitas? Pursuing a murder inquiry? There are three people dead here and one seriously injured. But on second thought I think your house might be the better venue."

"Oh, very well. If you insist."

This little exchange had served to inform Wexford of things he had not noticed at their first meeting. From his accent and his manner, the woodsman showed himself a considerable cut above the Harrisons. He was also extremely good-looking. He was the type of a Cold Comfort Farm hero. He had the looks of an actor some casting director might pick to play the male lead in a Hardy or Lawrence adaptation. Byronic but rustic too. His hair was black, his eyes very dark. The hands on the wheel were brown with black hairs on the backs of them and on the long fingers. The half-grin he had given Wexford when asked to drive down the by-road had shown a set of very white even teeth. He was a swashbuckler and of the type that is supposed more than any other to be attractive to women.

Wexford climbed into the passenger seat. "What time was it you told me you came home last night?"

"Eight twenty, eight twenty-five, that's the nearest I can make it. I didn't think I'd have any reason to be precise about the time." There was an edge of impatience to his tone. "I know I was back in my house when my clock struck the half-hour."

"Do you know Mrs. Bib Mew who works at the house?"

Gabbitas seemed amused. "I know who you mean. I didn't know she was called that."

"Mrs. Mew left here on her bicycle at ten to eight last night and reached home in Pomfret Monachorum at about ten past. If you reached home at twenty past, it's likely you might have met her on your way. She too used the by-road."

"I didn't meet her," Gabbitas said shortly. "I've told you, I met no one, I passed no one."

They had driven through the pinetum and reached the cottage where he lived. Gabbitas's manner, when ushering Wexford in, had become slightly more gracious. Wexford asked him where he had been on the previous day.

"Coppicing a wood near Midhurst. Why?"

It was a bachelor's house, tidy, functional, a little shabby. The living-room into which he took Wexford was dominated by objects which turned it into an office, a desk with lap-top computer, grey metal filing cabinet, stacks of box files. Bookcases full of encyclopaedias half filled a wall. Gabbitas cleared a chair for him by lifting off its seat an armful of folders and exercise books.

Wexford persisted, "And you came home along the by-road?"

"I told you."

"Mr. Gabbitas," said Wexford rather crossly, "you must have seen enough television, if you know it from no other source, to understand that a policeman's purpose in asking you the same thing twice is, frankly, to catch you out."

"Sorry," said Gabbitas. "Okay, I do know that. It's just that a . . . well, a law-abiding person doesn't much like to have it thought he's done anything to be caught out about. I suppose I expect to be believed."

"Yes, I daresay. That's rather idealistic in the world we live in. I wonder if you've been thinking about this business much today. While you've been in your woodland solitude near Midhurst, for instance? It would be natural to give it some thought."

Gabbitas said shortly, "I've been thinking of it, yes. Who could help thinking of it?"

"About the car these people who perpetrated this——this massacre, arrived in, for instance. Where was it parked while they were in the house? Where was it when you came home? Not making its escape by the by-road, or you would have passed it. Daisy Flory made her nine-nine-nine call at twenty-two minutes past eight, within a few minutes after they left. She made it as fast as she could crawl because she was afraid she might bleed to death." Wexford watched the man's face while he said this. It remained impassive but the lips tightened a little. "So the car can't have gone by the by-road or you would have seen it."

"Obviously it went by the main road."

"There happens to have been a squad car on the B 2428 at this time and it was alerted to block the road and note all vehicles from eight twenty-five. According to the officers in that car, no vehicle of any kind passed until eight forty-eight, when our own convoy with the ambulance came. A road-block was also set up on the B 2428 in the Cambery Ashes direction. Perhaps our block was put on too late. There's something you can perhaps tell me: Is there any other way out?"

"Through the woods, d'you mean? A jeep could perhaps

81

get out if the driver knew the woods. If he knew them like the back of his hand.'' Gabbitas sounded extremely dubious. ''I'm not sure I could do it.''

''But you haven't been here all that long, have you?''

As if he thought explanation rather than an answer was required, Gabbitas said, ''I teach one day a week at Sewingbury Agricultural College. I take private work. I'm a tree surgeon among other things.''

''When did you first come here?''

''Last May.'' Gabbitas put his hand up to his mouth, rubbed his lips. ''How is Daisy?''

''She's well,'' Wexford said. ''She's going to be very well—physically. Her psychological state, that's another thing. Who lived here before you came?''

''Some people called Griffin.'' Gabbitas spelt it. ''A couple and their son.''

''Was their work confined to the estate, or did they have outside jobs like you?''

''The son was grown up. He had a job, I don't know what. In Pomfret or Kingsmarkham, I should think. Griffin, I think his first name was Gerry or maybe Terry, yes, Terry, he managed the woodland. She was just his wife. I think she sometimes worked up at the house.''

''Why did they leave? It wasn't just a job to leave, it was a house too.''

''He was getting on. Not sixty-five but getting on. I think the work got too much for him, he took early retirement. They had a house to go to, a place they'd bought. That's just about all I know about the Griffins. I met them just the once, when I got this job and I was shown the house.''

''The Harrisons will know more, I imagine.''

For the first time, Gabbitas really smiled. His face was attractive and friendly when he smiled and his teeth were spectacular. ''They weren't on speaking terms.''

''What, the Harrisons and the Griffins?''

''Brenda Harrison told me they hadn't spoken since Griffin insulted her months before. I don't know what he said or did, that's what she told me.''

"Was that the real reason for their leaving?"

"I wouldn't know."

"Do you know where this house they moved to is? Did they leave an address?"

"Not with me. I think they said Myringham way. Not all that far. I have a distinct memory of Myringham. Would you like a coffee? Or tea or something?"

Wexford refused. He also refused Gabbitas's offer of a lift back to where his car was parked outside the incident room.

"It's dark. You'd better take a torch." He called after Wexford, "That was her place, Daisy's. Those stables, they were her private sort of sanctuary. Her grandmother had them done up for her." He had a kind of genius for minor bombshells, small revelations. "She spent hours in there on her own. Doing her own thing, whatever that was."

They had taken her sanctuary over without asking permission. Or, if permission had been asked and obtained, it was not from the stables' owner. Wexford walked along the winding path through the pinetum, aided by the lantern Gabbitas had lent him. It occurred to him as the now dark bulk, the unlit rear, of Tancred House came into sight, that all this now probably belonged to Daisy Flory. Unless there were other heirs, but if there were, newspaper articles and obituaries had made no mention of them.

She had come into all this narrowly. If the bullet had been an inch lower, death would have robbed her of her inheritance. Wexford wondered why he was so sure that her inheritance would be a liability to her, that when she knew of what some would call her good fortune, she would recoil from it.

Hinde had checked the items listed by Brenda Harrison with Davina Flory's insurance company. A string of jet beads, a rope of pearls that, whatever Brenda might insist on, were probably not real, a couple of silver rings, a silver bracelet, a silver-and-onyx-brooch, she had not bothered to insure.

On both lists were a gold bracelet valued at thirty-five hundred pounds, a ruby ring with diamond shoulders valued at five thousand pounds, another set with pearls and sapphires at two thousand, and a ring described as a diamond cluster, a formidable piece of jewellery this, valued at nineteen thousand pounds.

The whole seemed to be worth rather more than thirty thousand. They had taken the less valuable pieces as well, of course, not knowing. Perhaps they had been even more ignorant and had supposed their loot worth far more than it was.

Wexford poked at the grey furry cactus with his forefinger. Its colour and texture reminded him of Queenie the cat. No doubt she too had thorns concealed by silky fluff. He locked the door and went to his car.

CHAPTER EIGHT

Five cartridges had been used in the Tancred murders.

The cartridges, according to the ballistics expert who had examined them, had come from a .38 Colt Magnum revolver. The barrel of every pistol is scored inside by distinct lines and grooves which in turn leave their mark on the bullet as it leaves the gun. The interior of each barrel contains unique marks, as individual as a fingerprint. The marks on the .38 cartridges found at Tancred House—all had passed through the bodies of Davina Flory, Naomi Jones and Harvey Copeland—matched and could therefore be concluded to have come from the same gun.

Wexford said, "At least we know that only one gun was used. We know it was a Colt Magnum .38. The man Daisy saw did all the shooting. They didn't share it out, he did all the shooting himself. Is that odd?"

"They only had one gun," said Burden. "Or only one real gun. Do you know, I read somewhere the other day about a town in the United States where a serial killer was on the loose that all the students on the university campus were permitted to go out and buy guns for their own protection. Kids of nineteen and twenty they must have been. Think of that. Handguns are still hard to come by in this country, thank God.''

"We said that when poor Martin was shot, remember?"

"That was a .38 or .357 Colt too."

"I'd noticed," Wexford said sharply. "But the cartridges used in the two cases, Martin's killing and this one, don't match anyway."

"Unfortunately. If they did, we'd really be getting somewhere. One cartridge used and five left to go? Michelle Weaver's story wouldn't look quite so fantastic."

"Has it occurred to you it was odd using a handgun at *all*?"

"Occurred to me? It struck me at once. Most of them use a sawn-off shotgun."

"Yes. The great British answer to Dan Wesson. I'll tell you something else that's odd, Mike. Let's say there were six cartridges in the cylinder, it was full to capacity. Four people were in the house, but the gunman didn't fire four times, he fired five times. Harvey Copeland was the first to be shot, yet, knowing he had only six cartridges, he *fired twice at Copeland*. Why? Perhaps he didn't know there were three more people in the dining-room, perhaps he panicked. He goes into the dining-room and shoots Davina Flory, then Naomi Jones, one cartridge each, then Daisy. One cartridge remains in the cylinder, but he doesn't shoot Daisy twice to 'finish her off,' as Ken Harrison might put it. Why doesn't he?"

"Hearing the cat upstairs surprised him. He heard the noise and ran?"

"Yes. Maybe. Or there weren't six cartridges in the cylinder, there were only five. One had already been used before he came to Tancred."

"Not on poor old Martin, though," Burden said briskly. "Anything come in from Sumner-Quist yet?"

Wexford shook his head. "I suppose we must expect delays. I've put Barry on to checking where John Gabbitas was on

Tuesday, what time he left and so on. And then I'd like you to take him with you and find some people called Griffin, a Terry Griffin and his wife, living in the Myringham area. They were Gabbitas's predecessors on the Tancred estate. We're looking for someone who knew this place and the people who lived here. Possibly for someone with a grudge against them."

"A former employee then?"

"Perhaps. One who knew all about them and what they possessed, their habits and so on. One who's an unknown quantity."

After Burden had gone, Wexford sat looking at the scene-of-crime photographs. Stills from a snuff movie, he thought, the kind of pictures no one but himself would ever see, the results of *real* violence, *real* crime. Those great dark splashes and stains were *real* blood. Was he privileged to see them or unfortunate? Would the day ever come when newspapers displayed such photographs? It might. After all, it was not so long ago that no publication ever showed a picture of the dead.

He made the mental adjustment that shifted him from being a sensitive man with a man's feelings to a briskly functioning machine, an analyzing eye, a printer-out of question marks. In this avatar, he looked at the photographs. Tragic, appalling, monstrous as the scene in the dining-room might be, there was nothing incongruous about it. This was how the women would have fallen if one of them had been sitting at the table facing the door, the other, opposite her, standing up and staring past her. The blood on the floor in the empty corner near the foot of the table was Daisy's blood.

He saw what he had seen that night. The bloody napkin on the floor and the blood-dabbled napkin in Davina Flory's hand, clutched by her dying, contracting fingers. Her face lying dipped in a plate of blood and the dreadful ruined head. Naomi lay back in her chair as if in a swoon, her long hair trailed over the barred back of it and dipping nearly to touch the floor. Spangles of blood on the lampshades, the walls, black blotches on the carpet, dark spray spots on the bread in the basket, and the table-cloth dark where the blood had seeped in a dense smooth tide.

For the second time in this case—and he was later to experience it again and again—he had a perception of a prevailing order destroyed, of beauty outraged, of chaos come again. With no evidence for believing it, he thought he detected in this perpetrator a gleeful passion for destruction. But there was nothing incongruous in these photographs. Given the dreadful events, it was what he would expect. On the other hand, those of Harvey Copeland, showing him spread-eagled on his back at the foot of the staircase, his feet towards the front hall and door, presented a problem. One perhaps which Daisy's testimony would solve.

If the men had come downstairs and met him coming up to look for them, why had he, when the gunman shot him, not fallen *backwards* down those stairs?

Four was the hour he had in mind, it was at four that he had been to see her yesterday, though today he had named no definite time. The traffic was light and he reached the hospital rather early. It was ten to four when he stepped out of the lift and walked along the corridor towards MacAllister Ward.

This time there was no Dr. Leigh waiting to meet him. He had called Anne Lennox off her watch. There seemed no one about. Perhaps the staff were all having a quick breather (or choker) in the charge nurse's room. He came quietly to Daisy's room. Through the frosted glass panels he could see she had someone with her, a man in a chair on the left side of the bed.

A visitor. At least it wasn't Jason Sebright.

The pane of glass in the door clarified this man's image for him. He was young, about twenty-six, biggish and thickset, and such was his appearance that Wexford could immediately place him, or make a good guess at doing so. Daisy's visitor belonged to the upper middle class, had been to a distinguished public school but probably not to a university, was "something in the city," where he worked all his days with a computer and a phone. For this job he would be—as Ken Harrison might have said—finished before he was thirty, so he was coining in the maximum before that date. The clothes he wore were suitable to a man twice his age—navy blazer, dark-grey flannels, a white shirt and old school tie. The one concession he made to vague ideas of fashion and suitability was the wearing of his hair rather longer than that shirt and blazer required. It was fair curly hair, and from the way it was combed and the way it curled round his ear-lobes, Wexford guessed he was vain of it.

As for Daisy, she sat up in bed, her eyes on her visitor, her expression inscrutable. She was not smiling, nor did she look particularly sad. It was impossible for him to tell if she had begun to recover from the shock she had received. The young man had brought flowers, a dozen red roses in bud, and these lay on the bedcover between him and her. Her right hand, the good hand, rested on their stems and on the pink-and-gold-patterned paper in which they were wrapped.

Wexford waited for a few seconds, then tapped on the door, opened it and walked in.

The young man turned round, bestowing on Wexford precisely the stare he had expected. At certain schools, he had often thought, they teach them to look at you like that, with confidence, contempt, a degree of indignation, just as they teach them to talk with a plum in their mouths.

Daisy didn't smile. She managed to be polite and cordial without smiling, a rare feat. "Oh, hallo," she said. "Hi." Her voice today was subdued but measured, the edge of hysteria gone. "Nicholas, this is Inspector—no, *Chief* Inspector Wexford. Mr. Wexford, this is Nicholas Virson, a friend of my family."

She said it calmly, without a flicker of hesitation, though she had no family left.

The two men nodded to each other. Wexford said, "Good afternoon." Virson only gave a second nod. In his idea of a hierarchy, his great Chain of Being, policemen had their low place.

"I hope you're feeling better."

Daisy looked down. "I'm okay."

"Do you feel well enough for us to have a talk? To go into things rather more deeply?"

"I must," she said. She stretched her neck, lifted her chin. "You said it all yesterday when you said we had to, we didn't have a choice."

He saw her close her fingers round the paper that wrapped the roses, saw her clutch the stems tightly, and had the strange notion she was doing it to make her hand bleed. But perhaps they were thornless.

"You'll have to go, Nicholas." Men with this Christian name are almost always called by one of its diminutives, Nick or Nicky, but she called him Nicholas. "It was sweet of you to come. I adore the flowers," she said, squeezing their stems without looking at them.

Wexford had known Virson would say it or something like it, it was only a matter of time. "I say, I hope you aren't going to put Daisy through any sort of interrogation. I mean, at the end of the day, what can she in fact tell you? What can she remember? She's a very confused lady, aren't you, lovey?"

"I'm not confused." She spoke in a calm low monotone, giving each word equal weight. "I'm not at all confused."

"Now she tells me." Virson managed a hearty laugh. He got up, stood there, suddenly seeming not quite sure of himself. Over his shoulder he threw at Wexford, "She may manage a description of the villain she did see, but she never even caught a glimpse of the vehicle."

Now why had he said that? Was it simply that he needed something to say to fill up the time while he considered attempting a kiss? Daisy lifted her face to him, something Wexford hadn't expected, and Virson, bending down quickly, put his lips to her cheek. The kiss stimulated him to use an endearment.

"Is there anything I can do for you, darling?"

"There is one thing," she said. "On your way out, could you find a vase and put these flowers in it?"

This, evidently, was not at all what Virson had meant. He had no option but to agree.

"You'll find one in a place they call the sluice. I don't know where it is, down to the left somewhere. The poor nurses are always so busy."

Virson went off, carrying out the roses he had carried in.

Today Daisy had a white garment on, a hospital gown that fastened with tapes down the back. It covered and enclosed her left arm with the bandages and the sling. The IV line was still there. She followed his eyes.

"It's easier for putting drugs into you. That's why they keep it there. It's coming off today. I'm not *ill* any more."

"And you're not confused?" He was quoting her.

"Not in the least." She spoke for a moment like someone much older. "I have been thinking about it," she said. "People tell me not to think of it, but I have to. What else is there? I knew I'd have to tell you everything as best I could, so I've been thinking about it to get things straight. Didn't some writer say violent death wonderfully concentrates the mind?"

He was surprised but he didn't show it. "Samuel Johnson, but it was knowing one was going to be hanged on the morrow."

She smiled a little, a very little, narrowly. "You're not much like my idea of a policeman."

"I daresay you haven't met many." He thought suddenly, she looks like Sheila. She looks like my own daughter. Oh, she was dark and Sheila was fair, but it wasn't those things, whatever people said, that made one person look like another. It was similarity of feature, facial shape. It made him a bit cross when they said Sheila was like him because they had the same hair. Or had, before his went grey and half of it fell out. Sheila was *beautiful*. Daisy was beautiful and her features were like Sheila's. She was looking at him with a sadness close to despair. "You said you'd been thinking about it, Daisy. Tell me what you thought."

She nodded, her expression unchanging. She reached for the glass of something on the bedside cabinet—lemon squash, barley water—and drank a little. "I'll tell you what happened, everything I remember. That's what you want, isn't it?"

"Yes. Yes, please."

"You must interrupt me if something isn't clear. You'll do that, won't you?"

Her tone, suddenly, was that of someone used to telling servants, and not only servants, what she wanted and having them obey. She was habituated, he thought, to telling one to come and he cometh, to another to go and he goeth and to a third, to do this and he doeth it. Wexford suppressed a smile. "Of course."

"It's hard to know how far back to begin. Davina used to say that when she was writing a book. How far back to begin? You could start at what you thought was the beginning and then you'd realize it began long long before that. But here, in this case—shall I start with the afternoon?"

He nodded.

"I'd been to school. I'm a day student at Crelands. As a matter of fact, I'd love to have boarded, but Davina wouldn't let me." She seemed to recollect something, perhaps only that her grandmother was dead. *De mortuis* . . . "Well, it would have been silly really. Crelands is only the other side of Myfleet, as I expect you know."

He knew. This was also the alma mater of Sebright, apparently. A minor public school, it nevertheless belonged in the Headmasters' Conference, as Eton and Harrow did. The fees were similar to theirs. Exclusively a boys' school from its founding by Albert the Good in 1856, it had opened its doors to girls some seven or eight years ago.

"Afternoon school stops at four. I got home at four thirty."

"Someone fetched you by car?"

She gave him a glance, genuinely puzzled. "I drove myself."

The great British car revolution had not passed him by, but he could still recall very clearly the days when a three-or-four-car family was something he thought of as an American anomaly, when a great many women couldn't drive, when few people possessed a car until they were married. His own mother would have stared in astonishment, suspected mockery, if asked if she could drive. His mild surprise wasn't lost on Daisy.

"Davina gave me my car for my birthday when I was seventeen. I passed my test next day. It was a great relief, I can tell you, not having to depend on one of them or be driven by Ken. Well, as I was saying, I got home by four thirty and went to my place. You've probably seen my place. That's what I call it. It used to be stables. I garage my car there and there's this room that's mine, that's private."

"Daisy, I've a confession to make. We're using your place as an incident room. It seemed the most convenient. We do have to be there. Someone should have asked you and I'm very sorry we overlooked it."

"You mean there are lots of policemen and computers and desks and a—a blackboard?" She must have seen something like it on television. "You're sort of investigating the case from there?"

"I'm afraid so."

"Oh, don't be afraid. I don't mind. Why should I mind? Be my guest. I don't mind anything any more." She looked away, wrinkled up her face a little, said in the same cool tone, "Why would I care about a little thing like that when I've nothing to live for?"

"Daisy . . ." he began.

"No, don't say it, please. Don't say I'm young and I've all my life before me and this will pass. Don't tell me time is a great healer and this time next year I'll have put it all in the past. Don't."

Someone had been saying those things to her. A doctor? Some psychologist on the hospital staff? Nicholas Virson?

"All right. I won't. Tell me what happened after you got home."

She waited a little, drew in her breath. "I've got my own phone, I expect you've noticed. I expect you're using it. Brenda phoned to ask if I'd like tea and then she brought it. Tea and biscuits. I was reading, I get a lot of prep. A levels for me in May—or it was to have been."

He didn't comment.

"I'm no intellectual. Davina thought I was because I'm—well, quite bright. She couldn't bear to think I might take after my mother. Sorry, you won't want to hear about that. It doesn't matter any more, anyway.

"Davina expected us to change for dinner. Not dress, exactly, but change. My—my mother came home in her car. She works in a crafts gallery—well, she's a partner in a crafts gallery—with a woman called Joanne Garland. The gallery's called Garlands. I expect you think that's yucky, but it's the woman's name, so I suppose it's okay. She came home in her car. I think Davina and Harvey were home all afternoon, but I don't know. Brenda would know.

"I went to my room and put a dress on. Davina used to say jeans were a uniform and should be used as such, for work. The others were all in the *serre* having drinks."

"In the what?"

"The *serre*. It's French for "greenhouse," it's what we always called it. It sounds better than "conservatory," don't you think?"

Wexford thought it sounded pretentious but he said nothing.

"We always had drinks in there or in the drawing-room. Just sherry, you know, or orange juice or fizzy water. I always had fizzy water and so did my mother. Davina was talking about going to Glyndebourne, she is—was—a member or a friend or whatever, and she always went three times a year. Everything like that she went to, Aldeburgh, the Edinburgh festival, Salzburg. Anyway, her tickets had come. She was asking Harvey about what she should order for dinner. You have to order your dinner months in advance if you don't want to picnic. We never did picnic, it would be so awful if it rained.

"They were still talking about that when Brenda put her head round the door and said dinner was in the dining-room and she was off. I started talking to Davina about going to France in a fortnight's time, she was going to Paris to be in some television book programme and she wanted me to go with her and Harvey. It would have been Easter holidays for me but I didn't much want to go and I was telling her I didn't and—but you won't want to hear all this."

Daisy put her hand up to her lips. She was looking at him, looking through him. He said, "It is very hard to realize, I know that, even though you were there, even though you saw. It will take you time to accept what has happened.''

"No," she said remotely, "it's not hard to accept. I'm not in any doubt. When I woke up this morning I didn't even have a moment before I remembered. You know''—she shrugged at him—"how there's always that moment, and then everything comes back. It's not like that. Everything's there all the time. It'll always be there. What Nicholas said, about me being confused, that's absolutely not so. Okay, never mind, I'll go on, I'm digressing too much.

"My mother usually served dinner. Brenda left it all there for us on the trolley. We didn't have wine except at the weekends. There was a bottle of Badoit and a jug of apple juice. We had—let me see—soup, it was potato and leek, sort of vichyssoise, but it was hot. We had that and bread, of course, and then my mother cleared away the plates and served the main course. It was fish, sole something or other. Is it called sole *bonne femme* when it's in a sauce with creamed potatoes round?''

"I don't know," Wexford said, amused in spite of everything. "It doesn't matter. I get the picture."

"Well, it was that with carrots and French beans. She'd served us all and sat down and we'd started eating. My mother hadn't even started. She said, 'What's that? It sounds like someone upstairs.' ''

"And you hadn't heard a car? No one had heard a car?"

"They'd have said. You see, we were expecting a car. Well, not then, not till a quarter past eight, only she's always early. She's one of those people who are as bad as the unpunctual ones, always at least five minutes early."

"Who is? Who are you talking about, Daisy?"

"Joanne Garland. She was coming to see Mum. It was Tuesday, and Joanne and Mum always did the gallery books on a Tuesday, Joanne couldn't do them on her own, she's hopeless at arithmetic even with a calculator. She always brought the books and she and Mum worked on them, the VAT and all that."

"All right. I see. Go on, will you?"

"Mum said she heard a noise upstairs and Davina said it must be the cat. Then there was quite a lot of noise, more than Queenie usually makes. It was like something crashing onto the floor. I've thought about it since and I've thought maybe it was a drawer being pulled out of Davina's dressing table. Harvey got up and said he'd go and look.

"We just went on eating. We weren't worried—not then. I remember my mother looked at the clock and said something about how she wished Joanne would make it half an hour later on Tuesdays because she had to eat her meal too fast. Then we heard the shot and then another, a second one. It made this terrible noise.

"We jumped up, my mother and I, Davina went on sitting where she was. My mother sort of cried out, screamed. Davina didn't say anything or move—well, her hands sort of closed round her napkin. She clutched her napkin. Mum stood staring at the door and I pushed my chair away and started going to the door—or I think I did, I meant to—maybe I was just standing there. Mum said, 'No, no,' or 'No, don't' or something. I stopped, I was just standing there, I was sort of frozen to the spot. Davina turned her head towards the door. And then he came in.

"Harvey had left the door half-open—well, a little bit open. The man kicked it open and came in. I've tried to remember if anyone screamed but I can't remember, I don't know. We must have. He—he shot Davina in the head. He held the gun in both hands, like they do. I mean like they do on telly. Then he shot Mum.

"I haven't a clear memory of what happened next. I've tried hard to remember, but something blocks it off; I expect it's normal when you've had a thing like that happen, but I wish I could remember.

"I've a sort of idea I got onto the floor. I crouched on the floor. I know I heard a car start up. That one, the other one, had been upstairs, I think, he was the one we heard. The one who shot me, he was downstairs all the time, and when he shot us the other one got out fast and started the car. That's just what I think."

"The one who shot you, can you describe him?"

He was holding his breath, expecting her to say, fearing she would say, that she couldn't remember, that this too had been absorbed and destroyed by shock. Her face had been contorted, almost distorted, with the effort of concentration, the recollection of almost intolerably painful events. It seemed to clear, as if a little rest had come to her. Alleviation soothed her, like a sigh of relief.

"I can describe him. I can do that. I've *willed* myself to that. What I could see of him. He was—well, not too tall but thickset, heavily built, very fair. I mean his hair was fair. I couldn't see his face, he had a mask over his face."

"A mask? D'you mean a hood? A stocking over his head?"

"I don't know. I just *don't know*. I've been trying to remember because I knew you'd ask but I don't know. I could see his hair. I know he had fair hair, shortish, and thick, quite thick fair hair. But I wouldn't have been able to see his hair if he'd had a hood over it, would I? D'you know what's the impression I keep getting?"

He shook his head.

"That it was a mask like the sort people wear in smog, in pollution, whatever you call it. Or even one of those masks the woodsmen wear when they're using a chain-saw. I could see his hair and his chin. I could see his ears—but they were just ordinary ears, not big or sticking out or anything. And his chin was ordinary—well, it might have had a cleft in it, a sort of shallow cleft."

"Daisy, you've done very well. You've done supremely well to take all this in before he shot you."

At those words she shut her eyes and screwed up her face. The shooting, the attack on herself, he saw was still too much for her to discuss. He understood the terror it must evoke, that she too could so easily have died there in that death room.

A nurse put her head round the door.

"I'm all right," Daisy said. "I'm not tired, I'm not overdoing it. Really."

The head retreated. Daisy took another drink from the bedside glass. "We're going to have a picture made of him, based on what you've been able to tell me," Wexford said. "And when you're better and out of here, I'm going to ask you if you will say this all over again in the form of a statement. Also, with your permission, a tape will be made of it. I know it will be hard for you but don't say no now, think about it."

"I don't have to think," she said. "I'll make a statement, of course I will."

"In the meantime, I should like to come back and talk to you again tomorrow. But first, I'd like you to tell me one more thing. Did Joanne Garland in fact come?"

She seemed to be pondering. She was very still. "I don't know," she said at last. "I mean, I didn't hear her ring the bell or anything. But all sorts of things might have happened after—after he shot me, and I didn't hear them. I was bleeding, I was thinking of getting to the phone, I was concentrating on crawling to the phone and getting you, the police, an ambulance, before I bled to death; I really thought I'd bleed to death."

"Yes," he said, "yes."

"She could have come after they . . . the men . . . after they left. I don't know, it's no use asking me, I just don't know." She hesitated, said very quietly, "Mr. Wexford?"

"Yes?"

For a moment she said nothing. She hung her head and the copious dark-brown hair fell forward, covering face and neck and shoulders with its veil. Her right hand went up, that slim white long-fingered hand, and raked her hair, took a handful of it and threw it back. She looked up and looked at him, the expression taut, intense, her upper lip curled back in pain or incredulity.

"What's going to become of me?" she asked him. "Where will I go? What will I do? I've lost everything, everything's gone, everything that matters."

Now was not the time to remind her she would be rich, that not everything had gone. That which for many makes life worthwhile remained to her in abundance. He had never been a man to believe blindly in the adage which told him that money doesn't bring happiness. But he remained silent.

"I should have died. It would have been better for me if I'd died. I was terrified of dying. I thought I was dying when the blood was pumping out of me and I was terrified—oh, I was so frightened. The funny thing was, it didn't hurt. It hurts more now than it did then. You'd think something going into your flesh would hurt so terribly, but there wasn't any pain. But it would have been best if I'd died, I know that now."

He said, "I know I risk your thinking of me as one of those who hand out the old placebos. But you won't continue to feel like this. It *will* pass."

She stared at him, said rather imperiously, "I shall see you tomorrow then."

"Yes."

She held out her hand to him and he shook hands. The fingers were cold and very dry.

CHAPTER NINE

Wexford went home early. His feeling was that this might be the last time he got home by six for a long while.

Dora was in the hall, replacing the phone receiver, as he let himself in. She said, "That was Sheila. If you'd been a second sooner, you could have talked to her."

A sardonic retort rose to his lips and he suppressed it. There was no reason for being unpleasant to his wife. None of it was her fault. Indeed, at that dinner on Tuesday, she had done her best to make things easier, to dull the edge of spitefulness and soften sarcasm.

"They *are* coming," Dora said, her tone neutral.

"Who's coming where?"

"Sheila and—and Gus. For the weekend. You know Sheila said they might on Tuesday."

"A lot of things have happened since Tuesday."

At any rate, he probably wouldn't be home much during the weekend. But tomorrow was the weekend, tomorrow was

101

Friday, and they would arrive in the evening. He poured himself a beer, an Adnam's, which a local wine shop had begun to stock, and a dry sherry for Dora. She laid her hand on his arm, moved it to enclose the back of his hand. It reminded him of Daisy's icy touch. But Dora's was warm.

He burst out, "I've got to have that miscreant here for a whole weekend!"

"Reg, don't. Don't *begin* like that. We've only met him twice."

"The first time she brought him here," said Wexford, "he stood in this room in front of my books and he took them out one by one. He looked at them in turn with a little contemptuous smile on his face. He took out the Trollope and looked at it like that. He took out the short stories of M. R. James and shook his head. I can see him now, standing there with James in his hand and shaking his head slowly, very slowly from side to side. I expected him to turn his thumbs down. I expected him to do what the Chief Vestal did when the gladiator had the net-man at his mercy in the arena. Kill. That's the verdict of the supreme judge, kill."

"He has a right to his opinion."

"He hasn't a right to despise mine and show he despises it. Besides, Dora, that's not the only thing, and you know it isn't. Have you ever met a man with a more arrogant manner? Have you ever—well, as a friend in your own family circle or that you know well—have you ever come across anyone who so plainly made you feel he despised you? You and me. Everything he said was designed to show his loftiness, his cleverness, his wit. What does she see in him? *What does she see in him?* He's small and skinny, he's ugly, he's myopic, he can't see further than the end of his twitching nose . . ."

"You know something, darling? Women *like* small men. They find them attractive. I know big tall ones like you don't believe it, but it's true."

"Burke said—"

"I know what Burke said. You've told me before. A man's handsomeness resides entirely in his height, or something like that. Burke wasn't a woman. Anyway, I expect Sheila values him for his mind. He's a very clever man, you know, Reg. Perhaps he's a genius.''

''God help us if you're going to call everyone who was short-listed for the Booker Prize a genius.''

''I think we should make allowances for a young man's pride in his own achievements. Augustine Casey is only thirty and he's already seen as one of this country's foremost novelists. Or so I read in the papers. His books get half-page reviews on the fiction page of *The Times*. His first novel won the Somerset Maugham Award.''

''Success should make people humble, modest and kind, as the donor of that prize said somewhere.''

''It seldom does. Try to be indulgent towards him, Reg. Try to listen with—with an older man's wisdom when he airs his opinions.''

''And you can say that after what he said to you about the pearls? You're a magnanimous woman, Dora.'' Wexford gave a sort of groan. ''If only she doesn't really care for him. If only she can come to see what I see.'' He drank his beer, made a face as if the taste were after all not congenial to him. ''You don't think''—he turned to his wife, appalled—''you don't think she'd *marry* him, do you?''

''I think she might live with him, enter into—what shall I call it?—a long-term relationship with him. I do think that, Reg, really. You have to face it. She's told me—oh, Reg, don't look like that. I have to tell you.''

''Tell me what?''

''She says she's in love with him and that she doesn't think she's ever been in love before.''

''Oh, God.''

''For her to tell *me* that, she never tells me things—well, it has to be significant.''

Wexford answered her melodramatically. He knew it was melodramatic before the words were out, but he wouldn't stop it. The histrionics brought him a tiny consolation.

''He'll take my daughter from me. If he and she are together, that's the end of Sheila and me. She will cease to be my daughter. It's true. I can see it. What's the use of pretending otherwise, what is ever the use of pretending?''

He had blocked off that Tuesday evening's dinner. Or the events at Tancred House and their consequences had blocked them off for him, but now he opened his mind to them, the second beer he poured opened his mind, and he saw that man entering the little provincial restaurant, eyeing his surroundings, whispering something to Sheila. She had asked how her father, their host, would like them to sit at the table they were shown to, but Augustine Casey, before he had a chance to speak, had chosen his seat. It was the chair backing a corner of the room.

''I shall sit here where I can see the circus,'' he had said with a small private smile, a smile that was for himself alone, excluding even Sheila.

Wexford had understood him to mean he wanted to watch the behaviour of the other diners. It was perhaps a novelist's prerogative, though scarcely that of such an extreme post-post-modernist as Casey was. He had already written at least one work of fiction without characters. Wexford had still been trying to talk to him then, to get him to talk about something, even if the subject was himself. Back at the house he had spoken, had delivered some obscure opinions on poetry in Eastern Europe, every phrase he used consciously clever, but once in the restaurant he became silent, as if with boredom. He confined his speech to answering briefly requests that had to be made.

One of the things about him which had angered Wexford was his refusal ever to use an ordinary phrase or to indulge in the usage of good manners. When ''How do you do?'' was said to him he replied that he was not at all well but it was useless to inquire because he seldom was. Asked what he would drink, he requested an unusual kind of Welsh mineral water which came in dark-blue bottles. This unavailable, he drank brandy.

His first course he left after one mouthful. Halfway through the meal he broke his silence to talk about pearls. The view from where he sat had afforded him a sight of no fewer than eight women wearing pearls round their necks or in their ears. After using the word once he didn't repeat it but referred to "concretions" or "chitinous formations." He quoted Pliny the Elder, who spoke of pearls as "the most sovereign commodity in the whole world," he quoted Indian Vedic literature and described Etruscan jewellery, he delivered a thousand words or so on the pearls of Oman and Qatar that come from waters 120 feet deep. Sheila hung upon his words. What was the use of deceiving himself? She listened, gazing at Casey, with adoration.

Casey was eloquent on the subject of Hope's baroque pearl that weighed eleven ounces and on La Reine des Perles which was among the crown jewels of France stolen in 1792. Then he talked of the superstitions associated with "concretions," and with his eyes on the modest string round Dora's neck, spoke of the folly of older women who used to believe, and no doubt still did, that such necklaces would restore their lost youth.

Wexford had made up his mind then to speak, to rebuke, but his phone had started bleeping and he had left without a word. Or without a word of admonition. Naturally, he had said goodbye. Sheila kissed him and Casey said, as if it were some received rubric of farewell,

"We shall meet again."

Anger had fulminated, he had been boiling with rage, up through the dark, the cold woods. Enormous tragedy neutralized it. But the Tancred tragedy was not his, and this was, or might well be. The pictures kept on coming, the imagined future scenarios, *their* home. He thought of how it would be when he phoned her and that man answered. What message of arcane wit would that man have recorded on his and Sheila's answering machine? How would it be when, on some necessary trip to London, Sheila's father dropped in on Sheila as he so dearly loved to do and that man was there?

His mind was filled with it and when he went to bed he

expected a dream of Casey to be its natural consequence. But the nightmare which came, towards dawn, was of the massacre at Tancred. He was in that room, at that table, with Daisy and Naomi Jones and Davina Flory, Copeland having gone to investigate the noises upstairs. He could hear no noises, he was examining the scarlet table-cloth, asking Davina Flory why it was such a bright colour, why it was red. And she, laughing, told him he was mistaken, perhaps he was colour-blind, many men were. The cloth was white, as white as driven snow.

She didn't mind using a hackneyed expression like that one, he had asked her. No, no, she said and she smiled, she touched his hand with her hand, clichés like that were often the best way to describe something. You could be too clever.

The shot came and the gunman walked into the room. Wexford slipped out, he escaped unseen, the window with its panes of curved eight-ounce glass melted to allow his passage, so that he was in time to see the getaway car slide onto the courtyard, driven by the other man. The other man was Ken Harrison.

At the stables in the morning—he had stopped calling it an incident room, it was the stables—they showed him the composite picture made from Daisy's description. It would appear in television news programmes that evening, on all networks.

She had been able to tell him so little! The pictured face was blander and blanker than any real face ever can be. Those features she had been able to describe the artist seemed to have accentuated, perhaps unconsciously. After all, these were all he had to work on. So the man who looked out of the paper at Wexford had blank wide-apart eyes and a straight nose and lips neither full nor thin, but a strong chin with a cleft dividing it, large dramatic ears and a copious thatch of pale hair.

He gave Sumner-Quist's post-mortem reports a summary examination, then had himself driven down to Kingsmarkham to put in an appearance at the inquest. As he expected, it was opened, the pathologist's evidence heard, and the proceedings adjourned. Wexford walked across the High Street, down York Street and into the Kingsbrook Centre, to find Garlands, the craft gallery.

Although a notice inside the glass door informed prospective shoppers that the gallery would be open five days a week from 10 AM until 5.30 PM, on Wednesdays from 10 AM until 1 PM and closed on Sundays, it was shut. The windows on either side of this door contained a familiar assortment of pottery, dried flower arrangements, basketwork, marble photograph frames, shell pictures, ceramic cottages, silver jewellery, inlaid wooden boxes, glass baubles, carved, woven, moulded, knitted, blown-glass and sewn miniature animals; as well as a great quantity of household linens with birds and fish and flowers and trees printed on it.

But no lights were on to illuminate this plethora of uselessness. A dimness, becoming a darkness in the depths of the gallery, allowed Wexford just to make out larger items hanging from fake antique beams, gowns perhaps, shawls and robes, and a cash desk set up between a pyramid of what seemed like grotesque felt animals, the reverse of cuddlesome, and a display case showing, behind dim glass, terracotta masks and porcelain wall vases.

It was Friday and Garlands was closed. The possibility that Mrs. Garland had closed her gallery for the remainder of the week out of respect to the memory of Naomi Jones, her partner, who had died so dreadfully, did not escape him. Or she might have failed to open because she was simply too upset. The degree of her friendship with Daisy's mother was still unknown. But the purpose of Wexford's call had been to inquire about the visit she might or might not have paid to Tancred House on the Tuesday evening.

If she had been there, why had she not come to tell them? The publicity, the coverage had been enormous. Everyone with the least knowledge of events, everyone with the smallest connection with Tancred House had been appealed to. If she had been there, why had she not said so? If she had not been there, why had she not told them why not?

Where did she live? Daisy had not said, but it was a simple

matter to find out. Not over the gallery, at any rate. The three floors of the Centre were entirely devoted to the establishments of retailers, boutiques, hairdressers, a vast supermarket, a DIY place, two fast-food restaurants, a garden centre and a gym. He could call in to the incident room and get the address within minutes, but the main Kingsmarkham Post Office was only on the other side of the road. Wexford went in and, avoiding the queue for stamps, pensions and allowances, which coiled serpentinely around a roped-off winding lane, asked to see the electoral register. It was what he would have done long ago, before the advent of all this technology. Sometimes, defiantly, he liked doing these old-fashioned things.

The voters' list was arranged by street, not surname. It was a task for a subordinate, but he was there now, he had begun. Anyway, he wanted to know, he very much wanted to know, and as soon as possible, why Joanne Garland had closed her shop, and presumably closed it for three days.

He found her at last, and only a couple of streets from where he lived himself. Joanne Garland's house was in Broom Vale, a somewhat more spacious building and a rather superior location to his own. She lived alone. The register told him that. Of course, it wouldn't have told him if she had anyone under eighteen living with her, but this was unlikely. Wexford went back to the court where his car was. Parking in the town was not something to be engaged in lightly these days. He could just imagine the piece in the *Kingsmarkham Courier*, some bright young reporter—perhaps Jason Sebright himself?— spotting that it was Chief Inspector Wexford's car on the double yellow line, trapped in the jaws of the wheel clamp.

There was no one at home. Next door, on both sides, there was no one at home either.

When he had been young, you usually found a woman at home. Things had changed. For some reason, this reminded him of Sheila, and he sternly chased away the thought. He had a look at the house, which he had never bothered to study before, though he had passed it hundreds of times. It was quite ordinary, detached, set in its garden, well-kept, newly painted, probably four-bedroomed, two-bathroomed, with a television dish sticking out by an upstairs window. An almond tree was coming into bloom in the front garden.

He considered for a moment, then walked round the back. The house looked closed up. But at this time of the year, early spring, it *would* look closed up, windows wouldn't be open. He looked through the kitchen window. Inside it was tidy, though there were dishes on the draining board, washed and stacked against each other to dry.

Back to the front of the house and a squint through the keyhole in the garage door. There was a car inside but he couldn't make out what kind. A glance through the tiny window to the right of the door showed him newspapers on the floor and a couple of letters. Perhaps only this morning's papers? But no, he could see one *Daily Mail* masthead against the edge of the mat and another half-hidden by a brown envelope. Wexford twisted his head, striving to make out the name of the third paper, of which he could only see a corner and a section of a picture. The photograph was a full-length shot of the Princess of Wales.

Returning to Tancred House, he had the car stop at a news agent. As he had expected, the Princess of Wales's photograph was on today's *Mail*. Therefore, three newspapers had arrived for Joanne Garland since she had last been in the house. Therefore she had not been there *since Tuesday evening*.

Barry Vine said in his slow laid-back way, "Gabbitas may have been in that wood on Tuesday afternoon, sir, and he may not. Witnesses are what you might call thin on the ground out where he was. Or says he was. The wood's on land belonging to a man who owns five hundred acres. He calls it organic farming what he does on some of it, cattle just roaming around, if you know what I mean. He's planted some new woodland and he's got some of that set-aside the Government pays you not to grow things on.

"The point is, the wood where Gabbitas says he was is miles from anywhere. You go down this lane for two miles, it's like the end of the world, not a roof to be seen, not even a barn. Well, I've lived in the country all my life, but I wouldn't have believed there was anything like that in the Home Counties.

"They call it coppicing, what he was doing. It'd be pruning if it was roses, not trees. He's done some, that's for sure, and you can see he's been there—we checked the track marks with his Land Rover. But your guess is as good as mine, sir, if he was there on Tuesday."

Wexford nodded. "Barry, I want you to get down to Kingsmarkham and find a Mrs. Garland, Joanne Garland. Failing finding *her*—I don't think you'll find her—see if you can discover where she's gone, in fact her movements since Tuesday afternoon. Take someone with you, take Karen. She lives in Broom Vale, at number fifteen, and she's got one of those kitschy shops in the Centre. See if her car's gone, talk to the neighbours."

"Sir?"

Wexford put up his eyebrows.

"What's a kitschy shop?" Vine placed the stress on the first word, as in fish-shop. "I'm sure I ought to know, but it's slipped my mind."

Somehow, this reminded Wexford of distant days and his grandfather, who managed an ironmonger's in Stowerton, telling a lazy boy assistant to go out and buy a pound of elbow grease and the boy obediently going. But Vine was neither lazy nor stupid; Vine—*de mortuis* notwithstanding—was cuts above poor Martin. Instead of telling this tale to Vine, he explained the word he had used.

Wexford found Burden eating lunch at his desk. This was behind screens in the corner where Daisy's furniture, bookcases, chairs, floor cushions were carefully covered up in dust sheets. Burden was eating pizza and cole-slaw, not among Wexford's favourite foods, either apart or associated, but he asked where it came from just the same.

"Our caterers' van. It's outside and will be every day from twelve thirty till two. Didn't you fix it?"

"It's the first I've heard of it," said Wexford.

"Get Karen to go out and fetch you something. That's quite a selection they've got."

Wexford said Karen Malahyde had gone down to Kingsmarkham with Barry Vine but he'd ask Davidson to get his lunch. Davidson knew what he liked. He sat down opposite Burden with a mud-coloured coffee from the machine.

"How about these Griffins then?"

"The son's unemployed, living on the dole—well, no, Income Support, he's been unemployed too long for the dole. He lives at home with his parents. He's called Andrew or Andy. The parents are Terry and Margaret, late middle age to elderly."

"Like me," said Wexford. "What telling phrases you do use, Mike."

Burden ignored him. "They're retired people with not enough to do, they struck me as being at a loose end. And they're raving paranoiacs as well. Everything's wrong and everyone's against them. When we got there they were waiting for Telecom to fix their phone, that's who they thought we were, and they both gave us a blast before we got a chance to explain. Then, as soon as the name Tancred was mentioned, they started whingeing on about the best years of their lives they gave up to the place and the iniquities of Davina Flory as an employer, you can imagine. The funny thing was that although they must have known—I mean it was clear that they knew—all about what happened on Tuesday night, there was even yesterday's paper lying there with all the photos, they never said a word about it till we did. I mean, not even a comment on how terrible it was. Just an exchanged glance when I said I believed they'd worked there. Griffin said rather grimly that they'd worked there all right, they'd never forget it, and then they were off, the pair of them, until we had to—well, stem the tide."

Wexford quoted, " 'An event has happened on which it is difficult to speak and impossible to be silent.' " He got a suspicious look in return. "Did the Telecom man come?"

"Yes, he did at last. I was going spare, what with her

toddling to the front door every five minutes to look up and down the road for him. By the way, Andy Griffin wasn't there, he came in later. His mother said he was out jogging.''

They were interrupted by Davidson, coming round the screens with a waxed-paper carrier containing tandoori chicken, pilaf rice and mango chutney for Wexford.

''I wish I'd had that,'' said Burden.

''Too late now. No swaps, I hate pizza. Did you find out what they quarrelled about with the Harrisons?''

Burden looked surprised. ''I didn't ask.''

''No, but if they're so paranoid they might have volunteered the information.''

''They didn't mention the Harrisons. Maybe that's significant. Margaret Griffin went on about the immaculate state she'd left the cottage in and how the one time they met Gabbitas he'd had tar on his boots and it came off on their carpet. He'd soon turn the place into a tip, she could tell that.

''Andy Griffin came in. I suppose he might have been jogging. He's overweight, not to say fat. He was wearing a track suit but not everyone who wears them goes on tracks. He looks as if he couldn't run for a bus that was going at five miles an hour. He's shortish and fair, but there's no way you could stretch Daisy Flory's description to fit him.''

''She wouldn't have to describe him. She'd know him,'' said Wexford. ''She'd know him even behind a mask.''

''True. He was out on Tuesday night, he says with mates, and his parents confirm he went out at around six. I'm checking it out with the mates. They're supposed to have gone the round of pubs in Myringham and for Chinese in a place called the Panda Cottage.''

''Those names! Sounds like a haunt for gay endangered species. He's on the *dole*?''

''Like I say, one of those benefits. They're always changing the names. There's something funny about him, Reg, though I can't tell you what. I know that's not helpful, but what I'm really saying is, we have to keep our eye on Andrew Griffin. His parents give the impression of disliking everyone and they've got a lot of resentment built up for some reason—or no reason—against Harvey Copeland and Davina Flory, but Andy, he hates them. His whole manner and voice change when he talks about them. He even said he was glad they were dead—'scum' and 'shit' are the words he uses about them."

"Prince Charming."

"We'll know a bit more when we find out if he really was out round the pubs and this Panda Cottage on Tuesday."

Wexford glanced at his watch. "Time for me to get off over to the Infirmary. D'you feel like coming? You could put a few Griffin queries to Daisy yourself."

The moment the words were out of his mouth, he regretted them. Daisy was accustomed to him by now, she would almost certainly not want another policeman arriving with him and arriving unannounced. But he need not have worried. Burden had no intention of coming. Burden had an appointment for another interview with Brenda Harrison.

"She'll keep," he said of Daisy. "She'll feel easier about talking when she's out of there. By the way, where's she going when she *is* out of there?"

"I don't know," Wexford said slowly. "I really don't know. It hadn't occurred to me."

"Well, she can't go home, can she? If it's her home, I suppose it is. She can't go straight back where it happened. Maybe one day, but hardly now."

"I'll be back," said Wexford, as he went, "in time to see what the television networks do for us. I'll be back in time for the ITN news at five forty."

Once again, at the hospital, he did not declare himself but entered unobtrusively, almost secretly. No Dr. Leigh was about, and no nurses. He knocked on the door of Daisy's room, unable to see much through the frosted glass, the shape of the bed only, enough to tell him no visitor sat at the bedside.

No one said to come in. Of course, he was rather earlier than he had been on previous occasions. Alone, unescorted, he did not like to open the door. He knocked again, now certain, without evidence for his certainty, that the room was empty. They must have a day-room and she might be in it. He turned away and came face to face with a man in a short white jacket. The charge nurse?

"I'm looking for Miss Flory."

"Daisy went home today."

"She went *home*?"

"Are you Chief Inspector Wexford? She left a message that she'd phone you. Her friends came for her. I can give you the name, I've got it somewhere."

Daisy had gone to Nicholas Virson and his mother in Myfleet. That, then, was the answer to Burden's question. She had gone home to her friends, perhaps her closest friends. He wondered why she hadn't told him of this on the previous day, but perhaps she hadn't known. No doubt, they had been in touch with her, had invited her and she had agreed in order to escape. Almost every patient longs to escape from hospital.

"We'll be keeping an eye on her," the charge nurse said. "She has an appointment here for an examination on Monday."

Back at the stables, he watched television, one news broadcast after another. He was on himself, in the little video he had made that morning. The artist's impression of what the Tancred gunman looked like came onto the screen. Seeing it like that, enlarged, somehow more convincing than a drawing on paper could be, Wexford knew whom it reminded him of.

Nicholas Virson.

The face on the screen was exactly as he remembered Virson's face at Daisy's bedside. Coincidence, chance and something fortuitous on the artist's part? Or some unconscious displacement on Daisy's? Did that make the picture, which had now vanished from the screen, to be succeeded by some pop star's wedding, worthless? The mask the gunman had worn had served its purpose if the result of wearing it had been to make himself look like the witness's boyfriend!

Wexford sat in front of the television, unseeing. It was getting on for half past six, the time Sheila and Augustine Casey might be expected to arrive. He felt no compulsion to go home.

He went back to his own desk where a dozen messages awaited him. The top one told him what he already knew, that Daisy Flory could be found care of Mrs. Joyce Virson at The Thatched House, Castle Lane, Myfleet. It also gave him something he didn't know, a phone number. Wexford took his own phone out of his pocket and punched the digits.

A woman's voice answered, superior, sweeping, imperious. "Hallo?"

Wexford said who he was and that he would like to talk to Miss Flory on the following day, in the afternoon at about four.

"But it's Saturday!"

He agreed. There was no denying it.

"Well, I suppose so. If you must. Can you find this cottage? How do you intend to get here? The bus service isn't at all reliable . . ."

He said he would be there at four and pressed the cut-off button. There was much to be said for this new phone. The door opened, a strong draught of cold evening air swept in and Barry Vine appeared.

"Where have you sprung from?" Wexford said rather sourly.

"It sounds ridiculous, but she's disappeared. Mrs. Garland. Joanne Garland. She's missing."

"What d'you mean, missing? You mean she's not there? That's hardly the same thing."

"She's missing. She told no one she was going away, she left no messages or instructions for anyone. No one knows where she's gone. She hasn't been seen since Tuesday evening."

CHAPTER TEN

The old people were watching television. Their last meal of the day was over, it had been served at five, and this was evening for them, with bedtime scheduled for eight thirty not too far off.

Armchairs and wheelchairs were arranged in a semicircle in front of the set. The elderly viewers were confronted by a brutish face, the Identikit picture maker's idea of the Tancred gunman. It was the kind of face that once, long ago, was defined by the phrase "a blond beast." And this was the expression one of them used to describe him, uttering it in a loud stage whisper to the man next to her,

"Look at him, a real blond beast!"

She seemed one of the livelier inmates of the Caenbrook Retirement Home and Burden felt relief when it was to her chair that the thin worried-looking girl who had received them ushered him and Sergeant Vine. She looked round, smiled, surprise rapidly giving place to a very real delight when she understood that the visitors, whoever they might be, were for her.

"Edie, there's someone to see you. They're policemen."
The smile remained. It widened.

"Hey, Edie," said the old man she had whispered to, "what have you been up to then?"

"Me? Chance'd be a fine thing."

"Mrs. Chowney, my name is Inspector Burden and this is Detective Sergeant Vine. I wonder if we could have a word with you. We're anxious to find the whereabouts of your daughter."

"Which one? I've got six."

As Burden told Wexford later, that almost stunned him. It certainly silenced him, if briefly. Edie Chowney compounded matters by announcing proudly—to an audience who had evidently heard it many times before—that she also had five sons. All alive, all doing well for themselves, all in this country. It struck Burden then as dreadful, as something which in many other societies would be incomprehensible, that out of those eleven children none had taken their mother to live in their home, under their wing. Indeed, to avoid this, they had preferred to raise the money, among them all, most likely, which would keep her in this doubtless expensive end-of-the-road for the discarded old.

As they went along the corridor to Mrs. Chowney's room, a plan put forward by the thin warden, which drew forth more ribaldry from the old man, Burden reflected that one of those ten siblings of Joanne Garland might have been a better source of the information he was seeking. But there he was wrong, for Edie Chowney, walking to her room without assistance, ushering them in and complaining to the warden that the heating was less than adequate, showed herself as much in command of her mind and her speech as someone thirty years younger.

She looked in her late seventies, a small sprightly woman, thin but broad and rather bandy. It was a strong body that had borne many children. Her wispy hair was dyed dark brown. Only her hands, tree-root-like and with knobbed knuckles, revealed it must have been arthritis that betrayed her and committed her to Caenbrook.

The room had its basic furnishings and it had Edie Chowney's own things. Mostly framed photographs. They crowded onto the windowsill and the table-tops, the bedside cabinet and the little bookcase, these pictured people with their own posterity, their spouses, their dogs, their homes in the background, all of them aged between forty and fifty-five. One was very likely Joanne Garland, but there was no knowing which.

"I've got twenty-one grandchildren," said Mrs. Chowney when she saw him looking. "I've got four great-grandchildren, and with any luck, if Maureen's eldest gets on with it, I'll have a great-great-grandchild one of these fine days. What d'you want to know about Joanne?"

"Where she's gone, Mrs. Chowney," said Barry Vine. "We'd like the address of where she is. Her neighbours don't know."

"Joanne never had kids. Married twice but no kids. Women aren't barren in our family, so I reckon it was from choice. Didn't have much choice in my day, but times change. Joanne'd be too selfish, wouldn't put up with their noise and the mess. You get a lot of mess one way and another with kids. I should know, I've had eleven. Mind you, she was the eldest of the girls, so she *knew*."

"She's gone away, Mrs. Chowney. Can you tell us where?"

"Her first husband was a hard worker but he never made good. She divorced him, I didn't like that. I said, 'You're the first person in our family ever to go through the divorce court, Joanne.' Pam got divorced later and so did Trev, but at the time Joanne was the first. Anyway, she met this wealthy man. Do you know what he used to say? He used to say, 'I'm only a poor millionaire, Edie.' Oh, they lived it up, I can tell you, spend, spend, spend, but it all came to grief like the first time round. He had to pay up—ooh, she made him pay through the nose. That's how she's got that house and started that business she's got and bought that big car and all. It's her keeps me in here, you know. It costs as much to be in here as a posh hotel in London, which is a mystery when you look round you. But she pays, the others couldn't run to it."

Burden had to stem the tide. Edie Chowney had only paused to draw breath. He had heard of lonely people's verbosity when at last in company, but this (as he told himself) was ridiculous.

"Mrs. Chowney . . ."

She said, more sharply, "All right. I've done. I know I talk too much. It's not my age, it's my nature, I've always been a chatterbox, my husband used to go on at me. What was it you wanted to know about Joanne?"

"Where is she?"

"At home, of course, or at business. Where else would she be?"

"When did you last see her, Mrs. Chowney?"

She did a curious thing. It was as if she were reminding herself of which particular child they were inquiring. She viewed the photograph collection by the bed, paused for calculation, then selected a coloured one in a silver frame and looked at it, nodding.

"It would have been Tuesday evening. That's right, Tuesday, because it was the day the chiropodist comes and she always comes on a Tuesday. Joanne came in while we were having our teas. Five-ish. Maybe a quarter past five. I said, 'You're early, what about the shop?' And she said, 'Gallery, Mother, you always say that, the gallery's okay, Naomi's there till half past.' You know who she meant by Naomi? Naomi's one of them that got murdered—no, massacred like they say on the telly, massacred at Tancred House. Wasn't that a terrible thing? I suppose you've heard about it—well, you would, being policemen."

"While your daughter was with you, did she say anything about going to Tancred House that evening?"

Mrs. Chowney handed Burden the photograph. "She always went up there on Tuesday evening. Her and that poor Naomi, the one that was massacred, they did the shop accounts. That's her, that's Joanne, it was taken five years back, but she hasn't changed much."

The woman looked overdressed in a bright-pink suit with gilt buttons. A great deal of gold costume jewellery huddled round her neck and swung from her ears. She was tall with a good figure. Her blonde hair was rather rigidly and elaborately dressed and she seemed heavily made-up, though this was hard to tell.

"She didn't tell you she was going away on holiday?"

"She wasn't," Edie Chowney said sharply. "She wasn't going anywhere. She'd have told me. What makes you think she's gone away?"

That was something Burden hardly liked to answer. "When would you expect her to visit you again?"

Bitterness entered her voice. "Three weeks. A good three weeks. It wouldn't be sooner. Joanne never comes more than once every three weeks and sometimes it's a month. She pays up and she thinks she's done her duty. Comes once in three weeks and stops ten minutes and thinks she's the good daughter."

"And your other children?" It was Vine who asked. Burden had resolved not to.

"Pam comes. I mean, she only lives two streets away, so coming every day wouldn't kill her. Not that she does come every day. Pauline's in Bristol, so you can't expect it, and Trev's on one of them oil rigs. Doug's in Telford, wherever that may be. Shirley's got four kids and that's her excuse, though God knows they're all in their teens. John drops in when it suits him, which isn't often, and the rest of them crop up around Christmas. Oh, they all turn up together at Christmas, a whole troop of them. What's the use of that to me? I said that to them last Christmas, what's the good of you all coming at once? Seven of them on Christmas Eve in one go, Trev and Doug and Janet and Audrey and—"

"Mrs. Chowney," said Burden, "can you give me the addresses of"—he hesitated, hardly knowing how to put it—"one or two of your children who live nearest? Who live around here and might know where your daughter Joanne has gone?"

It was eight before Wexford finally left for home. When the car reached the main gates and Donaldson got out to open them, he noticed something tied to each gatepost. It was too dark under the crowding trees to make out more than shapeless bundles.

He switched on the headlamp beam, left the car and went to look. More bouquets, more tributes to the dead. Two this time, one on each gatepost. They were simple bouquets but exquisitely arranged, one a Victorian posy of violets and primroses, the other a sheaf of snow-white narcissi and dark-green ivy. Wexford read on one card: "In grief for the great tragedy of March 11." The other said: "These violent deaths have violent ends and in their triumph die." He returned to the car and Donaldson drove out through the gateway. The message on the first bunch of flowers left on the gatepost had seemed innocuous, a rather apt quotation from *Antony and Cleopatra*—well, apt if you had extravagantly admired Davina Flory. This later one had a faintly sinister ring. It too was probably Shakespeare, but he couldn't place it.

He had more important things to think about. Phone calls to John Chowney and Pamela Burns née Chowney had elicited only that they had no idea where their sister was and had not known she was going away. No neighbour had been told she would be absent. Her newsagent had not been alerted. Joanne Garland was not in the habit of taking a milk delivery. The manager of the card shop next door to Garlands in the Kingsbrook Centre had expected her to arrive and open the gallery on Thursday morning, one day's grace having been allowed from respect to Naomi Jones.

John Chowney named two women he called close friends of his sister. Neither was able to tell Burden anything of her whereabouts. Each was surprised to hear of her absence. She had not been seen since five forty on Tuesday evening, when she left the Caenbrook Retirement Home and the warden on duty saw her get into her car she had parked on the forecourt. Joanne Garland had disappeared.

In different circumstances, the police would hardly have noticed it. A woman who goes away for a few days without telling her friends or relatives is not a missing woman. That arrangement to call at Tancred House at eight fifteen on Tuesday evening altered things. If Wexford was sure of anything, it was that she had been there, she had kept her promise. Was her disappearance due to what she had seen at Tancred House or to what she had done?

He let himself into his house and immediately heard laughter from the dining-room, Sheila's laughter. Her coat was hanging up in the hall, it must be hers—who else would wear synthetic snow leopard with a petrol-blue fake fox collar?

In the dining-room they had had their soup and moved on to the main course. Roast chicken, not sole *bonne femme*. Why had he thought of that? It was an altogether different house, the whole of it would have got lost in the Tancred Hall, they were very different people. He apologized to Dora for his lateness, kissed her, kissed Sheila and held out his hand to Augustine Casey for Casey to ignore it.

"Gus has been telling us about Davina Flory, Pop," Sheila said.

"You knew her?"

"My publishers," said Casey, "don't belong among those whose policy is to pretend to one author that they have no others on their list."

Wexford hadn't known he and the dead woman shared a publisher. He said nothing but went back to the hall and took his hat and coat off. He washed his hands, telling himself to be tolerant, to be magnanimous, to make allowances, be kind. When he was back in there and sitting down, Sheila made Casey repeat everything he had said so far about Davina Flory's books, much of it unedifying as far as Wexford was concerned, and repeat, too, an unbelievable story that Davina Flory's editor had sent the manuscript of her autobiography to Casey for his opinion before they made her an offer for it.

"I'm not usually thick," said Casey, "I'm not, am I, love?"

Wexford, wondering what was coming, winced at that "love." Sheila's response when appealed to nearly made him cringe, it was so adoring, and at the same time he was so appalled that anyone, even the man himself, might deprecatingly suggest he was less than a genius.

"I'm not usually thick," Casey repeated, presumably expecting a further chorus of incredulous denial, "but I really had no idea that all that happened down here and that you . . ." He turned small pale eyes on Wexford. "I mean, Sheila's father, were in—what's the term, there must *be* a term—oh, yes, in *charge* of the case. I know nothing about these things, less than nothing, but Scotland Yard still exists, doesn't it? I mean, isn't there something called a Murder Squad? Why you?"

"Tell me your impressions of Davina Flory," Wexford said equably, swallowing a rage that filled his mouth with hot sourness and put up red screens before his eyes. "I'd be interested to hear from someone who had met her professionally."

"*Professionally*? I'm not an anthropologist. I'm not an explorer. I met her at a publisher's party. And no, thank you very much, I don't think I will tell you my *impressions*, I don't think that would be at all wise. I shall keep mum. It would only remind me of the time I was done for reckless driving and the funny little cop who chased me on his motor bike read back everything I said to him in court, the whole of it ineluctably distorted by the filtering process of semi-literacy."

"Have some wine, darling," said Dora smoothly. "You'll like it, Sheila brought it specially."

"You haven't put them in the same room, have you?"

"Reg, that's the kind of remark I should be making, not you. You're supposed to be the liberal one. Of course I've put them in the same room. I'm not running a Victorian workhouse."

Wexford had to smile in spite of himself. "That's typical unreason, isn't it? I don't mind my daughter sleeping under my roof with a man I like, but I hate the whole idea when it's a shit like him."

"I've never heard you use that word before!"

"There has to be a first time for everything. Me throwing someone out of my house, for instance."

"But you won't."

"No, I'm sure I won't."

Next morning Sheila said she and Gus would like to take her parents to dinner at the Cheriton Forest Hotel that evening.

It had recently changed hands and had a new reputation for wonderful food at high prices. She had booked a table for four. Augustine Casey remarked that it would be amusing to see that sort of thing at first hand. He had a friend who wrote about places like that for a Sunday paper, in fact about manifestations of nineties taste. The series was called "More Money Than Sense," a title which was his, Casey's, brainchild. He would be interested not only in the food and the ambience, but in the kind of people who patronized it.

Unable to resist, Wexford said, "I thought you said last night you weren't an anthropologist."

Casey gave one of his mysterious smiles. "What do *you* put on your passport? Police officer, I suppose. I've always kept *student*. It's ten years since I left my university, but I still have *student* in my passport and I suppose I always shall."

Wexford was going out. He was meeting Burden for a drink in the Olive and Dove. A rule, made to be broken, was that they never did this on a Saturday. He had to get out of the house for short spells, though he knew it was wrong of him. Sheila caught him up in the hall.

"Dear Pop, is everything all right? Are you okay?"

"I'm fine. This Flory case is a bit of a strain. What are you going to do with yourselves today?"

"Gus and I thought we'd go to Brighton. He's got friends there. We'll be back in heaps of time for dinner. You will be able to make it for dinner, won't you?"

He nodded. "I'll do my best."

She looked a little crestfallen. "Gus is marvellous, isn't he? I've never known anyone like him." Her face brightened. It was such a lovely face, as perfect as Garbo's, as sweet as Marilyn Monroe's, as transcendently beautiful as Hedy Lamarr's. In his eyes, at least. He thought so. Where did the genes dredge up from to create that? She said, "He's so clever. Half the time I can't keep up with him. The latest thing is he's going to be the writer-in-residence at a university in Nevada. They're building up a library of his manuscripts there, it's called the Augustine Casey Archive, they really appreciate him."

Wexford had scarcely heard the end of this. He was stuck—and blissfully—in the middle of her remarks.

"He's going to live in *Nevada*?"

"Yes—well, for a year. It's a place called Heights."

"In the *United States*?"

"He intends to write his next novel while he's there," said Sheila. "It will be his masterwork."

Wexford gave her a kiss. She threw her arms round his neck. Walking down the street, he could have burst into song. All was well, all was better than well, they were going to Brighton for the day and *Augustine Casey was going to America for a year*, the man was practically emigrating. Oh, why hadn't she told him last evening and given him a good night's sleep? It was useless worrying about that now. He was glad he had decided to go to the Olive on foot, he could have a real drink now and celebrate.

Burden was there already. He said he had come from Broom Vale where, on a warrant sworn out two hours before, they were searching Joanne Garland's house. Her car was in the garage, a dark-grey BMW. She kept no pets to be fed or walked. There were no house-plants to be watered, no flowers left dying in vases. The television set had been unplugged, but some people did this every night before they went to bed. It looked as if she had left the house of her own free will.

A desk diary, with engagements meticulously entered, told Burden only that Joanne Garland had been to a drinks party on the previous Saturday, to lunch on Sunday with her sister Pamela. Her visit to her mother was marked in for Tuesday March 11—and that was that. The following spaces remained blank. Her handwriting was small, neat and very upright, and she had managed to squeeze quite a lot of information into the one-by-three-inch space allowed for each entry.

"We've come across this sort of thing before," Wexford said, "someone apparently disappearing and it turns out they've been on holiday. But in neither of those cases had the missing person a host of relatives and friends, people, mark you, who in the past had been quite used to being told whenever the missing person was going away. The facts are that Joanne was going to Tancred House at eight-fifteen on Tuesday evening. She was an over-punctual person, we're told by Daisy Flory—in other words, too early for appointments as a general rule, so we may take it she got to the house soon after eight.''

''If she went there. What are you going to have?''

Wexford wasn't going to say anything to him about celebrations. ''I was thinking of Scotch, but I'd better think again. The usual half of bitter.''

When he came back with the drinks, Burden said, ''We've no reason to believe she went there.''

''Only the fact that she always did on a Tuesday,'' Wexford retorted. ''Only the fact that she was expected. If she hadn't been going, wouldn't she have phoned? There was no phone call received at Tancred House that evening.''

''But look, Reg, what are we saying? It doesn't add up. These are ordinary villains, aren't they? Trigger-happy villains after jewellery? One of them a stranger, the other possibly with special knowledge of the house and its occupants. That presumably is why only the blond beast, as Mrs. Chowney calls him, let himself be seen by the three he killed and the one he attempted to kill. The other, the familiar face, kept out of the way.

''But they're typical villains, they're not the sort who carry off a possible witness and dispose of her elsewhere, are they? You see what I mean about its not adding up? If she came to the door, why not shoot her too?''

''Because the chamber of the Magnum .357 was empty,'' Wexford said quickly.

''All right. If it was. There are other means of killing. He'd killed three people and wouldn't jib at killing a fourth. But no, he and his pal carry her off. Not as some sort of hostage, not for information she may have, just to get rid of her elsewhere. Why? It doesn't add up.''

''Okay. You've said that three times, you've made your point. If they killed her at Tancred House, what became of her car? They drove it home and put it neatly in her garage?''

"I suppose she could be involved. She could be the other one. We only assume it was a man. But, Reg, is it even worth considering? Joanne Garland is a woman in her fifties, a prosperous, successful businesswoman—because, God knows how or why, that gallery is successful, it does work. She's well enough off to be independent of it, anyway. Her car's a last year's BMW, she's got a wardrobe of clothes I know nothing about but Karen says are top designers, Valentino and Krizia and Donna Karan. Have you ever heard of them?"

Wexford nodded. "I do read the papers."

"She's got every kind of equipment there you can think of. One of the rooms is a gym full of exercising gear. She's obviously rich. What would she want with the sort of money some fence would give her for Davina Flory's pearls?"

"Mike, I've thought of something. Is there an answering machine? What's her phone number? There may be a message on it."

"I don't know the number," Burden said. "Can you get inquiries on that thing of yours?"

"Sure." Wexford asked for the number and was quickly given it. At their table in a dim corner of the Olive's lounge, he dialled Joanne Garland's number. It rang three times, then clicked softly and a voice that was not at all what they expected came on. Not a strong self-assertive voice, not confident and strident, but soft, even diffident:

"This is Joanne Garland. I am not available to speak to you now, but if you would like to leave a message I will get back to you as soon as I can. Please speak after the tone."

The routine statement of identity and availability recommended in most answering-machine literature.

"We'll check on what messages have been left, if any. I'm going to try it again and hope this time they realize and pick up the phone themselves. Is Gerry up there?"

"DC Hinde," said Burden, keeping a straight face, "is busy working but elsewhere. He has constructed what he calls a tremendous data base of all the crimes committed in this area in the past twelve months and he's mousing away in it—I've probably got the terminology all wrong—looking for coincidences. Karen's up there and Archbold and Davidson. You'd think one of them would have the sense to answer.''

Wexford dialled the number again. It rang three times and the message began to repeat itself. Next time, Karen Malahyde picked up the receiver after the second ring.

''About time too,'' said Wexford. ''You know who this is? Yes? Good. Play back the messages, would you? If you're not familiar with the working of these things, you should look for a button marked 'play.' Do it once only, note what's on it and take the tape out. It's probably the kind that will only play the same thing back twice. All right? Call me back on my personal number.'' He said to Burden, ''I don't think she's involved in Tuesday night's murders, of course not, but I do think she saw them. Mike, I'm wondering if instead of searching her house we should be looking for her body up at Tancred.''

''It's not in the vicinity of the house. It's not in the outbuildings. You know we've searched.''

''We haven't searched the woods.''

Burden gave a sort of groan. ''D'you want the other half?''

''I'll get them.''

Wexford went up to the bar, holding the empty glasses. Sheila and Augustine Casey would be on their way to Brighton now. With satisfaction—because it would soon come to an end, soon only be heard in Nevada—he imagined the conversation in the car, the monologue rather, as Casey gave vent to streams of wit and brilliance, esoterica, malicious anecdotes and self-aggrandizing tales, while Sheila listened enraptured.

Burden looked up. ''They might take her away with them because she saw them or was a witness to the murders. But take her where and kill her how? And how did her car get back into her garage?''

Wexford's phone bleeped. ''Karen?''

''I've taken the tape out like you said, sir. What would you like me to do with it?''

''Have it copied, phone me and play the copy to me, then bring it to me. At my home. The tape and the copy. What were the messages?''

''There are three. The first one's from a woman calling

herself Pam and I think that's Joanne's sister. I've written it down. It says to phone her about Sunday, whatever that means. The second's a man, it sounds like a sales rep. He's called Steve, no surname. He says he tried the shop but got no answer so he thought he'd phone her at home. It's about the Easter decorations, he says, and would she call him at home. The third's from Naomi Jones.''

''Yes?''

''This is it verbatim, sir: 'Jo, this is Naomi. I wish it was you sometimes and not always that machine. Can you make it eight thirty tonight and not earlier? Mother hates having dinner interrupted. Sorry about that but you understand. See you.'

Lunch at home, just the two of them.

''He's going to be writer-in-residence in the Wild West,'' said Wexford.

''You oughtn't to rejoice when it's making her so unhappy.''

''Is it? I don't see any signs of unhappiness. More likely the scales are falling from her eyes and she sees what a good miss he'll be.''

What Dora might have said in reply to these remarks was lost in the ringing of the phone. Karen said, ''Here it is, sir. You asked me to play it.''

Like the murmur of a ghost, the dead woman's voice spoke to him. ''. . . Mother hates having dinner interrupted. Sorry about that but you understand. See you.''

He shivered. Mother had had her dinner interrupted. An hour or so after that message was left, her life had been interrupted forever. He saw the red cloth again, the seeping stain, the head lying on the table, the head flung back to hang over the back of a chair. He saw Harvey Copeland spread-eagled on the staircase and Daisy crawling past the bodies of her dead, crawling to the phone to save her own life.

''You needn't bring it, thanks, Karen. It'll keep.''

At half past three he set off for Myfleet and the house where Daisy Flory had found her refuge.

CHAPTER ELEVEN

The first thing that came into his mind was that she was in the attitude of her dead grandmother. Daisy had not heard him come in, she had heard nothing, and she was slumped across the table with one arm stretched out and her head beside it. So had Davina Flory fallen across a table when the gun found its aim.

Daisy was abandoned to her grief, her body shaking, though she made no sound. Wexford stood looking at her. He had been told where she was by Nicholas Virson's mother, but Mrs. Virson had not accompanied him to the door. He closed it behind him and took a few steps into what Joyce Virson had called "the little den." What names these people had for parts of their houses others would have designated "greenhouse" or "sitting room"!

It was a thatched house, as its name indicated, something of a rarity in the neighbourhood. A kind of self-deprecatory snobbery might cause its owners to call it a cottage, but in fact it was a sizeable house, of picturesquely uneven construction and pargeted patterns on the walls. The windows were large or medium-sized or very small, and several peeped out under eyelid gables close up to the roof. The roof was a formidable reed construction, ornately done and with a woven design round where the ribbed and pargeted chimney-pots protruded. A garage, of the kind estate agents call "integral," was also roofed by this dense layer of thatch.

Their popularity on calendars had made thatched houses faintly absurd, the butt of a certain kind of wit. But if you cleared your mind of chocolate-box images, this house could be made to appear what it was, a beautiful English antiquity, its garden pretty with wind-blown spring flowers, its lawns the brilliant green result of a damp climate.

Inside, a certain shabbiness, an air of make-do-and-mend, made him doubt his own original assessment of Nicholas Virson's city successes. The little den where Daisy hung slumped over the table had a worn carpet and stretch nylon covers on the chairs. A weary house-plant on the windowsill had artificial flowers stuck into the soil around it to perk it up.

She made a little sound, a whimper, an acknowledgement perhaps of his presence.

"Daisy," he said.

The shoulder that was not bandaged moved a little. Otherwise she gave no sign of having heard him.

"Daisy, please stop crying."

She lifted her head slowly. This time there was no apology, no explanation. Her face was like a child's, puffy with tears. He sat down in the chair opposite her. There was a small table between them, such as might be used in a room of this kind for writing, for playing cards, for a supper for two. She looked at him in despair.

"Would you like me to come back tomorrow? I have to talk to you but it need not be now."

Crying had made her hoarse. In a voice he hardly recognized she said, "It may as well be now as any other time."

"How is your shoulder?"

"Oh, all right. It doesn't hurt, it's just sore." She said

something then which, if it had come from someone older or someone *else*, he would have found ridiculous. ''The pain is in my heart.''

It was as if she heard her own words, digested them and understood how they sounded, for she burst into a peal of unnatural laughter. ''How stupid I sound! But it's true—why does saying what's true sound false?''

''Perhaps,'' he said gently, ''because it isn't quite real. You've read it somewhere. People don't really have pains in their hearts unless they're having a heart attack, and then I believe it's usually in the arm.''

''I wish I was old. I wish I was as old as you and wise.''

This couldn't be treated seriously. ''Will you be staying here for a while, Daisy?'' he asked her.

''I don't know. I suppose so. I'm here now, it's as good a place as any. I made them let me out of the hospital. Oh, it was bad in there. It was bad being alone and worse being with strangers.'' She shrugged. ''The Virsons are very kind. I'd like to be alone, but I'm afraid of being alone too—do you know what I mean?''

''I think so. It's best for you to be with your friends, with people who'll leave you alone when you want to be on your own.''

''Yes.''

''Would you feel like answering some questions about Mrs. Garland?''

''Joanne?''

This, at any rate, was not what she had expected. She wiped her eyes with her fingers, blinked at him.

He had made up his mind not to tell her of their fears. She could know that Joanne Garland had gone away to some unknown destination but not that she was a ''missing person,'' not that they were already assuming her dead. Censoring what he said, he explained how she couldn't be found.

''I don't know her very well,'' Daisy said. ''Davina didn't like her much. She didn't think she was good enough for us.''

Recalling some of what Brenda Harrison had said, Wexford

was surprised and his astonishment must have shown on his face, for Daisy said, "Oh, I don't mean in a snobby way. It was nothing to do with class with Davina. I mean"—she lowered her voice—"she didn't much care for"—she cocked her thumb towards the door—"them either. She hadn't any time for people she said were dull or ordinary. People had to have character, vitality, something individual. You see, she didn't know any ordinary people—well, except the people who worked for her—and she didn't want me to either. She used to say she wanted me to be surrounded by the best. She'd given up on Mum, but she didn't like Joanne just the same, she'd never liked her. I remember one phrase she used, she said Joanne dragged Mum down into a 'quagmire of the commonplace.' "

"But your mother took no notice?" Wexford had observed that Daisy could now talk of her mother and grandmother without a break in her voice, without a lapse into despair. Her grief was stemmed while she talked of the past. "She didn't care?"

"You have to understand that poor Mum was really one of those ordinary people Davina didn't like. I don't know why she was, something to do with genes, I suspect." Daisy's voice was strengthening as she talked, the hoarseness conquered by the interest she could still take in this subject. She could be distracted from her sorrow for these people by talking of them. "She was just as if she was the daughter of ordinary people, not someone like Davina. But the strange thing was Harvey was a bit like that too. Davina used to talk a lot about her other husbands, number one and number two, saying how amusing and interesting they were, but I did wonder. Harvey never had much to say, he was a very quiet man. No, not so much quiet as passive. Easygoing, he called it. He did what Davina told him." Wexford thought he saw a spark burn in her eyes. "Or he tried to. He was dull; I think I've always known that."

"Your mother went on being friends with Joanne Garland in spite of your grandmother's disapproval?"

"Oh, Mum had had Davina disapproving of her and sort of

laughing at her all her life. She knew there was nothing she could do that would be right, so she'd got to do what she liked. She'd even stopped rising when Davina poked fun at her. Working in that shop suited her. You probably don't know this—why should you?—but Mum tried to be a painter for years and years. When I was little I can remember her painting and Davina coming into this studio they'd made for her and—well, criticizing. I remember one thing she said, I didn't know what it meant at the time. She said, 'Well, Naomi, I don't know what school you belong to, but I think we could call you a Pre-Raphaelite cubist.'

"Davina wanted me to be all the things Mum wasn't. Maybe she wanted me to be all the things *she* wasn't too. But you don't want to hear about that. Mum loved that gallery and earning her own money and being—well, what she called 'her own woman.' "

For the time being Daisy's tears were in abeyance. Talking did her good. He doubted whether she was right when she said the best thing for her was to be alone. "How long had they worked together?"

"Mum and Joanne? About four years. But they'd been friends forever, since before I was born. Joanne had a shop in Queen Street, and that was where Mum first started with her, then she got that place for the gallery when the Centre was built. Did you say she'd gone away? She didn't mean to go away. I remember Mum saying—well, on *the* day, that's how I think of it, as *the* day—Mum said she'd wanted to take Friday off for something but Joanne wouldn't let her because they'd got the VAT inspector coming in and she'd have to go through the books with him, I mean Joanne would. It took hours and hours and Mum would have to see to clients—they didn't call them customers."

"Your mother phoned her and left a message on her answering machine not to come before eight thirty."

Daisy said indifferently, "I expect she did. She often did, but it never seemed to make much difference."

"Joanne didn't phone during the evening?"

"No one phoned. Joanne wouldn't phone to say she'd come later. I don't think she *could* have come later even if she'd tried. Those extra-punctual people can't, they can't help themselves."

He watched her. A little colour had come into her face. She was perspicacious, she was interested in people, their compulsions, how they behaved. He wondered what they talked about, she and these Virsons, when they were alone together, at meals, in the evening. What had she in common with them? As if she read his mind, she said,

"Joyce—Mrs. Virson—is arranging about the funeral. Some undertakers came today. She'll speak to you, I expect. I mean, we can have a funeral, can we?"

"Yes, yes. Of course."

"I didn't know. I thought it might be different for murdered people. I hadn't thought anything about it till Joyce said. It gave us something to talk about. It's not easy talking when there's only one thing in your life to talk about and that's the one you have to avoid."

"It's fortunate you can talk about it with me."

"Yes."

She tried to smile. "You see, there aren't any family left. Harvey hadn't any relations, except a brother who died four years ago. Davina was . . . 'the youngest wren of nine,' and nearly all the rest are dead. Someone has to organize things, and I wouldn't know how on my own. But I'll say what I want the service to be and I'll go to the funeral, I will do that."

"No one would expect you to."

"I think you may be wrong there," she said thoughtfully. And then, "Have you found anyone yet? I mean, have you got any clues to who it was that . . . did it?"

"I want to ask you if you are quite sure of the description you gave me of the man you saw."

Indignation made her frown, her dark eyebrows push together. "What makes you ask? Of course I'm sure. I'll tell you it again, if you like."

"No, that won't be necessary, Daisy. I'm going to leave

you now, but I'm afraid this isn't likely to be the last time I'll want to talk to you.''

She turned away from him, twisting her body like a child turning its back out of shyness. ''I wish,'' she said, ''I wish there was someone, just one person, I could pour out my heart to. I'm so alone. Oh, if I could only open my heart to someone . . .''

The temptation to say, ''Open it to me,'' was resisted. He knew better than that. She had called him old and implied he was wise. He said, perhaps too lightly, ''You're talking of hearts a lot today, Daisy.''

''Because''—she faced him—''he tried to kill me in my heart. He aimed at my heart, didn't he?''

''You mustn't think of that. You need someone to help you not to,'' he said. ''It's not for me to advise you, I'm not competent to do that, but do you think you need some counselling? Would you consider it?''

''I don't need that!'' She uttered it scornfully, an adamant denial. He was reminded of a psychotherapist he had once met in the course of an inquiry who had told him that saying you don't need counselling is one sure way of estimating that you do. ''I need someone to . . . to *love me*, and there's no one.''

''Goodbye.'' He held out his hand to her. There was Virson to love her. Wexford was sure he did and would. The idea was rather dispiriting. She took his hand and her grip was strong, like a powerful man's. He felt in it the strength of her need, her cry for help. ''Goodbye for the time being.''

''I'm sorry to be such a bore,'' she said quietly.

Joyce Virson was not exactly hovering in the passage, though he guessed she had been. She emerged from what was probably a drawing-room, into which he wasn't invited. She was a big tall woman, perhaps sixty or rather less. The remarkable thing about her was that she seemed altogether on a larger scale than most women, taller, wider, with a bigger face, bigger nose and mouth, a mass of thick curly grey hair, man's hands, surely size-nine feet. A shrill affected upper-class voice went with all this.

"I simply wanted to ask you, I'm sorry but rather a delicate question—may we go ahead with the . . . well, the funeral?"

"Certainly. There's no difficulty about that."

"Oh, good. These things must be, mustn't they? In the midst of life we are in death. Poor little Daisy has some wild ideas but she can't do anything, of course, and one wouldn't expect it. I have actually been in touch with Mrs. Harrison, that housekeeper person at Tancred Hall, on this very subject. It seemed tactful to include her in, don't you think? I thought of next Wednesday or Thursday?"

Wexford said that seemed a sensible course to take. He wondered what Daisy's position would be. Would she need a guardian until she was eighteen? When would she be eighteen? Mrs. Virson shut the front door rather sharply on him, as befitted one who, in her estimation, would once, in better days, have been expected to come and go by a tradesman's entrance. As he walked to his car, an MG, old but stylish, swept in through the open gateway and Nicholas Virson got out of it.

He said, "Good evening," which made Wexford look at his watch in alarm, but it was only twenty to six. Nicholas let himself into the house without a backward glance.

Augustine Casey came downstairs in a dinner jacket.

If he had had any fears about the way Sheila's friend might dress himself for dinner at the Cheriton Forest, Wexford would have guessed at jeans and a sweat-shirt. Not that he would much have minded. That would have been Casey's business, to have put on the proffered tie the hotel produced or to have refused and the lot of them gone home. Wexford wouldn't have cared either way. But the dinner jacket seemed to invite comment, if only for a comparison with his own not very smart grey suit. He could think of nothing to say beyond offering Casey a drink.

Sheila appeared in a peacock-blue miniskirt and peacock-blue-and-emerald-sequin top. Wexford didn't much like the way Casey eyed her up and down while she told *him* how marvellous he looked.

The disquieting thing was that everything went very well for half the evening—the first half. Casey talked. Wexford was learning that things usually went well while Casey talked, while, that is, he talked about a subject chosen by himself, pausing to allow intelligent and appropriate questions from his audience. Sheila, Wexford noticed, was an adept at these questions, seeming to know the precise points at which to interject them. She had tried to tell them about a new part that had been offered her, a wonderful opportunity for her, the name part in Strindberg's *Miss Julie*, but Casey had little patience with that.

In the lounge, he talked about post-modernism. Sheila said, humbly resigned to no more interest being taken in her career, "Could you give us some examples, please, Gus," and Casey gave a large number of examples. They went into one of the several dining-rooms the hotel now boasted. It was full and not one of the men sitting at the tables was in a dinner jacket. Casey, who had already drunk two large brandies, ordered another and immediately went to the men's room.

Sheila had always appeared to her father as an intelligent young woman. He hated having to revise this opinion but what else could he do when she said things like this?

"Gus is so brilliant, it makes me wonder what on earth he sees in someone like me. I feel really inferior while I'm with him."

"What a bloody awful basis for a relationship," he said, at which Dora kicked him under the cloth and Sheila looked hurt.

Casey came back laughing, something Wexford hadn't seen him often doing. A guest had taken him for a waiter, had asked for two dry martinis, and Casey had said in an Italian accent that they were coming up, sir. This made Sheila laugh inordinately. Casey drank his brandy, made a big show of ordering some special wine. He was extremely jovial and began to talk of Davina Flory.

All talk of "keeping mum" and "funny little cops" was apparently forgotten. Casey had met Davina on several occasions, the first time at a launch party for someone else's book, then when she came into his publishers' offices and they encountered each other in the "atrium," a word for "hall" which occasioned a disquisition on Casey's part on fashionable words and otiose importations from dead languages. Wexford's interruption was received as well-timed.

"You didn't know I was published by the St. Giles's Press? I'm not, you're perfectly right. But we're all under the same umbrella now—or sunshade might be the more appropriate word. Carlyon, St. Giles Press, Sheridan and Quick, we're all Carlyon Quick now."

Wexford thought of his friend and Burden's brother-in-law, Amyas Ireland, an editor at Carlyon-Brent. He was still there, as far as he knew. This take-over hadn't squeezed him out. Would there be any point in phoning Amyas for information on Davina Flory?

For Casey's own reminiscences seemed not to amount to much. His third meeting with Davina had been at a party given by Carlyon Quick at their new premises in Battersea—or the "boondocks"—as Casey called it. Her husband had been with her, a rather too sweet and gracious old "honey" who had once been the Member for a constituency in which Casey's parents lived. A friend of Casey's had been taught by him some fifteen years before at the London School of Economics. Casey called him a "cardboard charmer." Some of this charm had been exercised on the hordes of publicity girls and secretaries who were always at such parties, while poor Davina had to talk to boring editors-in-chief and marketing directors. Not that she had taken any sort of back seat, but had thrown her opinions about in her nineteen-twenties Oxford voice, boring everyone with East European politics and details of some trip she and one of her husbands had made to Mecca in the fifties. Wexford smiled inwardly at this example of projection.

He, Casey, had personally liked none of her books with the possible exception of *The Hosts of Midian* (this was the novel Win Carver had described as the least successful or well-received by the critics), and his own definition of her was as the undiscerning reader's Rebecca West. What on earth made her think she could write novels? She was too bossy and didactic. She had no imagination. He was pretty sure she was the only person at that party who hadn't read his own Booker short-listed novel, or at any rate couldn't be bothered to pretend to have done so.

Casey laughed self-deprecatingly at this last remark of his. He tasted the wine. It was then that things began to go wrong. He tasted the wine, winced and used his second wineglass as a spittoon for receiving the offending mouthful. Then he gave both glasses to the waiter.

"This plonk is disgusting. Take it away and bring me another bottle."

Talking about it afterwards with Dora, Wexford said that it was odd nothing like this had happened on the previous Tuesday at La Primavera. Casey wasn't the host there, Dora said. And, after all, if you tasted wine and it was really unpalatable, where were you supposed to spit it out? On the cloth? She was always making excuses for Casey, though she was finding it difficult this time. She hadn't, for instance, much to say in Casey's defence when, after their starters had been sent back, with three waiters and the restaurant manager grouped round the table, he told the head-waiter he had about as much idea of nouvelle cuisine as a school-dinner lady with PMS.

Wexford and Dora were not the hosts but the restaurant was in their neighbourhood, they were in a sense responsible for it. Wexford felt too that Casey was not sincere in what he was doing, it was all for effect, or even what in his youth the old people called "devilment." The meal proceeded in miserable silence, broken by Casey, after he had pushed aside his main course, saying very loudly that he for one wouldn't let the bastards get him down. He returned to the subject of Davina Flory and began making scurrilous remarks about her sexual history.

Among them was the suggestion that Davina had still been a virgin eight years after her first wedding. Desmond, he said in a loud raucous voice, had never been able "to get it up," or not with her, and who could wonder at it? Naomi, of course, had not been his child. Casey said he wouldn't hazard a guess at who her father might have been, and then proceeded to hazard several. He had spotted an elderly man at a distant table, a man who was not, though he strongly resembled him, a distinguished scientist and Master of an Oxford College. Casey began speculating as to the possibilities of this man's *doppelgänger* being Davina Flory's first lover.

Wexford stood up and said he was leaving. He asked Dora to come with him and said the others could do as they pleased. Sheila said, "Please, Pop," and Casey asked what in Christ's name was the matter. To his chagrin, Sheila succeeded in persuading Wexford to stay. He wished very much he had stuck to his guns when the time came to pay the bill. Casey refused to pay it.

A frightful scene ensued. Casey had consumed a great deal of brandy, and though not drunk had become reckless. He shouted and abused the restaurant staff. Wexford had resolved that come what might, even if the *police* should be sent for, he would not pay that bill. In the end Sheila paid it. Stony-faced, Wexford sat by and let her. He said to Dora afterwards that there must have been times in his life when he felt more miserable but he couldn't remember them.

That night he had no sleep.

The missing pane of glass in the dining-room window was patched over with a sheet of plywood. It served its purpose of keeping out the cold.

"I've taken it upon myself to send away for some eight-ounce glass," Ken Harrison said gloomily to Burden. "Don't know how long they'll take coming up with that. Months, I shouldn't be surprised. These criminals, the villains who do this sort of thing, they don't think of the trouble they cause to the little folk like you and me."

Burden didn't much like being numbered among the "little folk," it made him feel (as he remarked to Wexford) like an elf, but he said nothing. They strolled towards the gardens at the rear, towards the pinetum. It was a fine sunny morning, cold and crisp, frost still silvering the grass and the box hedges. In the woods, among the dark leafless trees, the blackthorn was coming into flower, a white scattering on the network of dark twigs like sprinkled snow. Harrison had pruned the roses during the weekend, hard, nearly to the ground.

"We may be finished here for all I know," he said, "but you have to carry on, don't you? You have to carry on normal, that's what life's about."

"How about these Griffins, Mr. Harrison? What can you tell me about them?"

"I'll tell you one thing. Terry Griffin helped himself to a young cedar out of here for a Christmas tree. Couple of years back, it was. I came on him digging it up. No one'll miss that, he said. I took it upon myself to tell Harvey—Mr. Copeland, that is."

"Was that the cause of your falling out with the Griffins, then?"

Harrison gave him a sidelong look, truculent and suspicious. "They never knew it was me told on them. Harvey said he'd discovered it himself, he made a point of not involving me."

They passed among the trees into the pinetum, where the sun penetrated only in streaks and bars of light between the low coniferous branches. It was cold. Underfoot the ground was dry and rather slippery, a carpet of pine needles. Burden picked up a curiously shaped cone, as glossy brown and pineapple-shaped as if it had been carved from wood by a master hand. He said, "D'you know if John Gabbitas is at home or if he's off in the woods somewhere?"

"He goes out by eight but he's down there about a quarter of a mile ahead, felling a dead larch. Can't you hear the saw?"

The whine of it, coming then, was the first Burden had heard. From the trees ahead came the harsh cry of a jay. "Then what was it you and the Griffins did quarrel about, Mr. Harrison?"

"That's private," Harrison said gruffly. "A private matter between Brenda and me. She'd be finished if that got out, so I'm saying no more."

"In a murder case," Burden said with the deceptive smooth mildness he had learned from Wexford, "as I have already told your wife, there is no such thing as privacy for those involved in the inquiry."

"We're not involved in any inquiry!"

"I'm afraid you are. I'd like you to think about this matter, Mr. Harrison, and decide whether you'd like to tell us about it or your wife would or the two of you together. Whether you'd like to tell me or DS Vine and whether it's to be here or at the police station, because you're going to tell us and there'll be no two ways about it. See you later."

He walked off along the path through the pinetum, leaving Harrison standing and staring after him. Harrison called out something but Burden didn't hear what it was and he didn't look back. He rolled the fir cone between the palms of his hands like someone with a worry egg, and he found the feeling good. When he saw the Land Rover ahead and Gabbitas operating the chain-saw, he put the fir cone into his pocket.

John Gabbitas was dressed in the protective clothing, blade-repellent trousers, gloves and boots, mask and goggles, which sensible younger woodsmen put on before using a chain-saw. After the hurricane of 1987, surgical wards of the local hospitals, Burden recalled, had been populated by amateur tree-fellers with self-amputations of feet and hands. Daisy's description of the gunman, now on tape, returned to him. She had described the mask he wore as "like a woodsman's."

When he saw him Gabbitas switched off the saw and came over. He lowered his visor and pushed up the mask and goggles.

"We're still interested in anyone you might have seen when you were coming home last Tuesday."

"I've told you I didn't see anyone."

Burden sat down on a log, patted the smooth dry area of bark beside him. Gabbitas came reluctantly to sit there. He listened, his expression mildly indignant, while Burden told him of Joanne Garland's visit.

"I didn't see her, I don't know her. I mean, I didn't pass any car or see any car. Why don't you ask *her*?"

"We can't find her. She's missing," he said, though it was unusual for him to announce moves to possible suspects. "In fact, we start searching these woods today." He looked hard at Gabbitas. "For her body."

"I came home at twenty past eight," Gabbitas said doggedly. "I can't prove it because I was alone, I didn't see anyone. I came along the Pomfret Monachorum road and I didn't pass a car or meet a car. There were no cars outside Tancred Hall and no car at the side of it or outside the kitchens. I *know* that, I'm telling you the truth."

Burden thought, I find it hard to believe that coming at that time you didn't see both cars. That you saw neither, I find impossible to believe. You're lying, and your only motive for lying must be a very serious one indeed. But Joanne Garland's car was in her garage. Had she come in some other vehicle, and if so, where was it? Could she have come in a taxi?

"What did you do before you came here?"

The question seemed to surprise Gabbitas. "Why do you ask?"

"It's the kind of question," Burden said patiently, "that does get asked in a murder inquiry. For instance, how did you come to get this job?"

Gabbitas back-tracked. Having considered for a long silent moment, he reverted to Burden's first query. "I've got a degree in forestry. I told you I do a bit of teaching. The hurricane, as they call it, the storm of 1987, that got me started really. As a result of that, there was more work than all the woodsmen in the county could handle. I even made a bit of money, for a change. I was working near Midhurst." He looked up, slyly, it seemed to Burden. "At that place, as a matter of fact, where I was the evening this business happened."

"Where you were coppicing and no one saw you."

Gabbitas made an impatient gesture. He used his hands a lot to express his feelings. "I told you, mine is a lonely job. You haven't got people keeping an eye on you all the time. Last winter, I mean the winter before last, the major part of the work there was coming to an end and I saw this job advertised."

"What, in a magazine? In the local rag?"

"In *The Times*," said Gabbitas with a little smile. "Davina Flory interviewed me herself. She gave me a copy of her tree book but I can't say I actually read it." He moved his hands again. "It was the house which attracted me."

He said it quickly, for all the world, thought Burden, as if to forestall being asked if the attraction had been the girl.

"And now if you'll excuse me, I'd like to get this tree down before it falls down and does a lot of unnecessary damage."

Burden made his way back through the woods and the pinetum, this time crossing the garden and making for the wide gravelled area beyond which the stables were. Wexford's car was there, two police vans and DS Vine's Vauxhall, as well as his own car. He went inside.

Wexford he found in an uncharacteristic attitude, confronting and gazing at a computer screen. Gerry Hinde's computer screen. The Chief Inspector looked up and Burden was shocked by his face, by that grey look, those surely new ageing lines, something like misery in his eyes. It was as if Wexford were, for a brief moment, out of control of his face, but then he seemed to make some inner adjustment and his expression returned to normal, or nearly so. Hinde sat at the computer keyboard, having summoned onto the screen a long and, to Burden, impenetrable list.

Wexford, recalling Daisy Flory's sentiments, would have liked someone in whom he could freely confide. Dora was in this matter unsympathetic. He would dearly have liked someone he could talk to of Sheila's avowal that he, her father, was prejudiced against Augustine Casey and determined to hate him. That she was so in love with Casey as to be able to say, strange as it might sound, as to be discovering what that meant for the first time. That if it came to a choice—and this was the worst thing—she would "cleave" (her curious biblical word) to Casey and turn her back on her parents.

All this, expressed tête-à-tête while out on an unhappy walk, Casey being in bed recovering from the brandy, had cut him to the heart. As Daisy might put it. If there was any comfort to be found it was in the knowledge that Sheila had the offer of a role she couldn't forgo and Casey was off to Nevada.

His wretchedness showed in his face, he knew that, and he did his best to wipe it away. Burden saw the effort he made.

"They've started searching the woods, Reg."

Wexford moved away. "It's a big area. Can we rope in some of the locals to help?"

"It's only missing kids they're interested in. They won't turn out for adult corpses for love or money."

"And we're offering neither," said Wexford.

CHAPTER TWELVE

He's away," Margaret Griffin said.

"Away where?"

"He's a grown-up man, isn't he? I don't ask him where he's going and when he's coming home, all that. He may live at home but he's a grown man, he can do as he likes."

At mid-morning the Griffins had been drinking coffee and watching television. No coffee was offered to Burden and Barry Vine. Barry said to Burden afterwards that Terry and Margaret Griffin looked much older than they were, elderly already, set into a routine, which was apparent if not explicit, of television-watching, shopping, small regular meals, togetherness in solitude and early bedtimes. They answered Burden's questions with resigned truculence that threatened, at any moment, to yield to paranoia.

"Does Andy often go away?"

She was a small round white-haired woman with bulging blue eyes. "He's nothing to keep him here, has he? I mean, he's not going to get work, is he? Not with another two hundred laid off at Myringham Electrics last week.''

''Is he an electrician?''

''Turn his hand to anything, will Andy,'' said Terry Griffin, ''if he gets the chance. He's not one of your unskilled workers, you know. He's been PA to a very important businessman, has Andy.''

''An American gentleman. He placed implicit trust in Andy. Used to go backwards and forwards abroad and he left everything in Andy's hands.''

''Andy had the run of his house, had his keys, let to drive his car, the lot.''

Taking this with more than a grain of salt, Burden said, ''Does he go away looking for work, then?''

''I told you, I don't know and I don't ask.''

Barry said, ''I think you should know, Mr. Griffin, that though you told us Andy went out at six last Tuesday, according to the friends he said he was with, no one saw him that evening. He didn't do the round of the pubs with them and he didn't meet them in the Chinese restaurant.''

''What friends he said he was with? He never told us no friends he was with. He went to other pubs, didn't he?''

''That remains to be seen, Mr. Griffin,'' said Burden. ''Andy must know the Tancred estate very well. Spent his childhood there, did he?''

''I don't know about 'estate,' '' said Mrs. Griffin. '' 'Estate's' a lot of houses, isn't it? There's only the two houses there and that great place where *they* live. Lived, I should say.''

Demesne, Burden thought. How would it be if he had said that instead? A lifetime of police work had taught him never to explain if he could avoid it. ''The woods, the grounds, Andy knew them well?''

''Of course he does. He was a little kid of four when we first went there and that girl, that granddaughter, was a baby. Now you'd think it'd have been normal for them to play together, wouldn't you? Andy would have liked that, he used to say, 'Why can't I have a little sister, Mum?' And I had to say,

'God isn't going to send us any more babies, lovey.' But let her play with him? Oh, no, he wasn't good enough, not for little Miss Precious. There was only the two children there and they wasn't allowed to play together.''

"And him calling himself a Labour MP," said Terry Griffin. He gave a low hoot of laughter. "No wonder they kicked him out at the last election."

"So Andy never went in the house?"

"I wouldn't say that." Margaret Griffin was suddenly huffy. "I wouldn't say that at all. Why d'you say that? He'd come with me sometimes when I went to help out. They had a housekeeper woman living next door on her own before those Harrisons came but she couldn't do the lot, not when they had company. Andy'd come with me then, go all over the house with me, whatever they said. Mind you, I don't reckon he ever did after he was—well, ten like.''

This was her first mention of Ken and Brenda Harrison, the first indication either of them had given of the existence of their erstwhile neighbours.

"When he goes away, Mrs. Griffin," Barry put in, "how long is he usually away for?"

"Might be a couple of days, might be a week."

"I understand you weren't on speaking terms with Mr. and Mrs. Harrison at the time you left . . .''

Burden was cut short by the crowing Margaret Griffin made. More than anything else it was like the wordless utterance of a heckler at a meeting. Or, as Barry said afterwards, a child's jeer at a playmate proved wrong, a reiterated, "Aah, aah, aah!"

"I knew it! You said, didn't you, Terry, you said they'd get on to that. It'll come out now, you said, for all Mr. Harvey *Labour* Copeland's promises. They'll get hold of that to smear poor Andy after all this time."

In his wisdom, Burden didn't betray by the movement of a muscle or the flicker of an eyelid that he hadn't the faintest idea what she meant. He maintained a rather stern omniscient gaze as they told him.

. . .

The valuation of Davina Flory's jewellery joined the rest of Gerry Hinde's data on the computer.

Barry Vine discussed it with Wexford. "A lot of villains would consider thirty thousand pounds worth killing three people for, sir."

"Knowing they'd get maybe half that for it in the sort of markets they use. Well, yes, maybe. We've got no other motive."

"Revenge is a motive. Some real or imaginary injury perpetrated by Davina or Harvey Copeland. Daisy Flory had a motive. So far as we know, she inherits and no one else does. She's the only one left. I know it's a bit far-fetched, sir, but if we're talking of motives . . ."

"She shot her whole family and wounded herself? Or an accomplice did? Like her lover Andy Griffin?"

"All right. I know."

"I don't think the place interests her much, Barry. She hasn't realized yet what sort of money and property she's come into."

Vine turned from his computer screen. "I've been talking to Brenda Harrison, sir. She says she and the Griffins quarrelled because she didn't like Mrs. Griffin hanging washing out in the garden on a Sunday."

"You believe that?"

"I think it shows Brenda's got more imagination than I gave her credit for."

Wexford laughed, then became instantly serious. "We can be sure of one thing, Barry. This crime was committed by someone who didn't know this place and these people at all and by someone else who knew both very well indeed."

"One in the know and one to take instruction from him?"

"I couldn't put it better myself," said Wexford.

He was pleased with Burden's sergeant. You must not say, even to yourself, when someone has died a heroic death, or any death at all, that his replacement is a positive improvement or that tragedy was a blessing in disguise. But the feeling was there, or just the inescapable relief, that Martin's successor was so promising.

Barry Vine was a strong muscular man of medium height. If he had held himself less well, he might have been called short. Not exactly secretly but certainly privately, he went in for weight-lifting. He had reddish hair, short and thick, the kind that recedes but never goes bald, and a small moustache that had grown dark, not red. Some people always look the same and are instantly recognizable. Their faces can be conjured up by memory and screened on the inner eye. Barry's was not like that. There was something protean about him, so that in certain lights and at certain angles you would have called him a sharp-featured man with a hard jaw-line, while at others his nose and mouth looked almost feminine. But his eyes never varied. They were rather small, a fleckless, very dark blue, that fixed friend and suspect alike with an unvarying steady gaze.

Wexford, whom his wife called a liberal, tried to be tolerant and forbearing and often succeeded (or so he believed) in being merely irascible. Until his second marriage it had never occurred to Burden—or he had not listened when these things had been pointed out to him—that there might be any wisdom or virtue in holding views other than those of an inflexible conservative. He would have found nothing to dispute in the notion of the police force as the Tory Party with helmet and truncheon.

Barry Vine thought little about politics. He was the essential Englishman, more English in a curious way than either of his superiors. He voted for the party that had done most for him and his immediate circle in the recent past. It mattered very little whether they called themselves right- or left-wing. ''Most for him'' meant, in his book, most in the area of finance, saving him money, reducing taxes and prices, and making life more comfortable.

While Burden believed that the world would be a better place if others behaved more as he did, and Wexford that things would improve if people learned to think, Vine made no incursions into even such primitive metaphysics. For him there existed a large (but not large enough) population of decent law-abiding people who worked and owned houses and raised families in varying degrees of prosperity; and a swarm of others, instantly recognizable by him even if they had, as yet, committed no offence. The interesting thing was that this was not a matter of class, as it might be in Burden's case. He could spot, he said, a potential villain even if this person had a title, a Porsche or several millions in the bank; an accent like an art-history don at Cambridge or the intonation of the man who digs up the roads. Vine was no snob and often started off with a bias towards the road-digger. His villain-spotting rested on quite other pointers, something intuitive perhaps, though Vine called it common sense.

Therefore, when he found himself in the Myringham pub called the Slug and Lettuce, having discovered that this was where Andy Griffin's friends congregated most evenings, his antennae were quickly at work assessing the criminal potential of the four men for whom he had bought halves of Abbot.

Two of them were unemployed. That hadn't inhibited their regular attendance at the Slug and Lettuce, which Wexford would have excused on the grounds that human beings need circuses as well as bread, which Burden would have called fecklessness but Vine set down as characteristic of men on the lookout for lucrative ways to break the law. One of the others was an electrician, grumbling about a fall-off in work caused by recession, the fourth a messenger for an overnight delivery company who described himself as a "mobile courier."

A phrase particularly offensive to Vine's ears was that so often heard in court, uttered by defendants or even witnesses: "I might have been." What did it mean? Nothing. Less than nothing. Anybody, after all, might have been almost anywhere or done almost anything.

So when the unemployed man called Tony Smith said that Andy Griffin "might have been" in the Slug and Lettuce on the night of March 11, Vine ignored him. The others had already told him, days ago, that they hadn't seen him that evening. Kevin Lewis, Roy Walker and Leslie Sedlar were adamant that Andy hadn't been with them, nor afterwards at the Panda Cottage. They were less positive about his present whereabouts.

Tony Smith said he "might have been in the old Slug" on Sunday evening. The others couldn't say. That was one evening on which they gave the pub a miss.

"He goes up north," Leslie Sedlar offered.

"Is that what he tells you or do you know it?"

This was a distinction hard for any of them to make. Tony Smith insisted that he knew it.

"He goes up north with the lorry. He goes up regular, don't he?"

"He hasn't got a job any more," said Vine. "He hasn't had a job for a year."

"When he had his driving job he went up regular."

"How about now?"

He said he went up north, so he did. They believed him. The fact was they weren't much interested in where Andy went. Why should they be? Vine asked Kevin Lewis, whom he had assessed as the most sensible and probably the most law-abiding, where he thought Andy was now.

"Off on his bike," Lewis said.

"Where, then? Manchester? Liverpool?"

They barely seemed to know where those places were. To Kevin Lewis, Liverpool dredged up recollections of his "old man" talking about something popular in his youth called the Mersey Sound.

"He goes up north then. Suppose I said he doesn't, he hangs about down here?"

Roy Walker shook his head. "He don't. Not Andy. Andy'd be in the old Slug."

Vine knew when he was beaten. "Where does his money come from?"

"He gets the dole, I reckon," said Lewis.

"And that's it? That's all?" Keep it simple. No use asking about "supplementary sources of income." "He's no other money coming in?"

It was Tony Smith who answered. "He might have."

They were silenced. They had no more to offer. An enormous strain had been put on their imaginations and the result was to exhaust them. More Abbot might have helped—"might have"!—but Vine felt the game wasn't worth the candle.

Mrs. Virson's voice was loud, expansive, the product of an expensive girls' boarding-school attended some forty-five years before. She opened the front door of The Thatched House to him and welcomed him in with a kind of high graciousness. The floral printed dress she wore upholstered her like a voluminous chair cover. Her hair had been done that day. The scrolls and undulations looked as fixed as if they had been carved. It was unlikely that all this was for him, but something had happened to change her attitude to him since his previous visit—Daisy's own insistence on her willingness to see and talk to him?

"Daisy's asleep, Mr. Wexford. She's still very deeply shocked, you know, and I insist on her having plenty of rest."

He nodded, having no comment to make.

"She'll be awake in time for her tea. These young things have a very healthy appetite, I've noticed, however much they may have been through. Shall we go in here and wait for her? I expect there are things you want to chat to me about, aren't there?"

He was not the man to neglect such an opportunity. If Joyce Virson had something to say to him, which was what "chat" must mean, he would listen and hope for the best. But when they were in Mrs. Virson's drawing-room, sitting in faded chintz-covered chairs and facing each other across an arts-and-crafts coffee-table, she seemed to have no inclination to begin a conversation. She was not embarrassed or awkward or even diffident. She was simply thoughtful and perhaps doubted where to begin. He was wary of helping her. In his position any help would look like interrogation.

She said suddenly, "Of course what happened up there at Tancred House was a terrible thing. After I heard about it I didn't sleep for two whole nights. It was simply the most appalling thing I've ever heard in the whole course of my life.''

He waited for the ''but.'' People who began like that, with an admission of their appreciation of tragedy or extreme misfortune, usually went on to qualify it. Initial empathy was to be an excuse for subsequent abuse.

There was no ''but.'' She surprised him by her directness. ''My son wants Daisy to be engaged to him.''

''Really?''

''Mrs. Copeland didn't like the idea. I suppose I should call her Davina Flory or Miss Flory or something, but old habits die hard, don't they? I'm sorry, I suppose I'm old-fashioned, but a married woman will always be ''Mrs.'' and her husband's name to me.'' She waited for Wexford to say something and when he said nothing, continued, ''No, she didn't care for the idea. Of course I don't mean she had anything against Nicholas. It was just some silly notion—I'm sorry but I thought it silly—about Daisy having her life to lead before she settled down. I could have said to her that when she was Daisy's age, girls got married just as young as they could.''

''Did you?''

''Did I what?''

''You said you could have said this to her. Did you in fact say it?''

A pucker of wariness crossed Mrs. Virson's face. It passed. She smiled. ''It was hardly my business to interfere.''

''What did Daisy's mother think?''

''Oh, really, it wouldn't have mattered what Naomi thought. Naomi didn't have opinions. You see, Mrs. Copeland was much more like a mother than a grandmother to Daisy. *She* made all the decisions for her. I mean, where she went to school and all that. Oh, she had very big ideas for Daisy, or Davina, as she insisted on calling her, most confusing. She had her whole future mapped out, university first, Oxford, *naturally*, and then poor little Daisy was to have a year travelling. Not anywhere a young girl would want to go to, I mean not Bermuda or the south of France or anywhere nice, but places in Europe with art galleries and history, Rome and Florence and those sort of places. And then she was to go on doing something at another university, if you please, another degree or whatever they call them. I'm sorry, but I don't see the purpose of all this education for a pretty young girl. Mrs. Copeland's idea was for her to bury herself at some university, she wanted her to be a—what's the name I want?''

''An academic?''

''Yes, that's right. Poor little Daisy was to have got there by the time she was twenty-five and then she was supposed to write her first book. I'm sorry, but it just seems ridiculous to me.''

''What about Daisy herself? How did she feel?''

''What does a girl of that age know? She knows nothing about life, does she? Oh, if you go on talking about Oxford and make it sound a glamorous place and then you keep saying how wonderful Italy is and seeing this picture and that statue, and how much more you can appreciate things if you've been educated in this way and that—well, naturally, it has some effect on you. You're so impressionable at that age, you're just a baby.''

''Marrying,'' said Wexford, ''would of course put a stop to all that.''

''Mrs. Copeland may have been married three times but I don't think she was too keen on marriage just the same.'' She leaned towards him confidingly, lowering her voice and looking briefly over her shoulder as if someone else were in a far corner of the room. ''I don't know this, I mean I don't actually know it, it's pure guesswork, but I think it's pretty sound—I'm positive Mrs. Copeland wouldn't have turned a hair if Nicholas and Daisy had wanted to live together without marriage. She was obsessed with sex, you know. At her age! She'd probably have welcomed a relationship, she was all for Daisy having experience.''

''What sort of experience?'' he asked curiously.

''Oh, you mustn't take me up on every little thing I say, Mr.

Wexford. I mean, she used to say she wanted her to *live*. She'd really *lived*, she used to say, and I suppose she had, with all those husbands and all that travelling. But marriage? No, she wasn't at all happy about that idea.''

"Would you like your son to marry Daisy?"

"Oh, *yes*, I would. She's such a sweet girl. And clever, of course, and good-looking. I'm sorry, but I shouldn't like my son to marry a plain girl. I don't expect you think that's very nice but it does seem such a waste, a handsome man with a plain wife.'' Joyce Virson preened herself a very little. There was no other word for that slight elongating of her neck, for the way she ran a thick finger along her jaw-line. "We're a good-looking family on both sides.'' The smile she gave Wexford was arch, was nearly flirtatious. "Of course the poor little thing's madly in love with him. You've only got to see the way she follows him with her eyes. She adores him.''

Wexford thought she was going to preface her next remarks with her usual expression of sorrow for an opinion she very obviously did not in the least regret, but she only elaborated on Daisy's qualifications for a union with a member of the Virson family. Daisy was so fond of *her*, had such nice manners, was so even-tempered and good-humoured.

"And so rich,'' said Wexford.

Mrs. Virson actually jumped. She started as violently as someone in the early stage of a seizure. Her voice rose twenty or thirty decibels.

"That has nothing whatsoever to do with it. When you look at the size of this house and the standing we have in the community, you can hardly imagine there's any shortage of money, surely. My son has a very good income, he's quite able to support a wife in the . . .''

He thought she was going to add something about the style to which Daisy was accustomed but she checked herself and glowered at him. Sick of her hypocrisy and affectations, he had decided the time had come for a sharp thrust below the belt. It had gone home better than he hoped for. He smiled to himself.

"You're not worried she may be too young?" he said. Now the smile was extended to her as well, wide and disarming. "You called her a baby just now."

Joyce Virson was saved from answering by the entry of Daisy into the room. He had heard her footsteps on the hall floor as he spoke the word "baby." She gave him a wan smile. Her arm was still bandaged but less bulkily and the sling was lighter. This, he realized, was the first time he had seen her standing up, moving about. She was thinner than he had expected, her shape more fragile.

"What am I too young for?" she said. "I'm eighteen today, it's my birthday."

Mrs. Virson shrieked. "Daisy, you terrible girl, why didn't you tell us? I hadn't the least idea, you didn't say a word."

She attempted an astonished laugh but Wexford could tell she was very displeased. She was chagrined. Daisy's revelation gave the lie to her claims of an intimate knowledge of the young woman staying in her house.

"I suppose you just dropped a hint to Nicholas, so that he could plan a surprise."

"As far as I know, he doesn't know either. He won't remember. I have no one in the world now to remember my birthday." She looked at Wexford, said lightly, stagily, "Goodness, how sad!"

"Many happy returns of the day." He used the old-fashioned formula.

"Ah, you're tactful, you're careful. You couldn't say 'Happy birthday,' could you? Not to me. It would be frightful, it would be an insult. Will you remember my birthday next year, d'you think? Will you say to yourself on the eve of it, it's Daisy's birthday tomorrow? You may be the only one who will."

"What nonsense, dear. Nicholas will certainly remember. It'll be your job to keep him up to that. I'm sorry, but men need a hint, you know, not to say a little twist of the arm."

Joyce Virson's expression was ferociously arch. Daisy allowed her eyes to meet Wexford's for a short moment and looked away. Not looking at him, she said, "Shall we go in the other room, then?"

"Oh, why not stay here, dear? It's nice and warm in here and I won't listen to what you're saying, I'll be too wrapped up in my book. I won't hear a word."

Determined not to speak to Daisy in Mrs. Virson's presence, before making this point he waited to hear what Daisy would say. She looked so far away, so remotely sorrowful, that he expected an apathetic acquiescence, but instead she spoke firmly.

"No, it's better it should be private. We won't turn you out of your room, Joyce."

He followed her to the "little den," the room where they had been on Saturday. There she remarked, "She means well." He marvelled at how young she could be—and how old. "Yes, I'm eighteen today. After the funeral I think I'll go home. Quite soon after. I can do what I like now I'm eighteen, can't I? Absolutely what I like?"

"As far as any of us can, yes. Apart from breaking the law with impunity, you can do as you please."

She sighed heavily. "I don't want to break the law. I don't know what I want to do, but I think I'd be better at home."

Warningly he said, "Perhaps you don't quite realize how you'll feel confronting your home again. After what happened there. It will bring that night back to you very painfully."

"That night is always with me," she said. "It can't be there more strongly than it is every time I close my eyes. That's when I see the picture of it, you see. When I close my eyes. I see that table—before and after. I wonder if I'll ever be able to bear sitting at a dining-table again? She gives me my meals on a tray here. I asked for that." She was silent, smiled suddenly and looked at him. He saw a strange glow in her dark eyes. "We always talk about me. Tell me about you. Where do you live? Are you married? Have you got children? Have you got people who remember your birthday?"

He told her where he lived, that he was married, had two

daughters, three grandchildren. Yes, they remembered his birthday, more or less.

"I wish I had a father."

Why had he neglected to ask about this? "But surely you have? You see him sometimes?"

"I've never seen him. Or not that I remember. Mum and he were divorced when I was a baby. He lives in London but he's never shown any sign of wanting to see me. I don't mean I wish I had him, I wish I had a *father*."

"Yes, I expect your—er, your grandmother's husband filled the place of a father in your life."

It was unmistakable, the incredulity in the look she gave him. She made a sound in the back of her throat, somewhere between a snort and a cough. "Has Joanne turned up?"

"No, Daisy. We're worried about her."

"Oh, nothing will have happened to her. What could have?"

Her serene innocence only served to exacerbate his concern. "When she came to see your mother on Tuesdays," he said, "did she always come by car?"

"Of course." She looked surprised. "Oh, you mean, did she walk? It would be a good five miles. Anyway, Joanne never walked anywhere. I don't know why she lived here, she hated country things, everything to do with the country. I suppose it was on account of her old mum. I'll tell you what, she did sometimes come by taxi. It wasn't that her car had broken down. She liked a drink, did Joanne, and then she'd be scared to drive."

"What can you tell me about some people called Griffin?"

"They used to work for us."

"The son, Andy, have you seen him since they left?"

She gave him a curious look. It was as if she marvelled that he had hit on something so unexpected or secret. "I did once. How funny you should ask. It was in the woods. I was walking in the woods and I saw him. You probably don't know our woods at all but it was near the by-road, that little road that goes off to the east, it was near where the walnuts are. He may have seen me, I don't know, I should have said something to him, asked him what he was doing, but I didn't, I don't know why. It *frightened* me, seeing him like that. I didn't tell anyone. He was trespassing, Davina would have hated that, but I didn't tell her.''

"When was this?"

"Oh, last autumn sometime. October, I should think."

"How would he have got here?"

"He used to have a motor bike. I expect he still has."

"His father says he had a job with an American business-man. I had a hunch—that's all it was—they might have got in touch through your family."

She thought. "Davina would never have recommended him. I suppose it could be Preston Littlebury. But if Andy worked for him, it would only have been, well . . ."

"As a driver perhaps?"

"Not even that. Maybe to clean his car."

"All right. It's probably not important. One last question. Could the other man, the man you didn't see, leave the house and start the car—could that have been Andy Griffin? Think before you answer. Take it as a possibility and then think if there was anything, anything at all, that might have identified him with Andy Griffin."

She was silent. She seemed neither shocked nor incredulous. It was plain she was obeying his instruction and thinking it over. At last she said, "It *could* have been. Can I say there was nothing to make me certain it wasn't? That's all I can say."

He left her then, telling her he would be at the funeral on Thursday morning.

"I'll tell you my idea of what happened, if you like," Burden said. They were in his house, his son Mark in pyjamas on his lap, Jenny having gone to her evening class in advanced German. "I'll get you another beer and then I'll tell you. No, you can get the beer so I don't have to shift him."

Wexford came back with two cans and two steins.

"Those tankards, you see they're identical. There's a third one on the shelf. It's quite an interesting illustration in economics. The one you've got—let me have a closer look—yes, the one you've got, Jean and I bought on our honeymoon in Innsbruck for five shillings. Before decimal coinage, you see, well before. The one I've got, it's actually a fraction smaller, I bought ten years ago when we took the kids there. Same difference and it cost four quid. The one on the shelf's a good deal smaller and in my opinion not such a good piece of work. Jenny and I bought it in Kitzbühel while we were on holiday last summer. Ten pounds fifty. What does that tell you?''

''The cost of living's gone up. I didn't need three beer mugs to tell me that. Could we have your Tancred scenario instead of these disquisitions on comparative ceramics?''

Burden grinned. He said to his son rather sententiously, ''No, you can't have Daddy's beer, Mark, just as Daddy can't have your Ribena.''

''Poor old Daddy. I bet that's a real sacrifice. What happened on Tuesday evening, then?''

''The gunman in the bank, the one with the acne, I shall call him X.''

''That's really original, Mike.''

Burden ignored the interruption. ''The other man was Andy Griffin. Andy was the man with the knowledge, X had the gun.''

''Gun,'' said Mark.

Burden put him on the floor. The little boy picked up a plastic whistle from the heap of toys, pointed it at Wexford, said, ''Bang, bang.''

''Oh, dear, Jenny doesn't like him to have guns. He hasn't in fact got a gun.''

''He has now.''

''D'you think it would be all right for him to watch half an hour's television before I put him to bed?''

''For God's sake, Mike, you've more children than I have, you should know.'' When Burden still looked dubious, he said impatiently, ''So long as it's not more bloody than what you're going to tell me and it's unlikely to be.''

Burden switched the set on. ''X and Andy set off for Tancred House in X's jeep.''

"In *what*?"

"It has to be a vehicle that can handle rough ground."

"Where did they meet, these two, X and Andy?"

"In a pub. Maybe in the Slug and Lettuce. Andy tells X about Davina's jewellery and they make their plan. Andy knows Brenda Harrison's habits. He knows that she announces dinner every evening at seven thirty and goes home, leaving the back door unlocked."

Wexford nodded. "A good point in favour of Griffin's involvement."

Looking pleased, Burden went on, "They drive up by the main road through the gates from the B 2428, but take the left-hand branch just before the wall and the courtyard are reached. Brenda has gone home; Davina Flory, Harvey Copeland, Naomi Jones and Daisy Flory are all in that conservatory place. So no one hears a vehicle arrive or sees its lights, as Andy has calculated they won't. The time is twenty-five to eight."

"Cutting it fine. Suppose Brenda had been five minutes late leaving or the others five minutes early going into the dining-room?"

"They weren't," said Burden simply. He proceeded, "X and Andy enter the house by the back way and go up the back stairs."

"They can't have done. Bib Mew was there."

"You can get to the back stairs without passing through the main kitchen. That's where she was, working on the freezer. In Davina's bedroom they search for and find her jewellery and they also search the other women's bedrooms."

"They would need to in order to take twenty-five minutes over it. Incidentally, why leave the other women's bedrooms tidy but Davina's in a mess if they searched them all?"

"I'm coming to that. They went *back* to Davina's room because Andy believed there was some more valuable piece they had missed. It was while they were flinging the stuff about in there that they were heard by the people downstairs and Harvey Copeland went to investigate. They must have assumed he was coming up the front stairs, so they went down the back . . ."

"And out of the back door with their loot to make their get-away with no harm done beyond the loss to Davina of some heavily insured jewellery she didn't much care for anyway."

"We know it wasn't like that," Burden said very seriously. "They came through the house into the hall. I don't know why. Perhaps they had some reason to fear the return of Brenda or they believed Harvey was upstairs, intending to walk the length of the gallery and go down the back stairs. Whatever it was, they came into the hall and encountered Harvey, who was half-way up the stairs. He turned and saw them, immediately recognizing Andy Griffin. He took a couple of steps down, shouted some threat at Andy or called to the women to phone the police . . ."

"Daisy didn't hear him if he did."

"She's forgotten. She's admitted herself she can't recall details of what happened. She says on that tape we made, 'I've tried hard to remember but something blocks it off.' Harvey threatened Andy and X shot him. He fell backwards across the bottom stairs. Andy was now obviously terrified, *more* terrified, of being recognized. He heard a woman scream from the dining-room. While X kicked open the dining-room door, Andy ran to the front door and out.

"X shot the two women, he shot Daisy. From upstairs he heard someone racketing about. It was the cat but he didn't know that. Daisy was on the floor, he thought she was dead, he followed Andy out of the front door where the jeep had been brought round for him. Andy had fetched the jeep from where it was parked at the back . . ."

"It won't work, Mike. This was the time Bib Mew was leaving. She was leaving on her bike from the back of the house. Daisy heard a car start up, not 'brought round.' "

"It's a small point. Would she swear to that, Reg? Her mother and grandmother had been shot before her eyes, she was shot, she's on the floor wounded and bleeding—just imagine the noise that Magnum would have made, for one thing—and she can differentiate between a car starting up and one being driven?"

Turning his eyes from a nature programme on lions killing and disembowelling wildebeests, Mark said happily, "Wounded and bleeding." He nodded and pointed the whistle at his father.

"Oh, God, I must get him to bed. Just let me finish this, Mark. While Andy is round the back fetching the jeep and X is making mayhem in the dining-room, Joanne Garland arrives *in a taxi*. Once again she is afraid to drive because she has had a drink or two . . ."

"Where? Who with?"

"That remains to be seen. That remains to be discovered. She paid the driver and he left. Her intention was to phone for another taxi when she was through with her bookkeeping with Naomi. The time is ten past eight. She isn't supposed to be there until eight thirty, but we know she was one of these over-punctual people, always early.

"The front door is open. She steps inside, perhaps she calls out. She sees Harvey's body spread-eagled across the stairs, perhaps she hears the last shot. Does she turn and run? Perhaps. Andy has appeared by now with the jeep. He jumps out and seizes her. X comes out, kills Joanne, *with the sixth and last cartridge in the chamber*, and they put her body in the back.

"Fearing they might meet someone on the road, Gabbitas, us, some visitor, they take off *through* the wood, using paths negotiable by a jeep but not by your average saloon car." Burden picked up his son, switched off the television. The little boy was still grasping his whistle. "Subject to a few minor amendments, I suggest that's the only way it could have happened."

Wexford said, "What did the Harrisons and the Griffins quarrel about?"

Indignation had briefly contorted Burden's face. Was that all? Was that the only reception his analysis was going to get? He shrugged. "Andy tried to rape Brenda Harrison."

"What?"

"That's what she says. The Griffins say *she* made advances to him. Apparently, he tried a sort of blackmail on those grounds and Brenda told Davina Flory. Hence, if we were to be kept out of it, the Griffins had to go.''

"We'd better have him in, Mike."

"We will," said Burden, and he carried his son away to bed, Mark firing the whistle over his shoulder and shouting, "Wounded and bleeding, wounded and bleeding," all the way upstairs.

CHAPTER THIRTEEN

Had they no friends but the Virsons and Joanne Garland, this family who were wealthy and distinguished, whose nucleus was a famous writer and an economist and former MP? Where were Daisy's school friends? Their local acquaintances?

These questions had interested Wexford from the first. But the nature of the crime was such as to preclude hitherto law-abiding members of the public from being involved, and his usual investigation in a murder case of everyone known to the victims had not been carried out. It had simply occurred to him, while talking to Daisy, and to a lesser extent to the Harrisons and Gabbitas, that there seemed a dearth of Flory family friends.

The funeral showed him how right he had been—and how wrong. In spite of the fame of one of the dead and the distinction, by association with her, of the others, he had supposed those who mourned Davina Flory and her family would wait to attend the memorial service. Daisy, as well as Joyce Virson, had said a service would be held. St. James's, Piccadilly, had been suggested, in two months' time. The service in Kingsmarkham parish church would surely have a small congregation, a few people only proceeding to the distant cemetery. As it turned out, they were queuing up.

Jason Sebright from the *Kingsmarkham Courier* was taking names at the church gates when he arrived. Wexford quickly perceived that the queue was the press and he pushed past them, producing his warrant card. St. Peter's was very large, one of those English churches that would be called cathedrals anywhere else, with an enormous nave, ten side chapels and a chancel as big as a village church. It was nearly full.

Only the front pews on the right-hand side awaited occupants and a few scattered seats among the congregation. Wexford made his way to one of these, a vacant space next to the aisle on the left. The last time he was there had been to give Sheila away when she married Andrew Thorverton; the last time he had sat like this in the body of the church was to hear her banns called. A marriage come to grief, a love affair or two, and now Augustine Casey . . . He pushed it out of mind and eyed the congregation. A voluntary was playing, Bach probably.

The first person he recognized was someone he had met at a book launch, taken there by Amyas Ireland. The book, he recalled, had been a family saga with a policeman in every generation since Victorian times, its author's editor this man three rows in front of him. All the others in the pew looked like publishers to him, though he couldn't have said how. He identified (again without much to go on) a plump yellow-haired woman in a large black hat as Davina Flory's agent.

A preponderance of elderly women, some of them scholarly-looking, in groups or sitting alone, led him to believe these were old cronies of Davina, perhaps from as far back as Oxford days. From photographs he had seen in the newspapers, he recognized a distinguished woman novelist now in her seventies. Wasn't that the Minister for the Arts in the pew next to her? His name escaped Wexford for the moment, but that was who it was. A man with a red rose in his buttonhole—in questionable taste?—he had seen on television on the Opposition benches. An old parliamentary friend of Harvey Copeland's? Joyce Virson had secured herself a place very near the front. Of her son there was no sign. And there wasn't a young girl in sight.

Just as he was wondering who would take the empty pew next to him, Jason Sebright hurried in to sit in it.

"Hordes of glitterati here," he said happily, barely able to conceal his enjoyment of the occasion. "I'm going to do a piece called 'The Friends of a Great Woman.' Even if I get nine refusals out of ten, I should get at least four exclusive interviews."

"I'd rather have my job than yours," said Wexford.

"I've learned my technique from US TV. I'm half American, I spend my vacations there visiting with my mom." This he said in a horrible parody of a Midwest accent. "We've a lot to learn in this country. At the *Courier* they're dead scared all the time of treading on people's toes, everyone's got to be handled with gloves on, and what I—"

"Sshh, will you? It's going to start."

The music had stopped. A hush fell. There was no whispering. It was as if the congregation had even ceased to breathe. Sebright shrugged and put one finger up to his lips. The silence was of a kind that only ever prevails in a church: oppressive, cold, but for some transcendent. Everyone was waiting, expectant and gradually enclosed by awe.

The first chords from the organ broke the silence with a heavy and terrible multiplication of decibels. Wexford could hardly believe his ears. Not the "Dead March in Saul," no one ever had the "Dead March in Saul" any more. But that was what it was. "Dum-dum-de-boom-dum-de-dum-de-dum-dum-boom," he murmured under his breath. The three coffins were borne up the aisle with ineffable slowness in time to that wonderful and dreadful music. The men who supported them on their shoulders moved in the steps of a stately pavane. Someone with a sense of the dramatic had arranged for that, someone young and intense and steeped in tragedy.

Daisy.

She followed the three coffins and she was alone. Or, rather, Wexford thought, she was alone until he saw Nicholas Virson, who must have escorted her in, searching for an empty seat. She was in deepest mourning, or perhaps only in the clothes every girl her age had in abundance in her wardrobe, funereal garments habitually worn to discos and parties. Daisy's dress was a narrow black tube reaching to her black-booted ankles. Vague black draperies covered her, among them something that could almost be discerned as a coat of roughly coat shape. Her face was paper-white, her mouth painted crimson, and she stared ahead of her, moving at last alone into that empty front pew.

"I am the resurrection and the life, saith the Lord . . ."

Her sense of the dramatic—and of the fitting?—had prompted her also to make sure the Prayer Book of 1662 was used. Was he attributing too much to her and was that Mrs. Virson's work or even the parson's good taste? She was a remarkable girl. He was aware of a sense of warning, of alarm, whose source he couldn't trace.

"Lord, let me know mine end and the number of my days, that I may be certified how long I have to live . . ."

The wind had not been noticeable in the town. Perhaps, on the other hand, it had only got up in the past half-hour. Wexford remembered some sort of gale warning in the forecast of the night before. The wind had a knife-edge feel to it as it whistled across this place of burial that a few years ago had been a meadow on a hillside.

Why burial and not cremation? More of Daisy's dramatic ideas, perhaps, or else a wish expressed in wills. There was to be no will-reading after this, the solicitor had told him, no anything after this, none of that gathering together for sherry and cake. "In the circumstances," said the solicitor, "it would be wholly inappropriate."

No flowers. Daisy, it appeared, had asked for donations instead to a number of causes, none of them likely to meet with a sympathetic response from many of these people: charities for Bangladesh, a fund to counter famine in Ethiopia, the Labour Party and the Cats' Protection League.

A single grave had been prepared for the married couple. The one beside it was for Naomi Jones. Each was lined with sheets of artificial turf of a sicklier green than the grass. The coffins went down and one of those aged scholars stepped forward to cast a handful of earth upon the last of Davina Flory.

"Come, ye blessed children of my Father, receive the kingdom prepared for you from the beginning of the world . . ."

It was over, the drama past. The most significant thing now for all was the biting of the wind. Collars were turned up, arms hugged shivering bodies inside inadequate clothes. Undeterred, Jason Sebright was going from person to person, boldly putting his request. Instead of the notebook of former times, he had a receiver and recording device. Wexford wasn't altogether surprised to see how many people responded favourably. Some of them very likely thought they were going out live on radio.

He had not yet spoken to Daisy. He watched one mourner after another approach her and saw her lips move in monosyllabic response. One old woman pressed a kiss on her white cheek.

"Oh, my dear, and poor Davina wasn't even a believer, was she?"

Another said, "That lovely service, it does send shivers down one's spine."

An elderly man, speaking in what Wexford called an Ivy League voice, embraced her and, with an impulsive gesture, apparently an expression of sudden emotion, pressed her face into his neck. When she lifted her head Wexford saw her lips had left a crimson imprint on his white collar. He was a tall man, paper-thin, with a small grey moustache and a bow-tie. Preston Littlebury, the erstwhile employer of Andy Griffin?

"You have my deepest sympathy, my dear, you know that."

Wexford saw that he had been wrong about the young girls. One at any rate had braved the grimness of the day and the bad weather, a thin pale teenager in black trousers and a raincoat.

The elderly woman with her was saying, "I'm Ishbel Mac-samphire, my dear. Last year in Edinburgh? Remember? With poor Davina. And then I met you with your young man. This is my granddaughter . . ."

Daisy behaved beautifully to all of them. Her sadness gave her an enormous dignity. She managed the difficult feat he had seen her achieve before, of responding with courtesy yet without a smile. One by one they moved away from her and for a moment she was alone. She stood surveying the people as they moved towards their cars, as if searching for someone, her eyes wide, her lips a little parted. It was as if she was looking for a mourner whose presence she expected but who had not come, who had failed her. The wind snatched the long black scarf she wore and pulled it out in a fluttering streamer. She shivered, hunched herself for a moment before coming up to Wexford.

"That's over. Thank goodness. I thought I might burst out crying or faint, but I didn't, did I?"

"Not you. Were you looking for someone who hasn't come?"

"Oh, no. Whatever gave you that idea?"

Nicholas Virson was approaching them. In spite of her denial, it must have been he she had been looking for, her "young man," for she gave a little dip of the head as if bowing to some necessity, as if resigned. She took his arm and let him lead her to his car. His mother was already seated inside it, peering through the steamy glass.

Wexford thought, as he had occasionally thought of Sheila years ago, and thought of her with accurate foresight, what an actress she would make! Well, Sheila had made an actress, but Daisy wasn't acting, Daisy was sincere. She was simply one of those people who cannot help extracting drama from their personal tragedies. Hadn't Graham Greene said somewhere that every novelist has a splinter of ice in his heart? Perhaps she would follow in her grandmother's footsteps here too.

Grandmother's footsteps. He smiled to himself as he thought of the game children played, tiptoeing up close, seeing how near they could get, before the one in front with her back to them turned round, and they fled screaming . . .

"We found two sets of keys inside, sir," said Karen. "We found her cheque-book, but no cash or credit cards."

The house was lavishly furnished, the kitchen luxuriously appointed. In the bathroom, which was "en suite" with Mrs. Garland's bedroom, were a bidet and a power shower, a hair dryer attached to the wall.

"As in the best hotels," Karen said with a giggle.

"Yes, but I thought they only did that to stop the guests' stealing them. This is a private house."

Karen looked doubtful. "Well, you couldn't lose it this way, could you? You wouldn't wonder where you'd left it last time you washed your hair."

To Wexford it looked more as if Joanne Garland had spent money for the sake of spending it. She had hardly known what to spend her income on. An electric trouser press? Why not? Even though the clothes cupboard revealed only a single pair of trousers. A phone extension in the bathroom? No more running dripping into the bedroom, wrapped in a towel. The "gym" contained an exercise bicycle, a rowing machine, a contraption that looked to Wexford like nothing so much as pictures he had seen of the Iron Maiden of Nuremberg, and something that might have been a treadmill.

"They used to make poor devils in workhouses stomp up and down on those," Wexford said. "She has it for *fun*."

"Well, for her fitness, sir."

"And all this, is this for her fitness?"

They were back in the bedroom, where he confronted the most comprehensive collection of cosmetics and beauty products he had ever seen outside a department store. These items were not in the drawers of a dressing-table or on a shelf but contained in a large cabinet, there exclusively to accommodate them.

"There's another lot in the bathroom," said Karen.

"This looks more like something you'd stick up your nose,"

said Wexford, holding up a brown bottle with a gold top and dropper. He unscrewed the top from a jar and sniffed the contents, a thick sweet-scented yellow cream. "You could eat this one. They don't work, do they?"

"I suppose it gives the poor old things hope," said Karen with all the arrogant indifference of twenty-three. "You believe what you read, don't you think, sir? You believe what you read on labels. Most people do."

"I suppose so."

What struck him most was how tidy the place was. As if its owner were going away and had known well in advance she was going. But no one goes away without telling anyone. A woman with such a large family as Joanne Garland doesn't go away without a word to her mother, to her brothers and sisters. His mind went back to that evening and Burden's scenario. It hadn't been a satisfactory scenario but it had its points.

"How are we getting on with checking out all the cab companies in the district?"

"There are a lot of them, sir, but we're getting through them."

He tried to think of possible reasons for a wealthy, single, middle-aged woman suddenly taking off on a trip in March without telling her family, her neighbours or her business partner. Some lover from the past turned up and swept her off her feet? Unlikely in the case of a hard-headed business woman of fifty-four. A summons from the other side of the world that someone once close to her was dying? In that case, she would have told her family.

"Was her passport in the house, Karen?"

"No, sir. But she may not have had one. We could ask her sisters if she ever went abroad."

"We could. We will."

Back at the stables of Tancred House, a call was put through to him. It was no one he knew or had even heard of: the deputy governor of Royal Oak Prison outside Crewe in Cheshire. Of course he knew all about Royal Oak, the famous high-security, Category-B prison that was run as a therapeutic community and still, years after such theories ceased to be fashionable, held to the principle that criminals can be "cured" by therapy. Though with just the same rate of recidivism as any other British jail, it at least appeared not to make its inmates worse.

The deputy governor said he had a prisoner who wanted to see Wexford, who had asked for him by name. The prisoner was serving a long sentence for attempted murder and robbery with violence and at present he was in the prison hospital.

"He thinks he's going to die."

"Is he?"

"I don't know. He's called Hocking, James. Known as Jem Hocking."

"I've never heard of him."

"He's heard of you. Kingsmarkham, isn't it? He knows Kingsmarkham. Didn't you have a police officer shot dead down there getting on for a year ago?"

"Oh, yes," said Wexford. "Yes, we did."

O.k.a. George Brown. Was Jem Hocking the man who had bought a car in the name of George Brown?

Mrs. Griffin told them Andy hadn't come back yet. "But we had a phone call, didn't we, Terry? He rung up last night from up north. Where did he say he was, Terry? Manchester, was it?"

"He rung up from Manchester," Terry Griffin said. "He didn't want us to worry, he wanted us to know he was all right."

"Were you worried?"

"It's not a matter of whether we was worried or not. It's a matter of Andy thinking we might be worried. We thought it was very considerate. It's not every son that'd ring up his mum and dad to tell them he was all right when he'd only been away two days. You do worry when he's on that bike. A bike wouldn't be my choice, but what's a young boy to do with the price cars are? It was very considerate and thoughtful, ringing us up."

"Typical of Andy," said his mother complacently. "He was always a very considerate boy."

"Did he say when he was coming back?"

"I wouldn't ask. I wouldn't expect him to tell us his every movement."

"And you don't know his address in Manchester?"

Again Mrs. Griffin had been too sensitive and the relationship too finely tuned for her to risk disturbing it by bald inquiries of that nature.

The woman called Bib admitted Wexford to the house. She wore a red track suit with an apron over it. When Wexford said Mrs. Harrison was expecting him she gave a sort of grunt and she nodded but said not a word. She walked ahead of him with a rollicking gait like someone who has been too long on board ship.

Brenda Harrison was in the conservatory. It was very warm, faintly damp and sweet-smelling. The scent came from a pair of lemon trees in tubs of blue-and-white faience. They were simultaneously in flower and fruit, the flowers white and waxy. She had been busy with watering can, house-plant food and tissues for putting a gloss on leaves.

"Though who it's all for I'm sure I don't know."

The blue-and-white-printed blinds were drawn up in ruffles high up in the glass roof. Queenie, the Persian, sat on one of the sills, her hyacinth eyes fixed on a bird on a branch. The bird was singing in the rain and its cadences made the cat's teeth chatter.

Brenda got up off her knees, wiped her hands on her overalls and subsided into a wicker chair.

"I'd just like to hear their version, those Griffins. I'd really like to hear what they told you."

Here Wexford refused to oblige her. He said nothing.

"Of course I'd made up my mind I wasn't going to say a word. Not to you lot, I mean. It wasn't fair on Ken. Well, that's the way I saw it. Not nice for Ken, I thought. And when you think about it, what's that Andy Griffin taking a fancy to me for some reason and trying all that funny business, what's that got to do with criminals shooting Davina and Harvey and Naomi? Well, nothing, has it?"

"Tell me about it, will you, Mrs. Harrison?"

"I suppose I must. It's very distasteful. I know I look a lot younger than I am—well, people are always telling me—so maybe I shouldn't have been surprised when that Andy got fresh."

It was an expression Wexford hadn't heard for years. He marvelled at Mrs. Harrison's vanity, the delusion that made this shrivelled, lined woman imagine she looked younger than her fifty-odd years. And what was there, after all, to be so pleased and proud about in looking younger than one was? It had always perplexed him. As if there were some particular virtue attached to looking forty-five when one was fifty. And what anyway did fifty look like?

She was staring at him, seeking the words in which to reveal it or perhaps obfuscate it. "He touched me. I nearly jumped out of my skin." As if anticipating the question, she placed her hand against her left breast, looking away. "It was in my own house. He'd come in the kitchen, I was having a cup of tea, so of course I gave him one. Not that I liked him, don't think that.

"He's evil. Oh, yes, I'm not exaggerating. He's not just peculiar, he's evil. You've only got to look at his eyes. He was just a little kid when we first came here, but he wasn't like other kids, he wasn't normal. His mother, she wanted him allowed to play with Daisy—well, you can just see that happening, can't you? Even Naomi said no, not just Davina. He used to have these screaming tantrums, you'd hear him through the walls, it'd go on for hours. They couldn't do a thing with him.

"He can't have been a day over fourteen when I caught him here peering at me through the bathroom window. I'd got all my clothes on, thank God, but he didn't know that when he started looking, did he? That was the point, to catch me with no clothes on."

"The *bathroom*?" Wexford said. "What did he do, climb a tree?"

"The bathrooms are downstairs in these houses. Don't ask me why. They were built that way, with the bathrooms downstairs. He only had to come through from theirs through the hedge and hang about outside. It wasn't long after that his mother told me a lady in Pomfret had complained about him for the same thing. Called him a peeping Tom. Of course *she* said it was a wicked lie and the woman had got it in for her poor Andy, but I knew what I knew."

"What happened in the kitchen?"

"When he touched me, d'you mean? Well, I don't want to go into details and I won't. When it was done, after he'd gone, I thought to myself, it's only because he's madly attracted to you and he can't help himself. But he could help himself when he came back next day, asking for money, couldn't he?"

Queenie gave a tap with her paw on the glass. The bird flew away. The rain suddenly came down heavily, the water lashing against the panes. The cat got down and stalked towards the door. Instead of getting up to assist her, which Wexford would have expected from such a committed animal lover, Brenda sat intently watching. It soon became clear what she was waiting for. Queenie stood up on her hind legs, took hold of the door handle with her right paw and pulled it down. The door came open and she passed through, tail erect.

"You can't tell me they're not more intelligent than any human being," said Brenda Harrison fondly.

"I'd like to hear about this attempted rape, Mrs. Harrison."

She didn't care for the word. A deep blush coloured her worn face. "I'm sure I don't know why you're so keen on all these details." Having implied that Wexford's interest in the matter was of a prurient kind, she looked down, twisting her neck, and began kneading a corner of her overalls. "He touched me, like I said. I said, 'Don't.' He said, 'Why not? Don't you like me?' 'It's not a matter of like or dislike,' I said, 'I'm a married woman.' Then he got hold of me by the shoulders and he pushed me back against the sink and started rubbing up against me. Well, you said you wanted details. It doesn't give me any pleasure talking about it.

"I struggled but he was a lot stronger than me, it stands to reason he was. I said to let me go or I'd go straight in and tell his father. He said had I got anything on under my skirt, and he tried pulling at my skirt. I kicked at him then. There was a knife laying on the draining board, only a little knife I use for doing the veg, but I grabbed hold of it and I said I'd stick it in him if he didn't let go. Well, he let go then and called me a name. He called me an h-o-r-e, and said it was my fault for wearing my skirts tight.''

"Did you tell his father? Did you tell anyone?''

"I thought if I kept quiet it'd all blow over. Ken's a very jealous man, I suppose it's only natural. I mean, I've known him make a scene over a fellow just looking at me on a bus. Anyway, next day that Andy came back. He knocked on the front door and I was expecting the man to service the tumble-dryer, so naturally I opened it. He pushed his way in. I said, 'This is it, this time you've gone too far, Andy Griffin, I'm telling your dad *and* Mr. Copeland.'

"He didn't touch me. He just laughed. He said I was to give him five pounds down or he'd tell Ken I'd asked him to . . . well, to go with me. He'd tell his mum and dad and he'd tell Ken. And folks'd believe him, he said, on account of me being older than him. 'So much older' was what he said, if you must know.''

"Did you give him any money?''

"Not me. D'you think I'm daft? I wasn't born yesterday.'' The irony of this last remark was entirely lost on Brenda Harrison, who went on serenely, "I said, 'Publish and be damned!' I'd read that in a book and I'd always remembered it, don't know why. 'Publish and be damned,' I said, 'go on, do your worst.' He wanted five pounds down and five pounds a week till further notice. That's what he said, 'till further notice.'

"The minute Ken came in I told him everything. He said, 'Come along, my girl, we're going next door to have it out with those Griffins. That'll finish them with Davina,' he said. 'I know it's unpleasant for you,' he said, 'but it'll soon be over and you'll feel better for knowing you did the right thing.' So next door we went and I told them everything. In a quiet way, not getting excited, I just quietly told them what he'd done and about the peeping Tom too. Of course Mrs. Griffin went hysterical, shouting her precious Andy wouldn't do that, him so clean and pure and not knowing what a girl was for and all that. Ken said, 'I'm going to Mr. and Mrs. Copeland'—we never called them by their Christian names to those Griffins, of course, that wouldn't have been suitable—'I'm going to Mr. and Mrs. Copeland,' he said, and he did and me with him.

"Well, the upshot of it was Davina said Andy'd have to go. They could stay but he'd have to go. The alternative—that's what she said, the alternative—was calling the police and she didn't want to do that if she could help it. Mrs. Griffin wouldn't have that, she wouldn't be separated from her Andy, so they said they'd all go, he'd take early retirement, though what she meant by 'early' I don't know. He looked knocking seventy to me.

"Of course we had to put up with them next door for weeks and weeks after that, months. Mind you, Andy had a job then, some labouring job for an American friend of Harvey's he put him onto out of the goodness of his heart, so we never saw much of *him*. I'd said to Ken, 'Come what may,' I'd said, 'I shan't speak a word to any of them. I'll look through them if we happen to meet outside,' and that's what I did, and in the end they went like they were bound to, and Johnny Gabbitas came."

Wexford remained silent for a moment or two. He watched the rain. Drifts of crocuses made purple stains across the green grass. The forsythia was out, brilliant yellow like sunshine on this dull wet day. He said to Brenda Harrison,

"When did you last see Mrs. Garland?"

She looked surprised at this apparent change of subject. Wexford suspected that now the matter had been brought out into the open she was not at all averse to talking of her husband's jealousy and her own irresistible attractions. She answered him rather peevishly.

"Not for months, years. I know she came up here most Tuesday nights but I never saw her. I'd always gone home."

"Mrs. Jones told you she came?"

"I don't know as she ever mentioned it," Brenda said indifferently. "Why should she?"

"Then . . . ?"

"How did I know? Oh, I see what you mean. She used Ken's brother's cars, didn't she?" Wexford's obvious bewilderment fetched an explanation from her. "Between you and I, she liked a drink, did Joanne Garland. And sometimes two or three. Well, you can understand it, can't you? After a day in that shop. Beats me how they ever sold a thing. It really beats me how those places keep going. Anyway, sometimes when she'd had one too many, I mean when she reckoned she was over the limit, she wouldn't drive her car, she'd give Ken's brother a ring for one of his. Well, to bring her up here for one thing, and take her wherever else she might fancy going. She's rolling in money, of course, never thought twice about ringing up for a car."

"Your brother-in-law runs a taxi service?"

Mrs. Harrison put on a look of refinement, rarefied, slightly sour. "I wouldn't put it that way. He doesn't advertise, he has a private clientele, a few special selected clients." She became alarmed. "It's all above-board, you needn't look like that. I'll tell you his name, we've nothing to hide, I'll give you all the details you want, I'm sure you're welcome."

Occasionally in the past, when he had published a book he thought might interest his friend, Amyas Ireland had made a present of a copy to Wexford. It was always a pleasure, on arriving home in the evening, to find the parcel addressed to him, the padded bag with the publisher's name and logo on its label. But since the take-over of Carlyon-Brent he had received nothing, so it was a surprise to see a larger than usual parcel waiting for him. This time the logo was the St. Giles Press's lion with fritillary in its mouth, but inside, tucked among the books, was a letter on the familar-headed paper and an explanation from Amyas.

In the particular circumstances, he had thought Wexford might be interested in three of Davina Flory's books, which they were currently reissuing in a new format: *The Holy City, The Other Side of the Wall* and *The Hosts of Midian*. If Reg would like a copy of the first—and now, sadly, to be the only—volume of the autobiography, he had only to ask. He was sorry he hadn't been in touch before. Reg would be aware they had been taken over, but perhaps not of the subsequent shake-up and Amyas's fear for the fate of his own imprint. It had been an anxious time. However, all now seemed well, Carlyon Quick, as they were now to be known, had a wonderful autumn list in view. They were most specially delighted to have secured the rights in Augustine Casey's new novel, *The Lash*.

This was almost enough to spoil Wexford's pleasure in the Davina Flory books. The phone rang as he was glancing desultorily through the first of them. It was Sheila. Thursday was her evening for phoning. He listened to Dora speaking to her, indulging himself in a favourite pastime of trying to guess what she was saying from his wife's astonished, delighted or merely interested replies.

Dora's words fell into none of those categories this evening. He heard her expression of disappointment, "Oh, dear." And an intenser regret, "Is that a good idea? Are you sure you know what you're doing?" He had a feeling as of his heart growing heavy, a tension in his chest. He half got up from the table, sat down again, listened.

Dora said in the cold stiff tone he hated when it was directed at himself, "You'll want to talk to your father, I suppose."

He took the receiver. Before she spoke he found himself thinking, she has the most beautiful voice I ever heard from a woman's mouth.

The beautiful voice said, "Mother's cross with me. I expect you will be. I've turned down that part."

A glorious lightness, a splendid relief. Was that *all* it was? "In *Miss Julie*? I expect you know what you're doing."

"God knows if I do or not. The thing is I'm going to Nevada with Gus. I turned it down to go to Nevada with Gus."

CHAPTER FOURTEEN

At Kingsmarkham station illuminated digital letters announced that an experimental queuing system was in operation. In other words, instead of waiting comfortably, two or three to each ticket window, you lined up between ropes. It was as bad at Euston. In the concourse up near the platform from which the Manchester train would depart was a sign instructing travellers: "Form queue here."

Nothing about the train, nothing welcoming, nothing to say when it would leave, only the assumption made that there would be a queue. It was worse than wartime. Wexford could remember wartime—just—and then, while they might take queuing for granted, they at least put no official stamp on it.

Perhaps he should have let Donaldson drive him. He hadn't done so because of a weary dread of the motorways and their congestion. Trains were fast these days, trains didn't get into jams with other trains, and on weekdays at any rate railway tracks weren't being constantly excavated and mended as roads were. Unless there was snow or a hurricane, trains *ran*. He had bought himself a paper at Kingsmarkham and read it on the journey to Victoria. He could always buy another here, anything to keep his mind off Sheila and what had happened last night. On the other hand, *The Times* hadn't stopped him thinking about it, so why should *The Independent*?

The queue wound quite elegantly round the broad concourse. No one protested, just joined the tail of it, uncomplaining. It had formed a near-circle, as if these travellers were about to join hands and start singing "Auld Lang Syne." Then the barrier opened and everyone was let in, not exactly surging, but pushing a bit, impatient to reach the train.

A nice, newish, smart, modern train. Wexford had a reserved seat. He found it, sat down, looked at the front page of his paper and thought about Sheila, heard Sheila's voice. The ring of it, in his head, made him flinch.

"You'd made up your mind to hate him before you'd even met him!"

How she could rail! Like Petruchio's Shrew, a role of which she had oddly not made a success.

"Don't be ridiculous, Sheila. I've never made up my mind to hate anyone before I've met them."

"There's always a first time. Oh, I know why. You were jealous, you knew you had real cause. You knew none of the others meant a thing to me, not even Andrew. I was in love for the first time in my life and you saw the red light, you saw the danger, you were determined to hate anyone I loved. And why? Because you were afraid I'd love him better than you."

They had often quarrelled before. They were the kind of people who rowed hotly, lost their tempers, made up and forgot the cause of it within minutes. This time it was different.

"We're not talking about love," he had said. "We're talking about common sense and reasonable behaviour. You'd throw up maybe the best part you've ever had to tag along to the middle of nowhere just to be with that—"

"Don't say it! Don't abuse him!"

"I couldn't abuse him. What would be abuse to a miscreant like him? To that drunken foul-mouthed clown? The biggest insults I could find would flatter him."

"My God, whatever I've inherited from you I'm glad it isn't your tongue. Listen to me, Father . . ."

He gave a whoop of laughter. "Father? Since when have you called me Father?"

"Right, I'll call you nothing. Listen to me, will you? I love him with all my heart. I'll never leave him!"

"You're not on stage at the Olivier now," said Wexford very nastily. He heard her draw in her breath. "And if you go on like this, I frankly doubt if you ever will be again."

"I wonder," she said distantly—oh, she had inherited much from him!—"I wonder if it's ever occurred to you to think about how unusual it is for a daughter to be as close to her parents as I've been to you and Mother, how I phone you a couple of times a week, how I'm always coming down to see you. Have you ever wondered why?"

"No. I know why. It's because we've always been nice and sweet and loving to you, because we've spoiled you to hell and let you stomp all over us, and now that I've summoned up the nerve to confront you and tell you a few home truths about you and that ugly little pseud——"

He never finished the sentence. What he was going to cite as the consequence of his "nerve" he never reached and now he had forgotten what it was. Before he could get another word out she had slammed down the receiver.

He knew he shouldn't have spoken to her like that. His mother, long ago, had used a regretful phrase which was perhaps current in her youth: "Come back, all I said!" If only it were possible to call back all one had said! By saying those words of his mother's, to cancel out abuse and sarcasm, to make five minutes disappear. But it wasn't, and no one knew better than he that no word uttered could ever be lost; only, one day, like everything else that ever happened in human existence, it might be forgotten.

His phone was in his pocket. The train, as usual these days, was full of people using phones, mostly men making business calls. It had been a novelty not long ago, now it was commonplace. He could phone her, she might be at home. She might put the receiver down when she heard his voice. Wexford, who didn't usually care for the opinion of others, very much disliked the idea of his fellow-passengers witnessing the effect this would have on him.

A trolley came round with coffee and those ubiquitous sandwiches, the kind he liked in three-dimensional plastic boxes. In this world are two kinds of people—among the fed, that is—those who when worried eat for comfort and those whose appetite is killed by anxiety. Wexford belonged in the first category. He had had breakfast and presumably he would have lunch, but he bought a bacon-and-egg sandwich just the same. Eating it appreciatively, he found himself hoping that what he encountered at Royal Oak would to some extent drive Sheila from his mind.

At Crewe he got a taxi. The taxi driver knew all about the prison, where it was and what sort of institution it was. Wexford wondered who were the fares he habitually drove up there. Visitors perhaps, sweethearts and wives. There had been a move here a year or two ago to allow "conjugal visits in private," but this had been smartly vetoed. Sex was evidently rated highly among amenities not to be countenanced.

The prison turned out to be well out in the country, in, according to the driver, the valley of the river Wheelock. The name Royal Oak, he told Wexford in a practised guidelike way, came from an ancient tree, long since disappeared, in which King Charles had hidden from his enemies. Which King Charles he didn't say and Wexford wondered how many such trees proliferated in England, as many as there were beds slept in by Elizabeth I, no doubt. There was certainly one in Cheriton Forest, a favourite picnic spot. Charles must have spent years of his life climbing them.

Huge, sprawling, hideous. Surely what must be the highest and longest wall in the Midlands. No trees here. So barren, indeed, was the plain on which the cluster of crimson brick buildings stood as to make the name absurd. "Her Majesty's Prison: Royal Oak." He had arrived.

Would the taxi come back for him? Wexford was presented with the hire company's card. He could phone. The taxi disappeared rather quickly as if, unless a speedy escape was made, there might be problems about getting away at all.

One of the governors, a man called David Cairns, gave him a cup of coffee in a rather nice room with carpet on the floor and framed posters on the walls. The rest of the place looked like all such places, but smelt better. While Wexford drank his coffee Cairns said he supposed he knew all about Royal Oak and its survival in spite of official distrust and Home Office dislike. Wexford said he thought so, but Cairns proceeded to describe the system just the same. He was obviously proud of the place, an idealist with shining eyes.

Paradoxically, it was the most violent and recalcitrant prisoners who were referred to Royal Oak. Of course, they also had to want to come. So many wanted to come that there was currently a waiting list of over a hundred. Staff and inmates were on Christian-name terms. Group therapy and mutual counselling were the order of the day. Prisoners mixed, for, uniquely, there was no Rule 43 segregation here and no hierarchy of murderers and violent criminals at the top and sex offenders at the bottom.

All inmates came to Royal Oak on referral, usually the recommendation of a prison senior medical officer. Which reminded him, their own senior medical officer, Sam Rosenberg, would like to see him before he went to meet Jem Hocking. As he'd said, it was all first names here. None of your "Sir" this and "Dr." that.

A member of staff conducted Wexford to the hospital, which was just another wing. They passed men walking about freely—freely up to a point—dressed in track suits or pants and sweat-shirts. He couldn't resist a glance through an interior window where a group therapy session was in progress. The men sat round in a circle. They were opening their hearts and baring their souls, the member of staff said, learning how to bring to the surface all their inner confusions. Wexford thought they looked as hangdog and wretched as most incarcerated people.

A smell just like Stowerton Infirmary hung about the hospital: lime juice, Lysol and sweat. All hospitals smell the same, except private ones, which smell of money. Dr. Rosenberg was in his room, which was like the charge nurse's room at Stowerton. Only the cigarette smoke was absent. It commanded a view of the empty green plain and a line of electricity pylons.

Lunch had just arrived. There was enough for two, unexciting piles of brown slime on pillows of boiled rice, chicken curry probably. "Individual" fruit pies to follow and a carton of non-dairy creamer. But Wexford was eating for comfort and he accepted at once Sam Rosenberg's invitation to join him while they talked about Jem Hocking.

The medical officer was a short thickset man of forty with a round childlike face and a thatch of prematurely grey hair. His clothes were like those of the prisoners, a track suit and running shoes.

"What d'you think?" he said, waving a hand towards door and ceiling. "This place, I mean. Bit different from the 'System,' eh?"

Wexford understood the "System" to refer to the rest of the prison service and agreed that it was.

"Of course it doesn't seem to work. If by 'work' we mean stopping them doing it again. On the other hand, that's rather hard to tell because most of them hardly get the chance to do anything much again. They're lifers." Sam Rosenberg wiped up the remains of his curry with a hunk of bread. He seemed to be enjoying his lunch. "Jem Hocking asked to come here. He was convicted in September, was sent to the Scrubs or it may have been Wandsworth, and set about tearing the place apart. He was referred here just before Christmas and he got into what we do here, roughly an ongoing 'talking it through,' like a—well, a duck to water."

"What did he do?"

"What was his conviction for? He went to this house where the owner was supposed to keep her shop takings over the weekend, found five hundred pounds or so in a handbag and half-beat to death the woman who lived there. She was seventy-two. He used a seven-pound hammer."

"No gun involved?"

"No gun, so far as I know. Have one of these pies, will you? They're raspberry and red currant, not bad. We have the non-dairy creamer because I'm a bit of a cholesterol freak. I mean, I'm scared of it, I believe in battling against it. Jem's ill at the moment. He thinks he's dying but he's not. Not this time."

Wexford raised an eyebrow. "Not a cholesterol problem, I'm sure."

"Well, no. As a matter of fact, I've never tested his cholesterol." Rosenberg hesitated. "A lot of the Bill—sorry, didn't mean to be insulting, a lot of the police—still have gay prejudice. I mean, you'll hear coppers make these jokes about queens and queers and then they'll mince about. Are you one of those? No, I can see you're not. But you may still think homosexuals are all hairdressers and ballet dancers. Not *real men*. Ever read any Genet?"

"A bit. It was a long time ago." Wexford tried to remember titles and recalled one. *"Our Lady of the Flowers."*

"Querelle of Brest was what I had in mind. Genet, more than anyone, makes you understand gay men can be as tough and as ruthless as the heterosexual sort. Tougher, more ruthless. They can be killers and thieves and brutal criminals as well as dress designers."

"Are you saying Jem Hocking is one of those?"

"Jem doesn't know about closets, being in them or coming out of them, but one of the reasons he wanted to come here was to talk openly to other men about his homosexuality. Talk about it day after day, unchecked, in groups. The world he lived in is perhaps the most prejudiced of all worlds. And then he got ill."

"You mean he's got AIDS, don't you?"

Sam Rosenberg gave him a narrow look. "You see, you *do* associate it with the gay community. I tell you, it'll be as common among heterosexuals in a year or two. It is not a gay disease. Right?"

"But Jem Hocking has it?"

"Jem Hocking is HIV Pos. He's had a very bad go of flu. We've had a flu epidemic at Royal Oak and he just happened to get it worse than the others, badly enough to come in here for a week. With luck, he'll be back in the community by the end of the week. But he insists he's had AIDS-related pneumonia and he thinks I'm jibbing at telling him the truth. Hence he believes he's dying and he wants to see you."

"Why does he?"

"That I don't know. I haven't asked and if I asked he wouldn't tell me. He wants to tell you. Coffee?"

He was a man of the doctor's age but dark and swarthy, a week's growth of beard on cheeks and chin. Aware of modern hospital trends, Wexford had expected him to be up, dressing-gowned, seated in a chair, but Jem Hocking was in bed. He looked far more ill than Daisy ever had. The hands which rested on the red blanket were dark blue with tattoos.

"How are you?" Wexford said.

Hocking made no immediate reply. He put one blue-configured finger up to his mouth and rubbed it. Then he said, "Not good."

"Are you going to tell me when you were in Kingsmarkham? Is that what it's about?"

"Last May. That's making bells ring for you, isn't it? Only I reckon they've rung already."

Wexford nodded. "Some of them have."

"I'm dying. Did you know that?"

"Not according to the medical officer."

Derision altered Jem Hocking's face. He sneered. "They don't tell you the truth. Not even in here. Nobody ever tells the truth, not here, not anywhere. They can't, it's not possible to. You'd have to go into too much detail, you'd have to search your soul. You'd insult everyone and every word'd show you up for the bastard you are. Have you ever thought of that?"

"Yes," said Wexford.

Whatever Hocking had expected it wasn't a bald affirmative. He paused, said, "Most of the time you'd just say, 'I hate your guts, I hate your guts' over and over. That'd be what the truth is. And, 'I want to die but I'm fucking scared of dying.' '' He drew a breath. "I know I'm dying. I'll get another bout of what I've had but a bit worse and then a third and that one'll carry me off. It might be quicker than that. It was a fucking sight quicker for Dane."

"Who's Dane?"

"I reckoned on telling you before I died. Might as well. What can I lose? I've lost everything except my life and that's on the way out." Hocking's face narrowed and his eyes seemed to draw closer together. He suddenly looked one of the nastiest customers Wexford had ever come across. "D'you want to know something? It's the last pleasure I've got left, talking to people about me dying. It embarrasses them, see, and I enjoy that, them not knowing what to say."

"It doesn't embarrass me."

"Well, fucking Bill, what can you expect?"

A nurse came in, a man in jeans and a short white coat. In Wexford's youth he would have been called a "male nurse." That was what they said then: "male nurse" and "lady doctor." There was nothing particularly sexist about it but it shed a lot of bright illumination on people's expectations of the sexes.

The nurse heard Hocking's last words and said not to be rude, Jem, there was no call for that, mud-slinging didn't help, and it was time for his antibiotics.

"Fucking useless," said Hocking. "Pneumonia's a virus, right? You're all fuck-witted in here."

Wexford waited patiently while Hocking took his pills under feeble protest. He really looked very ill. You could believe this was death's threshold. He waited till the nurse had gone, hung his head, contemplated the designs on his blue hands.

" 'Who's Dane?' you said. I'll tell you. Dane was my mate. Dane Bishop. Dane Gavin David Bishop, if you want the lot. He was only twenty-four." *I loved him* hung unspoken in the air. Wexford could see it in Hocking's face, *I loved him*, but he wasn't a sentimentalist, especially about killers, especially about the kind who hammer old women. So what? Does loving someone redeem a man? Does loving someone make you good? "We did the Kingsmarkham job together. But you knew that. You knew that before you came or you wouldn't have come."

"More or less," said Wexford.

"Dane wanted money to buy this drug. It's American but you can get it here. Initials it goes by, doesn't matter."

"AZT."

"No, as a matter of fact, clever cop. DDI it's called, stands for dideoxyinosine. Not available on the fucking NHS, needless to say."

Don't give me your excuses, Wexford said to himself. You ought to know better. He thought of Sergeant Martin, foolish and foolhardy but quite bright by turns, a good man, an earnest, well-intentioned good man, the salt of the earth.

"This Dane Bishop, he's dead, is he?"

Jem Hocking just looked at him. It was a look full of hatred and pain. Wexford thought the hatred was due to the fact that the man couldn't embarrass him. Perhaps the sole purpose of the exercise, this "confession," was to cause an embarrassment in which Hocking had hoped to revel.

"Died of AIDS, I'd guess," he said, "and not long after.

"Dead before we could get the drug. It took him fast at the end. We saw that description you put out, spots on his face, all that. That wasn't fucking acne, that was Kaposi's sarcoma."

Wexford said, "He used a gun. Where did he get it?"

An indifferent shrug from Hocking. "Are you asking me? You know as well as I do, it's easy to get a shooter if you want one. He never said. He just had it. A Magnum, it was." The sly sidelong look came back. "He chucked it away, threw it down, getting out of the bank."

"Ah," said Wexford almost silently, almost to himself.

"Scared to be found with it. He was ill then, it makes you weak, weak like an old man. He was only twenty-four but he was weak as water. That's why he shot that fuckwit, too weak to keep up the pressure. I got us away; I wasn't even in there when he shot him."

"You were concerned with him. You knew he had a gun."

"Am I denying it?"

"You bought a car in the name of George Brown?"

Hocking nodded. "We bought a vehicle, we bought a lot of things with cash, we reckoned we could sell the vehicle again on account of we never dared keep any of the notes. I wrapped them in newspaper and stuffed them in a dump. We sold the vehicle—not a bad way of handling things, was it?"

"It's called laundering money," Wexford said coldly. "Or it is when done on a grander scale."

"He died before he got the drug."

"You told me before."

Jem Hocking heaved himself up in bed. "You're a frozen bastard, you are. If it was anywhere else in the System I was doing bird, they wouldn't have left you alone with me."

Wexford got up. "What could you do, Jem? I'm three times your size. I'm not embarrassed and I'm not impressed."

"Just fucking helpless," said Hocking. "The world's helpless against a dying man."

"I wouldn't say that. There's nothing in the law to say a dying man can't be charged with murder and robbery."

"You wouldn't!"

"I certainly will," said Wexford, leaving.

The train took him back to Euston in pouring rain. It was raining all the way down from Victoria to Kingsmarkham. As soon as he got in he tried to phone Sheila and got her voice, her Lady Macbeth voice, the one that said, "Give me the daggers," asking callers to leave a message.

CHAPTER FIFTEEN

It was a job Barry Vine might have done, or even Karen Malahyde, but he did it himself. His rank seemed to frighten Fred Harrison, a nervous man who looked an older and shorter version of his brother. Wexford asked him when he had last driven Joanne Garland to Tancred House and, looking through his book, he named a date four Tuesdays before.

"I wouldn't have touched her with a barge-pole if I'd known it was going to lead to trouble," Fred Harrison said.

In spite of himself and his wretched feelings, Wexford was amused. "I doubt if it's going to lead to trouble for you, Mr. Harrison. Did you see Mrs. Garland or hear from her on Tuesday, March the eleventh?"

"Nothing, not a dicky bird since whenever it was, what I said, February twenty-fifth."

"And on that evening, what happened? She phoned you and asked you to drive her to Tancred House at—what? Eight? Eight fifteen?"

"I'd not have taken her anywhere if I'd known it was going to lead to trouble. You've got to believe that. She rung up like she always did around seven, said she had to be at Tancred by half eight. I said like I always did I'd pick her up a few minutes after eight, be ample time, but she said no, she didn't want to be late, and to come at ten to. Well, I fetched up at Tancred eight ten, eight fifteen. Going the shortest way, I'd be bound to, but she never listened, she was scared stiff of being late. That always happened. Sometimes I'd wait for her, she'd ask me to wait, she'd be an hour, and I'd take the opportunity to pop in and see my brother."

Wexford was uninterested in this. He persisted. "You're sure she didn't phone you on March the eleventh?"

"Believe me, I'd make a clean breast of it. Trouble's the last thing I want."

"Do you think she ever used another taxi service?"

"Why would she? She's nothing to complain about with me. Time and time again she's said, 'I don't know what I'd do without you, Fred, to come to my rescue.' And then she'd say I was the only one round here she'd trust to drive her."

There seemed no more to be got out of the nervous Fred Harrison. Wexford left him to return to Tancred. He was driving himself and he took the Pomfret Monachorum road. This was only the second time he had been this way. After yesterday's rain it was a fine mild day and the woods were full of life, the quiet, stirring, fresh life of early spring. The road wound as it ascended the shallow wooded hill to Tancred. It was too soon for the trees to show leaf except for the hawthorns, which were already misted all over with green. Blossom hung on the wild plums like white-spotted veils.

He drove slowly. As soon as his mind emptied of Fred Harrison and his anxieties, Sheila came in to fill it. He could almost have groaned aloud. Every angry word that had been uttered during that hideous interchange was fresh in his memory, was persistently repeating itself.

". . . you were determined to hate anyone I loved. And why? Because you were afraid I'd love him better than you."

Driving on through the wood where aconites grew in yellow rings like patches of bright sunlight, he opened the car window to feel the sweet air against his face, the equinoctial air of the first, or maybe the second, day of spring. Last night, with the rain lashing against the windows, he had tried to ring her and Dora had tried. He wanted to apologize to her and ask her forgiveness. But the phone rang and rang unanswered and when he tried again, despairing, at nine and again at nine thirty, her answering-machine voice came on. Not one of her characteristic messages: "If that's someone offering me the female lead in the Scottish play or wanting to take me to dinner at the Caprice . . ." "Darling"—the actress's universal *darling* that would serve for him or Casey or the woman who cleaned—"Darling, Sheila's had to go out . . ." It was neither of those but, "Sheila Wexford. I'm out. Leave a message and there's a chance I'll get back to you." He hadn't left a message but at last had gone to bed, sick at heart.

He thought, I've lost her. It had nothing much to do with her going six thousand miles away. Casey would have taken her from him in the same way if they had both decided to buy a house and settle down in Pomfret Monachorum. He had lost her and things would never be the same for them again.

The lane made its last wind, coming to the straight and the level ground. On either side stretched acres of young trees, planted perhaps twenty years before, their slender branches that reached for the light a bright russet colour, the hawthorn and blackthorn amongst them bouquets of misty green and snow-white. The ground between, strewn with dry brown leaves, was dappled with spots of sunlight.

In the distance he saw a movement. Someone was walking towards him, along the lane, a long way ahead, someone young, a young girl. More and more was revealed as he approached and she approached. It was Daisy. Unlikely as it was that she should be here, in this place, at this time, it was undoubtedly Daisy.

She stopped when she saw the car. Of course, from that distance, she could have no idea who the driver was. She wore jeans and a Barbour jacket, the left sleeve empty, a bright-red scarf wound twice round her neck. He knew the precise moment when she recognized him by the way her eyes widened. She remained unsmiling.

He stopped and wound down the window. She didn't wait for the question.

"I've come home. I knew they'd try to stop me so I waited till Nicholas had gone off to work and then I said, 'I'm going home now, Joyce, thank you for having me,' and that was it. She said I couldn't, not on my own. You know how she talks, 'I'm sorry, dear, but you can't do that. What about your luggage? Who'll look after you?' I said I'd already phoned for a cab and I'd look after myself."

The thought came to Wexford that she had never in fact done much of that and, as in the past, Brenda Harrison would be looking after her. But she only had the kind of illusions all the young have. "And now you're taking a walk round your domain?"

"I've been out long enough. I'm going back. I soon get tired." The bleak look was back in her face, her sorrowful eyes. "Will you give me a lift?"

He reached across and opened the passenger door. "Now I'm eighteen," she said, though not enthusiastically, "I can do as I like. How d'you do up this seat-belt? My sling and all this padding gets in the way."

"You needn't put it on if you don't want to. Not on private land."

"Really? I never knew that. You've got yours on."

"Force of habit. Daisy, are you planning to stay here on your own? To *live* here?"

"It's mine." Her voice was as grim as it could get. It became bitter. "It's all mine. Why shouldn't I live in what's mine?"

He didn't answer. There was no point in telling her things she already knew, that she was young and a woman and defenceless, and things she might not have realized, that it might very well be in someone's interest to finish off the job he had begun two weeks before. If he took that seriously he would have to put a day-and-night guard on Tancred, not alarm Daisy with his fears.

Instead, he reverted to a subject they had discussed when he last saw her at the Virsons'. "I don't suppose you've heard from your father?"

"My *father*?"

"He *is* your father, Daisy. He must know about all this. There's no one living in this country could have missed it on television and in the papers. And unless I'm much mistaken, it'll revive today with the funeral all over the papers. I think you should expect him to get in touch."

"If he was going to, wouldn't he have already?"

"He wouldn't have known where you were. For all we know, he's been ringing up Tancred House every day."

Suddenly he wondered if it was this man she had looked for in vain at the funeral. That shadowy father no one talked of but who must exist. He parked the car beside the pool. Daisy got out and stared into the water. Perhaps because the sun was shining, several fish had come close to the surface, white, or colourless rather, with scarlet heads. She lifted her face to the statuary, the girl metamorphosed into a tree, a sheath of bark enclosing her limbs, the man closing upon her with uplifted yearning face, with arms outstretched.

"*Daphne and Apollo,*" she said. "It's a copy of the Bernini. Supposed to be a good one, I wouldn't know. I don't really care about things like that." She made a face. "Davina loved it. She *would*. I suppose the god was going to rape Daphne, don't you think? I mean, they have nice words for it, make it sound romantic, but that's what he was going to do."

Saying nothing, Wexford wondered what event in her own past prompted this sudden savagery.

"He wasn't going to *court* her, was he? Take her out to dinner and buy her an engagement ring? What fools people are!" She changed tack as she turned from the pool with a little toss of her head. "When I was younger I used to ask Mum about my father. You know how kids are, they want to know all that. She had this way, had my mother, if there was something she didn't like talking about she'd tell me to ask Davina. It was always, 'Ask your grandmother, she'll tell you.' So I asked Davina and she said—you won't believe this but it's what she said—'Your mother was a soccer groupie, darling, and she used to go and watch him playing football. That's how they met.' And then she said, 'Not to put too fine a point on it, he was among the low life.' She liked those expressions, sort of trendy slang, or what she thought was trendy slang, 'soccer groupie' and 'low life.' 'Forget him, darling,' she said. 'Imagine you were born by parthenogenesis like the algae,' and then she explained to me what parthenogenesis was. Typical of her, that was, to turn everything into a lesson. But it didn't exactly make me feel much love or respect for my father.''

''Do you know where he lives?''

''Somewhere in north London. He's married again. Come into the house, if you want, and we could find where he lives.''

The front door and the inner door were not locked. Wexford followed her in. The closing of the door behind them made the chandeliers tremble and ring. The lilies in the orangery had an artificial smell, like the perfumery department of a big store. Here in the hall she had crawled to the telephone, leaving a trail of blood across this shiny floor, had crawled past the body of Harvey Copeland, spread-eagled across those stairs. He saw her glance at the stairs where a great area of carpet had been cut away to show the bare wood beneath. She went to the door at the back which led into Davina Flory's study.

He had not previously entered it. Every wall was lined with books. Its single window gave onto the terrace, of which the *serre* formed one wall. He had expected this, but not the fine terrestrial globe of dark-green glass on the table, nor the bonsai garden in a terracotta trough under the window, nor the absence of word processor, typewriter, electronic equipment of any kind. On the desk, beside a leather writing-case, lay a gold Mont Blanc fountain pen. In a jar, made perhaps of malachite, were ball-points, pencils and a bone-handled paper knife.

''She wrote everything by hand,'' Daisy said. ''She couldn't type, never wanted to learn.'' She was searching a top drawer of the desk. ''Here. This is it. She called it her 'unfriendly' address book. She kept it for people she didn't like or it didn't—well, benefit her to know.''

There were an uncomfortably large number of names in the book. Wexford turned to the J's. The only Jones had the initials G. G. and an address in London N5. No phone number.

"I don't quite understand this, Daisy. Why would your grandmother have your father's address and not your mother? Or did your mother have it too? And why 'G. G.'? Why not his first name? After all, he'd been her son-in-law.''

"You really don't understand.'' She managed a fleeting smile. "Davina liked keeping tabs on people. She'd want to know where he was and what he was doing, even if she'd never see him again as long as she lived.'' At this she bit her lip but continued, "She was very manipulative, you know. Very organizing. She'd know exactly where he was, no matter how often he'd moved. You can be sure that's the right address you've got. I expect she thought he'd turn up sometime and—well, ask for money. She used to say that most people out of her past turned up sooner or later, she called it 'coming out of the woodwork.' As for Mum, I doubt if Mum even kept an address book.''

"Daisy, I'm trying to find a kind and tactful way of asking this and I'm not sure if there is one. About your mother.'' He hesitated. "Your mother's friends . . .''

"You mean, did she have boy friends? Lovers?''

Once again, he was astonished as her intuitiveness. He nodded. "She can't have seemed young to you, but she was only forty-five. Besides, I don't think age is of much importance in this area, in spite of what people say. People have friends of the opposite sex, friends in the romantic sense, at any age.''

"Like Davina would have had.'' Daisy grinned suddenly. "If Harvey had dropped off his perch.'' She realized what she had said, the awfulness of it. Her hand went up to cover her mouth and she gasped. "Oh, God! Forget I said that. I didn't say it. Why do we say these things?''

Instead of answering, for he couldn't answer ("Come back all I said''), he reminded her gently that she had been telling him about her mother.

She sighed. "I never knew her to go out with anyone. I never heard her mention a man. I just don't think she was interested. Davina used to tell her to get herself a man, that would 'take her out of herself,' and even Harvey had a go. I remember Harvey bringing some chap home, some political bloke, and Davina saying wouldn't he do for Mum. I mean, they didn't think I understood what they meant but I did.

"When we were all up in Edinburgh last year—you know we went up for the Festival, Davina was doing something at the Book Festival—Mum got flu, she spent the whole two weeks in bed, and Davina moaned about what a shame it was because she'd met this son of a friend of hers who would just have done for Mum. That's what she said to Harvey, that he'd just have done for Mum.

"Mum was all right as she was. She liked her life, she liked pottering about in that gallery and watching the telly and not having any responsibilities, doing her bit of painting and making her own clothes and all that. She couldn't be bothered with *men*." A look of extreme despair suddenly descended upon Daisy's face. It fell into a disconsolate childlike grief. She leaned forward across the table where the green glass globe was and pushed her fist up against her forehead. She pushed her fingers through her hair. He expected a sudden outburst of anger against life and the way things were, a cry of protest at what had happened to her simple, innocent, contented mother, but instead she lifted her head and said quite coolly, "Joanne's the same, so far as I know. Joanne spends thousands on clothes and having her face done and her hair and massage and whatever, but it's not for a man. I don't know what it's for. Herself, maybe. Davina was always on about love and men, she called it having a full life, she thought she was so *modern*, her word, but actually women don't care about that any more, do they? They're just as pleased to be seen about with women friends. You don't have to have a man to be a real woman, not any more."

It was as if she were justifying something in her own life, making it seem right. He said, "Mrs. Virson says your grandmother wanted you to be like her, to do all the same things."

"But without her mistakes, yes. I told you she was manipulative. I wasn't asked if I wanted to go to university and travel and write books and—and have sex with a lot of different people." Daisy looked away from him. "It was just taken for granted I would. I don't, as a matter of fact. I don't even want to go to Oxford and . . . and, well, if I don't even do my A levels, I *can't*. I want to be *me*, not someone else's creation."

So time had begun doing its stuff, he thought. It was working. And then what she said next made him revise.

"Insofar as I want to do anything. So far as I give a toss what happens."

He made no comment. "There's one thing you might want to do. Would you like to come and see how we've turned your sanctum into a police station?"

"Not now. I'd like to be alone now. Just me and Queenie. She was so pleased to see me, she jumped onto my shoulder from the banisters the way she used to, purring like a lion roaring. I'm going to go all over the house and just look at it, get re-acquainted with it. It's changed for me, you see. It's the same but it's quite different too. I shan't go into the dining-room. I've already asked Ken to seal up the door. Just for a while. He's going to seal it up so that I can't open it if I—if I forget."

It is rare to see people shiver. Wexford, watching her, did not see this galvanic movement of the body, only the outward signs of the inner shudder, the draining of colour from her face, a goose-pimpling on her neck. He considered explaining to her what he had in mind for her protection but thought better of it. Decidedly more sensible would be to present her with a *fait accompli*.

She had closed her eyes. When she opened them he saw she had made an effort not to cry. The lids were swollen. He thought that after he had gone she would allow herself a transport of grief but as he was leaving the telephone rang. She hesitated, lifted the receiver and he heard her say,

"Oh, Joyce. It's nice of you to phone but I'm quite all right. I'll be fine . . ."

. . .

Karen Malahyde would spend the night at Tancred House with Daisy, Anne Lennox the following night, Rosemary Mountjoy the next one, and so on. He thought of mounting a further guard from the stables, two men on duty throughout the twenty-four hours, but his heart quailed at the idea of the Deputy Chief Constable's response to that. They were short-handed anyway, they usually were. The girl had no business to be there on her own, she had friends to stay with, he could hear Freeborn saying it; it wasn't for them to spend public money for the protection of a young woman who had chosen to return to this great lonely place on a whim.

But Karen and Anne and Rosemary were only too pleased. None of them had ever slept under a roof that covered more than a three-bedroomed semi or a block of flats. His decision to let Karen tell Daisy was formed on the spur of the moment. He was protecting her but this was to protect himself. Whenever it was avoidable, he must not see her. Briefly, he thought he understood the meaning of that sense of warning and alarm he had experienced in St. Peter's.

It horrified him. For a whole ten minutes, sitting at his desk in the stables, staring at the Persian-cat cactus, but unseeing, unseeing, he believed he was in love with her. He saw it as some terminal disease Dr. Crocker might have enlightened him about, some fearful blight, he saw it as Jem Hocking saw the fate that would surely overtake him.

Of course there had been instances in the past. He had been married to Dora for more than thirty years, so of course there had been instances. That young Dutch girl, pretty Nancy Lake, others apart from his work. But he loved Dora, his was a happy marriage. And this was so ridiculous, he and this *child*. But how the whole day lit up for him when he saw her, when he saw her sad face! How happy he was when she talked to him, when they sat together talking! How beautiful she was, and clever, and good!

He put it to the test, the only test. He tried to imagine making love to her, her nakedness and wanting to make love to her, and the whole concept was grotesque. It wasn't that he *wanted* her, it wasn't that at all. A positive revulsion from that made him flinch. He couldn't have contemplated touching her with the tip of his finger, not even in some secret fantasy. No, he knew what it was he felt. Instead of groaning, which he had felt like doing ten minutes before, he let out a sudden guffaw, a bellow of laughter.

Barry Vine, previously glued to a report he was reading, turned round to stare. Wexford cut off the laughter and made his face grim. He thought Vine was going to say something, ask some fool question as poor Martin might have done, but he constantly underestimated DS Vine. The man was back to his clipboard and Wexford revelling now in the realization of what it was that had happened. Not sex, not being "in love," thank God. His mind had merely replaced the lost Sheila with Daisy. He had lost a daughter and found one. What a strange thing was the human psyche!

Thinking about it, he saw that this was exactly what had happened. He saw her as a daughter, for he was a man who needed daughters. Guilt touched him that he had not instead turned to that other, to Sylvia, his elder girl. Why go a-whoring after strange goddesses when he had his own near at hand? Because the feelings and the needs blow where they list, he thought, without regard for what is fitting and what is appropriate. But he made up his mind to see Sylvia soon, perhaps to take her a present. She was moving house, moving to some old Rectory in the countryside. He would go and ask her about her move, how he could help. And meanwhile that resolve to see less of Daisy might stand, lest the less dangerous love become as consuming as that other fearful sort.

He sighed and this time Barry Vine didn't turn round. The London phone directories had been brought here when they moved in and Wexford went to look in the book that used to be pink, E–K, and on whose cover pink still predominated in the picture. Of course there were hundreds of Joneses, but not too many G. G. Joneses. Daisy had been right when she said Davina would have the correct address for her father. Here it was: Jones, G. G., 11 Nineveh Road, N5, and a phone number on the 832 exchange. On the 071 area code, no doubt, it was inner London. But Wexford didn't pick up the phone. He sat wondering what those initials stood for, and wondering too why such an absolute breach had been established between Jones and his daughter.

He thought about inheritance too and the variously different outcomes there might have been if, say, Davina had been the one not to die, or Naomi had been. And what, if any, significance was there in the fact that neither Naomi nor her friend Joanne Garland had been interested in men, had apparently preferred each other's company?

A report in front of him expressed the opinion of a small-arms expert. His mind relieved, he read it again and more carefully. That first time, when he feared he was in the grip of the most overwhelming of obsessions, he hadn't taken it in. The expert was saying that though the cartridges used in the Martin killing appeared different from those used at Tancred House, they might not in fact be. It was possible, if you knew what you were doing, to tamper with the barrel of a pistol, to *engrave* on the inside of it lines that would be themselves imprinted on a cartridge passing through it. In his view this might well have been done in the present case . . .

He said, "Barry, it was true what Michelle Weaver said. Bishop threw down the gun. It skidded across the floor of the bank. Strange as it seems, there *were* two guns careering around that floor after Martin was shot."

Vine came over, sat on the edge of his desk.

"Hocking told me Bishop threw the gun down, the Colt Magnum. It was a Colt Magnum .357 or .38, no way of telling. Someone in the bank picked that gun up. One of the people who didn't hang around till we came. One of the men. Sharon Fraser had the impression the ones that went were all men."

"You only pick up a gun with malice aforethought," said Vine.

"Yes. But perhaps no particular malice. A mere generalized bias towards law-breaking."

"In case it might come in useful one day, sir?"

"Something like that. The way my old dad used to pick up every nail he saw lying in the gutter. In case it came in handy."

His phone was bleeping. Dora or the police station. Anyone who wanted them in connection with the Tancred murders would presumably know to call on the free-phone number that had daily appeared on television screens. It was Burden, who had not come up to the stables that day.

He said, "Reg, a call's just come through. Not a 999. A man with an American accent. Phoning on behalf of Bib Mew. She lives next door to him, hasn't got a phone, says she's found a body in the woods."

"I know who you mean. I've spoken to him."

"She found a body," said Burden, "hanging from a tree."

CHAPTER SIXTEEN

She let them in but said nothing. To Wexford she gave the same sort of blank hopeless stare she might have bestowed on a bailiff come to make an inventory of her goods. That typified her attitude from the beginning. She was stunned, despairing, unable to struggle against these waters which had closed over her head.

Oddly enough, she looked more masculine than ever in corduroy trousers, check shirt and V-necked pullover, the earring missing today. "I could find it in my heart to disgrace my man's apparel and cry like a woman," thought Wexford. But Bib Mew wasn't crying and wasn't that a fallacy anyway, that women wept and men did not?

"Tell us what happened, Mrs. Mew," Burden was saying.

She had led them into the stuffy little parlour that lacked for romantic authenticity only a shawled old woman in an armchair. There, without a word to them, she subsided onto the old horsehair sofa. Her eyes never left Wexford's face. He thought, I should have brought a WPC with me, for here is something I haven't understood till now. Bib Mew is not simply eccentric, slow, stupid if the term isn't too harsh. She's backward, mentally handicapped. He felt a rush of pity. For such people shocks were worse, they penetrated and somehow overturned their innocence.

Burden had repeated his question. Wexford said, "Mrs. Mew, I think you should have a hot drink. Can we get that for you?"

Oh, for Karen or Anne! But his offer had unlocked Bib's voice. "He give me that. Him next door."

It was no good expecting what Burden expected. This woman wasn't going to be able to give them any sort of factual account of what she had found. "You were in the woods," Wexford began. He looked at the time. "On your way to work?"

The nod she gave was more than frightened. It was the terrified movement of a creature cornered. Burden left the room silently, in search, Wexford guessed, of the kitchen. Now for the hard part, the bit that might set her off screaming.

"You saw something, *someone*? You saw something hanging from a tree?"

Again a nod. She had begun to wring her hands, a series of rapid dry washing movements. Speech from her surprised him. She said, very warily, "A dead person."

Oh, God, he thought, unless it's in her mind, and I don't think it's in her poor mind, this is Joanne Garland. "Man or woman, Mrs. Mew?"

She repeated what she had said. "A dead person," and then, "hanging up."

"Yes. Could you see it from the by-road?"

A fierce shake of the head and then Burden came in with tea in a mug printed with the faces of the Duke and Duchess of York. A spoon stuck out of it and Wexford guessed Burden had put enough sugar in to make the spoon stand up.

"I phoned in," he said. "Got Anne to come up here." He added, "And Barry."

Bib Mew held the mug close to her chest and closed her

hands round it. Incongruously Wexford recalled someone telling him how the people of Kashmir carry pots of hot coals under their clothes to warm them. If they hadn't been there he thought Bib would have put the mug up under her sweater. She seemed to take comfort from the tea as a heater rather than a drink.

"Went in the trees," she said. "I had to go."

It took Wexford a moment or two to understand what she meant. In court they still called it "for a natural purpose." Burden seemed baffled. She could only have been ten minutes from her own house, but of course it was possible even then one could be "caught short," that she might be troubled in that way. Or be in awe of using the bathrooms at Tancred House?

"You left your bike," he said gently, "and went in among the trees and then you saw it?"

She had begun to tremble.

He had to persist. "You didn't go on to Tancred, you came back?"

"Scared, scared, scared. I was scared." She pointed a finger at the wall. "I told him."

"Yes," Burden said. "Could you—could you tell us *where*?"

She didn't scream. The sound she made was a kind of gibbering and her body shook. The tea rocked in the cup and splashed over the side. Wexford took it gently from her. He said in the calmest, most soothing voice he could achieve, "It doesn't matter. Don't worry about it. You've told Mr. Hogarth?" She looked uncomprehending. He fancied her teeth had begun to chatter. "The man next door?"

A nod. Her hands went back to the mug of tea, clasped it. Wexford heard the car, nodded to Burden to let them in. Barry Vine and Anne Lennox had taken precisely eleven minutes to get there.

Leaving them with Bib, Wexford went next door. The young American's bicycle rested against the wall. There was no bell or knocker, so he flapped the letter-box lid up and down. The man inside took a long time coming and when he did he looked far from pleased to see Wexford. No doubt he resented this involvement.

"Oh, hi," he said rather coldly. And then, with resignation, "We've met before. Come on in."

It was a pleasant voice. Educated, Wexford supposed, though not up to the immaculate Ivy League standard of Mr. Littlebury's. The boy showed him into a grubby sitting-room, just what he would have expected someone of his age—twenty-three or -four?—to be living in on his own. There were a lot of books in bookcases made by resting planks on stacks of bricks, a smartish television set, a broken-down old green settee, a gateleg table weighed down with books, papers, typewriter, indefinable metal instruments of the clamp and wrench type, plates, cups and a half-empty glass of something red. Newspapers occupied the only other thing provided for sitting on, a Windsor wheelback chair. The young man swept them off and onto the floor, then removed, from the wheelback where they were hanging, a dirty white T-shirt and pair of muddy socks.

"Can I have your full name?"

"I guess." But he didn't give it. "Do I get to know what for? I mean, I'm not involved in all this."

"Routine, sir. Nothing for you to worry yourself about. Now I'd like your full name."

"Okay, if that's the way you want it. Jonathan Steel Hogarth." His manner changed and he became expansive. "They call me Thanny. Well, I call me Thanny, so everyone else does now. You can't all be Jon, can you? I figured if a girl named Patricia can be Tricia, I can be Thanny."

"You're an American citizen?"

"Yeah. Should I be calling my consul?"

Wexford smiled. "I doubt if that will be necessary. Have you been here long?"

"I've been in Europe since last summer. Since the end of May. I came to the U.K. in June. I guess I'm doing what they used to call the Grand Tour. I've lived *here* maybe a month. I'm a student. Well, I've *been* a student and hopefully I'm going to be one again. At USM in the fall. So I found this place—what would you call it? A cabin? No, a cottage—and settled in and the next thing there's this massacre on the property up there and the lady next door finds some poor guy hanging off of a tree.''

''A guy? It was a man?''

''Funny that, I don't know. I sort of presumed it was.''

He gave Wexford a rueful grin. It was a delicate face, not so much handsome as sensitive, the features fine as a girl's, large dark-blue eyes with thick long lashes, a short straight nose, rose-leaf skin—and the heavy stubble of a dark man who hasn't shaved for two days. The contrast was strangely arresting. ''You want me to tell you what happened? I guess it was lucky I was here. I'd just got back from USM . . .''

Wexford interrupted him. ''You said that before, USM. What's USM?''

Hogarth looked at him as if he must be simple-minded and Wexford quickly saw why. ''I'll be going to school there, right? University of the South, Myringham, USM. What do *you* call it? They do this post-grad creative-writing course and I've applied. I only minored in English literature at college, military history was my major, so I figured I needed more training if I'm going to write novels. I'd filled out the application and been over with it.'' He grinned. ''It's not that I don't have confidence in the British mails, I wanted to take a look at the campus. Well, like I said, I'd delivered my application and got back here—when? I guess around two, ten after two. There came this hammering on my door and the rest I guess you know.''

''Not quite, Mr. Hogarth.''

Thanny Hogarth put up his delicate dark eyebrows. He had recovered perfect command of himself, a remarkable command in one so young. ''She can't tell you herself?''

''No,'' Wexford said thoughtfully. ''No, it appears she can't. What exactly *did* she tell you?'' The idea had come to him, not too far-fetched, that Bib had been seeing ghosts, phantasms or bogies, that perhaps she had done this before. There was no body, or what hung from that tree was a sheet of plastic, a wind-blown sack. The English countryside, after wind and rain, was sometimes festooned with rags of grainy greyish polythene . . . "What did she say to you? Precisely?"

"Her exact words? It's hard to recall. She said there was a body, hanging . . . She told me *where* and then she started sort of laughing and crying." An idea struck him, it seemed with pleasure. He suddenly wanted to help. "I could show you. I guess I could find where she said and show you."

The wind had dropped and it was very silent and still in the woods. There was a little muted birdsong, but songbirds rarely live in forests and a more usual sound was the shriek of a jay and the woodpecker's distant drilling. They left the car at the point where the by-road twisted to the south. It was an old part of Tancred woods with old standing trees and many fallen.

Gabbitas or his predecessor had done some logging in here but had left a few tree trunks lying, overgrown now with brambles, as habitats for wildlife. So much light penetrated that whole areas of the forest floor were bright with spring grass, but deeper in, where the trunks crowded together, a dense leaf-mould lay underfoot, crisp on the surface with brown oak leaves.

Here it was that Bib Mew had come, according to Thanny Hogarth. He showed them where he calculated she had abandoned her bicycle. Modest, inhibited Bib must have gone a long way in among the trees before she was satisfied she had found privacy. So long a way, in fact, that Wexford's earlier notion returned to him: that they would find nothing—or nothing but a rag of plastic wrap flapping from a branch.

The silence they all maintained, the grim speechlessness would seem folly, a pointless over-reacting, when the hanging object, the fluttering rag, the empty sack, was found. He was thinking along these lines, beginning to think as if it were all over, Bib's bogy seen for what it was, the whole thing to be dismissed with an exasperated exclamation—when he saw it. They all saw it.

There were holly trees, a wall of them. They screened a clearing, and in the clearing, from one of the lower branches of a great tree, an ash or perhaps a lime, it hung by the neck. A bundle, tied up at the neck, but no rag or sack. It had weight, the weight of flesh and bones, to suspend it with a heavy ponderousness. This had once been human.

The policemen made no sound. Thanny Hogarth said, "Wow!"

It was sunny in the clearing. The sun lit the hanging body with a gentle golden gleam. Rather than swinging like a pendulum, it rotated to the extent perhaps of a quarter circle as a metal weight might on the end of a plumb-line. This was a beautiful place, a sylvan dell with budding branches around and the tiny yellow and white star flowers of spring underfoot. The body in this setting was obscene. An earlier thought returned to Wexford, that the man or men who did this took pleasure in destruction, delighted in spoliation.

Having stopped briefly to stare, they approached the pendent thing. The policemen went close up, but Thanny Hogarth hung back. His face was unchanged but he hung back and lowered his eyes. It wasn't in fact the exciting discovery he had envisaged, jaunty and eager back at the cottage, Wexford thought. At least, he wasn't going to throw up.

They were a yard from it now. A trousered body, track-suited, once fat, the neck stretched horribly by the noose, and Wexford saw that he had been wrong, so wrong.

"That's Andy Griffin," Burden said.

"It's not possible. His parents had a phone call from him on Wednesday night. He was up in the north of England somewhere and he phoned his parents Wednesday evening."

Sumner-Quist seemed unimpressed. "This man has been dead at least since Tuesday afternoon and very likely longer."

For further information they would await his report. Burden was indignant. You cannot directly reproach bereaved parents for telling you lies about their dead son. However much he longed to have it out with them, he would have to desist.

Freeborn was very keen on his officers' maintaining what he called "civilized and sensitive" relations with the public.

In any case, Burden could make an intelligent guess at what had happened. Terry and Margaret Griffin wanted to postpone any questioning of Andy for as long as possible. If they could maintain a fiction that he was far away—and how much of a fiction, after all, was it?—if they could, when he turned up, persuade him to go to ground again, by the time his reappearance was inevitable the case might be concluded and the whole thing have blown over.

"Where was he those three days, Reg? This 'up north' stuff is just a blind, isn't it? Where was he between Sunday morning and Tuesday afternoon? Staying with someone?"

"Better get Barry back to his favourite hostelry the Slug and Lettuce and see what Andy's mates have to suggest." Wexford pondered. "It's a horrible way to kill someone," he said, "but there are no 'nice' ways. Murder is horrible. If we can talk about it dispassionately, hanging has a lot of advantages for the perpetrator. No blood, for a start. It's cheap. It's certain. Provided you can immobilize your victim, it's easy."

"How was Andy immobilized?"

"We'll find out when we hear something final from Sumner-Quist. Could be whoever it was did it administered a Mickey Finn first, but that would have its own problems. Andy was the second man? The man Daisy didn't see?"

"Oh, I think so, don't you?"

Wexford made no answer. "Hogarth was distinctly put out when I came to his door. That may be natural enough, not wanting to get involved. He perked up when he appointed himself our guide, though. Probably just likes being the centre of attention. He looks about seventeen, though he's very likely twenty-three. They go to university for four years in the United States. He says he came here at the end of last May, so that would be after he'd graduated, they do that in May over there, and he'd have been twenty-two. Making the Grand Tour, he called it. Got a well-off father, I'd guess."

"Have we checked up on him?"

"I thought it wise," Wexford said rather austerely. He told

Burden of a call he had made privately to an old friend, the Vice-Chancellor of Myringham University, and of Dr. Perkins's equally private scanning of the enrolment applications computer.

"I wonder what Andy was up to?"

"You and me both," said Wexford.

He went to see Sylvia. He was too busy to take time to see her, and that was all the more reason. On the way he did something he had never done for her before, bought her flowers. In the florist's he found himself wishing for **one** of the gorgeous confections sent to dead Davina, a cushion or a heart of blossoms, a basket of lilies. There was nothing of that sort here and he had to settle for golden freesias and pheasant's-eye narcissi. The scent of them, stronger than any perfume in a glass flagon, filled his car overpoweringly.

She was strangely touched. He thought for a moment she was going to cry. Instead she smiled and buried her face in the yellow trumpets and the white petals.

"They're beautiful. Thank you, Dad."

Did she know of the quarrel? Had Dora told her?

"How are you going to feel about leaving this house?" It was a nice one, just off prestigious Ploughman's Lane. He knew why she kept moving, why she and Neil hankered after repeated change, and it added nothing to the sum of his happiness. "No regrets?"

"Wait till you see the Rectory."

He omitted to tell her he had driven past, back and forth, with her mother. He didn't tell her how appalled they had been by the size of it and its state of dilapidation. She made him tea and he ate her fruit-cake, though he didn't want it and it wasn't good for him.

"You and Mother absolutely mustn't fail to come to our house-warming."

"Why should we fail?"

"Now he asks me! You're famous for never going to parties."

"This will be the exception that proves the rule."

• • •

219

Three days had passed since he had seen Daisy. His only contact with her was to assure himself that the watch on her at Tancred House was maintained. To this end he spoke to her on the phone. She was indignant but not angry.

"Karen wanted to answer the phone! I can't be doing with that. I told her I wasn't afraid of heavy-breathers. Anyway, there haven't been any. I can't really be doing with Karen at all, or with Anne. I mean, they're very nice, but why can't I be here on my own?"

"You know why, Daisy."

"I just don't believe one of them's going to come back and finish me off."

"Nor do I, but I like being on the safe side."

He had tried several times to ring up her father, but there was no answer from G. G. Jones in Nineveh Road, wherever— Highbury? Holloway? That evening, having read Davina Flory's novel, *The Hosts of Midian*, the one Casey liked, he began her first book about Eastern Europe and found that he didn't much like Davina. She was a high-toned snob, both social and intellectual; she was bossy, she thought herself superior to most people; she was unkind to her daughter and feudal to her servants. Although avowedly left-wing, she referred not to a "working" but to a "lower" class. Her books revealed her as that always suspect creature, the rich socialist.

A mixture of elitism and Marxism imbued these pages. Down-to-earth humanity was conspicuously absent, as was humour, except in a single area. She appeared to be one of those people who relish the idea of unbridled sex for all, find the very notion of sex lubriciously, lip-lickingly delightful and the only provoker of fun, as readily available to the old (the intelligent and attractive old) as to the young. But in the case of the young indispensable, to be indulged in with fabulous frequency, as necessary as food and as positively nourishing.

As a result of his request in the matter of the enrolment computer, he and Dora were invited to the Perkinses' for drinks. The Vice-Chancellor of Myringham University surprised him by confessing a one-time close acquaintance with

Harvey Copeland. Harvey, years before, had been a visiting professor of business studies at an American university during the time he, Stephen Perkins, had taught a history class there while working for his Ph.D. According to Dr. Perkins, Harvey was at that time, in the sixties, a startlingly handsome man and what he called a "wow on campus." There was a minor scandal over a pregnant third-year student and a rather bigger one over his affair with the wife of a head of department.

"Pregnancy wasn't a commonplace among undergraduates then, especially not in the Midwest. He didn't have to leave, nothing like that. He stayed his full two years, but a good many sighs of relief were heaved when he took his departure."

"What was he like, apart from that?"

"Pleasant, ordinary, rather dull. He just looked amazing. They say a man can't tell that about another man but there was no escaping poor Harvey's looks. I'll tell you who he looked like. Paul Newman. But he was a bit of a bore. We went over there to dinner once, didn't we, Rosie? To Tancred, I mean. Harvey was just the same as he was twenty-five years ago, a terrible bore. Still looked like Paul Newman. I mean, the way Paul Newman looks *now*."

"He was gorgeous, poor Harvey," said Rosie Perkins.

"And Davina?"

"D'you remember a few years back that graffito the kids used to write up, 'Rambo Rules,' 'Pistols Rule,' that stuff? Well, that was Davina. You could have said, 'Davina Rules.' If she was there, she presided. Not so much the life and soul of the party as the boss. In a reasonably subtle way, of course."

"Why did she marry him?"

"Love. Sex."

"She used to talk about him in a very embarrassing way. Oh, I shouldn't tell him this, should I, darling?"

"How should I know when I don't know what it is?"

"Well, she was always saying very confidingly, you know, what a wonderful lover he was. She'd look sort of roguish and put her head on one side—it really was embarrassing—one would be alone with her, I mean, there wouldn't be any men

221

there, and she'd just say rather winsomely how he was a marvellous lover. I can't imagine saying such a thing to anyone about my husband.''

''Thank you very much, Rosie,'' Perkins laughed. ''She did in fact say it in my hearing once.''

''But she was in her mid-sixties when she married him.''

''Has age to do with love?'' said the Vice-Chancellor loftily in what sounded to Wexford like a quotation, though he couldn't place it. ''Mind you, she didn't pay him many other compliments. Let's say his intellect didn't stand very high in her regard. But she liked to surround herself with ciphers. People like that do. They acquire them, as in the case of Harvey, or create them, as in the case of that daughter of hers, and then they spend the rest of their lives railing at them for not being witty and scintillating.''

''Did Davina do that?''

''I don't know. I'm guessing. Poor woman's dead and in a hideous way.''

The four of them at the table, two ciphers, as Perkins called them, two sparklers, and then the gunmen entered the house and it was over, the railing and the wit, the dullness and the love, the past and the hope. He often thought of it, he thought about the *mise en scène* more than he ever had in any murder case before. The red-and-white table-cloth, red and white like those fishes in the pool, was a recurring image no one would believe a seasoned policeman like himself could keep seeing. As he read Davina's account of her travels in Saxony and Thuringia, he thought of that table-cloth, dyed with her blood.

''It's a horrible way to kill someone,'' he had said to Burden of Andy Griffin's hanging. ''Murder is horrible.'' But had it been a clever murder? Or a murder that was mystifying only through a concatenation of unforeseeable circumstances? Were they to believe that the gunman had been clever enough to engrave grooves in the barrel of a .38 or a .357? Some chum of Andy Griffin's had been clever enough for that?

Rosemary Mountjoy had stayed at Tancred House with Daisy on Monday night, Karen Malahyde on Tuesday and Anne Lennox on Wednesday. Dr. Sumner-Quist furnished Wexford with a full report on the post-mortem on Thursday and a national tabloid daily carried a story on its front page inquiring why the police had made no progress at all in the hunt for those responsible for the Tancred House massacre. The Deputy Chief Constable had Wexford up to his house, wanting to know how he had come to let Andy Griffin die. Or that was what it amounted to, couched differently.

The inquest on Andy Griffin was opened and adjourned. Wexford studied a detailed analysis from the forensic lab on the state of Andy's clothes. Particles of sand, loam, chalk and fibrous leaf-mould were found in the seams of his track-suit pants and top and the pockets of his jacket. A very small amount of jute fibre as used in the manufacture of ropes adhered to the neck of his track suit top.

Sumner-Quist had found no traces of any sedative or narcotic substance in the stomach or intestines. A blow had been struck to the side of the head prior to death. It was Sumner-Quist's opinion that this blow had been struck by a heavy instrument, probably a metal instrument, wrapped in cloth. The blow was not severe but would have been enough to stun Griffin, to lay him out cold for a few minutes. For long enough.

Wexford didn't shudder. He only felt like shuddering. It was an awful picture that this conjured up, somehow not of this modern world as he knew it, but of a long-past time, arcane, brutish and crudely rustic. He could see the unsuspecting man, the fat, stupid and foolishly confident man perhaps believing he had a henchman in his power, and the other creeping behind him with his prearranged weapon, his padded weapon. The blow to the head, quick and expert. Then, no time to waste, the prepared noose, the rope slung over the great limb of an ash tree . . .

Where had the rope come from? Gone were the days of small private ironmongers, ownership passed down in a family from generation to generation. Now you bought a rope at a DIY emporium or in the hardware section of some vast general supermarket. It made things harder, for a shop assistant remembers serving an individual customer who asks for specific items far better than does the girl or boy on the check-out. They look at the price rather than the nature of an object as it is lifted from the trolley, they may even pass it unseeing under the scrutiny of an electronic eye, and they may not look at the customer at all.

He had managed to get to bed early. Dora had a cold and was sleeping in the spare room. This had nothing, or not much, to do with the heated words they had had earlier over Sheila. Several times on the phone Dora had spoken to Sheila, but always in the daytime when her father was at work. She was bitter against him, Dora told Wexford, but willing to "talk it through." The terminology made Wexford snort. That sort of jargon was all very well at Royal Oak, quite another thing from the lips of his daughter.

Dora's idea was that Sheila should come down for another weekend. Of course, Casey would have to come too, they were a couple now, one of those unmarried couples who do everything together and put their names side by side on Christmas cards. Casey would come with her as naturally as Neil would with Sylvia. Over his dead body, said Wexford.

So Dora had sniffed and taken her cold into the spare room. With her went the pile of literature Sheila had sent—addressed pointedly to her mother—on the little town of Heights in Nevada where the university campus was. This included a prospectus of Heights University with details of the courses it offered and photographs of its amenities. A city guide presented panoramic views of the scenery in which it was set and pages and pages of advertisements from local traders to offset, no doubt, the cost of this glossy production. Wexford had given them both a miserable glance before handing these productions back to Dora without comment.

He sat up in bed with a fresh pile of books Amyas Ireland had sent. He read all the writing on the cover of the top one, which Ireland had told him was called "jacket copy." He read enough of the introduction to understand that *Lovely As a Tree* was going to be about Davina Flory's efforts with her first husband to replant the ancient woods of Tancred, before the onset of sleep dropped his eyelids and shook him with a violent galvanic start. He put out the light.

His phone was bleeping. He reached for it and knocked the tree book onto the floor.

Karen said, "Sir, this is DC Malahyde at Tancred House. I've phoned in." This was the term they all used for contacting the police station to summon help. "They're on their way. But I thought you'd want to know. There's someone outside, a man, I think. We heard him and then we—well, Daisy, she *saw* him."

"I'm on my way too," said Wexford.

CHAPTER SEVENTEEN

It was one of those rare nights when the moon shines nearly bright enough to read by. Up in the woods Wexford's car lights quenched it but once he emerged onto the open land and came into the courtyard, everything showed as clear as day in the white still radiance. No breath of wind stirred the trees. To the west of the great pile of the house and behind it showed the tops of the pines and firs and cedars in the pinetum, serrated, spired, pinnacled, fronded; black silhouettes against that gleaming pearl-grey sky. A single greenish star shone very brightly. The moon was a white sphere, alabasterlike and glowing, so that you could understand the ancients believing a light burned inside it.

The arc lamps under the wall were out, had perhaps gone out on a time clock. It was twenty to one. Two police cars were parked on the flagstones, one of them Barry Vine's Vauxhall. Wexford put his car alongside Barry's. In the still dark water of the pool the moon was reflected, a white globe. The front door was open, the inner glass door closed but not locked.

Karen opened it to him as he approached. She told him, before he could get a word out, that four men from the uniformed branch were searching the woods nearest to the house. Vine was upstairs.

He nodded, went past her into the drawing-room. Daisy was walking up and down, clenching and unclenching her hands. He thought for an instant that she was going to throw herself into his arms. But she only came close to him, about a yard from him, bringing her fists up to her face and holding them to her mouth as if she meant to gnaw her knuckles. Her eyes were enormous. He understood at once that she had been frightened almost unendurably, was near hysteria with terror.

"Daisy," he said gently. And then, "Won't you sit down? Come and sit down. Nothing is going to happen. You're quite safe."

She shook her head. Karen went up to her, hazarded a touch on her arm, and when that was not repulsed, took her arm and led her to a chair. Instead of sitting down, Daisy turned fully to face Karen. Her wound must be nearly healed by now, only a slight padding on the shoulder showed through her sweater. She said,

"Hold me. Please hold me for a minute."

Karen put her arms round her and held her tight. Wexford noticed that Karen was one of those rare people who can hug another without patting shoulder blades. She held on to Daisy like a mother with a child that has been endangered and newly restored to her, then she released her gently and propelled her into the chair, *placed* her in the chair.

"She's been like this ever since she saw him, haven't you, Daisy?" Nurselike, Karen went on, "I don't know how many times I've cuddled you, it doesn't seem to do much good. Would you like another cup of tea?"

"I didn't want the first cup!" Wexford had never before heard Daisy sound like this, her voice all over the place, jagged, like the run-up to a scream. "Why do I have to have tea? I'd like something to stun me, I'd like something to make me go to sleep forever!"

"Make us all a cup of tea, would you, Karen?" He disliked making this request of women officers, it smacked too much of the old days, but he told himself he would have asked for tea to be made if it had been Archbold standing there or Davidson. "For you and me and Sergeant Vine and whoever else is about. And would you bring Daisy a small brandy? I think you'll find it in the cabinet in the"—not for anyone was he going to call it the *serre*—"the greenhouse."

Daisy's eyes darted this way and that, to the windows, to the door. When the door swung slowly and silently inwards she drew in her breath in a long tremulous gasp, but it was only the cat, the big dignified blue cat, walking majestically in. The cat gave Wexford one of those stares of a contempt that only a spoilt pet can achieve, went up to Daisy and leaped lightly into her lap.

"Oh, Queenie, oh, Queenie!" Daisy hung forward, burying her face in the dense blue fur.

"Tell me what happened, Daisy."

She went on nuzzling the cat, murmuring feverishly. Queenie's purr was a deep heavy throb.

"Come on," Wexford said more roughly. "Get a grip on yourself." He talked to Sheila like that when she tried his patience, *had* talked to her like that.

Daisy lifted her head. She swallowed. He saw the delicate movement of the thorax between the curtains of shining dark hair.

"You must tell me what happened."

"It was *so* awful." Still the ragged voice, hoarse, shrill, broken. "It was *terrible*."

Karen came in with the brandy in a wineglass. She held it to Daisy's lips like medicine. Daisy took a sip and choked.

"Let her drink it herself," said Wexford. "She's not ill. She's not a child or a geriatric, for God's sake. She's just had a fright."

That shook her. Her eyes flashed. She took the glass from Karen as Barry Vine came in with four cups of tea on a tray and threw the brandy down her throat in a bold defiant gesture.

A violent choking ensued. Karen banged her on the back and the tears came into Daisy's eyes, overflowed and streamed down her face.

Having watched this performance inscrutably for a few seconds, Vine said, "Good morning, sir."

"I suppose it is morning, Barry. Yes, well, it must be. Now, Daisy, dry your eyes. You're better now. You're all right now."

She rubbed at her face with the tissue Karen handed her. She stared at him rather mutinously but it was in her old voice that she spoke.

"I've never had brandy before."

It rang a bell. Years and years before, he remembered Sheila uttering those same words and the young ass who was with her saying, "Another virginity gone, alas!" It made him sigh. "Okay, where were you both, you and Karen? In bed?"

"It was only just after eleven thirty, sir!"

He had forgotten that to these young things eleven thirty was mid-evening. "I asked Daisy," he said sharply.

"I was in here, watching the telly. I don't know where Karen was, in the kitchen or somewhere, making herself a drink. We were going to go to bed when the programme finished. I heard someone outside but I thought it was Karen."

"What do you mean, you heard someone?"

"Footsteps out in the front. The outside lights had just gone off. They're set to go off at half past eleven. The footsteps came right up to the house, to the windows there, and I got up to look. The moon was very bright, you didn't need lights. I saw him, I saw him out there in the moonlight as near as you are to me now." She paused, breathing quickly. "And I just started screaming, I screamed and screamed, till Karen came."

"I'd already heard him, sir. I heard him before Daisy did, I think, footsteps outside the kitchen door and then going round the back of the house, along the terrace. I ran through the house and into the—the conservatory, and I heard him again but I never saw him. That was when I phoned in. I phoned in before I heard Daisy screaming. I came in here and found Daisy at the window screaming and hammering on the glass and then I—I phoned you.''

Wexford turned to Daisy again. She had grown calm, the brandy apparently having had that stunning effect she craved. ''What exactly did you see, Daisy?''

''He had a thing over his head, like a sort of woolly helmet with eyeholes. He looked like those pictures you see of terrorists. The thing he was wearing, I don't know, maybe a track suit, dark, could have been black or dark blue.''

''Was it the same man as the gunman who killed your family and tried to kill you here on March the eleventh?''

Even as he uttered it he thought what a terrible question it was to have to put to an eighteen-year-old, a sheltered girl, a gentle frightened girl. Of course she couldn't answer him. The man had been masked. She returned his look with one of despair.

''I don't know, I don't know. How can I tell? It might have been. I couldn't tell anything about him, he might have been young or not so young, he wasn't *old*. He looked big and strong. He seemed—he seemed to know this place, though I don't know how I knew that, it's just that he seemed to know what he was doing and where he was going. Oh, what will become of me, what will happen to me!''

Wexford was saved from trying to find an answer by the entry into the room of the Harrisons. Though Ken Harrison was fully dressed, his wife was in the kind of garment Wexford had heard, long ago, called a ''housecoat,'' red velvet with whitish swansdown round the neck, the front open from the waist to show blue-spotted pyjama legs. In time-honoured fashion, she was carrying a poker.

''What's going on?'' said Harrison. ''There's men everywhere. The place is bristling with cops. I said to Brenda, 'You know what this could be? This could be those villains come back to finish Daisy off.' ''

''So we put some things on and came straight here. I wasn't walking, I made Ken get the car out. You're not safe here, I wouldn't count on being safe even *inside* a car.''

231

"Mind you, we should have *been* here. I said it from the first, when we first heard there was going to be some policewoman stopping in the house. Why didn't they get us? You don't want some bit of a girl, policewoman or no policewoman so-called. Johnny and us, we should have been called in, God knows there's bedrooms enough, but oh, no, nobody suggested it, so I never said a word. If Johnny and us had been here and the word had gone round we was here, d'you reckon any of this would have happened? D'you reckon that gunman would have had the nerve to come back here with ideas of finishing her off? Not a—"

Daisy cut him short. Wexford was astonished by what she did. She jumped up and said with cold clarity, "I'm giving you notice. You must be on some sort of notice and I don't know what it is, but a month's if possible. I want you out of here and the sooner the better. If I had my way, you'd be out tomorrow."

She was her grandmother's granddaughter all right. She stood with her head thrown back, confronting them contemptuously. And then, quickly, her voice broke and slurred. The brandy had done its work and now it was doing work of a different kind.

"Haven't you any feelings? Haven't you any care for me? Talking about finishing me off? I hate you! I hate you both! I want you out of my house, off my land, I'm going to take your cottage away from you . . ."

Her cry disintegrated into a wail, a hysterical sobbing. The Harrisons stood dumbfounded, Brenda's mouth actually hanging open. Karen went up to Daisy and Wexford thought for a moment she was going to administer one of those slaps that are supposed to be the best remedy for hysteria. But instead she took Daisy in her arms and, with one hand on the dark head, brought it to rest against her own shoulder.

"Come, Daisy, I'm going to take you up to bed now. You'll be quite quite safe now."

Would she? Wexford wished he could have provided such a confident reassurance. Vine's eyes met his and the sedate sergeant performed the action most nearly possible to him of casting up the gaze. He moved his eyeballs a few millimetres to the north.

Ken Harrison said excitedly, "She's overwrought, she's in a state, she didn't mean that. She didn't mean that, did she?"

"Of course she didn't mean it, Ken, we're all a family here, we're part of the family. Of course she didn't mean it—did she?"

"I think you'd better go back home, Mrs. Harrison," said Wexford. "Both of you should go home." He rejected saying that things would seem different in the morning, though they undoubtedly would. "Get on home and get some sleep."

"Where's Johnny?" said Brenda. "That's what I'd like to know. If we could hear those men, and they were making enough racket to wake the dead, why didn't Johnny hear them? Why's he laying low? That's what I'd like to know." She went on with venom, "Can't even be bothered to come up here and see what's going on. If you ask me, if someone's going to get the push it should be him, lazy devil. What's he got to lay low about?"

"He slept through it." Wexford couldn't resist adding, "He's young."

Karen Malahyde, twenty-three years old, far from fitting Ken Harrison's image of a "policewoman," that now derogatory and disused term, was a black belt who taught a judo class. Wexford knew that if she had encountered the Tancred intruder on the previous night and that man had either been unarmed or slow on the draw, she would have been capable of rendering him harmless very rapidly. Once she had described how she went alone everywhere fearlessly at night, having proved herself by throwing a mugger the width of a street.

But was she an adequate bodyguard for Daisy on her own? Were Anne or Rosemary adequate? He must persuade Daisy to leave the house. Not exactly to go into hiding but certainly to go some distance and hole up with friends. Still, he confessed to himself and later to Burden that this was a development he hadn't expected. He had supplied a "minder" for Daisy but only to be on the safe side. That one of those men, the gunman necessarily if the other, the unseen, had been Andy Griffin, should in fact come back to "get her" was the stuff of dreams, of fiction, of wild imaginings. *It did not happen.*

"It did," said Burden. "She's not safe here and she ought to go. I don't see how it's going to make much difference if we move the Harrisons and Gabbitas into the house. There were four people in the house that first time, remember? That didn't deter him."

The white table-cloth with the glass on it and the silver. The food on the heated trolley. The curtains cosily drawn against the March night. The first course finished, the soup, Naomi Jones serving the fish, the sole *bonne femme*, and when everyone has a plate, as everyone begins to eat, the sounds from overhead, the noises Davina Flory says are made by the cat Queenie on the rampage.

But Harvey Copeland goes to look, handsome Harvey who looked like Paul Newman and had been a "wow on campus," whom his elderly wife had married for love and for sex. Silence outside, no car, no footsteps, only a distant commotion overhead.

Harvey has gone upstairs and come down again or has never reached upstairs, but turned at the foot as the gunman comes out of the passage . . .

How long had all this taken? Thirty seconds? Two minutes? And in those two minutes what was going on in the dining-room? They were calmly eating their fish in Harvey's absence? Or simply waiting for him, talking about the cat, the way the cat ran up the back stairs and down the front stairs, the way it always played every night. Then the shot and Naomi getting to her feet, Daisy getting to her feet, starting for the door. Davina remained where she was, seated at the table. Why? Why would she do that? Fear? Simple fear holding her fast to the spot?

The door flies open and the gunman enters and the shots are fired and the table-cloth is no longer white but scarlet, dyed by a dense stain that was to spread across nearly the whole of it . . .

"I'll talk to her in a minute," Wexford said. "Of course I can't force her to leave if she doesn't want to. Come with me, will you? We'll both have a go."

"She may be very anxious to go by now. Morning makes all the difference."

Yes, but it doesn't make that kind of difference, thought Wexford. The light of day makes you less afraid, not more. Sunshine and the morning make you dismiss last night's terrors as exaggerated. Light is practical and dark is occult.

They went outside, crossed the yard and came slowly round the side of the house, the west wing. He had not used those words to himself metaphorically. The sun shone with a hard strong light where the moon had shed a pale glow. The sky was a deep blue without a cloud. It might have been June, for the air felt mild, as if the chill had been lifted for an assured stretch of months.

"He came round the back here, then," Burden said. "What was he trying to do, find a way in? An open window downstairs? It wasn't a cold night."

"There were no open windows downstairs. All the doors were locked. Unlike that previous time."

"It was a bit funny, wasn't it, pattering round the house so that two people inside could plainly hear you? With all the windows closed, they could still hear? You disguise yourself in a hood but you don't mind making a hell of a racket while you're looking for a way in."

Wexford said thoughtfully, "I wonder if the truth is he didn't mind if he was heard or seen? If he believed Daisy was alone and he meant to kill her, so what if she did see him?"

"In that case, why wear a mask?"

"True."

An unfamiliar car was parked a few yards from the front door. That door opened as they approached the car and Joyce Virson came out, with Daisy behind her. Mrs. Virson was in a fur coat, the kind of garment neither favoured nor fashionable, that the Oxfam shop balked at and church sales couldn't sell, unmistakably made from the pelts of many foxes.

Never had Wexford seen Daisy so punkish. There was something defiant about her gear, the black tights and lace-up boots, black sweat-shirt with something white printed on it, the scuffed black leather motor-bike jacket. Her face was a mask of misery, but her hair, heavily jelled, stuck out in spikes all over her head like a forest of burnt tree stumps. She seemed to be making a statement—perhaps only that this was Daisy *contra mundum*.

She looked at him, she looked at Burden, in silence. It took Joyce Virson a moment or two to recall who this was. A big toothy smile transfigured her as she came up to Wexford with both hands outstretched.

"Oh, Mr. Wexford, how are you? I'm so pleased to see you. You're just the man to persuade this child to come back with me. I mean, she can't stay here on her own, can she? I was so utterly horrified when I heard what happened here last night, I came straight over. She should never have been allowed to leave us."

Wexford wondered how she had heard. Not through Daisy, he was sure.

"I'm sorry, but I don't understand the way things are allowed to be these days. When I was eighteen I wouldn't have been permitted to stay anywhere on my own, let alone in a great lonely house like this one. You can't tell me things have changed for the better. I'm sorry, but as far as I'm concerned the old days were the best."

Stony-faced, Daisy had watched her through half this speech, then turned aside to fix her eyes on the cat which, perhaps seldom permitted to escape from the front of the house, was sitting on the stone coping of the pool, watching the white-and-red fish. The fish swam in concentric circles and the cat watched.

"Do say something to her, Mr. Wexford. Persuade her. Use your authority. You can't tell me there's no way of bringing pressure to bear on a *child*." Mrs. Virson was rapidly forgetting that persuasion necessarily must include elements of niceness and perhaps flattery if it is to succeed. Her voice rose. "It's so stupid and downright foolhardy! What does she think she's playing at?"

The cat dipped a paw into the pool, found an element different from what it expected and shook water drops from its pads. Daisy bent down and lifted it up in her arms. She said, "Goodbye, Joyce." And with an edge of irony, not lost on Wexford, "Thank you so much for coming." She stalked into the house with her fluffy armful, but left the door open.

Burden followed her in. With no idea what to say, Wexford muttered something about having it all in hand, the police had it under control. Joyce Virson gave him a scathing glare, as well she might.

"I'm sorry, but that's just not good enough. I'm going to have to see what my son says about that."

From her it sounded like a threat. He watched her making heavy weather of turning the little car round and positioning it without—just without—scraping its near side wing on the gateway post as she drove off. Daisy was in the hall with Burden, sitting in a high-backed, velvet-cushioned chair with Queenie on her lap.

"Why do I care so much if he does kill me?" she was saying. "I don't understand myself. After all, I want to die. I've nothing to live for. Why did I scream and make all that fuss last night? I should have walked out there and gone up to him and said, 'Kill me, go on, kill me. Finish me off, like that horrible Ken says.' "

Wexford shrugged. He said with some taciturnity, "Don't mind me, will you? If you get done in, I'll have to resign."

She didn't smile but made a sort of grimace. "Talking of resigning, what d'you think? It was that Brenda phoned her, Joyce, I mean. She phoned her up first thing this morning and told her I'd given them the sack and to *make* me keep them on. How about that? As if I was a child or a psychiatric case. That's how Joyce knew about last night. There's no way I'd have told her, interfering old bat."

"You must have other friends, Daisy. Isn't there someone else you could stay with for a little while? For a couple of weeks?"

"You'll have caught him in two weeks?"

"It's more than probable," Burden said stoutly.

"It makes no difference to me, anyway. I'm staying here. Karen or Anne can come if they like. Well, it's if *you* like, I suppose. But it's a waste of time, they needn't bother. I shan't be afraid any more because *I want him to kill me*. That'll be the best way out, to die."

She hung her head forward and buried her face in the cat's fur.

Tracing Andy Griffin's movements from the time he left his parents' house proved impossible. His usual drinking companions from the Slug and Lettuce knew nothing of any other address he might have, though Tony Smith spoke of a girl friend "up north." That empty expression always came up in conversation concerning Andy. Now there was a girl friend in that vague region, that Never Never Land.

"Kylie, she was called," said Tony.

"I reckon he made her up," Leslie Sedlar said with a sly grin. "He got her off the telly."

Until losing his job just over a year before, Andy had been a long-distance lorry driver for a company of brewers. His usual route had taken him from Myringham to various London outlets and to Carlisle and Whitehaven.

The brewers had few good words to say of Andy. They had in the past two or three years been enlightened as to the reality of sexual harassment. Andy had spent little time in the office but on the few occasions he had been there he had made offensive remarks to a woman marketing executive and had once taken hold of her secretary from behind in an arm lock round her neck. Status did little to deter Andy Griffin, it was apparently enough that his quarry should be female.

The girl friend seemed a myth. There was no evidence of her and the Griffins denied her existence. Terry Griffin gave reluctant permission for a search of Andy's bedroom in

Myringham. He and his wife were stunned by the death of their son and both looked as if aged by ten years. They sought the remedy of television as others in their situation might look to sedatives or alcohol. Colours and movement, faces and violent action flowed across the screen to provide a solace that needed only to be *there*, not absorbed or even comprehended.

The whitewashing of her son's reputation was now Margaret Griffin's only aim. It might have been said that this was the last best thing she could do for him. Accordingly, still watching the flowing images, she denied all knowledge of any girl. There had never been a girl in Andy's life. Taking hold of her husband's hand and gripping it tightly, she repeated this last phrase. She managed, in the way she repudiated Burden's suggestion, to make a girl friend sound like a venereal disease, in a mother's eyes as disgraceful, as irresponsibly acquired and as potentially damaging.

"And you last saw him on Sunday morning, Mr. Griffin?"

"Early morning. Andy was always up with the lark. About eight, it was. He made me a cup of tea." The man was dead and he had been a thug, a sexual menace, idle and stupid, but his father would continue pathetically to do for him this splendid public-relations job. Even post-mortem his mother would advertise the purity of his conduct and his father eulogize over his punctual habits, his thoughtfulness and his altruism. "He said he was off up north," Terry Griffin said.

Burden sighed and suppressed his sigh.

"On that bike," said the dead man's mother. "I always hated that bike and I was right. Look what's happened."

From some curious emotional need, she was beginning the metamorphosis of her son's murder into death in a road accident.

"He said he'd give us a ring. He always said that, we didn't have to ask," said Terry Griffin.

"We never had to ask," his wife said wearily.

Burden put in gently, "But he didn't in fact phone, did he?"

"No, he never did. And that worried me, knowing he was on that bike."

Margaret Griffin held on to her husband's hand, drawing it

into her lap. Burden went down the passage to the bedroom where Davidson and Rosemary Mountjoy were searching. The stack of pornography an exploration of Andy's clothes cupboard had revealed didn't surprise him. Andy would have known that his mother's discretion where he was concerned would have kept herself and her vacuum cleaner honourably away from the inside of that cupboard.

Andy Griffin had not been a correspondent, nor had he been attracted by the printed word. The magazines relied on photographs solely for effect and the briefest of crudely titillating captions. His girl friend, if she had existed, had never written to him and if she had given him a photograph of herself he had not kept it.

The only discovery they made of real interest was in a paper bag in the bottom drawer of a chest of drawers. This was ninety-six American dollars in various denominations, tens, fives and singles.

The Griffins insisted they knew nothing about this money. Margaret Griffin looked at the notes as if they were phenomenal, currency from some remote culture perhaps, a find from an archaeological dig. She turned them over, peering, her grief temporarily forgotten.

It was Terry who put the question she perhaps thought asking would make her look foolish. "Is it money? Could you use it to buy things?"

"You could in the United States," Burden said. He corrected himself. "You could use it almost anywhere, I daresay. Here in this country and in Europe. Shops would take it. Anyway, you could take it to a bank and change it into sterling." He put it more simply. "Into . . . well, pounds."

"Why didn't Andy spend it then?"

Burden balked at the idea of asking them about the rope but he had to ask. In the event, to his relief, neither of them seemed to make the awful connection. They knew the means by which their son had died but the word "rope" did not immediately conjure for them the notion of hanging. No, they possessed no rope and they were sure Andy had not. Terry Griffin harked back to the money, the haul of dollars. Once the idea of it was planted in his mind, it seemed to take precedence over everything.

"Those notes you said could be changed into pounds, they belonged to Andy?"

"They were in his room."

"Then they'll be ours, won't they? It'll be like compensation."

"Oh, Terry," said his wife.

He ignored her. "How much d'you reckon they're worth?"

"Forty to fifty pounds."

Terry Griffin considered. "When can we have them?" he said.

CHAPTER EIGHTEEN

He answered the phone himself.

"Gunner Jones."

Or that was what Burden thought he said. He might have said "Gun*nar* Jones." Gunnar was a Swedish name but such as might possibly be held by an Englishman if, say, his mother had been a Swede. Burden had been at school with someone called Lars who had seemed as English as himself, so why not Gunnar? Or else he *had* said "Gunner" and it was a nickname he'd got through having been in the Royal Artillery.

"I'd like to come and see you, Mr. Jones. Would later on today be convenient? Say six?"

"You can come when you like. I'll be here."

He didn't ask why or mention Tancred or his daughter. It was slightly disconcerting. Burden didn't want a wasted journey.

"You *are* Miss Davina Jones's father?"

"So her mother told me. We have to believe the ladies in these matters, don't we?"

243

Burden wasn't getting himself involved with that one. He said he'd see G. G. Jones at six. "Gunner"—on an impulse he looked it up in the dictionary from which Wexford was never parted for long and found it could also be another name for a gunsmith. A *gunsmith*?

Wexford's phone call was to Edinburgh.

Macsamphire was such an odd name, though unmistakably Scots, that he had counted on the single one in the Edinburgh telephone directory being Davina Flory's friend, and he was right.

"Kingsmarkham *Police*? What help can I possibly be to you?"

"Mrs. Macsamphire, I believe Miss Flory and Mr. Copeland with Mrs. Jones and Daisy all stayed with you last August when they came up for the Edinburgh Festival?"

"Oh, no, whatever can have given you that idea? Davina very much disliked staying in private houses. They all stayed in an hotel, and then when Naomi was taken ill, she had a really severe flu, I suggested she be moved here. So dreadful being ill in an hotel, don't you think, even a grand one like the Caledonian? But Naomi wouldn't, afraid of giving it to me, I expect. Davina and Harvey were in and out, of course, and we all went to a good many of the shows together. I don't think I saw poor Naomi at all."

"Miss Flory was taking part in the Book Fair herself, I believe?"

"That's so. She gave a talk on the difficulties which arise in the writing of autobiography and she also took part in a writers' panel. The subject was something about the practicalities of writers being versatile—that is, writing fiction as well as travel and essays and so on. I attended the lecture and the panel and both were really most interesting . . ."

Wexford managed to cut her short. "Daisy was with you as well?"

Her laugh was musical and rather girlish. "Oh, I don't think Daisy was much interested in all that. As a matter of fact, she'd promised her grandmother she'd come to the lecture but I don't believe she turned up. She's such a sweet unaffected girl, though, you'd forgive her anything.''

This was the kind of thing Wexford wanted to hear from her—or he could persuade himself he wanted to hear it.

"Of course, she had this young man of hers there with her. I only saw him once and that was on their last day, the Saturday. I waved to them across the street."

"Nicholas Virson," said Wexford.

"That's right. Davina did mention the name Nicholas."

"He was at the funeral."

"Oh, was he? I was rather upset at the funeral. I don't remember. Was that all you wanted to ask me?"

"I haven't begun to ask you what I really want, Mrs. Macsamphire. It's to do me a favour." Was it? Or to exact from him a great sacrifice? "Daisy should be away from here for various reasons I needn't go into. I want to ask if you'd invite her to stay with you. Just for a week"—he hesitated—"or two. Would you ask her?"

"Oh, but she wouldn't come!"

"Why not? I'm sure she likes you. I'm sure she would like to be with someone she could talk to about her grandmother. Edinburgh is a beautiful and an interesting city. Now, what's the weather like?"

Again that pretty giggle. "I'm afraid it's *pouring*. But of course I'll ask Daisy, I'd love to have her, it's just that I never thought of asking her myself."

The drawbacks of the system sometimes seemed to outweigh the points in favour of setting up an incident room on site. Among the advantages were that you could see with your own eyes who came calling. Not a Virson vehicle this morning, drawn up between the pond and the front door, not one of the Tancred cars, but a small Fiat Wexford couldn't immediately place. He had seen it before, but whose was it?

This time he was to be granted no timely opening of the door and egress of the visitor. There was nothing of course to stop him pulling the sugar-stick bell-pull, gaining admittance and making a third at whatever tête-à-tête was in progress. He disliked the idea. He mustn't take over her life, rob her of all her privacy, her right to be solitary and free.

Queenie, the Persian, sat on the coping of the pool, looking into the mirrorlike surface of the water. A lifted paw briefly distracted its attention. The cat contemplated the underside of fat grey pads, as if deciding on the paw's fitness as a fishing implement, then tucked both paws under its chest, folded itself into the sphinx position and resumed its staring at the water and the circling fish.

Wexford walked back past the stables, round the house and onto the terrace. He had a vague feeling of trespassing, but she knew they were there, she wanted them there. While he was here she was protected, she was safe. He looked up at the back of the house and saw for the first time that the Georgianization had not reached so far. This was much the way it had been in the seventeenth century, the half-timbering exposed, the top windows mullioned.

Had Davina built the conservatory? Before Listed Building consent was needed? He thought he disapproved, without knowing enough about architecture to have a firm opinion. Daisy was in there. He caught sight of her getting up from where she had been sitting. Her back was to him and he quickly left the terrace before she had seen him. Her companion was invisible.

It was chance that allowed Wexford an encounter with him an hour later. He was coming out in his own car and he told Donaldson to wait when he saw someone getting into the Fiat.

"Mr. Sebright."

Jason gave him a broad smile. "Did you read my piece on the mourners? The sub cut it to bits and changed the title. They called it 'A Farewell to Greatness.' What I don't like about local journalism is the way you have to be nice about everybody. You can't be *acerbic*. For instance, the *Courier* has a gossip column but there's never a snide line in it. I mean, the sort of thing you want is speculation about who's screwing the Mayoress and how the Chief Constable wangled his holiday in Tobago. But that's anathema on a local paper."

"Don't worry," said Wexford. "I doubt if you'll be there long."

"That sounds a bit double-edged. I've had an amazing interview with Daisy. 'The Masked Intruder.' "

"She told you about that?"

"Everything. The works." He gave Wexford a sidelong look, a little smile twitching. "I couldn't help thinking, anyone could do that, couldn't they? Come up here in a mask and frighten the ladies?"

"Appeals to you, does it?"

"Only as a story," said Jason. "Well, I'll be off home."

"And where's home?"

"Cheriton. I'll tell you a story. I only read it the other day, I think it's wonderful. Lord Halifax said to John Wilkes, 'Upon my word, sir, I do not know if you will first perish on the gallows or of the pox,' and Wilkes said back, quick as a flash, 'That depends, my lord, on whether I first embrace your Lordship's principles or your Lordship's mistress.' "

"Yes, I've heard it before. Is it apt?"

"It sort of reminds me of *me*," said Jason Sebright. He waved to Wexford, got into his car and drove off rather too fast down the by-road.

Gunther, or Gunnar, appears in the saga of the Nibelungen. Gunnar is the Norse form, Gunther the German or Burgundian. Gunther resolved to ride through the flames that encircled Brunhild's castle and thus win her for his wife. He failed and it was Siegfried who succeeded in Gunther's shape, remaining with Brunhild for three nights, lying beside her but with a sword between. Wagner composed operas about it.

This account was given Burden by his wife before he set off for London. Burden sometimes thought his wife knew everything—well, everything *of that sort*. Far from resenting this, it met with his unqualified admiration and it was very useful. She was better than Wexford's dictionary and, he told her, much nicer-looking.

"How did they do that, d'you think? The sword, I mean. It

wouldn't have been much of a hindrance if they laid it down flat. You could just have pulled the sheet up over it and you'd hardly have known it was there.''

"I think," said Jenny gravely, "they must have laid it sharp side upwards, the hilt resting on the bedhead, if you can imagine. Only I expect they only wrote about it, never actually did it.''

Barry Vine drove. He was one of those who enjoy driving, whose wives are never allowed to drive, who will drive distances of enormous and terrible lengths and still appear to enjoy themselves. Barry had once told Burden how he had driven all the way home from the west of Ireland single-handed and without a break except for the bit on the ferry to Fishguard. This time he only had to drive fifty miles.

"You know that expression, sir, 'kissing the gunner's daughter'?"

"No, I don't." Burden was beginning to feel an ignoramus. Was DS Vine about to tell him the further adventures of all these Wagnerian people, who seemed to find their way from Norse sagas into German operas and back?

"It's a phrase that means something completely different, only I can't remember what.''

"Does it come in an opera?"

"Not so far as I know," said Barry.

Daisy's father's house was near Arsenal football ground, a small grey brick Victorian house in a street of terraces. There was no restriction on parking and Vine could leave the car by the kerb in Nineveh Road.

"Be light this time tomorrow," Barry said, feeling for the latch on the gate. "Clocks go on tonight.''

"They go on, do they? I never can remember when they go on and when they go back.''

"Spring forward, fall back," said Barry.

Burden, tiring of always being the one at the receiving end of instruction, was about to protest that you might as well say, fall forward, spring back, when a brilliant flood of light from the front door suddenly washed over them and made them blink.

A man came out onto the step. He held out his hand to each of them as if they were invited guests or even old friends.

"You found your way all right then?"

It was one of those remarks which must have received a preambulatory affirmative in order to be made at all, but people go on making them. G. G. Jones even made another.

"Put your car somewhere, have you?"

His tone was jolly. He was a younger man than Burden had expected, or he looked younger. Inside, with the light on him rather than behind him, he was revealed as not much more than forty. Burden had also expected a resemblance to Daisy but there was none, or none that an early cursory study showed. Jones was fair, his face ruddy. The look of youth was partly due to that face's being round and babyish, snub-nosed, wide at the cheek-bones. Daisy was no more like him than she was like Naomi. She was her grandmother's child.

He was also overweight, too much overweight for his big frame to carry it well. The beginnings of a formidable belly swelled out his sweater in a barrel shape. He seemed perfectly at ease, with nothing to hide, and the impression of their being invited, even honoured, guests was enhanced by his producing a bottle of whisky, three cans of beer and three tumblers.

Both policemen refused. They had been shown into a living room that was comfortable enough but lacked what Burden would have called "a woman's touch." He was aware that this was (mysteriously to him, since he could only see it as flattering women) a sexist theory. His wife would have told him off for holding it. But secretly he adhered to it, it was a *fact*. Here, for example, was a comfortable, decently furnished room with pictures on the walls and a calendar hanging up, a clock on the mantelpiece over the Victorian fireplace, even a rubber plant struggling to survive in a dim corner. But there was nothing of care or taste, nothing of interest in what a place looked like, no symmetry, no arrangement, no home-making. No woman lived in this house.

He was aware that he had been silent too long, even though Jones had filled the interval with fetching the Diet Coke he had pressed Barry into accepting and with pouring his own beer. Burden cleared his throat.

"D'you mind telling us your name, Mr. Jones? What do the initials stand for?"

"My first name's George but I'm always called Gunner."

"*E-r* or *a-r?*"

"I'm sorry?"

"Gunn*er* or Gunn*ar*?"

"Gunner. On account of I used to play for Arsenal. Didn't you know?"

No, they didn't know. Barry's lips twitched. He took a swig of his Diet Coke. So Jones had once, maybe twenty years ago, played for Arsenal, the Gunners, and Naomi the "soccer groupie" had hero-worshipped from the stand . . .

"George Godwin Jones, that's my full name." Gunner Jones's face wore a pleased look. "I've been married since Naomi," he said unexpectedly, "but that one wasn't a roaring success either. She packed her bags five years ago and I'm not thinking of taking the plunge again. Not when it's like the song says and you can have it all and not get hooked."

"What do you do for a living, Mr. Jones?" Barry asked.

"Sell sports equipment. I've got a shop in the Holloway Road, and don't talk to me about recessions. As far as I'm concerned, business is booming, never better." He wiped the broad, self-satisfied smile from his face as if with some swift inner switch. "That was a bad business at Tancred," he said, his voice dropping an octave. "That's what you're here about, yes? Or let's say you wouldn't be here if it hadn't happened?"

"I don't believe you've had much contact with your daughter?"

"I haven't had any, my friend. I haven't had sight nor sound of her for a good seventeen years. How old is she now? Eighteen? I haven't seen her since she was six months old. And the answer to your next question is, no, not a lot. No, I don't care. It doesn't worry me one way or the other. Men may get to like their kids when they're older, fair enough, but babies? Don't mean a thing, do they? I washed my hands of the lot of them and I've never had a moment's regret."

It was startling how fast his bonhomie could become belligerence. His voice rose and fell as the subject matter changed, a crescendo when he spoke of things personal to himself, a low purr when paying lip-service to society's requirements.

Barry Vine said, "You didn't think of getting in touch when you heard your daughter had been injured?"

"No, sport, I didn't." Only a momentary hesitation preceded Gunner Jones's opening of a second pint can. "No, I didn't think about it and I didn't do it. Get in touch, I mean. Since you ask, I was away when it happened. I went fishing, a not unusual pastime with me, in fact it's what I'd call my hobby if anyone was interested in knowing what my hobby is. It was the West Country this time, I was staying in a cottage on the river Dart, nice little place I often go to for a few days at this time of the year." He spoke with a self-confident aggressiveness. Or perhaps this amount of pugnacity was never really confident? "I'm there to get away from it all, so the last thing I do is watch the news on TV. The first I knew of it was on the fifteenth, when I got back." His tone altered a little. "Mind you, I'm not saying I wouldn't have felt a pang if the kid'd gone the same way as the rest of them, but you'd feel like that about any kid, doesn't have to be your own.

"I don't mind telling you something else. Maybe you think I'm incriminating myself but I'm saying it just the same. Naomi was nothing, *nothing*. I'm telling you, *there wasn't anything there*. There was quite a pretty face and what you might call an affectionate nature. A hand-holder and a cuddler. Only the cuddling strictly stopped at bedtime. As for empty-headed, well, I'm not educated and I don't reckon I've read more than say six books in all my life, but I was a bloody genius compared to that one. I was the personality of the year—"

"Mr. Jones . . ."

"Yes, sport, you can have your say in a minute. Don't cut me short in my own house. I haven't said what I started to say yet. Naomi was nothing and I never had the pleasure of Mr. Copeland MP's acquaintance, but I'll tell you something, I'll tell you what I'm working up to. Any bloke who'd take on Davina Flory, *any* bloke, he'd have to be a soldier, a fighting soldier, gentlemen. He'd have to be brave as a lion and strong as a horse and with a skin as thick as a bleeding hippo. Because that lady was some queen-sized bitch and she *never got tired*. You couldn't tire her, she only needed about four hours sleep and then she was raring to go—or raring to attack, I should say.

"I had to live there. Well, they called it 'staying there while we found somewhere,' but it was plain Davina'd never let go, especially after the baby came along." He barked at Burden, "D'you know what a Goth is?"

Something like Gunnar and those Nibelungen, Burden thought. "You tell me."

"I looked it up." Gunner Jones had evidently, long ago, learned the definition by heart. " 'One who behaves like a barbarian, a rude, uncivilized or ignorant person.' That's what she used to call me, 'the Goth' or just 'Goth.' She'd use it like a Christian name. I mean, I had those initials, didn't I? G. G. She wasn't common, oh, dear, no, or she'd have called me Horse. 'What's Goth going to sack and pillage today?' she'd say. And, 'Have you been battering at the gates of the city again, Goth?'

"She set out to break up the marriage, she once actually told me how she saw me, as someone who'd give Naomi a child, and once that was done my usefulness was over. Just an animal at stud, that's me. A champion Goth. I had the face to complain once, said I was sick of living there, we wanted a place of our own, and all she said was, 'Why not go off and find somewhere, Goth? You can come back in twenty years and tell us how you've got on.'

"So I went but I never came back. I used to read the ads in the papers for her books, the things they said. 'Wise and witty, compassion combined with a statesmanlike grasp, humanity and a deep empathy for the humble and the oppressed . . .' Christ, but that made me laugh. I wanted to write to that paper and say, 'You don't know her, you've got it all wrong.' Well, I've got that off my chest and maybe I've given you some idea of why wild horses wouldn't have driven me to make contact with Davina Flory's daughter and Davina Flory's grandchild."

Burden felt slightly winded by it all. It was as if a juggernaut of hatred and bitter resentment had rolled through the little room, leaving him and Barry Vine to recover gradually from the flattening they had had. Gunner Jones had the look of a man who has been through a catharsis, liberated and pleased with himself.

"Have another of those Diet Cokes?"

Vine shook his head.

"Time for a chaser." Jones poured himself a generous two fingers of whisky into the third glass. He was writing something down on the back of an envelope he had taken from behind the mantelpiece clock. "There you are. The address of the place I was in on the Dart and the name of the people at the pub next door, the Rainbow Trout." He had suddenly grown enormously good-humoured. "They'll give me an alibi. You check up all you want, be my guest.

"I don't mind freely admitting something, gentlemen. I would gladly have killed Davina Flory if I'd thought I could do it and get away with it. But that's when you come to the crunch, isn't it? Getting away with it? And I'm speaking of eighteen years ago. Time heals all, or so they say, and I'm not the crazy young madcap, I'm not the Goth I was in the days when I thought once or twice I'd wring Davina's neck and to hell with the fifteen years inside."

You could have fooled me, thought Burden, but he said nothing. He wondered if Gunner Jones was the stupid man Davina Flory had believed him to be, or very very clever. He wondered if he was acting or all this was real, and he couldn't tell. What would Daisy have made of this man if she had ever met him?

"As a matter of fact, I may be called Gunner but I can't handle a gun. Never so much as fired an airgun. I ask myself if I could even find my way to that place, that Tancred House, these days and I don't know, I honestly don't know. I reckon there'll have been some trees grown up and others fallen down. There were some folk there—Davina called them the 'help,' I reckon she thought that a fraction more democratic than 'servants'—lived in a cottage, name of Triffid, Griffith, something of that sort. They had a kid, some kind of retard, poor little sod. What became of them? The place'll go to my daughter, I suppose. Lucky little lass, eh? I don't reckon she'll have been crying her eyes out, whatever she may say. Does she look like me?''

"Not a bit," said Burden, though by this time he had seen Daisy in the turn of Gunner Jones's head, a certain lift to the corner of his mouth, the slant of his eyes.

"So much the better for her, eh, my friend? Don't think I can't tell what's going on behind that blank look of yours. If you've done, seeing it's Saturday night, I'll bid you a fond farewell and be off to my local watering hole.'' He opened the front door and ushered them out. "If you're thinking of lying low for a bit, keeping an eye on me, I'll be leaving my vehicle where it's parked right outside there and taking what the old folks call Shanks's pony.'' As if they were traffic police, he added, "I'd hate to give you the satisfaction of finding me over the limit, as by now I surely am.''

"D'you want me to drive?" said Burden when they were in the car, knowing his offer would be refused.

"No, thanks, sir, I enjoy driving.''

Vine started the ignition.

"Is there a map-reader's light in this car, Barry?''

"Under the dashboard shelf. It pulls out on a flexible what-d'you-call-it.''

It was impossible to turn here. Barry took the car a hundred yards down the street, swung round in the entrance to a side street and returned the way they had come. The place was too much of an unknown, a mystery, for him to attempt the experiment of getting back to the crossroads by a sortie round the block.

Gunner Jones went across a pedestrian crossing in front of them. There was no one else on foot and they were the only car. Jones put up his hand in an imperious gesture to halt them but he didn't look into the car or give any other sign that he knew who the driver and passenger were

"A strange man," Barry said.

"This is a very odd thing, Barry." Burden had the map-reader's light trained on the envelope Gunner Jones had given him and on which he had written the two addresses. But it was the other side, the previously used side with the stamp, that he was looking at. "I noticed it when he first took it off the mantelpiece. It's addressed to him, here at Nineveh Road, to Mr. G. G. Jones, nothing peculiar about that. But the handwriting, it's a very distinctive handwriting, I last saw it in a desk diary, I'd know it anywhere. It's Joanne Garland's writing."

CHAPTER NINETEEN

It was broad daylight now at six. Nothing could have made it feel more like spring, the late sunsets, the lengthening evenings. Less pleasing, according to the Deputy Chief Constable, Sir James Freeborn, was the length of time Wexford's team had been quartered at Tancred House without results. And the bills they were running up! The cost! A day-and-night guard on Miss Davina Jones? What was it going to cost? The girl shouldn't be there. He had never heard of such a thing, an eighteen-year-old imperiously insisting on staying alone in that barrack of a place.

Wexford came out from the stables just before six. The sun was still shining and the evening air untouched by chill. He heard a sound ahead that might have been made by heavy rain, but rain couldn't be falling out of that unclouded sky. As soon as he came to the front of the house he saw that the fountain was playing.

Until now he had scarcely known it *was* a fountain. The water spouted from a pipe that came up somewhere between Apollo's legs and the tree trunk. It cascaded through slanting

257

sunbeams to make rainbows. In the little waves the fish cavorted. The fountain in full play transformed the place so that the house no longer looked austere, nor the courtyard bare, nor the pool stagnant. The sometimes oppressive silence had given place to a delicate musical plashing.

He tugged at the sugar-stick bell-pull. Whose car was that on the drive behind him? A sports car, an uncomfortable-looking, by no means new MG. Daisy came to let him in. Her appearance had undergone another alteration and she was feminine again. In black, of course, but a clinging, flattering black with a skirt and not trousers, shoes and not boots, the back of her hair hanging loose, the sides looped up, like an Edwardian girl's.

And there was something else different about her. He was unable at first to say what this was. But it was in all of her, her step, her demeanour, the lift of her head, her eyes. A light shone out of her. "You meaner beauties of the night, That poorly satisfy our eyes . . . What are you when the moon shall rise?"

"You answered the door," he said reproachfully, "when you didn't know who it was. Or did you see me from the window?"

"No, we're in the *serre*. I turned on the fountain."

"Yes."

"Isn't it lovely? Look at the rainbows it makes. With the water washing down you can't see that nasty leer on Apollo's face. You can believe he loves her, you can see he only wants to kiss her . . . Oh, please don't look like that. I knew it would be all right, I sensed it. I sensed it was someone nice."

With less faith in her intuition than she had herself, he followed her through the hall, wondering who the other half of "we" was. The entrance to the dining-room was still sealed up, door taped to architrave. She walked ahead of him with springy step, a different girl, a changed girl.

"You remember Nicholas," she said to him, pausing on the threshold of the conservatory. And to the man inside, "This is Chief Inspector Wexford, Nicholas, that you met in the hospital."

Nicholas Virson was sitting in one of the deep wicker arm-chairs and he didn't get up. Why should he? He didn't extend a hand, but nodded, said, "Ah, good evening," like a man twice his age.

Wexford looked about him. He looked at the prettinesses of the place, the green plants, an early azalea in flower in a tub, the lemon trees in their blue-and white china, a pink cyclamen, burdened with blossoms in a bowl on the glass table. At Daisy, who was back in the seat she must have vacated a moment before, close to Virson's chair. Their two drinks, gin or vodka or plain spring water, were side by side, no more than two inches apart, beside the cyclamen flowers. He knew quite suddenly what had caused the change in her, brought pink into her cheeks and removed the pain from her anxious eyes. If it hadn't been impossible in these circumstances, after what had happened and she had gone through, he would have said she was happy.

"Can I offer you a drink?" she said.

"Better not. If that's mineral water, I'll accept and have a glass."

"Let me do it."

Virson spoke as if the request Wexford had made implied some gargantuan task, for the water to be fetched from a well, for instance, or brought up a dangerous ladder out of the cellar. Daisy must be saved from an exertion Wexford had no right to ask of her. A reproachful glance accompanied his handing over of the half-full glass.

"Thank you. Daisy, I've come to ask you if you won't reconsider your decision to stay here."

"How funny. So has Nicholas. I mean, come here to ask me that." She turned on the young man a smile of great candle-power. She took his hand and held it. "Nicholas is so good to me. Well, you all are. Everyone's so kind. But Nicholas would do anything for me, wouldn't you, Nicholas?"

It was a strange thing to say. Was she serious? Surely the irony was in his imagination?

Virson seemed a little taken aback, as well he might be. An uncertain smile trembled on his mouth. "Anything in my power, darling,'' he said. He had seemed reluctant to have more to do with Wexford than he could help, but now he forgot prejudices and what was perhaps snobbism and said almost impulsively, ''I want Daisy to come back to Myfleet with me. She should never have left us. But she's so absurdly stubborn—can't you do something to make her see she's in danger here? I worry about her day and night, I don't mind telling you. I can't sleep. I'd stay here myself, only I suppose it wouldn't be quite the thing.''

That made Daisy laugh. Wexford didn't think he had ever heard her laugh before. Nor did he believe he had ever heard a young man make such a remark, not even in the old days when he was young himself and people still found something improper in unmarried persons' of opposite sexes sleeping under the same roof.

''It wouldn't be at all the thing for you, Nicholas,'' she said. ''All your things are at home. And it takes yonks to get to the station from here, you've no idea till you try it.'' She spoke fondly, she still held his hand. Momentarily, her face blazed with happiness when she looked at him. ''Besides, you're not a policeman.'' She spoke teasingly. ''Do you think you could defend me?''

''I'm a bloody good shot,'' said Virson like an old colonel.

Wexford said drily, ''I don't think we want any more guns here, Mr. Virson.''

That made Daisy shiver. Her face went dull, like a shadow crossing the sun. ''An old friend of my grandmother's rang up at the weekend and asked me to go and stay with her in Edinburgh. Ishbel Macsamphire. You remember my pointing her out to you, Nicholas? She said she'd invite her granddaughter as well and that was supposed to be an attraction! I shuddered. Of course I said no. Maybe later in the year, but not now.''

''I'm sorry to hear that,'' Wexford said, ''very sorry.''

''She's not the only one. Preston Littlebury invited me to his house in Forby. 'Stay as long as you like, my dear. Be my guest.' I don't think he knows 'Be my guest' is a sort of joke thing to say. Two girls from school have asked me. I'm really popular, I suppose I'm a kind of celebrity.''

"You've turned all these people down?"

"Mr. Wexford, I'm going to stay on here in my own house. I know I'm going to be safe. Don't you see that if I ran away now I might never come back?"

"We shall catch these men," he said stoutly. "It's only a matter of time."

"An extremely long time." Virson drank his water or whatever it was in slow sips. "It's getting on for a month."

"Just three weeks, Mr. Virson. Another idea that occurred to me, Daisy, was that when you go back to school in whenever it is the Crelands term starts—two or three weeks' time, you might think of boarding for your final term."

She answered him as if she saw the suggestion as extremely odd, almost improper. The gap of temperament and taste he had always sensed between her and Virson was quickly closed. They suddenly became highly compatible young people with the same values and reared in an identical culture. "Oh, I'm not going back to school! Why would I ever do that? After everything that's happened? A levels aren't something I'm likely to need in my future life."

"Haven't you got a university place consequent on how well you do in your A levels?"

Virson gave Wexford a look implying that it was impertinent of him to believe anything of the sort. "University places," said Daisy, "don't have to be taken up." She spoke strangely. "I only tried for it to please Davina, and now—now there's no pleasing her any more."

"Daisy has left school," said Virson. "All that's over."

Wexford was suddenly sure some revelation was to be offered or announcement made. *Daisy has just promised to be my wife*—something old-fashioned and pompous but nevertheless a bombshell. No revelatory statement was made. Virson sipped his water. He said, "I think I'll stay on a while, darling, if you'll let me. Could you give me a spot of dinner, or shall we go out?"

"Oh, the place is groaning with food," she said lightly. "It always is. Brenda was cooking all the morning, she doesn't know what to do with herself now—now there's only me."

"You're feeling better" was all Wexford said to her as she saw him to the door.

"I'm getting over it, yes." But she looked as if things had gone farther than that. He had the impression that from time to time she tried to revert to her old misery, for form's sake, for decency. But to be miserable was no longer natural. Naturally, she was happy. Yet she said, as if feelings of guilt had caught up with her, "In a way I'll never get over it, I'll never forget."

"Not for a while, anyway."

"It would be worse somewhere else."

"I wish you'd reconsider. Both about going away from here and about university. Of course, university—that's no business of mine."

She did something astonishing. They were on the doorstep, the door was open and he was about to leave. She flung her arms around his neck and kissed him. The kisses landed, warm and firm, on both his cheeks. He felt against the length of him a body seething with delight, with joy.

Firmly, he disengaged himself. "Please me," he said as he had sometimes said to his daughters, long ago and usually to no avail, "please me by doing what I ask."

The water continued to splash steadily into the pool and the fish leaped in the little waves.

"Are we saying," said Burden, "that the vehicle they used left, and perhaps arrived, through the woods themselves? It was a jeep or a Land Rover or something built for use on rough ground and the driver knew those woods like the back of his hand."

"Andy Griffin certainly knew them," said Wexford. "And his father does, perhaps better than anyone else. Gabbitas knows them, and so, to a lesser extent, does Ken Harrison. No doubt the three dead people knew them and, for all we know, Joanne Garland may have done, members of her family may do."

"Gunner Jones says he doesn't think he could find his way

through them now. Why say that to me if he wasn't pretty confident he *could*? I didn't ask him. It was simply a piece of gratuitous information. And we're talking about someone *driving* through the woods, not running through on foot, which, provided you followed your nose or a compass, would be bound to bring you out on a road sooner or later. This guy would have to be prepared to drive a cumbersome four-wheel-drive vehicle through woods in the dark and the only lights he'd dare have on would be sidelights and maybe not even those.''

"The other one walked in front of him with a lantern," Wexford said drily, "like in the early days of motoring."

"Well, perhaps he did. I find it all hard to picture, Reg, but what alternative is there? There's no way they wouldn't have passed Bib Mew or Gabbitas wouldn't have met them if they were on the Pomfret Monachorum road—unless Gabbitas was one of them, unless he was the other one."

"How d'you like the idea of a motor bike? Suppose they made their way through the woods in the dark on Andy Griffin's motor bike?"

"Wouldn't Daisy distinguish between the sound of a motor bike starting up and the sound of a car? I can't somehow see Gabbitas riding pillion on Andy's bike. Gabbitas, I don't need to remind you, has no alibi for the afternoon and early evening of March eleventh."

"You know, Mike, something rather strange has happened to alibis in recent years. It's getting progressively more difficult to establish hard and fast ones. That works against villains, of course, but it also works for them. It's got something to do with people leading more isolated lives. There are more people than ever before, but individual lives are more lonely."

The glazed look appeared on Burden's face which often settled there when Wexford began to talk what he categorized as "philosophy." Wexford was becoming ultra-sensitive to this change of expression and, since he had nothing more to say of value in the present case, he cut short his remarks and bade Burden good night. But his thoughts on alibis remained with him as he drove home, how suspects were able to call on less and less corroboration in support of their claims.

Men, in times of recession and high unemployment, went to the pub less frequently than they used to. Cinemas were empty as television lured away their audiences. The Kingsmarkham cinema had closed five years before and been converted into a DIY emporium. More people lived singly than ever before. Fewer grown-up children lived at home. In the evenings and by night the streets of Kingsmarkham, of Stowerton, of Pomfret were empty, not a car parked, not a pedestrian, only freight traffic rolling through, each truck with a lone driver. At home, in single rooms, or tiny flats, a lone man or a lone woman sat watching television.

This accounted, in some measure, for the problems in establishing the certain whereabouts of almost all these people on that date in March. Who was there to support the claims of John Gabbitas and Gunner Jones, or, come to that, Bib Mew? Who could corroborate where Ken Harrison had been, or John Chowney or Terry Griffin but, in the case of two of them, their wives, whose testimony was useless? They had all been at home, or on their way home, alone or with their wives.

To say that Gunner Jones had disappeared would be putting it too strongly. A call to the sports-equipment shop in the Holloway Road ascertained that Gunner had gone on a few days' holiday, he hadn't said where, he often went away. Wexford could hardly help seeing the coincidence here, if coincidence it was. Joanne Garland kept a shop and had gone away. Gunner Jones, who knew her, who corresponded with her, kept a shop and "often went away." Another thing, which Wexford was prepared to admit might be seen as way-out, had struck him. Gunner Jones sold sports equipment. Joanne Garland had converted a room in her house to a gym and filled it with sports equipment.

Were they together, and if so, why?

The proprietors of the Rainbow Trout Inn at Pluxam on the Dart were most willing to tell DS Vine everything they knew about Mr. G. G. Jones. He was a regular customer when in the neighbourhood. They let a few rooms to visitors and he had once stayed there, but only once. Since then he had always rented the cottage next door. It was not exactly next door, in Vine's eyes, but a good fifty yards down the lane that led to the river bank.

The eleventh of March? The licensee of the Rainbow Trout knew exactly what Vine was talking about and needed no explanation. His eyes sparkled with the excitement of it. Mr. Jones had certainly been there from the tenth to the fifteenth. He knew because Mr. Jones never paid for his drinks till he left and there was a record of his expenditure for those days. To Vine it seemed an incredibly large sum for one man. As to the eleventh, the licensee couldn't say, he had no record of Mr. Jones's coming in that evening, he didn't write the dates on his "slate."

Since then he hadn't seen Gunner Jones and hadn't expected to. There was no one in the cottage at present. The landlord told Vine he had no further bookings for Gunner Jones in the current year. He had rented the cottage four times and had always been alone. That is, he had never moved into it with someone else. The landlord had once seen him having a drink in the Rainbow Trout with a woman. Just a woman. No, he couldn't describe her beyond saying she hadn't impressed him as being too young for Gunner or, come to that, too old. The probability was that Gunner Jones was at present off fishing in some other part of the country.

But what had been contained in the envelope on the mantelpiece in Nineveh Road? A love letter? Or the outline of some kind of plan? And why had Gunner Jones kept the envelope when he had evidently discarded the letter? Why, above all, had he written those addresses on it and handed it so insouciantly to Burden?

Wexford ate his dinner and talked to Dora about going away for the coming weekend. She could go if she liked. He saw no prospect of his getting away. She was reading something in a magazine and when he asked her what interested her so deeply, she said it was a profile of Augustine Casey.

Wexford made the sound the Victorians wrote as "Pshaw!"

"If you've finished with *The Hosts of Midian*, Reg, can I read it?"

He handed her the novel, opened *Lovely as a Tree*, which he still hadn't got very far with. Without looking up, his head bent, he said, "Do you speak to her?"

"Oh, for God's sake, Reg, if you mean Sheila why can't you say so? I speak to her the same as always, only you aren't here to snatch the receiver from me."

"When is she going to Nevada?"

"In about three weeks' time."

Preston Littlebury had a small Georgian village house in the middle of Forby. Forby has been called the fifth prettiest village in England, which he explained as his reason for having a weekend house there. If the so-called prettiest village in England were as near to London, he would have lived there, but it happened to be in Wiltshire.

It was not strictly a weekend house, of course, or he wouldn't have been there on a Thursday. He smiled as he made these pedantic remarks and held his hands together up under the chin, the wrists apart and the fingertips touching. His smile was small and tight and patronizing in a twinkling way.

Apparently, he lived alone. The rooms in his house reminded Barry Vine of the partitioned-off areas in an antiques emporium. Everything looked like a beautifully preserved, well-tended antique, not the least silver-haired Mr. Littlebury in his silver-grey suit, his pink Custom Shop shirt and his rose-and-silver-spotted bow-tie. He was older than he looked at first, as is also true of some antiques. Barry thought he might be well into his seventies. When he spoke he sounded like the late Henry Fonda playing a professor.

His circumlocutory style of speaking left Vine very little the wiser as to what he did for a living than when he began describing his occupation. He was an American, born in Philadelphia, and had been living in Cincinnati, Ohio, while Harvey Copeland had been teaching at a university there. That was how they came to meet. Preston Littlebury was also acquainted with the Vice-Chancellor of the University of the South. He had been some sort of academic himself, had worked at the Victoria and Albert Museum, had a reputation as an art expert and had once written a column about antiques for a national newspaper. It seemed that he now bought and sold antique silver and porcelain.

This much Vine managed to sort out from Littlebury's obscurities and digressions. All the while he talked he was nodding like a Chinese mandarin.

"I travel rather a lot, back and forth, you know. I pass a considerable amount of time in Eastern Europe, a fecund marketplace since the cessation of the Cold War. Let me tell you of rather an amusing thing that happened as I was crossing the frontier between Bulgaria and Yugoslavia . . ."

An anecdote on the perennial theme of bureaucratic bumbling threatened. Vine had endured three already and hastily cut him short.

"About Andy Griffin, sir. You employed him at one time? We're anxious to know his whereabouts during the days before he was killed."

Like most raconteurs, Littlebury was not happy to be interrupted. "Yes, well, I was coming to that. I haven't set eyes on the man for nearly a year. You're aware of that?"

Vine nodded, though he wasn't. If he demurred he might get to hear the further adventures of Preston Littlebury in the Balkans during that year. "You did employ him?"

"In a manner of speaking." Littlebury spoke very carefully, weighing each word. "It depends on what you mean by 'employ.' If you mean, did I have him on what I believe in common parlance is called a 'payroll,' the answer must be an emphatic no. There was, for instance, no question of making National Insurance contributions on his behalf or applying myself to certain income-tax adjustments. If, on the other hand, you refer to *casual labour*, to a role as *odd-job man*, I must tell you that you are right. For a short time Andrew Griffin was in receipt of what I will call an elementary emolument from me."

Littlebury put the tips of his fingers together and twinkled at Vine over the top of them. "He performed such menial tasks as washing my car and sweeping my yard." The use of this word was the first hint he had given of his Philadelphian origins. "He took my little dog—now, alas, passed on to the rabbit warren in the sky—for walks. Once, I recall, he changed a wheel when I had a flat—a puncture, I should say to you, Sergeant."

"Did you ever pay him in dollars?"

If anyone had told Vine that this man, this epitome of refinement and pedantry, or, as he himself would doubtless put it, of civilization, would use the old lag's favourite phrase, he wouldn't have believed it. But that was what Preston Littlebury did.

"I might have done."

It was uttered in as shifty a way as Vine had ever heard. Now, he thought, the man would probably start using those other give-aways: "To be perfectly honest with you" was one of them; "To tell you the absolute truth" another. Littlebury would doubtless have no occasion to use the defendant's biggest whopper: "I swear on the lives of my wife and children I'm innocent." He appeared, anyway, to have neither wife nor children and his dog was dead.

"Did you, sir, or didn't you? Or can't you remember?"

"It was a long time ago."

What was he afraid of? Not much, Vine thought. No more than the Inland Revenue catching up with his back-pocket transactions. Very likely he dealt in dollars. Countries in Eastern Europe liked them better than sterling, far better than their own currencies.

"We found a certain number of dollar notes . . ." He corrected himself. ". . . Er, bills, in Griffin's possession."

"It's a universal currency, Sergeant."

"Yes. So you may have paid him occasionally in dollars, sir, but you can't remember?"

"I may have done. Once or twice."

No longer tempted to illustrate every rejoinder with an amusing tale, Littlebury seemed suddenly ill at ease. He was bereft of words. He no longer twinkled and his hands fidgeted in his lap. Vine was inspired and said quickly,

"Do you have a bank account in Kingsmarkham, sir?"

"No, I do not." It was snapped out. Vine remembered that he lived in London, this was only a weekend or occasional retreat. No doubt, though he sometimes stayed on over Mondays and needed cash . . . "Have you anything else you want to ask me? I was under the impression this inquiry was concerned with Andrew Griffin, not my personal pecuniary arrangements."

"The last days of his life, Mr. Littlebury. Frankly, we don't know where he spent them." Vine told him the relevant dates. "A Sunday morning till a Tuesday afternoon."

"He didn't spend them with me. I was in Leipzig."

Greater Manchester Police confirmed the death of Dane Bishop. The death certificate gave the cause as heart failure and the contributory cause as pneumonia. He had been twenty-four years old and living at an address in Oldham. The reason for his failing to come to Wexford's notice before had been his lack of a record. There was only one offence recorded against him and that had taken place some three months after the death of Caleb Martin: shop-breaking in Manchester.

"I'm going to have that Jem Hocking charged with murder," Wexford said.

"He's already in jail," Burden half-objected.

"Not my idea of jail. Not real jail."

"That doesn't sound like you," said Burden.

CHAPTER TWENTY

If Miss Jones had died, Miss Davina Jones, that is," said Wilson Barrowby, the solicitor, "there is no question but that her father, Mr. George Godwin Jones, would have inherited the estate, would indeed have inherited everything.

"No other heirs exist. Miss Flory was the youngest of her family." He gave a rueful smile. "Indeed, we know she was the 'youngest wren of nine,' and was in fact five years younger than her youngest sibling and no less than *twenty* years younger than her eldest sister.

"There were no first cousins. Professor Flory and his wife were both only children. They were not a prolific family. Professor Flory might well have expected to have eighteen or twenty grandchildren. In fact, he had six, one of those being Naomi Jones. Only one of Miss Flory's siblings had more than one child, and of those two, the elder died in infancy. Among Miss Flory's four surviving nieces and nephews ten years ago, three were not much younger than herself and the fourth was only two years younger than she. That niece, Mrs. Louise Merritt, died in Menton in the south of France in February.''

''And their children?'' Wexford asked. ''The great-nieces and -nephews?''

''Great-nieces and -nephews don't inherit under an intestacy or, if a will exists as in this case, unless they are specifically named in that will. There are only four, the children of Mrs. Merritt, both living in France, and the son and daughter of an elder nephew and niece. But as I've told you, there was no question of their inheriting. Under the terms of the will, as I believe you already know, everything was left to Miss Davina Jones with the proviso that Mr. Copeland have a life interest in Tancred House and be allowed to live there for life, and the same in the case of Mrs. Naomi Jones, who was to be allowed to live there until her own death. I believe you also know that in addition to the house and grounds and the extremely valuable furniture and the jewellery, alas lost, a fortune of just under a million pounds had accumulated, not, I'm afraid, a vast sum in these days. There are also the royalties from Miss Flory's books, what I believe is called a 'backlist,' amounting to some fifteen thousand pounds per annum.''

It seemed big enough to Wexford. It justified his description to Joyce Virson of Daisy as ''rich.'' He was paying this belated visit to Davina Flory's solicitors because it was only now that he had come fully to believe that the Tancred murders were in a sense an ''inside job.'' Gradually, he had come to see that robbery, at least actual on-the-spot robbery of jewels, had little to do with these deaths. The motive was closer to home. It lay somewhere in this web of relationships, yet where? Was there somewhere somehow a relative who had slipped through Barrowby's net?

''If a blood relation of Davina Flory's wouldn't have inherited,'' he said, ''I mean a great-niece or -nephew, I don't quite see why George Jones would have done. By all accounts, Miss Flory hated Jones and he hated her and he's not named in the will.''

''You could say it had nothing to do with Miss Flory,'' said

Barrowby, "and everything to do with Miss Jones. I'm sure you know how the order of deaths is presumed to be when several people who are related to each other are killed. We assume that the youngest survives longest."

"Yes, I know that."

"Therefore, in this case, though it hasn't come to that, the assumption would be that Davina Flory died first, then her husband, then Mrs. Jones. In fact, we know that it wasn't so from the testimony of Miss Jones. We know that Mr. Copeland died first. But let us say that the perpetrator was successful and Miss Jones had died. Then assumptions of this kind would have had to be made, since there would be no surviving witness to help us. We would assume, in the absence of precise medical evidence of the time of death, in this case obviously not forthcoming, that Davina Flory died first, her granddaughter immediately inheriting under the will with the proviso that Mr. Copeland and Mrs. Jones have a life interest in the house.

"Then, in order of age, we suppose Mr. Copeland to die, then Mrs. Jones, thus by death forfeiting their life interest. The property, in those few crucial moments, perhaps seconds only, is Miss Davina Jones's alone in its entirety. Therefore, if and when she should die, her natural heirs would inherit under an intestacy, regardless of whether they were of Miss Flory's blood or anyone else's. Davina Jones's *only natural heir*, after her mother's death, is her father, George Godwin Jones.

"If she had died, as she might well have done, the entire property would have passed to Mr. Jones. I cannot see that there would be any dispute about it. Who would contest such a thing?"

"He's never seen her since she was a baby," Wexford said. "He hasn't seen or spoken to her for over seventeen years."

"No matter. He is her father. That is, he most probably is her father and certainly he is in the law. He was married to her mother at the time of her birth and his paternity has never been disputed. He is her natural heir as much as, in the event of his death, if he died without making testamentary disposition, she would be his."

The engagement would be announced any day, Wexford had begun to believe. *Nicholas, only son of Mrs. Joyce Virson and the late whatever-it-was Virson, and Davina, only daughter of Mr. George Godwin Jones and the late Mrs. Naomi Jones . . .* Virson's car was outside Tancred House even earlier today, soon after three. He must be taking time off work; perhaps, with acute opportunism, part of his annual holiday. But Wexford really had no doubt that neither opportunism nor luck was needed. Daisy had been persuaded, Daisy would be Mrs. Virson.

He found himself very much disliking the idea. Not only was Virson a pompous ass with absurd notions of his own importance and status, but Daisy was too young. Daisy was only just eighteen. His own daughter Sylvia had been married at that age, rather against his and Dora's wishes at the time, but she had gone ahead in spite of them and the wedding had taken place. She and Neil were still together but, Wexford sometimes suspected, only for the children's sake. It was an uneasy marriage, full of tensions and incompatibilities.

Of course Daisy had turned to Nicholas Virson to console her in her grief. And he had consoled her. The change in her had been remarkable, she was as nearly happy as anyone in her situation could be. The only explanation for that happiness had been a declaration of love on Virson's part and of acceptance on hers.

He was one of the few young people she appeared to know, apart from those schoolfellows who may have invited her to stay but were certainly conspicuous by their absence from Tancred House. Well, there was Jason Sebright, if you could count him. Her family had approved of Nicholas Virson. At any rate, they had permitted him to accompany them to Edinburgh last year as Daisy's acknowledged escort. It might have been true that Davina Flory would have smiled more graciously on a plan for the two of them to live together rather than marry, but that was itself approval. He was a good-looking man, of suitable age, with a satisfactory job, who would make a good, dull, and very likely faithful husband. But for Daisy, at eighteen?

It seemed to Wexford a great waste. The kind of life Davina Flory had mapped out for her, though perhaps imperiously conceived, was surely the life that would just have suited her with its potential for adventure, for study, for meeting people, for travel. Instead, she would marry, bring her husband to live at Tancred and, Wexford had little doubt, after a few years divorce him, when it was growing too late for the education and the self-discovery.

He was reflecting on all this as he had himself driven from the solicitors to the Caenbrook Retirement Home. He had not yet met Mrs. Chowney, though he had spent an unproductive half-hour with her daughter Shirley. Mrs. Shirley Rodgers was the mother of four teenagers, her excuse for seldom visiting her mother. She seldom visited her sister Joanne either and seemed to know very little about her life. "At *her* age?" was her immediate rejoinder when Wexford asked her if her sister had men friends. But he hadn't been able to forget the wardrobe of clothes, the cosmetic aids to beauty and the gym full of fitness equipment.

Edith Chowney was in her own room but not alone there. A woman on the staff, receptionist or nurse, took him up to the room and knocked on the door. It was opened a crack by a woman who might have been Shirley Rodgers's twin. She admitted him, he was expected, and Mrs. Chowney in a bright-red wool dress, red-ribbed tights covering her bandy legs and pink bedsocks on her feet, was all smiles.

"Are you the head one?" she said.

He thought he might reasonably say he was. "That's right, Mrs. Chowney."

"They've sent the head one this time," she said to the woman she then proceeded to introduce as her daughter Pamela, the good daughter who came most often, though she didn't say this. "My daughter Pam. Mrs. Pamela Burns."

"I'm glad you're here, Mrs. Burns," he said with some diplomacy, "because I think you too may be able to help us.

It's now more than three weeks since Mrs. Garland went away. Have either of you heard from her?''

''She's not gone away. I told the others—didn't they tell you? She's not gone away, she wouldn't go away and not say a word to me. She's never done such a thing.''

Wexford balked at telling this old woman they were by now seriously worried not simply for Mrs. Garland's whereabouts but for her life. He was expecting any day another one of those calls that announced a gruesome discovery. At the same time he wondered if Mrs. Chowney might not take it all in her stride. What a life hers must have been! The eleven children and all the consequent worries and stresses and even tragedies. Unwelcome marriages, even less acceptable divorces, partings, deaths. And yet he hesitated.

''Wouldn't you have expected her to have been in to see you by now, Mrs. Chowney?''

''What I expect,'' she retorted sharply, ''and what they do are two different things altogether. She's been gone three weeks before without showing her face in here. Pam's the only one you can rely on. The only one in the whole lot of them isn't for self, self, self, morning, noon and night.''

Pamela Burns looked a little smug. A small modest smile appeared on her lips. Mrs. Chowney said shrewdly, ''This is about that Naomi, isn't it? It's got something to do with what happened up there. Joanne was worried about her. She used to talk to me about it, when she wasn't talking about herself.''

''Worried in what way, Mrs. Chowney?''

''Said she had no life, ought to find a man. Said her life was empty. Empty, I thought to myself, and her living in that house, never known money worries, playing at selling china animals, never had to fend for herself. 'That's not an empty life,' I said, 'that's a sheltered life.' Still, she's gone and it's all water under the bridge.''

''Your daughter had a man in her own life, did she?''

''Joanne,'' said Mrs. Chowney. He remembered too late that with so many, it was necessary to specify. ''My daughter Joanne. She'd had two, you know, two husbands.'' She spoke as if some kind of rationing scheme existed in this area of life and her daughter had already used up the best part of her allocation. "There might be someone, she wouldn't tell me, not if he wasn't loaded. What she'd do is show me the things he'd given her and there was nothing of that, was there, Pam?"

"I don't know, Mother. I wasn't told and I wouldn't ask."

Wexford came to the question that was the point of his visit. He trembled on the brink of it. So much depended on a guilty or defensive or indignant response.

"Did she know Naomi's ex-husband, Mr. George Godwin Jones?"

They both looked at him as if such sublime ignorance were only to be pitied. Pamela Burns even leaned a little towards him as if to encourage him to repeat what he had said, as if she had not, could not, have heard aright.

"Gunner?" said Mrs. Chowney at last.

"Well, yes. Mr. Gunner Jones. Did she know him?"

"Of course she knew him," said Pamela Burns. "Of course she did." She made a gesture of locking her forefingers. "They were like that, thick as thick, her and Brian and Naomi and Gunner, weren't they? Used to do everything together."

"Joanne had just got married for the second time," put in Mrs. Chowney, "oh, it'll be getting on for twenty years ago."

They were still incredulous that all this might not be widely known. It was as if he had to be indignantly reminded of the facts, not be told them for the first time.

"It was through Brian Joanne got to know Naomi. He was a pal of Gunner's. I remember her saying what a coincidence it was, Gunner marrying a girl from round here, and I thought, not just a girl from round here, come on, a girl from that background! Still, Joanne had got a leg up in the world. Brian used to say he was just a poor millionaire, but that was him trying to be funny."

"They were that close," said Mrs. Chowney. "I said to Pam, 'I wonder Gunner and Naomi don't take those two on their honeymoon with them.' "

"And the closeness persisted after the two divorces?"

"Pardon?"

"I mean, did these four people continue to know each other after their marriages ended? Of course I know Mrs. Garland and Mrs. Jones remained friends."

"Brian went to Australia, didn't he?" Mrs. Chowney asked the question in the tone she might have used to ask Wexford if the sun had risen in the east that morning. "They couldn't be hob-nobbing with him even if they'd wanted to. Anyway, Gunner and Naomi'd split up long before. That marriage was doomed from the start."

"Joanne took Naomi's part," said Pamela Burns eagerly. "Well, you would, wouldn't you? A close friend like that. She lined herself up with Naomi. She and Brian were together then and even Brian took against Gunner." She added sententiously, "You don't give up on a marriage just because you can't get on with your wife's mother, especially when you've got a baby. That baby was only six months old."

The caterer's van, as was its daily habit, was drawn up on the courtyard between Tancred House and the stables. It was fragrant with curry and the scent of Mexican spices.

"Freebee would have a word to say about that, too, if he did but know about it," said Wexford to Burden.

"We have to eat."

"Yes, and it's a cut above the station canteen or any of our cheaper haunts in town." Wexford was eating chicken pilaf and Burden an individual ham-and-mushroom quiche.

"Funny to think of that girl, only a few yards away from us really, being waited on by a servant, her meals cooked for her, just as a matter of course."

"It's a way of life, Mike, and one we don't happen to be used to. I doubt if it contributes much to personal happiness or detracts from it. When does that shop of his expect Gunner Jones back?"

"Not till Monday. But that doesn't mean he won't be home sooner. Unless he skipped off, left the country. I wouldn't put it past him."

"Gone to join her, d'you reckon?"

"I don't know. I was certain she was dead, but now I just don't know. I'd like to be able to make another of what you call my scenarios for those two, but when I try it it doesn't work. Gunner Jones has the best motive of anyone for these killings—provided Daisy had died and no doubt whoever shot her thought she would die. In that case, he would have inherited everything. But where does Garland come in? Was she his girl friend, going to share the loot with him? Or was she an innocent visitor who interrupted him—and who else? We've established no connection at all between Jones and Andy Griffin beyond Gunner's seeing him a couple of times as a kid. Then there's the vehicle they came in. Not Joanne Garland's car. The forensic boys have been over that with a tooth-comb. Not the BMW. There's not a sign to indicate anyone but Joanne herself had been in it for months."

"And where does Andy come in?"

Bib Mew had returned to work at Tancred House and there Wexford and Vine had each had a further go at talking to her. Mention of the body hanging from the tree, however carefully couched in soothing language, resulted in more trembling fits and once in a kind of attack that manifested itself in a series of short sharp screams.

"She won't go past where it was," Brenda Harrison volunteered with ghoulish relish. "She goes all that long way round. All the way down to Pomfret and along the main road and up to Cheriton. Takes her hours and it's no joke when it's raining. Daisy"—here a loud sniff—"says to Ken to fetch her in the car, it's the least we can do, she says. 'Let her fetch her herself if she's so keen,' I said. 'We're under notice,' I said, 'I don't see why we should put ourselves out.' 'I hope you're still baking our own bread, Brenda,' she says, and 'I've got someone for dinner tonight, Brenda.' And we're getting pushed out into the street. Davina would turn in her grave if she knew."

The next time Wexford tried to see her Bib hid in the room off the kitchen where the freezer was and locked herself in.

"I don't know what you've done to scare her," Brenda said. "She's a bit simple, you know. You did know that?" She tapped her head with two fingers. A silent mouthing offered: "Damage to her brain in the birth."

There were a good many things Wexford would have liked to know. If Bib had seen anyone near the hanging tree. If she had seen anyone at all in the woods on Tuesday afternoon. Thanny Hogarth was his only link with what might have happened; Thanny Hogarth must be her interpreter.

"Accordingly," Wexford said, finishing his pilaf, "I've got him coming up here this afternoon to make a statement. On what happened when Bib arrived at his door and told him about finding Andy Griffin's body. But I don't think it's going to supply any shattering revelations."

Thanny Hogarth arrived on his bicycle. Wexford saw him from the window. He came across the courtyard towards the stables no hands, pedalling away, his arms folded, his face rapt as he listened to the Walkman clamped to his head.

The headset was draped round his neck when he sauntered in. Karen Malahyde intercepted him and brought him over to Wexford. Thanny's hair was tied back today, apparently with a shoe-lace, in that style which Wexford loathed on a man, while recognizing his dislike as prejudice. He was unshaven to exactly the same degree as he had been last time they met, that is, with two or three days' growth of beard. Was it always so? Wexford allowed himself to wonder how he managed it. Did he trim it to that level with scissors? In a pair of Western boots, chestnut brown, stitched and studded, and with a red scarf knotted round his neck, he looked like a handsome young pirate.

"Before we begin, Mr. Hogarth," Wexford said, "I'd like you to satisfy my curiosity on one point. If your creative-writing course doesn't start until the autumn, why are you here six months early?"

"Summer school. It's a preliminary course for students taking the M.A."

"I see."

He would check that with Dr. Perkins, but he had no doubt

he would find all above-board. Karen had a shorthand notebook and took down Thanny Hogarth's statement. It was also recorded on tape.

"For what it's worth," he said cheerfully, and Wexford was inclined to agree with him. What was it worth, this brief account of a few blurted-out terrified words?

"She said, 'A dead person. Hanging up. Hanging up off of a tree.' I guess I didn't believe her. I said, 'Come on,' or something like. Maybe I said, 'Wait a minute.' I said to tell me again. I'd just made coffee and I made her have some, though I guess she didn't care for it. Too strong. She spilt it all down her, she was kind of shaking.

"I said, 'How about you take me and show me?' But that was the wrong thing to say. It started her off again. 'Okay, then,' I said, 'you have to call the police, right?' It was then she said she hadn't a phone. Isn't that incredible? I said to use mine but she wouldn't. I mean, naturally I see she wouldn't want to do that, so I said okay, I'll do it, and I guess I did."

"She said nothing about seeing anyone else in the woods? Then or on a previous occasion near where the body was?"

"Nothing. You have to understand she didn't talk much, not actual *talk*. She made a whole lot of noises, but real speech, no."

In addition to the other means of recording this statement, Wexford had been noting down some of it when his ball-point ceased to work. The tip of it began making grooves instead of marks on the page. He looked up, reached for another pen out of the jar beside the furry cactus and saw that Daisy had come into the stables and was standing just inside the door, looking rather wistfully about her.

She saw him a fraction after he saw her and immediately came over, smiling and holding out her hands. This might have been a social visit, long-promised, that she was paying. That it was, to all intents and purposes, a police station, that these were police officers conducting a murder inquiry, had not in the least deterred her. She was unaware of the implications and innocent of the knowledge which would have inhibited others.

"You asked me to come the other day, and I said no, I was

tired or I wanted to be alone or something, and ever since I've thought how rude that was. So I thought, today I'll go and see the place and here I am!''

Karen was looking scandalized and Barry Vine not much less so. The open-plan arrangement of the stables had its disadvantages. Wexford said, ''I'll be delighted to give you a conducted tour in ten minutes' time. Meanwhile, Sergeant Vine will show you our computer system and how it works.''

She was looking at Thanny Hogarth, just a glance she gave him before taking her eyes away, but it was a glance full of curiosity and speculation. Barry Vine said to come this way, please, and he'd explain the computer phone link with the police station. Wexford had the impression she didn't want to go but that she realized she hadn't much choice.

''Who was that?'' said Thanny.

''Davina, called Daisy, Jones, who lives at the house.''

''You mean the girl who was shot?''

''Yes. I'd like you to read this statement, please, and if you find everything satisfactory, to sign it.''

Half-way through his reading, Thanny lifted his eyes from the sheet to have another look at Daisy, who was being instructed by Vine in the formatting of software. A line came into Wexford's head: ''What lady is that which doth enrich the hand of yonder knight?'' *Romeo and Juliet* . . . Well, why not?

''Thank you very much. I shan't need to trouble you any longer.''

Thanny seemed not at all anxious to go. He asked if he too could be shown the computer system. It was interesting to him because he was considering replacing his typewriter. Wexford, who wouldn't have got where he was if unable to deal with this kind of thing, said no, sorry, they were far too busy.

With a shrug, Thanny ambled off towards the door. There he lingered for a moment as if deep in thought. There he might have stood until Daisy herself had taken her leave, had not DC Pemberton opened the door for him and firmly ushered him out.

''Who was that?'' said Daisy.

"An American student called Jonathan Hogarth."

"What a nice name. I do like names with *th* sounds in them." For a moment, a disconcerting moment, she sounded exactly like her grandmother. Or as Wexford guessed her grandmother must have sounded. "Where does he live?"

"In a cottage at Pomfret Monachorum. He's here to do a creative-writing M.A. at the University of the South."

Wexford thought she looked wistful. If you like the look and the sound of him, he felt like saying, go to university and you'll meet plenty like him. He felt like saying it but he didn't. He wasn't her father, however paternal he might feel, and Gunner Jones was. Gunner Jones couldn't have cared less whether she went to Oxford or she went on the streets.

"I don't suppose I'll ever use this place again," she said. "Well, not as my own special private place. I won't need to. It would be a funny thing to do now I've got the whole house. But I shall always have happy memories of it." She spoke like someone of seventy, grandma again, looking back to a distant youth. "It was really nice, getting home from school and having here to come to. And I could bring my friends, you know, and no one would disturb us. Yet I'm sure I didn't appreciate it as I should have done when I had it." She looked out of the window. "Did that boy come on a bike? I saw a bike leaning up against the wall."

"Yes, he did. It's not all that far."

"Not if you know the way through the woods, though I suppose he wouldn't. And, anyway, not on a bike."

After she had gone back to the house, Wexford permitted himself a small fantasy. Suppose they were really attracted to each other, those two. Thanny might ring her up, they might meet and then——who could tell? Not marriage or a serious relationship, he wouldn't want that for Daisy at her age. But to put Nicholas Virson's nose out of joint, to change Daisy's repudiation of Oxford to enthusiastic acceptance, how desirable all that seemed.

Gunner Jones returned home rather earlier than expected. He had been in York, staying with friends. Burden, on the phone, asked him for the name and address of these friends and he refused to give these details. In the meantime, he had learned from the Metropolitan Police that, far from being unable to handle a gun, Jones was a member of the North London Gun Club and had been issued with firearms certificates for a rifle and a hand-gun, in respect of both of which he was subject to periodic inspections by the police.

The hand-gun was not a Colt but a Smith & Wesson Model 31. Nevertheless, all this led Burden to ask him, in no uncertain terms, to come to Kingsmarkham police station. At first Jones again refused but something in Burden's tone must have made it clear to him that he had little choice.

To the police station, not to Tancred House. Wexford would talk to him in the austerity of an interview room, not up here with his daughter only a stone's throw away. He hardly knew how he came to the decision to drive home by the Pomfret Monachorum road. It was much farther, a very long way round. The beauty of the sunset perhaps or, more practically, to avoid, by driving eastwards, heading straight for that flaming red ball whose light blinded as it penetrated the woodland in dazzling shafts. Or simply to see how spring had begun to veil the young trees with green.

After half a mile he saw them. Not the Land Rover. That was either hidden among the trees or not in use today. And John Gabbitas was not dressed in his protective clothing, there was no chain-saw or other tools to be seen. He was in jeans and a Barbour jacket and Daisy too wore jeans with a heavy sweater. They stood on the edge of a recent plantation of young trees, a long way away, glimpsed only because there happened to be an aisle here, a swatch cut through. They were talking, they were close together and they did not hear his car.

The sun gilded them with red-gold so that they looked like painted figures brushed into a landscape. Their shadows were dark and stretched out on the reddened grass. He saw her lay her hand on Gabbitas's arm and her shadow copy the gesture, and then he drove on.

CHAPTER TWENTY-ONE

A woodsman uses rope. Burden remembered "surgery" being performed on a tree in a neighbour's garden. It was during his first marriage, when his children were young. They had all watched from an upstairs window. The tree surgeon had roped himself to one of the great limbs of the willow before beginning the work of sawing off a dead branch.

Whether or not John Gabbitas would be working he didn't know, but he made a point of getting to the cottage early just in case. It was only a minute or two past eight thirty. A repeated ringing of the doorbell failed to rouse him. Gabbitas either wasn't yet up or had already gone out.

Burden walked round the back and looked at the various outbuildings, a wood-shed and a machinery shed and a structure for keeping wood dry while it seasoned. All had been searched at the beginning of the case. But when they searched, what had they been looking for?

Gabbitas appeared as he returned to the front of the house.

He seemed not to have come along the path through the pinetum but from among the trees themselves, from that area of woodland that lay to the south of the gardens. Instead of working boots, he was wearing running shoes and instead of protective clothing or even his Barbour, jeans and a heavy sweater. If there was a shirt under it, this was not apparent.

"May I know where you've been, Mr. Gabbitas?"

"A walk," Gabbitas said. It was short and sharp. He looked affronted.

"A fine morning for a walk," Burden said mildly. "I want to ask you about rope. Do you use rope in your business?"

"Sometimes." Gabbitas looked suspicious, he looked as if he was going to ask why, but he must have thought better of it—or remembered how Andy Griffin had died. "I haven't used any lately, but I've always got it to hand." As Burden had expected, he was in the habit of roping himself to a tree if the work he had to do was above a certain height or otherwise dangerous.

"It'll be in the machinery shed," he said. "I know exactly where. I could put my hand on it in the dark."

But he couldn't. Not in the dark or broad daylight. The rope had gone.

Wexford, who had wondered where those features of Daisy's appearance came from that were not direct hand-me-downs from Davina Flory, saw them uncannily present in the man before him. But no, not perhaps uncannily. Gunner Jones was her father, a fact manifest to all except those who saw likenesses only in physical size and in colour of hair and eye. He had her—or, rather, Daisy had *his*—way of looking sideways with a tilt to eye and mouth, the curve of his nostrils, the short upper lip, the straight eyebrows that described a curve only at the temples.

His weight obscured other possible resemblances. He was a big heavy man with a truculent look. When he was brought to the interview room where Wexford was, he behaved as if on a social visit or even a fact-finding mission. Eyeing the window (which gave onto a backyard and repository for wheelie-bins), he remarked breezily that the old place had changed out of all conscience since he was last here.

There was an insolent defiance in the way he spoke, Wexford thought. He ignored the hand that was extended to him with a false cordiality, and pretended to be studying a folder of papers on the table between them.

"Sit down, please, Mr. Jones."

It was a cut above the usual interview room, that is the walls were not whitewashed roughcast, the window had a blind and no metal grille, the floor was not concrete but tiled and the chairs in which the two men sat had padded backs and seats. But there was nothing to raise it to "office" standard, and over by the door sat a uniformed policeman, PC Waterman, trying to look insouciant and as if sitting in the corner of a bleak chamber in the police station were the way he preferred to spend his Saturday mornings.

Wexford added a note to the notes in front of him, read what he had written, looked up and began to speak about Joanne Garland. He fancied Jones was surprised, perhaps even disconcerted. This was not what he had expected.

"We were friends once, yes," he said. "She was married to my pal Brian. We used to go about a bit together, the two couples, I mean. Me and Naomi, Brian and her. As a matter of fact, I was working for Brian while I lived here, I had a job with his company as a sales rep. I did my leg in, as you may know, and the world of sport was closed to me at the tender age of twenty-three. Hard cheese, wouldn't you reckon?"

Treating the question as rhetorical, Wexford said, "When did you last see Mrs. Garland?"

Jones's laughter was a honking sound. "See her? I haven't seen her for whatever it is, seventeen, eighteen years? When me and Naomi split up she took Naomi's side, which I daresay you could call being loyal. Brian took her side too, and that was the end of my job. What you'd call that, my friend? I don't know but I'd call it treachery. Nothing was bad enough for those two to say about me—and what had I done? Not a lot, to be honest with you. Had I beaten her up? Did I go with other women? Did I drink? No way, there was none of that. All I'd done was get driven round the bend by that old bitch till I couldn't stand another bloody day of it.''

"You haven't seen Mrs. Garland since then?"

"I told you. I haven't seen her and I haven't spoken to her. Why would I? What was Joanne to me? I never fancied her, for a start. As you may by now have gathered, bossy meddling women don't exactly turn me on, besides her being a good ten years older than me. I haven't seen Joanne and I haven't been near this place from that day to this."

"You may not have seen or spoken to her but you've communicated," Wexford said. "You recently had a letter from her."

"Did she tell you that?"

He should have known better than to ask. Wexford wouldn't have described his blustering manner and quick protests as good acting. But perhaps they were not acting at all.

"Joanne Garland is missing, Mr. Jones. Her whereabouts are unknown."

His expression was the extreme of incredulity, the look of a character in a horror comic confronted by disaster.

"Oh, come *on*."

"She's been missing since the night of the murders at Tancred House."

Gunner Jones pushed out his lips. He lifted his shoulders in a massive shrug. He no longer looked surprised. He looked guilty, though Wexford knew this meant nothing. It was merely the air of a person who is not habitually honest and straightforward. His eyes fixed themselves on Wexford's but the gaze soon faltered and fell.

"I was in Devon," he said. "Maybe you haven't heard that. I was fishing at a place called Pluxam on the Dart."

"We've found nobody to support your story that you were there during March the eleventh and twelfth. I'd like you to come up with the name of someone who might corroborate that. You told us you had never handled a gun, yet you're a member of the North London Gun Club and hold firearms certificates in respect of two weapons.''

"It was a joke," said Gunner Jones. "I mean, come on, surely you can see that? It's funny, isn't it, being called Gunner and never had a gun in my hand?''

"I think I must have a different sort of sense of humour from yours, Mr. Jones. Tell me about the letter you had from Mrs. Garland.''

"Which one?" said Gunner Jones. He went on as if he hadn't asked the question. "It doesn't matter because they were both about the same thing. She wrote me three years ago—it was when I got divorced from my second wife—and said Naomi and me should get back together. I don't know how she knew about the divorce, someone must have told her, we still knew some of the same people. She wrote to say now I was 'free,' her word, there was nothing to stop me and Naomi 're-making our marriage.' I'll tell you something, I reckon these days folk only write letters when they're scared to talk on the phone. She knew what I'd say to her if she phoned me.''

"Did you reply?"

"No, sport, I didn't. I consigned her letter to the bin." A look of ineffable shiftiness took command of Jones's face. It was pantomimic. It was also, probably, unconscious. He had no idea how sly he looked when he lied. "I had another one like it around a month ago, maybe a bit more. That went the same way as the first.''

Wexford began questioning him about his fishing holiday and his prowess with guns. He took Gunner Jones over the same ground as when he had first asked him about the letter, and got similar evasive answers. For a long time Jones refused to say where he had been staying in York but he yielded at last and admitted sulkily that he had a girl friend there. He provided a name and an address.

"However, I shan't be taking the plunge again.''

"Until today you haven't been to Kingsmarkham for getting on for eighteen years?''

"That's right.''

"Not on Monday, May thirteenth of last year, for instance?"

"Not on that day, *for instance*, or any other instance."

It was the middle of the afternoon and two hours since a sandwich lunch had been provided from the canteen when Wexford asked Jones to make a statement and reluctantly and inwardly decided he must let him go. He had no hard evidence on which to hold him. Jones was already talking about "getting a lawyer down here," which seemed to tell Wexford that he knew more about crime from American television imports than from actual experience, but again he could be acting.

"Now I'm here I might think about taking a cab up to meet my daughter. How about that?"

Wexford said neutrally that this, of course, would be up to him. The idea was not pleasant but he had no doubt Daisy would be perfectly safe. The place was swarming with police officers, the stables still fully staffed. In advance of his own arrival, he put through a call to Vine, alerting him to Jones's intention.

In the event, Gunner Jones, who had come by train, returned to London at once by the same means, putting up no resistance to the offer of police transport to Kingsmarkham British Rail station. Wexford found himself uncertain as to whether Jones was really quite clever or deeply stupid. He concluded that he was one of those people to whom lies are as reasonable an option as the truth. What is chosen is that which makes life easier.

It was growing late and it was Saturday, but he had himself driven back to Tancred just the same. Another floral offering had been hung on the right-hand post of the main gate. He wondered who might be the donor of these flowers, this time a heart composed of dark-red rose-buds, if it was a series of people or always the same person, and he got out of the car to look while Donaldson opened the gate. But on the card was written only the message, "Good night, sweet lady," and there was no name or signature.

Half-way up the woodland road a fox ran across in front of them but far enough away for Donaldson not to have to brake. It disappeared into the thick greening underbrush. On the banks, among the grass and new April growth, primroses were opening. The car window was open and Wexford could smell the fresh mild air, scented with spring. He was thinking of Daisy, as the fear of her father's surprise visit had led him to do. But thinking of her—he realized with careful self-analysis—with no excessive anxiety, no passionate fear, no absolute love, to speak truly.

He felt slightly shaken. He had no great desire to see Daisy, no need to be with her, place her in that daughter's position, be her father and have that role acknowledged by her. His eyes were opened. Perhaps by the fact that he had not been horrified or angered by Gunner Jones's declared intention of coming up here. He had been no more than annoyed and on his guard. For he was fond of Daisy but he did not love her.

It was self-revelation that the experience brought him. He had been taught the difference, the huge division, between love and being fond of someone. Daisy had been there when, for the first time in her life, Sheila defected. No doubt, any amiable pretty young woman who was nice to him would have served the purpose.

He had been given his allotment of love, for wife, children and grandchildren, and that was it, there would be no more. He wanted no more. What he felt for Daisy was a tender regard and a hope that all would go well with her.

This final reflection was forming itself in his mind when he caught sight, from the car window, of a running figure in the distance among the trees. The day was fair and shafts of sunlight penetrated the woods everywhere in slanting misty rays, in places almost opaque. These hindered his view rather than helped him to see whose the figure might be. It ran, apparently joyously and with abandon, through the clear spaces and into the dense bars of light, then between them again. Impossible to tell whether the flying figure was a man or a woman, young or middle-aged. Wexford could only be confident that the runner was not old. It disappeared in the vague direction of the hanging tree.

• • •

When the phone rang Gerry Hinde was talking to Burden, asking him if he had seen the flowers on the gate. You never saw flowers like that in a flower shop. When you wanted to buy some for your wife, for instance, you got them all bunched together, not looking very attractive, and she had to arrange them. His wife said that she didn't really like people bringing her flowers because the first thing she had to do, whatever else she might be doing, was put them in water. And that might take ages when the chances were she was cooking a meal or getting one of the kids to bed.

"It would be a useful thing to know. I mean, where whoever he is got those flowers from. Done like that."

Burden didn't like to say they would very likely be beyond DC Hinde's means. He picked up the phone.

The puritan ethic still played an important role among the forces that ruled his thinking. It told him not to use a car if you could walk the distance and that phoning the people next door was almost a sin. Therefore, when Gabbitas said he was at home in his cottage, Burden was on the point of asking sharply why he couldn't have come over if he had something to say. A note of gravity and perhaps of shock in the woodsman's voice stopped him.

"Could you come here, please? Could you come and someone with you?"

Burden didn't say what he might have, that Gabbitas had seemed far from keen on his company that morning. "Give me some idea of what this is about, would you?"

"I'd rather wait until you're here. It's nothing to do with the rope." The voice wavered a little. It said awkwardly, "I haven't found a body or anything."

"For God's sake," said Burden to himself as he put the receiver back.

He emerged onto the courtyard and walked round the front of the house. Nicholas Virson's car was parked on the flagstones. The sunshine was still very bright but the sun by now quite low in the sky. Its oblique rays turned the car approaching along the main road out of the woods to a dazzling globe of white fire. Burden was unable to look at it, so that it had drawn up not far from him and Wexford was getting out before he saw who this was.

"I'll come with you."

"He said to bring someone with me. I thought it a bit of a nerve."

They took the narrow road through the pinetum. On either side the placid sunshine of early evening showed the varying colours of the conifers, smooth spires, serrated cones, Christmas-tree spruces and sweeping cedars, green, blue, silver, gold and almost black. The sunlight stood in pillars and hung in bands between the symmetrical shapes. There was a strong aromatic tarry scent.

Underfoot it was dry and rather slippery, for brown needles covered the road surface as well as the interstices of the wood. The sky was a great blue-white dazzlement above them. How lucky they were to live here, Wexford thought, those Harrisons and John Gabbitas, and how much they must fear the loss of it. Uneasily, he remembered his homeward journey of the previous evening and the woodsman and Daisy standing side by side in the sunlit aisle. A girl might lay her hand on a man's arm and look up into his face in that confiding way and it all mean nothing. They had been a long way distant from him. Daisy was a "toucher," she tended to touch you as she talked, to lay a finger on your wrist, pass her hand lightly across your arm in a gesture near a caress . . .

John Gabbitas was out in his front garden waiting for them, his right hand beating time with a frenzied impatience as if he found this delay intolerable.

Once again Wexford was struck by his looks, a spectacular handsomeness which, if it had belonged to a woman, would have led you to call it a waste, buried in such a place. The same sort of comment simply never applied to a man. He was reminded suddenly of Dr. Perkins's remarks about Harvey Copeland and his appearance, and then Gabbitas was ushering them into the little house, into the living-room and pointing, with the same quivering finger that had beat time, at something which lay on a woven raffia-topped stool in the middle of the room.

"What is this, Mr. Gabbitas?" Burden asked him. "What's going on?"

"I found it. I found *that*."

"Where? Where it is now?"

"In a drawer. In the chest of drawers."

It was a large hand-gun, a revolver, of a dark leaden colour, the metal of the barrel of a slightly paler and browner shade. They looked at it in a moment of silence.

Wexford said, "You took it out and put it there?"

Gabbitas nodded.

"You know, of course, that you shouldn't have touched it."

"Okay, I know now. It was a shock. I opened the drawer, I keep paper and envelopes in there, and it was the first thing I saw. It was lying on top of a packet of paper for printing out. I know I shouldn't have touched it, but it was instinctive."

"May we sit down, Mr. Gabbitas?"

Gabbitas cast up his eyes, then nodded furiously. These were the gestures of a man wondering at the triviality of the request at such a time. "It's the gun they were all killed with, isn't it?"

"It may be," said Burden. "It may not. That remains to be established."

"I phoned you as soon as I found it."

"As soon as you'd removed it from where you found it, yes. That would have been at five fifty. When was the last time you looked in that drawer, prior to five fifty?"

"Yesterday," Gabbitas said after a small hesitation. "Yesterday evening. About nine. I was going to write a letter. To my parents in Norfolk."

"And the gun wasn't there then?"

"Of course it wasn't!" Gabbitas's voice was suddenly ragged with exasperation. "I'd have got in touch with you then if it had been. There was nothing in the drawer but what's always in it, paper, notepaper, envelopes, cards, that sort of thing.

The point is the gun wasn't there. Can't you understand? I've never seen it before."

"All right, Mr. Gabbitas. I should try to keep calm if I were you. Did you in fact write to your parents?"

Gabbitas said impatiently, "I posted the letter in Pomfret this morning. I spent the day felling a dead sycamore in the centre of Pomfret and I had two kids doing community service to help me. We finished at four thirty and I was back here by five."

"And fifty minutes later you opened the drawer because you meant to write another letter? You seem to be an enthusiastic correspondent."

It was with a scarcely restrained fury that Gabbitas turned on Burden. "Look, I didn't have to tell you about this. I could have chucked it out with the rubbish and no one the wiser. It's nothing to do with me, I simply found it, I found it in that drawer *where someone else must have put it*. I opened the drawer, if you must know, for a piece of paper on which to write an invoice for the job I did today. To the Borough Council's environment department. That's the way I work. I have to. I can't hang about for weeks and weeks. I need the money."

"All right, Mr. Gabbitas," Wexford said. "But it was unfortunate you handled this weapon. I suppose it was with bare hands? Yes. I'm going to put through a call to DC Archbold to come over here and take care of it. It'll be wiser for no other unauthorized person to touch it."

Gabbitas was sitting down, leaning forward, his elbows resting on the arms of the chair, his expression truculent and peevish. It was the look of someone who has been balked of his desire to have authority thank him for his services. Wexford considered that there were two possible views to take. One was that Gabbitas was guilty, perhaps only of possessing this gun, but guilty of that and now afraid to hang on to it. The other was that he simply did not realize the gravity of the matter or understand what this meant, if the revolver on the stool was indeed the murder weapon.

He made his call, said to Gabbitas, "You were out all day?"

"I told you. And I can give you the names of dozens of witnesses to prove it."

"It's a pity you can't give us the name of one to corroborate where you were on March the eleventh." Wexford sighed. "All right. I suppose there are no signs of a break-in? Who else has a key to this house?"

"Nobody, so far as I know." Gabbitas hesitated, and quickly amended what he had said. "I mean, the lock wasn't changed when I moved in. The Griffins might still have a key. It's not my house, it doesn't belong to me. I suppose Miss Flory or Mr. Copeland had a key." More and more names seemed to come to mind. "The Harrisons had a key between the Griffins going and me coming. I don't know what happened to it. I never go out and leave the house unlocked, I'm careful about that."

"You might as well not bother, Mr. Gabbitas," said Burden drily. "It doesn't seem to make much difference."

You lost a rope and found a gun, Wexford reflected when he was alone with Gabbitas. Aloud he said, "I suppose much the same applies to the keys to the machinery shed. A lot of people have keys?"

"There's no lock on the door."

"That settles that, then. You came here last May, Mr. Gabbitas?"

"At the beginning of May, yes."

"No doubt you have a bank account?"

Gabbitas told him where, told him without hesitation.

"And when you came here you immediately transferred your account to the Kingsmarkham branch? Yes. Was this before or after the murder of the police officer? Can you remember that? If it was before or after DS Martin was murdered in that bank branch?"

"It was before."

Wexford fancied Gabbitas sounded uneasy, but he was used to his imagination telling him things like that. "The gun you found just now was almost certainly the weapon used in that murder.'' He watched Gabbitas's face, saw nothing there but a kind of blank receptiveness. ''Of the public who were in the bank that morning, May the thirteenth, not all came forward to make statements to the police. Some left before the police came. One took that gun with him.''

''I know nothing about any of this. I wasn't in the bank that day.''

''But you had already come to Tancred?''

''I came on May the fourth,'' Gabbitas said sullenly.

Wexford paused, then said in a conversational way, ''Do you like Miss Davina Jones, Mr. Gabbitas? Daisy Jones?''

The change of subject caught Gabbitas off guard. He burst out, ''What's that got to do with it?''

''You're young and apparently unattached. She's young too and good-looking. She's very charming. As a result of what has happened she's in possession of a considerable property.''

''She's just someone I work for. All right, she's attractive, any man would find her attractive. But she's just someone I work for, so far as I'm concerned. And may not be working for much longer.''

''You're leaving this job?''

''It's not a matter of leaving the job. I'm not employed here, remember? I did tell you. I'm self-employed. Is there anything else you want to know? I'll tell you one thing. Next time I find a gun I won't tell the police, I'll chuck it in the river.''

''I wouldn't do that if I were you, Mr. Gabbitas,'' Wexford said mildly.

In the *Sunday Times* Review Section was an article by a distinguished literary critic on material he had collected for a biography of Davina Flory. Most of this was correspondence. Wexford glanced at it, then began to read with mounting interest.

Many of the letters had been in the possession of the niece in Menton, now dead. They were from Davina to her sister, the niece's mother, and indicated that Davina's first marriage to Desmond Cathcart Flory had never been consummated. Long passages were quoted, instances of unhappiness and bitter disappointment, all written in Davina's unmistakable style that alternated between the plain and the baroque. The author of the article speculated, basing his argument on evidence in later letters, as to who might have been Naomi Flory's father.

This accounted for something Wexford had wondered about. Though Desmond and Davina had married in 1935, Davina's only child had not been born until ten years later. He called to mind, painfully, that horrible scene at the Cheriton Forest Hotel when Casey had loudly averred that Davina had still been a virgin eight years after her marriage. With a sigh, he finished the piece and turned over to the double-page spread on the newspaper's Literary Banquet held at Grosvenor House on the previous Monday. Wexford looked at it only in the hope of seeing a photograph of Amyas Ireland, who had been at the banquet the previous year and might be again.

The first face he saw, that leaped at him from a page of photographs, was Augustine Casey's. Casey was sitting at a table with four other people. At any rate, there were four other people in the picture. Wexford wondered if he had spat in his wineglass, and then he read the caption. "From left to right: Dan Kavanagh, Penelope Casey, Augustine Casey, Frances Hegarty, Jane Somers."

All were smiling pleasantly except Casey, whose face wore a sardonic smirk. The women were in formal evening gowns.

Wexford looked at the picture and reread the caption, looked at the other pictures on the two pages, returned to the first one. He sensed Dora's silent presence at his left shoulder. She was waiting for him to ask but he hesitated, not knowing how to frame what he wanted to say. The question came carefully.

"Who is the woman in the shiny dress?"

"Penelope Casey."

"Yes, I know. I can see that. What is she to him?"

"She's his wife, Reg. It looks as if he's gone back to his wife or she's come back to him."

"You knew this?"

"No, darling, I didn't know. I didn't know he had a wife

until the day before yesterday. Sheila didn't phone this week, so I phoned her. She sounded very upset, but all she told me was that Gus's wife had come back to their flat and he'd gone back there 'to talk it through.' "

That expression again . . . He put his hand up to his eyes, perhaps to hide the picture from sight. "How unhappy she must be," he said. And then, "Oh, the poor child . . ."

CHAPTER TWENTY-TWO

I can't tell you if this is the same weapon as was used in the bank killing last May,'' the expert witness said to Wexford. "It certainly is the weapon that was used at Tancred House on March eleventh.''

"Then why can't you say if it was the same gun?''

"It probably is. Evidence in favour of that theory is that the chamber accommodates six cartridges—it's a classic 'six-gun'—and one of these was used at the bank killing, while five were used at Tancred House. Very likely the remaining five in the chamber. In a society where hand-guns appear constantly as murder weapons, one would hardly care to hazard that. But I think it's an intelligent guess here.''

"But you still can't be sure it's the same gun?''

"As I've said, I can't be sure.''

"Why not?''

"The barrel's been changed,'' the expert said laconically. "It's not such an amazing task to undertake, you know. The Dan Wesson line of revolvers, for instance, with their variety of barrel lengths, are all capable of being changed at home by any amateur. The Colt Magnum might be more difficult. Whoever embarked on that would have to have the tools. Well, he must have had because this is definitely not the barrel this gun started life with.''

''Would a gunsmith have them?''

''Depends on what kind of gunsmith, I should say. Most specialize in shotguns.''

''And that's what makes the marks on the five cartridges fired at Tancred House different from the one that killed Martin? A change of barrel?''

''Right. That's why I can only say this and that is probable, not that it definitely happened. This is Kingsmarkham, after all, not the Bronx. There aren't going to be unlimited caches of firearms about. It's the numbers really that point to it, the one for that poor fellow who was one of you, and the five for Tancred. And the calibre, of course. And his intent to deceive. How about that? He wasn't changing gun barrels for fun, it wasn't his hobby.''

He was angry. The relief he might have felt that Sheila had been divided from that man, that she would no longer go to Nevada, was subsumed in anger. For Casey she had turned down *Miss Julie*, for Casey she had changed her life and, it seemed to him, her very personality. And Casey had gone back to his wife.

Wexford hadn't spoken to her. Only the answering machine replied when he dialled her number and there were no more cheerful messages, only the clipped name and request for a message to be left. He left a message, asking her to phone. Then, when she didn't, he left another, one that said he was sorry—for her, for what had happened, and for all the things he had said.

He called into the bank on the way to work. It was the branch where Martin had been killed, not his bank, but the nearest to the route Donaldson took and it had its own small car-park at the back. Wexford had his Transcend card that enabled him to draw cash at all banks and all branches in the United Kingdom. The name made him grind his teeth at the misuse of words but it was a useful card.

Sharon Fraser was still there. Ram Gopal had obtained a transfer to another branch. The second cashier this morning was a very young and pretty Eurasian woman. Wexford, who had resolved not to do this, could not keep his eyes from turning to the place where Martin had stood and had died. There should be some mark, some lasting memorial. He half expected to see Martin's blood still there, some vestige of it, while castigating himself for such nonsensical ideas.

Four people were in the queue ahead of him. He thought of Dane Bishop, ill and frightened, perhaps not even of sound mind by that time, shooting Martin from about this spot, running out and throwing down his gun as he went. The frightened people, the screams, those men who had not remained but had quietly slipped away. One of them, standing perhaps where he was standing now, had, according to Sharon Fraser, been holding a bunch of green banknotes in his hand.

Wexford looked round to see the length of the queue behind him and saw Jason Sebright. Sebright was trying to write a cheque where he stood instead of using one of the bank's tables and chained-up ball-point. The woman in front of him turned round and Wexford heard him say, "Do you mind if I rest my cheque-book on your back, madam?"

This aroused uneasy giggles. Sharon Fraser's light came on and Wexford went up to her with his Transcend card. He recognized the look in her eyes. It was apprehensive, unwelcoming, the look of someone who would rather attend to anybody except you because, by your profession and your searching questions, you endanger her privacy and her peace and perhaps her very existence.

When Martin died, people had come into the bank and laid flowers on the spot where he fell, donors as anonymous as whoever had brought these bouquets to hang on the Tancred gates. The latest offerings were dead. Night frosts had blackened them until they looked like a nest made by some untidy bird. Wexford told Pemberton to remove them and throw them on Ken Harrison's rubbish heap. No doubt they would soon be replaced by others. Perhaps because his mind was dwelling abnormally on love and pain and the perils of love that he had begun speculating who the donor of these flowers might be. A fan? A silent—and rich—admirer? Or more than that? The sight of the withered heart of roses made him think of those early letters of Davina's and her loveless years until Desmond Flory went away to war.

As he approached the house, he saw a workman at the west-wing window, replacing the pane of eight-ounce glass. It was a dull still day, the kind of weather the meteorologists had taken to calling "quiet." The mist that hung in the air showed itself only in the distance where the horizon was blurred and the woods turned to a smoky blue.

Wexford looked through the dining-room window. The door to the hall was open. The seals had been taken off and the room opened up. On the ceiling and walls the blood splash marks still showed but the carpet was gone.

"We'll be making a start in there tomorrow, governor," the workman said.

So Daisy was beginning to come to terms with her loss, with the horror of that room. Restoration had begun. He walked across the flagstones, past the front of the house, towards the east wing and the stables behind. Then he saw something he hadn't noticed when he first arrived. Thanny Hogarth's bicycle was leaning up against the wall to the left of the front door. A fast worker, Wexford thought, and he felt better, he felt more cheerful. He even felt like speculating as to what might happen when Nicholas Virson arrived—or was Daisy too good a manager in these matters to let that happen?

"I think Andy Griffin spent those two nights here," Burden said to him as he walked into the stables.

"What?"

"In one of the outbuildings. We searched them, of course, when we did the general search of the house after it happened, but we never went near them again."

"Which outbuilding are you talking about, Mike?"

He followed Burden along the sandy path behind the high hedge. A short row or terrace of cottages, not dilapidated but not well-maintained either, stood parallel to this hedge, the roadway a sandy track. You might be quartered here for a month, as they had been, without ever knowing the cottages were there.

"Karen came out here last night," Burden said. "She was doing her rounds. Daisy said she heard something. There was no one, in fact, about, but Karen came this way and looked through that window."

"She shone a torch, d'you mean?"

"I suppose so. There's no electricity to these cottages, no running water, no amenities at all. According to Brenda Harrison, they've not had anyone living in them for fifty years—well, since before the war. Karen saw something which made her go back this morning."

"What d'you mean, 'saw something'? You're not in court, Mike. This is me, remember?"

Burden made an impatient gesture. "Yes, sure. Sorry. Rags, a blanket, remains of food. We'll go in. It's still there."

The cottage door opened on a latch. The most powerful of a variety of smells that greeted them was the ammoniac one of stale urine. It was a floor of bricks on which a makeshift bed had been contrived from a pile of dirty cushions, two old coats, unidentifiable rags, a good thick and fairly clean blanket. Two empty Coke cans stood in the grate in front of the fireplace. An iron fire basket contained grey ash and on top of the ash, thrown there perhaps after the cinders had cooled, was a wad of greasy screwed-up paper that had wrapped fish and chips. The smell of this was marginally more unpleasant than that of the urine.

"You think Andy slept here?"

"We can try the Coke cans for prints," Burden said. "He could have been here. He would have known about it. And if he was here on those two nights, March the seventeenth and the eighteenth, no one else was."

"Okay. How did he get here?"

Burden beckoned him through the unsavoury room. He had to duck his head, the lintels were so low. Beyond the hole of a scullery and the back door, bolted top and bottom but not locked, was a wired-in plot of overgrown garden and a small walled area that might have been a coal-hole or a pigsty. Inside, half-covered by a waterproof sheet, was a motor bike.

"No one would have heard him come," Wexford said. "The Harrisons and Gabbitas were too far away. Daisy hadn't come back home. She didn't come until several days later. He had the place to himself. But, Mike, why did he *want* the place to himself?"

They strolled along the path that bordered the wood. In the distance, to the south of the by-road, the whine of Gabbitas's chain-saw could be heard. Wexford's thoughts reverted to the gun, to the extraordinary thing that had been done to the gun. Would Gabbitas have had the means and the knowledge to change the barrel on a revolver? Would he have the tools? On the other hand, would anyone else?

"Why would Andy Griffin want to sleep up here, Mike?" he said.

"I don't know. I'm starting to wonder if this place had some sort of particular fascination for him."

"He wasn't our second man, was he? He wasn't the one Daisy heard but didn't see?"

"I don't see him in that role. That would have been too big for him. Beyond his class. Blackmail was his line, small petty blackmail."

Wexford nodded. "That's why he was killed. I think he started in a small way and it was all for cash. We know that from his Post Office savings account. He may have operated from here quite a bit while he and his parents still lived here. I don't suppose he began on Brenda Harrison. He may well have tried it successfully on other women. All he had to do was pick an older woman and threaten to tell her husband or her friends or some relative that she'd made advances to him. Sometimes it would work and sometimes it wouldn't."

"Do you think he tried something on the women here? Davina herself, say, or Naomi? I can still hear the venom in his voice when he talked to me about them. The choice language he used."

"Would he dare? Perhaps. It's something we're never likely to know. Who was he blackmailing when he left home that Sunday and camped here? The gunman or the one Daisy didn't see?"

"Maybe."

"And why did he have to be here to do that?"

"This sounds more like one of your theories than mine, Reg. But as I've said, I think he was fascinated by this place. It was his *home*. He may have bitterly resented being turned away from it last year. We may well discover that he spent far more time up here and in the woods and just spying out the land than anyone's dreamt of. All those times he was away from home and no one knew where, I reckon he was up here. Who knew this place and these woods? He did. Who could have driven through them and not got bogged down or hit a tree? He could."

"But we've said we don't see him as our second man," said Wexford.

"Okay, forget his ability to drive through the wood, forget any involvement in the murders. Suppose he was camping in here on March the eleventh? Let's say he intended to stay here for a couple of nights for purposes we as yet know nothing of. He left home on the motor bike at six and brought his stuff up here. He was in the cottage when the two men arrived at eight—or maybe he wasn't in the cottage but outside, prowling about or whatever he did. He saw the gunman and one of them he recognized. How about that?"

"Not bad," said Wexford. "Who would he recognize? Gabbitas, certainly. Even under a woodsman's mask. Would he recognize Gunner Jones?"

The bicycle was still there. The workman was still there, putting the finishing touches to his mended window. A thin persistent drizzle began to fall, the first rain for a long time. The water washed down the stables windows and made it dark inside. Gerry Hinde had an angled lamp on above the computer on which he was building a new data base: every subject or suspect they had interviewed with his or her alibis and corroborative witnesses.

Wexford had begun to wonder if there was any point in their remaining so close to the scene of the murders. It would be four weeks tomorrow since what the newspapers called "the Tancred Massacre," and the Deputy Chief Constable had made an appointment for an interview with him. Wexford was to go to his house. It would seem like a social engagement, a glass of sherry featuring somewhere in the proceedings, but the purpose of it all was, he was sure, to complain to him about the lack of progress made and the cost of it all. The suggestion would be made, or more likely the order given, that they move back to Kingsmarkham, to the police station. He would again be asked how he could continue to justify the night guard on Daisy. But how could he justify to himself the removal of that guard?

He phoned home to ask Dora if there had been any sign from Sheila, got a worried negative and walked outside into the rain. The place had a dismal look in wet weather. It was curious how the rain and the greyness changed the appearance of Tancred House, so that it seemed like a building in one of those rather sinister Victorian engravings, austere, even dour, its windows dull eyes and its walls discoloured with water stains.

The woods had lost their blueness and grown pebble-grey under a scummy sky. Bib Mew came out from round the back, wheeling her bicycle. She dressed like a man, walked like a man, you would unhesitatingly put her down as male from here or nearer. Passing Wexford, she pretended not to see him, twisting her head round awkwardly and looking skywards, studying the phenomenon of rain.

He reminded himself of her handicap. Yet she lived alone. What must her life be? What had it been? She had been married once. He found that grotesque. She mounted her bike in man's fashion, swinging one leg over, pushed hard on the pedals, swung off along the main drive. It was apparent that she was still avoiding the by-road and the proximity of the hanging tree and this brought him a little inner shiver.

Next morning the builders arrived. Their van was on the flagstones by the fountain before Wexford got there. Not that they called themselves builders, but "Interior Creators of Brighton." He went carefully through his case notes, filling by now a large file. Gerry Hinde had them all on a small disc, smaller than the old single record, but useless to Wexford. He saw the case slipping through his fingers now that so much time had elapsed.

Those irreconcilables remained. Where was Joanne Garland? Was she alive or dead? What connection was hers with the murders? How did the gunmen get away from Tancred? Who put the gun in Gabbitas's house? Or was this some ploy of Gabbitas's own?

Wexford read Daisy's statement again. He played over Daisy's statement on tape. He knew he would have to talk to her again, for here the irreconcilables were most obvious. She must try to explain to him how it was possible for Harvey Copeland to have climbed those stairs, yet be shot as if he were still at the foot of them and facing the front door; account for the long time—a long time measured in seconds—between his leaving the dining-room and being shot.

Could she also account for something he knew Freeborn would laugh to scorn if he heard the matter raised? If the cat Queenie normally, indeed, it seemed invariably, galloped about the upper floors at six in the evening, *always* at six, why had Davina Flory thought the noise upstairs was Queenie when she heard it at eight? And why had the gunman been frightened off by sounds from upstairs, which were, in fact made by nothing more threatening than the cat?

There was another question he had to ask, though he was almost sure time would have blotted out her accurate memory of this, just as trauma had begun to do so immediately after the event.

The car on the flagstones, as far away from "Interior Creators of Brighton'' as could possibly be managed without parking on the lawn, was one he thought he recognized as Joyce Virson's. He was probably right in thinking Daisy would welcome a respite from Mrs. Virson, perhaps an excuse for getting rid of her altogether. He rang the bell and Brenda came.

A sheet had been hung up over the dining-room door. From behind came muffled sounds, not bangs, not scraping noises, but soft liquid floppings and sluicings. Accompanying these was the builders' invariable *sine qua non*, but turned low, the mindless dribble of pop music. You couldn't hear it in the morning-room nor in the *serre* where they were sitting, not two but three people: Daisy, Joyce Virson and her son.

Nicholas Virson took time off whenever he felt like it, Wexford thought, saying an austere good morning. Whatever he did, was business so bad in this recession time that it mattered very little whether he went in or not?

They had been talking when Brenda brought him in and he fancied their talk had been heated. Daisy was looking determined, a little flushed. Mrs. Virson's expression was more than usually peevish and Nicholas seemed put out, balked in some endeavour. Were they here for lunch? Wexford hadn't previously noticed that it was past noon.

Daisy got up when he came in, hugging close to her the cat, which had been lying in her lap. Its fur was almost the same shade as the blue denim she wore, a bomber jacket, tight jeans. The jacket was embroidered and between the coloured stitching were a multiplicity of gilt and silver studs. A black-and-blue-checked T-shirt was under the jacket and the belt in the jeans' waistband was of metal, woven silver and gold with bosses of pearly and clear glass. Inescapable was the feeling that this was a statement she was making. These people were to be shown the real Daisy, what she wanted to be, a free spirit, even an outrageous spirit, dressing as she pleased and doing as she liked.

The contrast between what she wore and Joyce Virson's clothes—even allowing for the great age difference—was so marked as to be ludicrous. It was a mother-in-law's uniform, burgundy wool dress with matching jacket, round her neck a silver rhomboid on a thong, trendy in the sixties, her only rings her large diamond engagement ring and her wedding band. Daisy had an enormous ring on her left hand, a two-inch-long turtle in silver, its shell studded with coloured stones, which looked as if it were creeping down her hand from first finger joint to knuckle.

Having an objection to the word "intrude," Wexford apologized for disturbing them. He had no intention of leaving and agreeing to come back later, and he indicated that he was sure Daisy wouldn't expect this. It was Mrs. Virson who answered for her.

"Now you're here, Mr. Wexford, perhaps you'll come in on our side. I know how you feel about Daisy being here alone. Well, she's not alone, you put girls in here to protect her, though what they could do in an emergency . . . I'm sorry but I really can't imagine. And frankly, as a ratepayer, I rather resent our money being spent on that sort of thing."

Nicholas said unexpectedly, "We don't pay rates any more, Mother, we pay Poll Tax."

"It's all the same thing. It all goes the same way. We came here this morning to ask Daisy to come back and stay with us. Oh, it's not the first time, as you know as well as I do. But we thought it worth another try, particularly as circumstances have changed as regards—well, Nicholas and Daisy."

Wexford watched a terrible blush suffuse Nicholas Virson's face. It wasn't a blush of pleasure or gratification but, to judge by the wince that accompanied it, of intense embarrassment. He was nearly sure circumstances hadn't changed except in Joyce Virson's mind.

"It's obviously absurd for her to be here." Mrs. Virson reflected and her remaining words came out in a rush. "As if she was *grown up*. As if she was able to make her own decisions."

"Well, I am," Daisy said calmly. "I am grown up. I *do* make decisions." She seemed quite untroubled by all this. She looked faintly bored.

Nicholas made an effort. His face was still pink. Wexford suddenly remembered the description of the masked gunman Daisy had given him, the fair hair, the cleft chin, the big ears. It was almost as if it was this man she had been thinking of when she described him. And why would she do that? Why would she do it even unconsciously?

"We thought," Nicholas said, "that Daisy might come over to dinner with us and . . . and stay the night and sort of see how she felt. We were planning to give her her own sitting-room, a sort of suite, you know. She wouldn't actually have to live with us, if you see what I mean. She could be absolutely her own woman, if that's what she wants."

Daisy laughed. Whether it was at the whole idea or Nicholas's use of the fashionable absurdity Wexford couldn't tell. He had thought her eyes troubled and the disturbance, the anxiety in them remained, but she laughed and her laughter was full of merriment.

"I've already told you, I'm going out to dinner tonight. I don't expect to be back until quite late and my friend will certainly bring me home."

"Oh, Daisy . . ." The man couldn't help himself. His misery broke through the pompous manner. "Oh, Daisy, you might at least tell me who you're going to dinner with. Is it someone we know? If it's a friend, can't you bring her with you to us?"

Daisy said, "Davina used to say that if a woman talks about her friend, or her cousin even, or 'someone' she works with or 'someone' she knows, people will always assume it's another woman. Always. She said it's because deep down they don't really want women to have relationships with the opposite sex."

"I haven't the faintest idea what you're talking about," Nicholas said and Wexford could see he hadn't. He really hadn't.

"Well, I'm sorry," said Joyce Virson, "but all this is beyond me. I should have thought a girl who had an understanding with a young man would want to spend time with him."

Her temper was going and with it her self-control. It was always a tremulously balanced function. "The truth is that when freedom and a lot of money come to people too soon, it goes to their heads. It's power, you see, they become power-mad. It's the greatest pleasure in life some women have, exercising power over some poor man whose only crime is he happens to be fond of them. I'm sorry, but I hate that sort of thing." She grew wilder, her voice tipping over the edge of control. "If that's women's lib or whatever they call it, women's something, horrible nonsense, you can keep it and much good may it do you. It won't find you a good husband, that I do know."

"Mother," said Nicholas, with a flash of strength. He spoke to Daisy, "We're on our way to lunch with . . ." he named some local friends ". . . and we hoped you'd come too. We do have to go very soon."

"I can't come, can I? Mr. Wexford's here to talk to me. It's important. I have to help the police. You haven't forgotten what happened here four weeks ago, have you? Or have you?"

"Of course I haven't. How could I? Mother didn't mean all that, Daisy." Joyce Virson had turned her head away and was holding a handkerchief up to her face while apparently staring with great concentration at the newly opened tulips in the terrace tubs. "She'd set her heart on your coming and so . . . well, so had I. We really thought we could win you over. May we come back later, on our way home from this lunch? Can we just drop in again and try to explain to you just what we had in mind?"

"Of course. Friends can call on each other when they want, can't they? You're my friend, Nicholas, surely you know that?"

"Thank you, Daisy."

"I hope you'll always be my friend."

They might not have been there, Wexford and Joyce Virson. For a moment the two were alone, enclosed in whatever their relationship was, had been, whatever secrets of emotion or events they shared. Nicholas got up and Daisy gave him a kiss on the cheek. Then she did a curious thing. She strode to the door of the *serre* and flung it open. Bib was revealed on the other side of it, taking a step backwards, clutching a duster.

Daisy said nothing. She closed the door and turned to Wexford. "She's always listening outside doors. It's a passion with her, a sort of addiction. I always know she's there, I can hear her start breathing very fast. Strange, isn't it? What can she get out of it?"

She returned to the theme of Bib and eavesdropping as soon as the Virsons had gone. "I can't sack her. How would I manage with no one?" She sounded suddenly like someone twice her age, an embattled housewife. "Brenda's told me they're going. I said I only sacked them in a rage, I didn't mean it, but they're going just the same. You know his brother runs that hire-car business? Ken's going in with him, they plan to expand and they can have the other flat over Fred's office. John Gabbitas has been trying to buy a house in Sewingbury since last August and he's just heard his mortgage has come through. He'll still look after the woods, I suppose, but he won't live here." She gave a kind of dry giggle. "I'll be left alone with Bib. D'you think she'll murder me?"

"You've no reason to think . . . ?" he began seriously.

"None at all. She just looks like a bloke and never speaks and listens at doors. She's feeble-minded too. As a murderer she makes a really good cleaner. Sorry, that wasn't funny. Oh God, I sound like that awful Joyce! You don't think I ought to go there, do you? She persecutes me."

"You wouldn't do what I thought anyway, would you?" She shook her head. "Then I shan't waste my breath. There are one or two things, as you rightly guessed, I'd like to talk to you about."

"Yes, of course. But there's something I have to tell you first. I was going to before, but they kept on and on." She smiled rather ruefully. "Joanne Garland phoned."

"What?"

"Don't look so amazed. She didn't *know*. She didn't know any of it had happened. She came back last night and went down to the gallery this morning and saw it all shut up, so she phoned me."

He realized Daisy might not be aware of their fears for Joanne Garland, might not know anything beyond the fact that she had gone away somewhere. Why should she?

''She thought she was phoning Mum. Wasn't that awful? I had to tell her. That was the worst part, telling her what had happened. She didn't believe me, not at first. She thought it was some ghastly joke. This was only—well, half an hour ago. It was just before the Virsons came.''

CHAPTER TWENTY-THREE

She was in tears.

It was because she was crying on the phone, incoherent with tears and gasps, that he had relented and, instead of asking her to come to the police station, had said he would go to her. In the house in Broom Vale he sat in one armchair and Barry Vine in another while Joanne Garland, incapacitated by the first question he had asked her, sobbed into the sofa arm.

The first thing Wexford noticed when she admitted them to the house was that her face was bruised. They were old marks, fast healing now, but the vestiges were there, greenish, yellow-ish, bruises around the mouth and nose, darker abrasions, plum-coloured at the eyes and the hair-line. Her tears couldn't disguise them, nor were they the aftermath of tears.

Where had she been? Wexford asked her that before they sat down and the question drew more tears. She gasped out, "America, California," and threw herself down on the sofa in floods of weeping.

"Mrs. Garland," he said after a while, "try to get a grip on yourself. I'll get you a drink of water."

She sat bolt upright, her bruised face streaming. "I don't want *water*." She said to Vine, "You could get me a whisky. In that cupboard. Glasses in there. Have yourselves one." A heavy choking sob cut the end of the last word. From a large red leather handbag on the floor she pulled a handful of coloured tissues and rubbed at her face. "I'm sorry. I *will* stop. When I've had a drink. My God, the shock."

Barry showed her the soda bottle he had found. She shook her head fiercely and took a swig of the neat whisky. She seemed to have forgotten all about the offer she had made them, which in any case would have been refused. The whisky was evidently welcome. The effect it had on her was quite different from that on someone who seldom drinks spirits. It was not so much as if she had been in need of a drink—that is, an alcoholic drink—as thirsty. Some special kind of thirst seemed quenched by what she drank and relief spread through her.

The tissues came out again and once more she wiped her face, but carefully this time. Wexford thought she looked remarkably young for fifty-four, or if not exactly young, remarkably smooth-faced. She might have been a tired and rather battered thirty-five. Her hands, though, were those of a much older woman, webs of stringy tendons, wormed with veins. She wore a jersey suit of goose-turd green and a great deal of gold costume jewellery. Her hair was a bright pale-gold, her figure shapely if not quite slim, her legs excellent. In anyone's eyes she was an attractive woman.

Breathing deeply now, sipping the whisky, she took a powder compact and lipstick out of the bag and restored her face. Wexford could see her gaze arrested by the worst of the bruises, one under her left eye. She touched it with a fingertip before applying powder in an attempt at concealment.

"We have a lot of things we'd like to ask you, Mrs. Garland."

"Yes. I suppose." She hesitated. "I didn't know, you know, I didn't have a clue. They don't have foreign news—well, it's foreign to them—in American papers. Not unless it's a war or something. There wasn't anything about this. The first

I knew was when I phoned that girl, Naomi's girl.'' Her lip trembled when she spoke the name. She swallowed. ''Poor thing, I suppose I should be sorry for *her*, I should have told her I was sorry, but it threw me, it just flattened me. I could hardly speak.''

Vine said, 'You told no one you were going away. You didn't say a word to your mother or your sisters.''

''Naomi knew.''

''Maybe.'' Wexford didn't say what he felt, that they would never know the truth of that, since Naomi was dead. The last thing he wanted was a fresh gush of tears. ''Would you mind telling us where you went and why?''

She said, like children do, ''Do I have to?''

''Yes, I'm afraid you do. Eventually. Perhaps you'd like to think about your answer. I have to tell you, Mrs. Garland, that your vanishing into thin air like this has caused us considerable trouble.''

''Could you get me some more Scotch, please.'' She held the empty glass up to Vine. ''Yes, all right, you needn't look like that, I do like a drink but I'm not an alcoholic. I specially like a drink in times of stress. Is there anything wrong with that?''

''I'm not in the business of answering your inquiries, Mrs. Garland,'' Wexford said. ''I'm here so that you can answer mine. I'm doing you the courtesy of coming here. And I want you capable of answering. Is that clear?'' He half-shook his head at Vine, who was standing with the glass in his hand and a what-did-your-last-servant-die-of expression on his face. Joanne Garland looked shocked and truculent. ''Very well. This is a very serious matter. I'd like you to tell me when you got home and what you did.''

She said sulkily, ''It was last evening. Well, the plane from Los Angeles gets to Gatwick at half two, only it was late. We weren't through Customs till four. I meant to get the train but I was too tired, I was clapped out, so I had a car all the way. I was here about five.'' She looked hard at him. ''I had a drink . . . well, two or three. I needed them, I can tell you. I went to sleep. I slept the clock round.''

"And this morning you went down to the shop, found it closed up and looking as if it had been closed up for a long while."

"That's right. I was mad with Naomi—God forgive me. Oh, I know I could have asked someone, I could have phoned one of my sisters. It never crossed my mind. I just thought, Naomi's screwed it up again—well, like I said, God forgive me. I hadn't got the shop keys, I thought it'd be open, so I shlepped home and phoned Daisy. Well, I reckoned I was phoning Naomi to tear her off a strip. Daisy told me. That poor kid, it must have been hell having to tell me, sort of relive it all over again."

"The evening you went away, March the eleventh, you went to see your mother in the Caenbrook Retirement Home between five and five-thirty. Would you tell us what you did after that?"

She sighed, cast a glance at the empty glass Vine had placed on the table and passed her tongue across her freshly painted lips. "I finished my packing. It was the next day I was flying on, the twelfth. The flight didn't leave till eleven AM and I was to check in at nine thirty but still I thought, well, I'll go tonight. The trains haven't been very reliable lately, I thought, what if the trains are delayed in the morning? It was just a decision I made on the hop really. When I was packing. I thought, I'll ring up a hotel at Gatwick and see if they'll take me and I did and they could. I'd promised to go up and see Naomi, though we'd actually made all the arrangements during the day. And we weren't going to do the books, Naomi said she'd keep the VAT up to date. But I'd said I'd go just to show willing, you know . . ." Joanne Garland's voice faltered. "Well, all that. I thought, I'll go to Tancred, have half an hour with Naomi, and then drive home and get myself to the station. It's five minutes' walk to the station from here."

This fact was well known to Wexford and he made no comment on it. It was Vine who persisted. "I don't see why you had to go that night. Not if the plane didn't leave till eleven. Say you had to check in by nine thirty. It can't be half an hour in the train, if that."

She gave him a sidelong aggrieved look. It was evident Joanne Garland had taken against his sergeant. "If you must know, I didn't want to run the risk of seeing anyone in the morning." Vine's expression remained unenlightened. "Okay, don't bend over backwards to understand, will you? I didn't want people seeing me with cases, I didn't want questions, my sisters just happening to phone up—right?"

"We'll leave the magical mystery tour for the time being, Mrs. Garland," said Wexford. "What time did you go to Tancred House?"

"Ten to eight," she said quickly. "I always know the times of things. I'm very time-conscious. And I'm never late. Naomi was always trying to get me to go up there later but that was only her mother flapping. She'd leave these messages on my answering machine but I was used to that, I never played the messages back on a Tuesday. I mean, why shouldn't I be considered as much as Lady Davina? Oh, God, she's dead, I shouldn't say it. Well, like I said, I left at ten to eight and got up there at ten past. Eleven minutes past, in fact. I looked at my watch while I was ringing the doorbell."

"You rang the bell?"

"Over and over. I knew they heard. I knew they were there. God, I mean, I *thought* I knew." The colour drained from her face and left it paper-white. "They were dead, weren't they? It had just happened. My God." Wexford watched her as she briefly closed her eyes, swallowed. He gave her time. She said in a changed, thicker voice, "The lights were on in the dining-room. Oh, God forgive me, I thought, Naomi's told Davina we've done all that needs to be done and Davina's said, 'In that case it's time that woman learned not to come disturbing me while I'm having my dinner.' She was like that, she would say that." Again came a vivid recollection of what had happened to Davina Flory. Joanne Garland put her hand up to her mouth.

To frustrate any further calls for God's forgiveness, Wexford said quickly, "You rang again?"

"I rang three or four times altogether. I went round to the

dining-room window but I couldn't see in. The curtains were drawn. Look, I was a bit cross. It sounds terrible to say that now. I thought, okay, I won't hang about and I didn't, I drove home.''

"Just like that? You drove all the way up there and then, when they didn't answer the bell, you drove home again?"

Barry Vine received a very peevish look. "What did you expect me to do? Break the door down?"

"Mrs. Garland, please think very carefully. Did you pass any vehicle or meet any vehicle on your way to Tancred?"

"No, definitely not."

"Which way did you come?"

"Which way? By the main gate, of course. That's the way I always went. I mean, I know there's another way, but I've never used it. It's a very narrow lane, that other way."

"And you saw no other vehicle?"

"No, I've said. I hardly ever did, anyway. Well, I think I met John what's-his-name once, Gabbitas. But that was months ago. I definitely met no one on March the eleventh."

"And going back?"

She shook her head. "I didn't meet or pass another vehicle when I was coming or going."

"While you were at Tancred, was there another car or van or vehicle of some kind parked in front of the house?"

"No, of course there wasn't. They always put their cars away. Oh, I see what you mean, oh, God . . ."

"You didn't go round to the side of the house?"

"You mean, round the bit past the dining-room? No, no, I didn't."

"You heard nothing?"

"I don't know what you mean. What would there be to hear? Oh—oh, yes. *Shots.* My God, no."

"By the time you left, it would have been—what? A quarter past?"

She said in a low subdued voice, "I told you, I always know the time. It was sixteen minutes past eight."

"If it helps, you can have another drink now, Mrs. Garland."

If she was expecting Barry to wait on her she waited in vain. She gave a contrived sigh, got up and went to the drinks cupboard. "Sure you won't have one?"

It was clear only Wexford was being asked. He shook his head. "How did you get those bruises on your face?" he said.

The drink cradled in her lap, she sat upright on the sofa with her knees pressed together. Wexford tried to read her face. Was it coyness he saw there? Or embarrassment? Not, at any rate, the memory of some kind of abuse.

"They've almost gone," she said at last. "You can hardly see them any more. I wasn't coming home until I was sure they'd faded."

"I can see them," Wexford said bluntly. "No doubt I'm wrong, but it looks to me as if someone punched you in the face pretty savagely about three weeks ago."

"You've got the date right," she said.

"You're going to tell us, Mrs. Garland. There are a lot more things you're going to tell us, but we'll start with what happened to your face."

It came out in a rush. "I've had cosmetic surgery. In California. I stayed with a friend. It's usual there, everyone has it— well, not everyone. My friend had and she said to come and stay with her and go into this clinic . . ."

Wexford interrupted with the only term familiar to him. "You mean you've had your face lifted?"

"That," she said sulkily, "and my eyelids tucked back and a peel on my upper lip, all that stuff. Look, I couldn't have it done here. Everybody would have known. I wanted to get away, I wanted to go somewhere warm and I didn't—well, if you must know, I didn't like the look of my face any more. I used to like what I saw in the mirror and suddenly I didn't— right?"

Things began falling into place very rapidly. He wondered if the time would come when Sheila would want something like this done and feared she would. Could you, anyway, make a mockery of Joanne Garland or disapprove or sneer? She could afford it and it had no doubt achieved what she aimed at. He could understand how she might not want that aggressive gossipy family to know or her neighbours to notice, but present them all with a *fait accompli* to which they might react by attributing her new appearance to good health or the rarely precedented kindness of time. Vague, out-of-this-world Naomi might be allowed to know. Someone had to be in her confidence, to hold the fort and run the shop. Who better than Naomi, who knew the business inside out and whose reaction to a face-lift might be no more than another woman's to a hair tinting or a shortened hemline?

"I don't suppose you've talked to my mother," said Joanne Garland. "Well, why would you? But if you had, you'd know why I wouldn't want her getting hold of something like this."

Wexford said nothing.

"Are you going to let me off the hook now?"

He nodded. "For the time being. Sergeant Vine and I are going to get our lunch. You'll probably want to have a rest, Mrs. Garland. I'd like to see you later. We have an incident room up at Tancred House. I'll see you there at—shall we say four thirty?"

"*Today?*"

"Today at four thirty, please. And if I were you I'd give Fred Harrison a call. You won't want to be driving over the permitted limit."

More flowers on the gatepost. Crimson tulips this time, about forty of them, Wexford estimated, their stems concealed by the heads of those below, the whole mass of them laid on a pillow of green branches to form a lozenge shape. Barry Vine read the words on the card to him.

" 'Hereat the hardest stones were seen to bleed.' "

"Curiouser and curiouser," said Wexford. "Barry, when I've done with Mrs. G., I want you and me to conduct an experiment."

As they proceeded through the woods, he phoned home and spoke to Dora. He might be late. "Oh, no, Reg, not tonight, you mustn't, it's Sylvia's house-warming." Had he forgotten? He had. What time were they due there? Eight thirty at the latest.

"If I can't make it before, I'll be home by eight."

"I'll go out and buy her something. Champagne, unless you've got something more interesting in mind."

"Only a pillow of forty red tulips, but I'm sure she'd prefer champagne. I don't suppose Sheila rang?"

"I would have told you."

The woods were sheened with green, coming alive with spring. In the long green alleys between the trees, white and yellow flowers starred the grass. There an oniony scent from the wild garlic with its stiff jade-coloured leaves and lilylike blossoms. A jay, pink and speckled blue, flew low under the oak branches, uttering its screeching cry. The rain that pattered down filled the woods with a soft rustling susurration.

They emerged into the open parkland, passed through the space in the low wall. A sudden increase in rain power came as a violent cloudburst, water pounding on the stones, streaming down the windscreen and the sides of the car. Through the shivering glassy greyness, Wexford saw Joyce Virson's car back again outside the front door. A sudden premonition, which came to him of something momentous in the offing, he dismissed as absurd. They meant nothing, those feelings.

He went into the stables, thinking of the sender of flowers, of John Gabbitas, who had never mentioned his plans to buy a house, of the defection of the Harrisons, of that strange half-witted woman who listened outside doors. Were any of these anomalies of significance in the case?

When Joanne Garland arrived he took her into the corner where Daisy's two armchairs had been stowed. Since their earlier meeting she had applied pancake make-up and powder to her face. His knowledge of the reason for her trip had made her self-conscious. She looked at him anxiously, sat in one of the chairs, holding her hand up to her cheek in a way designed to hide the worst purple mark.

"George Jones," he said. "Gunner Jones. You know him?"

He must be getting naïve. What had he expected? A deep blush? Another collapse into tears? She gave him the sort of look he might have given her had she asked him if he knew Dr. Perkins.

"I haven't seen him for years," she said. "I used to know him. We were pals, him and Naomi and me and Brian—that's my second husband. Like I say, I haven't seen him since him and Naomi split up. I've written to him a couple of times—is that what you're getting at?"

"You wrote to him suggesting he and Naomi Jones got together again?"

"Is that what he told you?"

"Isn't it true?"

She paused for thought. A scarlet nail scratched at her hairline. Perhaps the invisible mending itched. "It is and it isn't. The first time I wrote, that's what it was about. Naomi's been a bit . . . well, wistful, sort of moping. Once or twice she said to me how maybe she should have tried harder with Gunner. Anything was better than loneliness. So I wrote. He never answered. Charming, I thought. Still, by then I could see it wasn't all that good an idea. I'd been a bit premature. Poor Naomi, she wasn't made for marriage. Well, that applies to relationships in general. I don't mean she liked women. She was best on her own, pottering about with her bits and pieces, her paints and all that."

"But you wrote to him again, at the end of last summer."

"Yes, but not about that."

"About what then, Mrs. Garland?"

How many times had he heard the words she was about to utter? He could forecast them, the precise form of the rebuttal. "It's got nothing to do with this business."

He responded as he always did. "I'll be the judge of that."

She became suddenly angry. "I don't want to say. It's embarrassing. Can't you understand? They're dead, it doesn't matter. In any case, there wasn't any—what d'you call it?—abuse, violence. I mean, that's laughable, those two old people. Oh, God, this is so *stupid*. I'm *tired* and it's got nothing to do with any of this."

"I'd like you to tell me what was in the letter, Mrs. Garland."

"I want to see Daisy," she said. "I must go to the house

and see Daisy and tell her I'm sorry. For God's sake, I was her mother's best friend.''

"Wasn't she yours?''

"Don't twist my words all the time. You know what I mean.''

He knew what she meant. "I've got plenty of time, Mrs. Garland.'' He hadn't, he had Sylvia's party that he had to go to. Let the heavens fall, he had to go to that party. "We're going to stay here in these two quite comfortable armchairs until you decide to tell me.''

By now, anyway, apart from its relevance to the case, he was dying to know. She hadn't just awakened his curiosity with her prevarications; she had pulled it out of sleep and set its nerves on stalks.

"I gather it's not personal,'' he said. "It's not something about you. You need not be embarrassed.''

"Okay, I'll fess up. But you'll see what I mean when I tell you. Gunner never answered that letter either, by the way. Fine father he is. Well, I should have known that, never taking a scrap of interest in the poor kid from the time he scarpered.''

"This was about Daisy?'' Wexford asked, inspired.

"Yes. Yes, it was.''

"Naomi told me,'' Joanne Garland said. "I mean, you have to have known Naomi to realize what she was like. Naïve's not exactly the word, though she was that too. Sort of not like other people, vague, not having a clue about what goes on. I don't suppose I'm making myself clear. She didn't act like other people, so I don't reckon she really knew how other people did act. Not when they were doing things that were . . . well, wrong or not on or downright disgusting. And she didn't know when they were doing something—well, successful or clever or special either. Am I making any sense?''

"Yes, I think so.''

"She started talking about this business when we were in the shop one day. I mean, talking about like she might have said Daisy'd got a new boy friend or she was going on some school trip abroad. That's how she came out with it. She said—

I'm trying to think of her actual words—yes, she said, 'Davina thinks it would be nice if Harvey made love to Daisy. To sort of start her off. Initiate her.' That was the word. 'Because Harvey's a wonderful lover. And she doesn't want Daisy to go through what happened to her.' You see what I mean by embarrassing.''

Wexford wasn't shocked but he could see that it was shocking. "What was your reply?"

"Wait. I'm not done. Naomi said the fact was Davina was too old now for . . . well, I don't have to spell it out, do I? Sort of physically, if I make myself clear. And it worried her for Harvey because he—this is what Davina said—was young still and a vigorous man. Yuck, I thought, yuck, yuck. Davina really thought, apparently, that it would be great for both of them and she and Harvey had actually put it to the girl. Well, she told the girl and that same day horrible old Harvey made a sort of pass.''

"What did Daisy do?"

"Told him to get lost, I imagine. That's what Naomi said. I mean, Naomi wasn't indignant or anything. She just said Davina was sex-mad, always had been, but she ought to understand not everybody felt like she did. But Naomi wasn't the way I'd have been—well, I imagine I'd have been—if it was my kid, if I'd had a kid. She just said it like she was talking about some difference of opinion we might have had, like whether we were going to show clothes in the gallery or not, she just said it was up to Daisy. I got mad. I said a lot of things about Daisy being in moral danger, all that, but it wasn't any use. Then I got to see Daisy. I met her when she was coming out of school, said my car had broken down and would she give me a lift home.''

"You discussed this with her?"

"She laughed but you could tell she was—well, disgusted. She'd never liked Harvey much and I got the impression she was disillusioned about her grandma. She kept saying she wouldn't have expected that of Davina. She didn't a bit mind me knowing, she was very sweet, she's a very sweet girl. And that sort of made it worse.

"They were all going off on holiday. It really worried me, I didn't know what else I could do. I kept having this picture of old Harvey . . . well, raping her. It was silly, I know, because I don't suppose he could have, and anyway, whatever they were, they weren't that sort."

Wexford had no clear idea what sort she meant but he wouldn't interrupt. All Joanne Garland's initial shame and reticence had gone as she warmed enthusiastically to her tale.

"They were nearly due back when I ran into that chap Nicholas—Virson, is he called?—I knew he was a sort of boy friend of Daisy's, the nearest she had to a boy friend, and I thought of telling him. It was on the tip of my tongue but he's such a pompous ass I could just picture him going scarlet and sort of blustering out of it. So I didn't. I told Gunner. I wrote him a letter.

"After all, he *is* her father. I thought even bloody Gunner would rise to this. But I was wrong, wasn't I? Couldn't have cared less. I just had to rely on Daisy—well, on her good sense. And it wasn't as if she was a child, not really, she was seventeen. But that Gunner—what kind of a fine bloody father is that?"

Seven gunsmiths in the Yellow Pages for Kingsmarkham, five for Stowerton, three in Pomfret alone, a further twelve in the surrounding countryside.

"It's a wonder we've any wildlife left," said Karen Malahyde. "What exactly are we looking for?"

"Someone who had Ken Harrison working for him on a part-time basis and who taught him how to change a gun barrel and lent him the tools."

"You're joking, aren't you, sir?"

"I'm afraid so," said Burden.

CHAPTER TWENTY-FOUR

Fred Harrison in his taxi passed him as he drove to the main gates. On his way to fetch Joanne Garland, paying her visit of condolence to Daisy, he thought as he returned the man's salute. Condolence? Yes—why not? It was amazing what abuses love survived. You had only to look at battered wives, maltreated children. She had probably kept the old admiring awe of her grandmother, tempered as it was by a real affection, and as for Harvey, she had plainly never cared for him. As to her mother, such people as Naomi Jones, eccentric in their unworldliness, their soft, contented passivity, were often very lovable.

What Wexford knew about and Joanne Garland probably did not were what the letters cited in the *Sunday Times* review revealed. The unconsummated first marriage to Desmond Flory. Those years of living "like brother and sister," as the euphemism of the time had it, the impossibility in those days and that environment of seeking help. The best years of her sexual life, in anyone's estimation, from twenty-three to thirty-three, wasted, lost, perhaps never to be compensated for adequately later on. And towards the end of the war, in whose last days Desmond Flory was to be killed, the meeting with a lover took place, the man who was to be Naomi's father.

The unused energy of those years she had put into the planting of these woods. It was interesting to speculate as to whether the woods would be here now if Flory had not been incapable with his wife. Wexford wondered if Davina Flory's oversexedness wasn't perhaps due to ten years of frustration, if they had always been there in her past, those years, standing empty. She knew that whatever happened in the future, they could never be filled, the gap never closed.

From something like that she had wanted to save Daisy. That was the charitable view. Wexford could think of so many other disastrous consequences of a liaison between Daisy and her grandmother's husband that the charitable view came to look like what it was, an empty excuse. She should have known better, he told himself. Good taste and common decency should have taught her better, these and something she claimed to be so keen on, *civilized* behaviour.

Who had the lover been? Who was this man who, like the prince in the story, had ridden up to liberate the woman in the sleeping wood? Some fellow writer, he supposed, or an academic. It wasn't hard to see Davina in the Lady Chatterley role and Naomi's father a servant on the estate.

The rain had stopped. It was damp and misty in the woods but when he left the forest road and was heading towards Kingsmarkham, a late sun had come out. The evening was fine and warm, all those clouds drawn in dense billowing masses to the horizon. The car splashed through a lingering puddle up onto his garage drive. Dora he found on the phone and hope sprang up, to be dispelled by her quick shake of the head. It had only been Neil's father, asking if she wanted a lift.

"What about me? Why shouldn't I want a lift?"

"He assumed you weren't going. People do take it for granted, darling, that mostly you aren't going."

"Of course I'm going to my own daughter's house-warming party."

It was unreasonable to be put out of temper by this. Wexford was enough of a psychologist to know that if he was disconcerted, this was due to guilt. Guilt that he took Sylvia for granted, loved her routinely, put her second to her sister, had to make himself think of her lest he came half-way to forgetting her existence. He went upstairs and changed. He had intended putting on a sports jacket and cords but rejected these in favour of his best suit, his only really good suit.

Why did he worry so much about that stupid girl, that affected actressy ridiculous Sheila? Using those terrible adjectives about her, even to himself, nearly made him groan aloud. Alone in the hall, he picked up the phone and dialled her number. Just on the chance. When it rang more than three times and the recorded voice hadn't come on, he felt another resurgence of hope. But no one answered. He let it ring twenty times and then he put the receiver back.

Dora said, "You look very smart." And, "She won't do anything silly, you know."

"I'd never even thought of that," he said, though he had.

The house Sylvia and her husband had bought was on the other side of Myfleet, about twelve miles away. A Rectory was what it had been in the days when the Church of England thought nothing of putting the incumbent of a benefice into a damp, unheated, ten-bedroomed mansion on five hundred pounds a year. Sylvia and Neil had wanted it, had the late-twentieth-century scorn of anything suburban and had hardly been able to wait until they could afford to leave their five-roomed semi-detached. This longing for a "real house" was one of the few matters they agreed on, as Wexford and Dora had observed in a recent discussion. But no incompatible couple could have striven more earnestly to stay together than these two, accumulating more and more joint possessions, contriving to depend more and more on each other's services and support.

Sylvia, now she had her Open University degree, had a rather good job in the County Education Department. She seemed to like putting impediments in her own way so that she had to rely on Neil's presence and Neil's promises, just as he took on more entertaining and more foreign trips so that he could rely on hers. But buying this house, a further ten miles away from where she worked and in the opposite direction to his grandsons' school, seemed to Wexford to be going too far. He remarked on it to Dora as he drove carefully along the winding lanes to Myfleet.

"Life's hard enough without turning it into an obstacle race."

"Yes. Has it occurred to you Sheila might be there tonight? She's invited."

"She won't be there."

She wasn't. Sylvia told him she wasn't coming—well, she had told him a week ago she wasn't coming—before he could ask. He wouldn't have asked, anyway. From past scenes and shows of bitter resentment, he knew the consequences of asking.

"You're looking very smart, Dad."

He kissed her, said the house was lovely, though it seemed bigger and starker than he remembered from the one occasion on which he had seen it before, but there was no denying it was a great place to have a party. He walked into the drawing-room, which was already crowded. The whole place wanted decorating, cried out with icy tears for central heating. A great log fire in the Victorian mock baronial fireplace looked good and the heat of fifty bodies would provide the warmth. Wexford said hallo to his son-in-law and accepted a glass of Highland Spring, much embellished with ice, lime slices and mint leaves.

Everybody knew who he was. It was not exactly unease he could sense as he moved among them so much as caution, a drawing in upon themselves, a perfunctory self-examination. This was truer now than it had once been, with the current campaign against drinking and driving, and he could see men glance at glasses holding an obvious inch of whisky as they wondered whether they could pass it off as apple juice or fall back on the old justification: "My wife's driving."

Then he saw Burden. Part of a group that included Jenny and some of Sylvia's fellow educationists, the inspector stood silent, the large glass in his hand really containing apple juice.

If it wasn't, Mike had gone mad and asked for half a pint of Scotch. He edged his way over, having found a congenial companion for the best part of the evening.

"You're looking very smart."

"You're the third one who's seen fit to comment on my appearance. In those very words. Am I generally such a rag-bag? The head model of the Oxfam catwalk?"

Burden made no reply but gave Wexford one of his small tight half-smiles accompanied by a little lift of the eyebrows. Himself dressed in charcoal cashmere sweater over a white polo neck, charcoal washed-silk bomber jacket and designer jeans, he had perhaps not quite achieved the desired effect. Not, at least, in Wexford's eyes.

"Since we're into personal remarks," Wexford said, "that get-up makes you look like a trendy vicar. The proper occupant of this house. It's the dog-collar effect."

"Oh, nonsense," Burden said huffily. "You always say something like that, just because I don't invariably look as if I've got 'fuzz' stamped all over me. Come in here. Bring your glass. This house is a real warren, isn't it?"

They found themselves in a place that might once have been morning-room, sewing-room, study or "snug." An oil heater burned in one corner, making a smell but not much heat.

Wexford said, "Look at these things in my glass. They look like marbles. Now what would you call them? Not ice cubes because they're round. How about ice spheres?"

"No one would know what you meant. You'd say 'round ice cubes.' "

"Yes, but that's a contradiction in terms, you'd have to—"

Burden interrupted him firmly. "The DCC phoned while you were with that Joanne woman. I talked to him. He says it's a farce talking about a 'murder room' four weeks after the event and he wants us out of Tancred by the end of the week."

"I know. I've an appointment to see him. Who calls it a murder room, anyway?"

"Karen does and Gerry, when they answer the phone. Worse than that. I heard Gerry say, 'Massacre room here.' "

"It doesn't matter much. We don't have to be there. I feel

it's in my grasp, Mike, I can't say more than that. I need one or two things to fall into place, I need one spark of enlightenment . . .''

Burden was looking at him suspiciously. "I need a whole lot more than that, I can tell you. D'you realize we haven't even got past the first hurdle—that is, how they got away from Tancred without someone seeing them?''

"Yes. Daisy made her 999 call at twenty-two minutes past eight. This, she says, was somewhere between five and ten minutes after they had gone. But she doesn't know and this is a very rough estimate indeed. If it was as much as ten minutes, the maximum time, I should think, they must have left at eight twelve, which is four minutes before Joanne Garland left. I believe that woman, Mike. I think she knows about time, like these punctuality addicts do. If she says she left at sixteen minutes past, that's when she left.

"But if they left at eight-twelve she must have seen them. That was the time she was walking about the front of the house, trying to see into the dining-room window. So they left later and it took Daisy nearer five minutes than ten to reach the phone. Say they left at seventeen or eighteen minutes past eight. In that case they must have followed Joanne Garland and might well be supposed to be driving faster than she—''

"Unless they took the by-road.''

"Then Gabbitas would have seen them. If Gabbitas is guilty of some involvement in this, Mike, it would be in his interest to say he had seen them. He doesn't say that. If he's innocent and he says he didn't see them, they weren't there. But to get back to Joanne Garland.

"When she reached the main gate she would have had to get out of her car and open it. Then she would have to drive through, get out and close it again. Is it conceivably possible that, with the killers' car close behind her, she could have done this and the other car not caught up with her?''

"We could try it out,'' Burden said.

"I have tried it. I tried it this afternoon. Only we left three minutes, not two, between the departure of car A and that of car B. I was driving car A at between thirty and forty miles per hour and Barry was in car B, driving as fast as he felt he safely could, forty to fifty, sometimes over fifty. He caught up with me as I got out the second time, to close the gates."

"Could their car have left *before* Joanne Garland arrived?"

"Hardly. She got there at eleven minutes past eight. Now Daisy says they didn't hear the gunmen in the house until a minute or two after eight. If they left at ten past, that allows them nine minutes at most in which to go upstairs and turn the place over, come down again, kill three people and wound a fourth and make their getaway. It could be done—just. But if they got away by the main road through the wood, they must have met Joanne coming in. And if they took the by-road road at, say, seven minutes past eight, they would have overtaken Bib Mew on her bicycle, since she left Tancred at ten to eight."

Burden said thoughtfully, "You make it sound impossible."

"It is impossible. Unless there's a conspiracy between Bib and Gabbitas and Joanne Garland and the gunmen, which is patently not so, it's impossible. It's impossible that they left at any time between five past eight and twenty past eight, yet we know they must have done so. We've been making an assumption all this time, Mike, based on a very flimsy piece of evidence. And that is that they came and left *in a car*. In or on some sort of motor vehicle. We've assumed there was a vehicle involved. But suppose there wasn't?"

Burden stared at him. At that moment the door opened and a crowd of people came in, all carrying plates of food, all in search of somewhere to sit. Instead of answering his own question, Wexford said, "It's supper. Shall we go and get something to eat?"

"We oughtn't to stay in here, anyway. It's not fair on Sylvia."

"You mean it's the party guest's duty to circulate and thus earn his fizzy water and taco chips?"

"Something like that." Burden grinned. He looked at his watch. "D'you know, it's gone ten. We've only got our baby sitter till eleven."

"Just time for a sandwich," said Wexford, who was pretty sure that such favourites of his wouldn't be on offer.

While consuming salmon mayonnaise, he talked to two of Sylvia's colleagues, then to a couple of old school friends. There was something in what Burden said about doing one's bit as a guest. Dora he could see involved in an amiable argument with Neil's father. He kept half an eye on Burden all the while and edged in his direction when the school friends went off for more chicken salad.

Burden took up their discussion at the precise point they had left it. "There must have been some sort of vehicle."

"Well, you know what Holmes said. When everything else is impossible, that which remains, however improbable, must be so."

"How did they get there without transport? It's miles from anywhere."

"Through the woods. On foot. It's the only way, Mike. Think about it. The roads were positively clogged with traffic. Joanne Garland going up and down the main way in. First Bib, then Gabbitas, on the by-road. But that doesn't bother them because they're making their way out in perfect safety—on foot. Why not? What had they to carry? A gun and some bits of jewellery."

"Daisy heard a car start up."

"Of course she did. She heard Joanne Garland's car start up. Later than she says, but she can hardly be expected to be precise about the time. She heard the car start up after both gunmen had gone and she was crawling to the phone."

"I believe you're right. And those two could have got away without anyone seeing them?"

"I didn't say that. Someone saw them. Andy Griffin. He was up there that night, bedding down in his hidey-hole, and he saw them. Close enough, I imagine, to know them again. The result of his attempt to blackmail them, or one of them, was that they strung him up."

After Burden and Jenny's departure, Wexford began to think about leaving himself. They had left it late, their sitter would be obliged to stay on for a further quarter-hour. It was almost eleven.

Dora had gone with a crowd of other women, under Sylvia's leadership, to be shown over the house. They were supposed to keep very quiet, so as not to wake the little boys. Wexford didn't want to ask Sylvia if she had heard from her sister because such a question might provoke a scene of jealousy and resentment. If Sylvia was feeling good about her new house and her present style of life, she would answer his inquiry like a rational person. But if she wasn't—and he couldn't tell what her state of mind was this evening—she would round on him with those old accusations of a preference for her younger sister. He managed to make his way over to Neil and ask him.

Of course Neil had no idea whether Sylvia had recently spoken to Sheila, only vaguely knew that Sheila had been having a relationship with a novelist he had never previously heard of and was unaware this relationship was over. Without this intention, he made Wexford feel foolish. He said he knew everything would be all right and excused himself to fetch a tray of coffee.

Dora came back, said that if he would like a real drink now, she would drive home. No, thanks, Wexford said, he'd found that once you'd had two of these mineral waters, you didn't really fancy alcohol. Shall we go then?

They had both become so delicately careful with this difficult child, bending over backwards not to offend her. But other people were leaving. Only a hard core of nocturnals would linger after midnight. They waited patiently for other people's coats to be brought, for those last-minute pleasantries to be exchanged with departing guests who stand upon their going.

At last Wexford was kissing his daughter and saying good-night, thank you, lovely party. She kissed him back, gave him a nice, warm, unresentful hug. He thought Dora was going a bit far saying, "Happy house"—what an expression!—but anything that helped along the aim to please.

There were various ways home. Through Myfleet itself or a slight detour north to bypass Myfleet, or south the long way via Pomfret Monachorum. He took the bypassing route, though that made it sound like a well-lit twin-track highway instead of what it really was, a cat's-cradle of lanes in which you had to know how to pick up the right threads.

It was very dark. There was no moon and the stars were hidden by a thick overcast. In these villages the residents had campaigned against street lighting, so that at this hour they appeared uninhabited, every house in darkness but for the occasional square of drawn-curtain gleam, behind which some night-bird stayed up.

Dora heard the wail of sirens a fraction before he did. She said, "Do your lot have to? At past midnight?"

They were on one of the long stretches of tree-bordered lane between habitations. The banks on either side reared up like defensive walls. In this dark canyon his car lights made a greenish radiance.

"That's not us," he said. "That's the fire service."

"How can you tell?"

"A different kind of howl."

The volume of sound increased and for a moment he thought the engine was coming this way, would meet them head-on. He had already begun to brake and was edging as close as he could to the near side, when the wail died again and he knew the engine—appliances, they called them—was on some other road ahead.

The car gathered speed and came up out of the trough of rampart-like banks and dense bushes and sheltering trees, out of the well of darkness. The banks fell away, the road widened and a plain, a spread of downland, opened before them. The sky ahead was red. On the horizon and seeping across the massed clouds was a smoky redness as it might be above some city. But there was no city.

A new wailing began. Dora said, "It's not in Myfleet. It's this side of Myfleet. Is it a house on fire?"

"We shall soon see."

He knew before they got there. It was the only thatched house in the neighbourhood. The redness intensified. From a dull smoky rust it grew richer until the glow in the sky was like a fire of coals, like the bright spaces between burning coal. Then they could hear it. A crackling, licking, rhythmic roar.

Already the road was cordoned off. On the other side of the barrier the two appliances were parked. The firemen were hosing with what looked like water but very likely wasn't. The noise the burning house made was like waves of the sea crashing on shingle in a storm, like the rushing tug-back of the tide. It deafened, it made speech impossible, commentary on the blaze, the urgent, streaming flames, silenced by it.

Wexford got out of the car. He went over the barrier. A fire officer started telling him to get back, to take the Myfleet road, and then he recognized who this was. Wexford shook his head. He wasn't going to attempt shouting above this noise. The heat from the fire reached out here, robbing the air of cold, of damp, blazing like some vast domestic hearth in an abode of giants.

Wexford gazed. He was near enough to imagine it seared his face. In spite of the recent rain, rain that had come too sparsely, the thatch had gone up like paper and kindling. Where it had been, where vestiges of it still were, the blackened roof-beams could be seen through the fierce roaring flames. The house had become a torch, but the fire was more alive than a torch flame, animal-like in its greed and determination, its passion to burn and destroy. Sparks spiralled up into the sky, dipping and dancing. A great burning ember, a lump of seething thatch, suddenly blew out of the roof and eddied towards them like a rocket. Wexford ducked and backed away.

When the burning thing was smouldering at their feet, he said to the fire officer, "Was there anyone in there?"

The arrival of the ambulance saved the man from answering. Wexford saw Dora reversing the car to make room. The fire officer moved the barrier and the ambulance came in.

"It was hopeless attempting anything," the fireman said.

A car followed. It was Nicholas Virson's MG. The car slowed and stopped, but not as if under control, not as if the driver had braked and gone into neutral and put the hand-brake on. It shuddered to a stop and stalled with a jump. Virson got out and stood looking at the fire. He put his hands over his face.

Wexford went back to Dora. "You can go on home if you like. Someone will bring me."

"Reg, what's happened?"

"I don't know. I can't imagine it started by chance."

"I'll wait for you."

The ambulance were bringing someone out on a stretcher. He had expected a woman but it was a man, the fire officer who had made a hopeless attempt. Nicholas Virson turned a stricken face to Wexford. Tears were running out of his eyes.

CHAPTER TWENTY-FIVE

The house was in part very old and had been strongly built in that distant past on a timber frame. Two of the main posts survived. They were of oak and nearly indestructible, standing up among the ashes like burnt trees. There had been no foundations and, like trees, these great uprights had been planted deep in the ground.

The blackened site looked more like the leavings of a forest fire than a burnt house. Wexford, surveying the ruins from his car, remembered how he had thought the Virsons' home pretty the first time he had seen it. A chocolate-box cottage with roses round the door and a garden fit for a calendar. The man who had done this took pleasure in the destruction of beauty, enjoyed defacement for its own sake. For by now Wexford had no doubt this was a deliberate act of arson.

To wreak death might have been the primary motive, but the lust for spoliation was there as well. It gilded the lily, it iced the cake.

. . .

The garage at the Thatched House had contained twenty two-gallon cans of petrol and about half that number of gallon cans of paraffin. These cans had been lined up against the sides of the garage, most of them against the common wall with the house. The thatched roof extended across the garage as well as the house itself.

Nicholas Virson had an explanation. Trouble in the Middle East had prompted his mother to lay in a store. Which particular trouble he couldn't remember but the oil had been there for years, against a "rainy day."

The days, Wexford thought, hadn't been rainy enough. A long severe drought had preceded the drizzle of the past few days. Investigators had found little evidence in that garage, there was very little left. Something had ignited those cans, a simple fuse. The discovery of the stub of an ordinary household candle, near-miraculously rolled away and out under the doors, led them to believe this was a vital item in the arson. What the investigator had in mind wouldn't always work, but in this case it *had* worked. Soak a piece of string not in petrol, but in paraffin, and insert one end in a can of paraffin. The single can of paraffin would be surrounded by cans of petrol. Tie the other end of the string round a candle halfway down, light the candle and two, three, four hours later . . .

The fire officer was badly burnt but would recover. Joyce Virson was dead. Wexford had told the press they were treating it as murder. This was arson and murder.

"Who knew about that petrol, Mr. Virson?"

"Our cleaner. The chap who comes to do the garden. I expect my mother told people, friends. I may have told people. I mean, for one thing, I remember a very good friend of mine who'd come over and was very low on juice. I put enough in his tank to get him home. Then there were the chaps who came to patch up the thatch, they went in there, used to have their sandwiches in there at lunch-time . . . ."

And a smoke, thought Wexford. "You'd better let us have some names."

While Anne Lennox was taking the names down, Wexford thought about the interview he had just had with James Freeborn, the Deputy Chief Constable. How many more murders were they to expect before a perpetrator was found? Five people had died so far. It was more than a massacre, it was a hecatomb. Wexford knew better than to correct the Chief Constable, to say something sarcastic, for instance, about hoping there wouldn't be another ninety-five deaths. Instead, he asked for the incident room at Tancred to be maintained just till the end of the week and permission was reluctantly granted.

But no more guards on the girl. Wexford had to assure him that there had been none that week.

"Something like that could go on for years."

"I hope not, sir."

Nicholas Virson asked if they were finished with him, if he might go.

"Not yet, Mr. Virson.

"I asked you yesterday, before we had much idea of the cause of this fire, where you were on Tuesday night. You were very distressed and I didn't press the question. I'm asking you again now. Where were you?"

Virson hesitated. At last he made that answer that is never true but nevertheless often given in these circumstances. "To be perfectly honest with you, I was just driving around."

Two of those phrases in conjunction. Do people ever "just drive around"? Alone, by night, in early April? In their home countryside where there is nothing new to see and no beauty spots to discover and go back to see in daylight? On a holiday trip perhaps, but in their own neighbourhood?

"Where did you drive?" he asked patiently.

Virson was no good at this. "I don't remember. Just around the lanes." He said hopefully, "It was a fine night."

"All right, Mr. Virson, what time did you leave your mother and start out?"

"I can tell you that. Nine thirty. On the dot." He added, "I'm telling the truth."

"Where was your car?"

"Outside, on the gravel, and my—my mother's beside it. We never put them in the garage."

No, you couldn't get them in. There wasn't room. The

garage was full of cans of fuel oil, waiting to go up when a flame reached them, running along a piece of string.

"And where did you go?"

"I've told you, I don't know, I just drove around. You know when I got back . . ."

Three hours later. It looked nicely timed. "You drove around the countryside for three hours? In that time you could have got to Heathrow and back."

An attempt at a sad smile. "I didn't go to Heathrow."

"No, I don't suppose you did." If the man wouldn't tell him he would have to guess. He looked at the sheet of paper on which Anne had written the names and addresses of those people who knew about the petrol *cache*: Joyce Virson's close personal friends, Nicholas Virson's friend who ran out of "juice," their gardener, their cleaner . . . "I think you've made a mistake here, Mr. Virson. Mrs. Mew works at Tancred House."

"Oh, yes. She works for us—er, me, as well. Two mornings a week." He seemed relieved at the change of inquiry. "That's how she came to help out at Tancred. My mother recommended her."

"I see."

"I swear by my life and all I hold sacred," Virson said passionately, "I had nothing to do with any of this."

"I don't know what you hold sacred, Mr. Virson," Wexford said mildly, "but I doubt if it's relevant in this case." He had heard the like of this often before, respectable men as well as villains swearing on their children's heads and as they hoped for heaven in a life to come. "Let me know where I can find you, won't you?"

Burden came up to him after Nicholas Virson had gone. "I went home that way too, you know, Reg. The place was in total darkness at eleven fifteen."

"No candle flame glimmering through the chinks in the garage door?"

"The aim wasn't to kill Mrs. Virson, was it? I mean, our perpetrator's quite ruthless, he wouldn't care if he killed her or not, but she was incidental, she wasn't his primary quarry?"

"No, I don't think she was."

"I'm going to get lunch. D'you want some? Today it's Thai or steak-and-kidney pie."

"You sound like the lowest form of TV commercial."

Wexford went outside with him and joined the short queue. From here only the end of the house was visible, the high wall and windows of the east wing. The shape of Brenda Harrison could be dimly seen behind one of these, rubbing at the glass with a duster. Wexford held out his plate for a wedge of pie with mashed potatoes and stir-fry. When he looked up again Brenda had disappeared from the window and Daisy had taken her place.

Daisy was not, of course, polishing the glass, but standing with her hands hanging by her sides. She seemed to be gazing into the distance, into woods and forest and far blue horizon, and to him her expression, as far as he could see, was ineffably sad. She was a figure of loneliness standing there, and it brought him no surprise to see her put up her hands and cover her face before she turned away.

His head lifted, Burden too had seen. For a moment he said nothing but took his plate of the rather brightly coloured scented food and a can of Coke with the glass upturned over it. Back in the stables, he said laconically,

"He was after her, wasn't he?"

"Daisy?"

"He's always been after her from the first. When he rigged up that fire it was Daisy he was after, not Joyce Virson. He thought Daisy would be there. You told me the Virsons had been here to persuade her to come to them on Tuesday night, dinner and stay the night."

"Yes, but she refused. She was adamant."

"I know. And we know she didn't go there. But our perpetrator didn't. He knew the Virsons had tried to persuade her and knew too that *they went back in the afternoon to renew their attempt*. Something must have happened to make him certain Daisy would be spending that night at the Thatched House."

"Not Virson then? He knew she wouldn't be there. You keep saying 'he,' Mike. Must it be a 'he'?"

"It's something one takes for granted. Perhaps one shouldn't."

"Perhaps one should take nothing for granted."

"Bib Mew worked for the Virsons as well as up here. She knew about the petrol in the garage."

"She listens outside doors," said Wexford, "and perhaps hears only imperfectly what is said on the other side of them. She was here on the evening of March the eleventh. A lot of the—shall we say manoeuvres?—of that night depend on her evidence. She's not very bright but she's sharp enough to live alone and hold down two jobs."

"She looks like a man. Sharon Fraser said the people who left the bank were all men, but if one of them had been Bib Mew, would she know this wasn't a man?"

"One of the men in the bank stood in the queue with a handful of green banknotes. Since the pound went, we don't have green notes in this country. Which country does? Exclusively green banknotes?"

"The United States," said Burden.

"Yes. Those notes were dollars. Martin was killed on May the thirteenth. Thanny Hogarth is an American who may well have had dollars in his possession when he came here but he didn't arrive in this country until June. How about Preston Littlebury? Vine tells us he does most of his transactions in dollars."

"Have you seen Barry's report yet? Littlebury deals in antiques, that's correct, and he imports them from Eastern Europe. But his main source of income at the present time is from the sale of East German army uniforms. He was a little shy of admitting it but Barry got it out of him. Apparently, there's a terrific market for that sort of memorabilia here, tin hats, belts, camouflage gear."

"But not guns?"

"Not guns, so far as we know. Barry also says that Littlebury has no bank account here. He has no account with that bank."

"Neither do I," Wexford retorted, "but I've got my famous Transcend card. I can use any branch or any bank I like.

Besides, the man in the queue with the notes was there simply *to change those notes into sterling*, wasn't he?''

"I've never seen this Littlebury, but from what I hear of him he's not the sort to pick up a gun and make off with it. I'll tell you what, Reg, it was Andy Griffin in that queue, with the dollars Littlebury paid him in.''

"Then why did he never change them? Why did we find them in his parents' house?''

"Because he never reached the head of the queue. Hocking and Bishop came in and Martin was killed. Andy picked up the gun and made off with it. He took it to sell it and he did sell it. That was what he blackmailed the purchaser about, possession of the incriminating gun.

"He never changed those dollar bills. He took them home and hid them in that drawer. Because he had a . . . well, a sort of superstitious fear of being seen with them after what had happened. One day maybe he'd change them but not now, not yet. He'd get far more for that gun than fifty pounds, anyway.''

Wexford said slowly, "I believe you're right.''

The kind, hospitable gesture would have been an offer to put Nicholas Virson up. Perhaps Daisy had made the offer and it had been declined. On the same grounds as Virson's refusal to stay the night once before?

Now, though, things were surely different. The man had nowhere to go. But in Daisy's sky his star was setting, no matter how brightly it had once shone, when it had occasioned that wonder and that adoring gaze. Thanny Hogarth had displaced it. What are you when the moon doth rise?

It was normal behaviour for someone of her age. She was eighteen. But a tragedy had happened, Nicholas Virson's mother was dead, his house had burnt down. Daisy must have offered hospitality, and her offer, simply because of the existence of Thanny Hogarth, been spurned.

Until he found somewhere more permanent, Nicholas Virson had taken a room at the Olive and Dove. Wexford found him in the bar. Where he had acquired the dark suit he wore Wexford couldn't guess. He looked sombre and lonely and much older than when they had first met at the Infirmary, a sad man who had lost everything. As Wexford approached he was lighting a cigarette and it was to this act that he made reference.

"I gave up eight months ago. I was on holiday with Mother in Corfu. It seemed a good time, no stress and all that. It's a funny thing, when I said nothing would make me start again, I couldn't have foreseen this. I've been through twenty today already."

"I want to talk to you about Tuesday night again, Mr. Virson."

"For God's sake, must you?"

"I'm not going to ask you, I'm going to tell you. All you have to do is confirm or deny. I don't think you'll deny it. You were at Tancred House."

The unhappy blue eyes flickered. Virson took a long draw on his cigarette, like a smoker who has rolled up something stronger than tobacco. After a hesitation he made the classic reply of those he would have defined as of the criminal classes. "What if I was?"

At least it wasn't, "I might have been."

"Far from 'driving around,' you drove straight up there. The house was empty. Daisy was out and no police officer was there. But you knew all that, you knew how it would be. I don't know where you parked your car. There are plenty of places where it would be hidden from those coming in up the main drive or along the by-road.

"You waited. It must have been cold and boring but you waited. I don't know when they came in, Daisy and young Hogarth, or how they came. In his van or her car—one of her cars. But they came at last and you saw them."

Virson murmured into his drink, "Just before twelve."

"Ah."

He was muttering now, sullenly. "She came back just before midnight. There was a young chap with long hair driving." He lifted his head. "He was driving *Davina's* car."

"It's hers now," said Wexford.

"It isn't right!" He hammered with his fist on the table and the barman looked round.

"What? Not to drive her grandmother's car? Her grandmother's dead."

"Not that. I don't mean that. I mean, she's mine. We were practically engaged. She said she'd marry me 'one day.' She said that the day she came out of hospital and came to our house."

"These things happen, Mr. Virson. She's very young."

"They went into the house together. The fellow had his damned arm round her. A fellow with hair down on his shoulders and two days' growth of beard. I knew he wouldn't come out again that night, I don't know how, but I knew. There was no point in waiting any longer."

"Perhaps it was as well for him he didn't come out."

Virson gave him a defiant glare. "Perhaps it was."

Wexford believed part of it. He thought he could easily believe all of it. Believe but not prove. He was nearly there, anyway, he nearly knew what had happened on March the eleventh, he knew the motive and the name of one of the two who had carried it out. As soon as he got home he was going to phone Ishbel Macsamphire.

The post had come late, after he had left for work. Among the things for him was a parcel from Amyas Ireland. It contained Augustine Casey's new novel, *The Lash*, in proof. Amyas wrote that this proof copy was one of five hundred Carlyon Quist were issuing, Wexford's number 350, and he should hang on to it as it might be worth something one day. Especially if he could get Casey's signature on it. Amyas was right, wasn't he, in thinking Casey was a friend of Wexford's daughter?

An instinct to hurl it into the log fire Dora had lighted he suppressed. What quarrel did he have with Augustine Casey? None. Once Sheila was over the worst, the man had done them all a favour.

He tried the Edinburgh number but no one answered. She was out and might not be in till ten, say, or ten thirty. If someone was out at eight you could be pretty sure she'd be out till past ten. He would while away the time with Casey's book. Even if Mrs. Macsamphire said yes to all his questions, it was such a little thing to go on, so thin on its own . . .

He read *The Lash*, or tried to. After a time he realized he had understood nothing, and this wasn't because his attention was elsewhere, he simply found it incomprehensible. A good deal of it was in verse and the rest seemed to be a conversation between two unnamed persons, probably but not certainly male, who were deeply concerned about the disappearance of an armadillo. He had a look at the end, could make nothing of it, and, turning the pages back, saw that this verse alternating with talk about the armadillo persisted through the pages, apart from one which was covered with algebraic equations and one which contained the single word "shit" repeated fifty-seven times.

After an hour he gave it up and went upstairs to find Davina Flory's tree book, which was on his bedside cabinet. The place he had reached he saw he had marked with the guide to the town of Heights, Nevada, which Sheila had given him, the town where Casey was to be, doubtless by now had become, writer-in-residence at the university.

At least she was no longer going there. Love was a strange business. He loved her and therefore should have wished for her what she wished for herself, to be with Casey, to follow him to the ends of the earth. But he didn't. He was overwhelmingly glad she was to be denied what she wanted. He sighed a little and turned the pages, looking at the colour plates of forest and mountain, a lake, a waterfall, the city centre with a gold-domed capitol building.

The advertisements were more entertaining. Here was a company which made Western boots to order "in all the radiant colours of the spectrum, in this world and outer space." Coram Clark Inc. was a gunsmith in Reno, Carson City and Heights. He sold all kinds of weaponry that made Wexford's eyes open wide. Rifles, shotguns, hand-guns, airguns, ammo, reloading, scopes, black powder, said the advertisement. The whole spectrum of Browning, Winchester, Luger, Beretta, Remington and Speer. Highest prices paid for used guns. Buy, sell, trade, gunsmithing. You didn't need a licence in some American states, you could carry a gun with you in your car, provided you displayed it openly on the seat. He remembered what Burden had said about students being allowed unrestrictedly to buy guns for self-defence when a serial killer was rumoured on some campus . . .

Here was an ad for the finest popcorn in the West and another for personalized licence plates in iridescent colours. He tucked the guide into the back of *Lovely As a Tree* and read for half an hour. It was nearly ten and he tried Ishbel Macsamphire again.

Of course, he couldn't ring her at all much after ten. That was a rule he tried to stick to, that you phone no one after ten at night. Two minutes to ten and someone was ringing the doorbell. The rule about not calling anyone after ten applied equally to calling *on* them, in Wexford's opinion. Well, it wasn't quite ten.

Dora went to the door before he could stop her. He never thought it wise for a woman to go alone to answer the door in the evening. Not a sexist attitude but prudent, until the day all women went to Karen's trouble and learned a martial art. He got up and went to the living-room door. A woman's voice, very low. So that was all right. A woman collecting something.

He sat down again, opened *Lovely As a Tree* at the place where the marker was and his eye fell once more on the gunsmith's advertisement. Coram Clark Inc . . . One of those names he had heard recently in some quite other context. Clark was a common name. But whose name was Coram? *Coram*, he remembered from long-ago school days when Latin was obligatory, meant "on account of"—no, "in the presence of." There was a mnemonic they learned of prepositions which took the ablative:

> *a, ab, absque, coram, de,*
> *Palam, clam, cum, ex and e,*

Sine, tenus, pro and prae,
Add super, subter, sub and in,
When state, not motion, 'tis they mean.

Amazing to remember that after all these years . . . Dora came in with a woman behind her. It was Sheila.

She looked at him and he looked at her and he said, "How marvellous to see you."

She went up to him and put her arms round his neck. "I'm staying with Sylvia. I got the night of the party wrong and came yesterday. But, darling, what a fabulous house! And what's come over them, abandoning suburbia at last? I'm loving it but I thought I'd tear myself away and sort of pop over."

At ten fifteen. It was just like her. "Are you all right?" he said.

"Well, no. I'm not all right. I'm wretched. But I'll be okay."

He could see the proof of Casey's book lying on one of the sofa cushions. Casey's name wasn't in letters an inch high as it might be on a finished copy, but it was plain enough to see. "*The Lash* by Augustine Casey, uncorrected proof, probable price in UK £14.95."

"I said a lot of horrible things. Do you want to talk it through?"

Wexford's involuntary shudder made her laugh.

"I'm sorry, Pop, for all the things I said."

"I said worse things and I'm sorry."

"You've got Gus's book." There was a look in her eyes that recalled the adoration he had hated to see, the slavish spellbound devotion. "Did you like it?"

What did it matter now? The man was gone. He would lie to be kind. "Yes, very good. Very fine."

"I didn't understand a word of it myself," said Sheila.

Dora burst out laughing. "For goodness' sake, let's all have a drink."

"If she has a drink she'll have to stay the night," said Wexford the policeman.

• • •

Sheila stayed for breakfast, then went back to the Old Rectory. It was long past Wexford's usual time for going to work but he wanted to speak to Mrs. Macsamphire before he left. For some reason, not fully comprehended, he wanted to speak to her from here, not the stables or his own phone in the back of a car.

Just as ten seemed the latest you could phone anyone, so nine was the earliest. He waited till Sheila was gone, dialled the number and got a young woman with a very thick Scots accent who said Ishbel Macsamphire was in the garden and could she call him back? Wexford didn't want that. The woman might be one of those who grudged every penny spent on long-distance calls, who might *have* to grudge every penny.

"Would you mind asking her if she could spare the time to speak to me now?"

While he waited something strange happened. He remembered quite clearly who it was shared his name with a gunsmith in Nevada, who it was had Coram for a middle name.

CHAPTER TWENTY-SIX

It took him all day because he couldn't start until the late afternoon. All day and half the night because when it was midnight in Kingsmarkham it was still only four in the afternoon in the Far West of the United States.

Next day, after four snatched hours of sleep and enough transatlantic phone calls to give Freeborn apoplexy, he was driving along the B 2428 towards the main gate of Tancred. The night had been very cold, laying a sharp silvering on wall and fencepost and a shimmering hoar frost to outline young leaves and twigs that were still leafless with glitter. But the frost was gone now, melted in strong spring sunshine, the sun high and dazzling in a bright-blue sky. Much the same as in Nevada.

Every day the trees grew greener. A sheen of green became a mist, the mist a veil, the veil a deep brilliant cloak of it. All the weariness of winter was being covered up by green, dirt and damage concealed as the new growth hid accumulated litter and detritus. A dark grim picture, a grey lithograph had its spaces gradually filled in by a brush loaded with soft viridian. The forest to the right of him and the woods to the left were no longer dark masses but a variegated shimmering green that the wind stirred, lifting branches and swaying them to let in gusts of light.

A car was parked ahead, by the gate. Not a car, a van. Wexford could just make out the figure of a man who seemed to be tying something to the gatepost. They approached slowly. Donaldson stopped the car and got out to open the gate, pausing as he did so to examine the confection of blues, greens and violets of which the latest offering was composed.

The man had returned to his van. Wexford got out of the car and went over to it, necessarily passing behind it in order to speak to the occupant of the driving seat. This viewpoint afforded him the sight of a bunch of flowers painted on the van's side.

The driver was young, no more than thirty. He wound down the window.

"What can I do for you?"

"Detective Chief Inspector Wexford. May I ask if all the flowers on the gate have come from you?"

"So far as I know. Other people may have brought floral tributes but not so far as I know."

"You're an admirer of Davina Flory's books?"

"My wife is. I don't have time to read."

Wexford wondered how many times he had heard those two statements before. Particularly in the country, a certain kind of man found it macho to make these disclaimers. Blame it on the wife. Reading, specially fiction, was for women.

"So all these have been tributes from your wife?"

"Eh? You have to be joking. They're my advertising campaign, aren't they? The wife wrote out the bits to put on the cards. It looked like a good place. Constant comings and goings. Whet their appetites and when they're really intrigued, tell 'em where they can order similar for themselves. Right? Now, if you'll excuse me, I've got a date at the crematorium."

Wexford read the label on this fan-shaped bouquet of irises, asters, violets and forget-me-nots, a peacock's-tail design. No quotation from the poets this time, no apt line from Shakespeare, but: "Anther Florets, First Floor Kingsbrook Centre, Kingsmarkham" and a phone number.

Burden, when Wexford told him, said, "Drawing a bow at a venture, isn't it? And a pretty expensive bow. Would it ever work?"

"It has, Mike. I saw Donaldson surreptitiously taking down the address. And you surely remember all the people who said they wished they could get flowers like that. Hinde, for another. You did yourself. You wanted them for your wedding anniversary or something. So much for my sentimental speculations."

"What sentimental speculations?"

"I'd got as far as imagining this was some ancient who'd been Davina's lover in the dim past. Might even have been Naomi's dad." He said to Karen, who walked by with a clipboard, "We can get this lot packed up today, ready to move out. Mr. Graham Pagett can have his technology back with the grateful thanks of Kingsmarkham CID. Oh, and a polite letter thanking him for doing his bit to fight crime."

"You've found the answer," said Burden. It was a statement, not a question.

"Yes. At last."

Burden looked hard at him. "Are you going to tell me?"

"It's a lovely morning. I'd like to go outside somewhere, in the sun. Barry can drive us. We'll take the car down through the woods somewhere—and we'll make it a long way from the hanging tree. That gives me the creeps."

His phone started bleeping.

The small amount of rain that had come had done little to soften the ground. A track indented by the wheels of Gabbitas's Land Rover showed tyre-marks that had probably been made last autumn, penetrating the wood. Vine slid the car along this path, careful not to break down the verges. This was in the north-eastern part of the Tancred woods, the track branching northwards off the by-road, not far from where Wexford had seen Gabbitas and Daisy standing side by side in the evening light, her hand touching his arm.

And as the car followed the winding track through a break in the clustering hornbeams, the great sweep of a green ride opened before them. This grassy road, cut between the central and the eastern woodland, opened a long vista, a green canyon or roofless tunnel, at the end of which was a U-shape of sunlit blue dazzle. At this end and all the way between the walls of tree trunks the sun lay unbroken on the smooth turf, shadows shortened to nothing at noon.

Wexford remembered the figures in a landscape, the air of something romantic that had pervaded the scene that evening, and he said, "We'll park here. It's a fine view."

Vine put on the hand-brake and the engine died. The silence was broken by the chattering, tinny, unmusical song of birds in the giant limes, ancient survivors of hurricanes. Wexford wound down the window.

"We know now that the killers who came here on March the eleventh didn't come in a car. It would have been impossible to have done so and to have got away unobserved. They didn't come in a car or a van or on a motor bike. We only assumed they did, but the evidence for doing so was strong. I think I can say anyone would have made that assumption. However, we were wrong. They came on foot. Or one of them did."

Burden looked up at him sharply.

"No, Mike, there were two involved. And no motor transport or any other sort of transport was used. The time too, we've known that from the beginning. Harvey Copeland was shot at a few minutes past eight, say two or three minutes past, the two women and Daisy at perhaps seven minutes past. The get-away was at ten past or a minute or so earlier, at which time Joanne Garland was still on her way to Tancred.

"She reached the house at eleven minutes past. When the get-away was made she would have been coming up the main drive. While she was ringing and knocking at the door, trying to see in the dining-room window, while she was doing all these things, those three people were already dead. And Daisy was crawling across the dining-room and hall floors to reach the phone.''

"She didn't hear the bell?"

"She thought she was dying, sir," said Vine. "She thought she was bleeding to death. Perhaps she did hear it, perhaps she can't remember."

Wexford said, "It would be wrong to put much credence on what Daisy said happened. For instance, it's unlikely anyone suggested the noise upstairs was made by the cat when the cat normally rampaged about at six, not eight. It's very unlikely her grandmother suggested the noise came from the cat. We should also discount everything Daisy said about a get-away car.

"We'll leave these circumstantial things for a moment and enter a more speculative area. The reason for Andy Griffin's murder was certainly to silence him after he had made a blackmail attempt. What was the reason for the murder of Joyce Virson?"

"The perpetrator thought Daisy would be in the house that night."

"You believe that, Mike?"

"Well, Joyce Virson wasn't blackmailing him," Burden said with a grin, which he decided was misplaced and changed to a scowl. "We've agreed he was after Daisy. He must have been after Daisy."

"It seems a roundabout way of doing things," said Wexford. "Why go to the trouble of fixing a timed arson, risk killing others, when Daisy was most of the time totally alone at Tancred and easily accessible? On Freeborn's orders she was no longer protected by night and the stables were empty. I have never believed the burning of the Thatched House was designed to kill Daisy.

"It was designed to kill someone but not Daisy." He paused and looked from one to the other speculatively. "Tell me, what have Nicholas Virson, John Gabbitas, Jason Sebright and Jonathan Hogarth in common?"

"All male, all young," said Burden, "all English-speaking . . ."

"They live round here. Two are American or part American."

"All Caucasian, middle-class, quite good-looking or very good-looking . . ."

"They're Daisy's admirers," said Vine.

"That's right, Barry. You've got it. Virson is in love with her, Hogarth is very keen, and Gabbitas and Sebright, I think, are considerably attracted. She's an attractive girl, a lovely girl, it's not surprising she should have many admirers. Another one was Harvey Copeland, rather old for her, more than old enough, in fact, to be her grandfather, but a handsome old fellow for his age and once a 'wow on campus.' And a real prince in bed, according to Davina."

Burden was making his Puritan Father face, mouth pulled down, eyebrows drawn together. Laid-back Vine's dead-pan look didn't change.

"Yes, I know the idea of old Harvey initiating Daisy sexually is disgusting. It's disgusting and it's also a bit of a joke. Remember there was no coercion, probably not even much persuasion. Just a thought, wasn't it? You can hear Davina saying it: 'It was just a thought, my dear.' Only a monomaniac with ideas of revenge very different from most people's would have held it viciously against Harvey Copeland. And who, anyway, would have known?"

"Her father knew," Burden put in. "Joanne Garland wrote and told him."

"Yes. And no doubt Daisy told people. She would have told a man who loved her. She didn't, however, tell me. I had to find it out from her mother's best friend. Let's go to Edinburgh now, shall we?" Burden's involuntary glance out of the window made Wexford laugh. "Not literally, Mike. I've brought you far enough for one morning. Let's imagine ourselves in Edinburgh at the Festival in the last week of August and the first of September.

"Davina always went to the Edinburgh Festival. Just as she went to Salzburg and Bayreuth, to the Passion Play at

Oberammergau every ten years, to Glyndebourne and to Snape. But last year the book festival was held, as it is every other year, and she was due to speak on the subject of autobiographers and also to appear on some literary panel. As a matter of course, Harvey went with her and she also took Naomi and Daisy along.

"This time they took Nicholas Virson as well. An unlikely devotee of the arts but that wouldn't, of course, be his reason for going. He merely wanted to be with Daisy. He was in love with Daisy and took every opportunity of being near her.

"They didn't stay with Ishbel Macsamphire, an old college friend of Davina's, but they visited her, or Davina and Harvey did. Naomi was ill in the hotel with flu. Daisy had her own occupations. No doubt Davina talked to Ishbel about her hopes for Daisy, mentioning, in what terms we don't know but can guess at, that she had a boy friend called Nicholas.

"Then one day Mrs. Macsamphire saw Daisy across the street with her boy friend. They weren't near enough to be introduced but no doubt she waved and Daisy waved back. It wasn't until the funeral that they met again. I overheard Mrs. Macsamphire say to Daisy that they hadn't seen each other since the festival, 'when I saw you with your young man.' Of course I thought she meant Nicholas, I have always believed she meant Nicholas."

"She didn't?"

"Joanne Garland said she met Nicholas Virson in the street at the end of August and thought of speaking to him about this sex-initiation business with Copeland. She didn't in fact do this, but that's irrelevant here. Virson later told me that he and his mother were in Corfu around the end of August. Now none of this meant much. He could have been in Kingsmarkham and next day he could have been in Corfu, but it did make it unlikely he was in Edinburgh as well at much the same time."

"You asked him?" Burden said.

"No, I asked Mrs. Macsamphire. I asked her this morning if it was a fair-haired man she'd seen with Daisy and she said, no, he was dark and very good-looking."

Wexford paused and said, "Shall we get out and walk a bit?

I've a fancy to walk the length of this ride and see what's at the end. There's something in human nature, isn't there, always wanting to know what's at the end?''

The scenario he had dreamt about took a new shape. He saw the sequence re-form itself as he got out of the car and began to walk along the grassy path. Rabbits had cropped it close so that it resembled mown turf. The air was very soft and mild, scented with something fresh and vaguely sweet. Blossom was coming out on the cherry trees among the uncurling copper-coloured leaves. He saw the table again, the woman lying across it with her head in a plateful of blood, her daughter opposite her in a swoon of death, the young girl crawling, bleeding. Something like a rewind mechanism took him back one minute, two, three, to the first sounds in the house, the deliberately created noise as things in Davina's room were overturned, the jewellery already taken earlier in the day . . .

Burden and Vine walked in silence beside him. The end of this roofless tunnel showed itself slowly approaching but with no opening vista of further woods, further wide green path. It was as if the sea might be beyond or the termination of the ride a cliff edge, a precipice you would step off into nothing.

"There were two of them," he said, "but only one came into the house. He came on foot and entered by the back door at five minutes to eight, well-primed, knowing his way, knowing exactly what he would find. He was wearing gloves and carrying the gun he had bought from Andy Griffin, who picked it up in the bank after Martin was shot.

"Perhaps he would never have thought of doing any of this but for the gun. He had the gun, so he had to use it. The gun gave him the idea. The barrel he had already changed, he knew all about that, how to do it, he'd been doing it since he was a boy.

"Armed with the gun, containing the five cartridges which remained in the chamber, he came into Tancred House and went upstairs by the back stairs to carry out the plan of disarranging Davina's bedroom. The people downstairs heard him and Harvey Copeland went to look, but by that time the man with the gun had come down the back stairs and was approaching the hall along the passage from the kitchen regions. Harvey, on the bottom stair, turned round when he heard footsteps and the gunman shot him, so that he fell backwards over the lowest stairs.''

"Why shoot him twice?" Vine asked. "According to the report the first shot killed him.''

"I said something just now about a monomaniac with ideas of revenge very different from most people's. The gunman knew what had been proposed for Harvey Copeland and Daisy. He fired two shots into Davina's husband in a passion of jealousy, to be revenged on him for his temerity.

"He then proceeded into the dining-room, where he shot Davina and Naomi. Lastly, he shot Daisy. Not to kill her, only to wound.''

"Why?" said Burden. "Why only to wound? What happened to disturb him? We know it wasn't the noise the cat made upstairs. You say the get-away was at ten past or a minute earlier, while Joanne Garland was still coming up the main drive, but in a sense there was no get-away at all. Only an escape on foot. Wasn't it Joanne ringing the front-door bell that sent him running for the back way out?''

Vine said, "If it was her, she'd have heard the shots or she'd have heard the last one. He left because he had no more cartridges in the gun. He couldn't shoot her again just because he missed first time.''

The green ride had come to an end and in a way it was a cliff edge, a precipice. The borders of the forest, the meadows beyond, in the distance the downs, rolled away below them. A huge bank of cumulus welled up from the horizon but a long way from the sun, too far away to diminish its brightness. They stood and gazed at the view.

"Daisy crawled to the phone and made her 999 call,'' Wexford said. "She was not only in pain and in a state of terror, of fear for her life, but in mental anguish too. In those minutes she may have been afraid to die, but she wanted to die too. For a long time afterwards, days, weeks, she wanted to die, she had nothing to live for.''

"She had lost her whole family,'' said Burden.

"Oh, Mike, that had nothing to do with it," Wexford said with sudden impatience. "What did she care for her family? Nothing. Her mother she despised just as Davina despised her, a poor feeble thing who had made a foolish marriage, never got any sort of career together, had been dependent on her own mother all her life. Davina I think she positively disliked, hated her domination of her, those plans for university and travel, even making up her mind what Daisy should study, even arranging her sex life for her. She must have regarded Harvey Copeland with a mixture of ridicule and revulsion. No, she disliked her nearest relations and felt no grief for them after they were dead."

"She grieved, though. You told me you'd seldom seen such grief. She was constantly crying and sobbing and wishing she was dead. You just said so."

Wexford nodded. "But not because she'd seen the brutal murder of her family. She grieved because the man she loved and who she believed loved her had shot her. The man she loved, the only person in the world she loved, and who she thought would risk everything for love of her, had tried to kill her. That's what she thought.

"When she crawled to that phone, in those minutes, the whole world was overturned for her because the man she was passionately in love with had tried to do to her what he had done to those others. And she went on grieving—for that. She was alone, abandoned, first in the hospital, then with the Virsons, lastly alone in the house that was now hers, and he never got in touch, he never tried, he never came to her. He had never loved her, he had wanted to kill her too. No wonder she said to me with great melodrama: 'The wound is in my heart.' "

As the clouds peaked to reach the sun and the chill came quickly, they turned and began to walk back. It was immediately cold, a hard April breeze cutting the air.

They came to the car, got into it and drove back up the by-road to pass the front of the house. Vine brought the car across the flagstones very slowly. The blue cat was on the stone coping of the pool with one of the goldfish between its paws.

The scarlet-headed fish floundered and flapped, twisting its body this way and that. Queenie patted it pleasurably with the paw that was not holding it down. Vine started to get out of the car but the cat was much too quick for him. She was a cat and he was only a man. She snatched up the flailing fish in her mouth and ran for the front door, which was a crack ajar.

Someone inside closed it behind her.

CHAPTER TWENTY-SEVEN

Most of the technology was gone. The blackboard was gone, and the phones. The two men Graham Pagett had sent were carrying out the master computer and Hinde's laser printer. Someone else was carrying a tray of cacti in pots. One end of the stables had been restored to what it had once been, a young girl's private retreat.

Wexford had never seen it this way before. He had never seen what Daisy had here, the taste that had governed the furnishings, the kind of pictures she had on the walls. A Klimt poster, glazed and framed, showed a nude in shimmering, all-revealing gold drapery; another was of cats, a huddle of cuddly Persians nestled together inside a satin-lined basket. The furniture was wicker, white, and prettily upholstered in blue-and-white-check cotton.

Was this her taste or Davina's for her? A house-plant, unwatered and the worse for wear, stood drooping in a blue-and-white Chinese pot. The books were all Victorian novels, their covers pristine, doubtless unread, and works on a variety of subjects from archaeology to present-day European politics, from language families to British Lepidoptera. All chosen by Davina, he thought. The only book that looked as if it had ever been taken out of that bookcase was *The World's Greatest Cat Photos*.

He motioned Burden and Vine to sit down in the little sitting-room area that had been created by the impending move. For the last time the caterers' van had arrived outside, but that must wait. He thought once more, angry with himself, how Vine had guessed and spoken up only a day or two after the murders.

"There were two," Burden said. "All the time you've insisted there were two of them, but you've only mentioned one. That leaves only one conclusion, as far as I can see."

Wexford looked sharply at him. "Does it?"

"Daisy was the other one."

"Of course she was," Wexford said and he sighed.

"There were two of them, Daisy and the man she loved," Wexford went on. "You told me, Barry. You told me at the start and I didn't listen."

"I did?"

"You said, 'She inherits, she's got the best motive,' and I said something sarcastic about supposing she'd got her lover to wound her in the shoulder and that she wasn't interested in property."

"I don't know that I was altogether serious," said Vine.

"You were right."

"It was done for the property then?" Burden asked.

"She wouldn't have thought of it if he hadn't put the idea into her head. And he wouldn't have done it if she hadn't backed him up. She wanted freedom too. Freedom and the place hers and the money, doing what she liked, unconstrained. Only she didn't know what it would be like, what murder *is*, what people look like when they are killed. She didn't know about the blood."

He thought suddenly about Lady Macbeth's words. No one had bettered them in four hundred years, no one had said anything more psychologically profound. Who would ever think people had so much blood in them?

"She told me very few lies. She didn't have to, she hardly had to act. Her misery was real. It's not hard to imagine what that would be like, trusting someone absolutely, your lover, your accomplice, knowing exactly what he will do and what your own part is. And then it goes wrong and he shoots you too. He's a different person. For a split second before he shoots you, you can see it in his eyes, not love but hatred; you know you've been deceived all along the line.

"So her unhappiness was real—no wonder she kept saying she wanted to die and what would become of her—until one night, when she was here alone with Karen, he came back. He didn't know about Karen and he came at the first opportunity to tell her he loved her, he had only wounded her to make it look real, to put her in the clear. He had always meant to do that and he knew it would be all right, he was a crack shot, he never missed. It was in the shoulder he shot her, taking the smallest risk. But he couldn't have warned her, could he? He couldn't have told her in advance, he couldn't have said, 'I'm going to shoot you too, but trust me.' "

"But he had to take risks, didn't he? For the Tancred estate and the money and the royalties, all to be theirs and no one else's? He couldn't phone her, he didn't dare. The first chance he got, assuming she'd be alone, he came to the house to see her. Karen heard him but she didn't see him. Daisy did. He wasn't masked, that was Daisy's own invention. She saw him and no doubt, remembering how he had betrayed her, how he had shot her too, she thought he had come back to kill her."

Burden objected, "Shooting her at all was a hell of a risk. She could have taken against him and told us everything."

"He calculated that she was too deep in it herself for that. Give us a clue as to who he was, arrest him, and he would tell us of her part in it. And he counted on her being too much in love with him to betray him. He was right, wasn't he?

"The day after he had come to the house in the dark, he came back when she really was alone. He told her why he had shot her, that he loved her, and of course she forgave him. After all, he was all she had. And after that she was a changed girl, she was happy. I've never seen such a transformation. In spite of everything, she was happy, she had her lover back, all would be well. I'm a fool, I thought it was for Virson. Of course it wasn't. She turned on the fountain. The fountain played to celebrate her happiness.

"For a day or two the euphoria persisted—until the memory of that night began coming back. The red table-cloth and Davina's face in a plate of blood and her harmless silly mother dead and poor old Harvey spread out on the stairs—and that crawl to the phone.

"It wasn't, you see, what she had meant at all. She hadn't known it would be like that. It was a kind of game in the planning and the rehearsing. But the reality, the blood, the pain, the dead bodies, this she hadn't meant at all.

"I'm making no excuses for her. There are no excuses. She may not have known what she was doing, but she knew three people would be murdered. And it was a case of *folie à deux*. She couldn't have done it without him but he wouldn't have done it without her. They egged each other on. Kissing the gunner's daughter is a dangerous business."

"That expression," Burden said. "What does it mean? Someone said it to me the other day, I can't think who it was . . ."

"It was me," said Vine.

"What does it mean? It means being flogged. When they were going to flog a man in the Royal Navy, they first tied him to a cannon on deck. Kissing the gunner's daughter was therefore a dangerous enterprise.

"I don't think she knew Andy Griffin would have to be killed. Or, rather, would be killed because this lover of hers saw killing as the way out of difficulties. Someone annoys you? Then kill him. Someone happens to look at your girl friend? Kill him.

"It wasn't Daisy he was after when he rigged up that candle-and-string contraption among the petrol cans at the Thatched House. It was Nicholas Virson. Nicholas Virson dared to look at Daisy, dared in fact to think Daisy might actually marry him. Who would have supposed that Virson, who had asked Daisy to stay with him and his mother, wouldn't in fact be home that night but keeping tabs on Daisy up at Tancred?

"She's more like her grandmother than she knows. Did you notice how few friends she has? Not a single young woman has been to the house all this while—apart from the young women *we* put there. There was just one young woman at the funeral, a granddaughter of Mrs. Macsamphire.

"Davina had a few friends from the distant past, but *their* friends were Harvey Copeland's. Naomi had friends. Daisy hasn't one young woman to confide in, to be a companion to her now. But men? She's very good with men." Wexford said it ruefully. He thought for a moment how very good she had been with him. "Men quickly become her slaves. An interesting point is how short-sighted Davina Flory must have been in believing she would have to provide a lover for Daisy, as if Daisy wasn't ably equipped to provide her own. But they were self-absorbed, both these women, grandmother and granddaughter, and therefore unable to see further than their own noses.

"Daisy met her lover in Edinburgh, at the Festival. We shall find out how eventually. Perhaps at a fringe theatre or a pop concert. Her mother was ill and no doubt she escaped from her grandmother whenever she could. She was very sore at the time. Davina's suggestion about Harvey was rankling. Not, I think, because she was shocked or even disgusted but because she was coming more and more to hate all this interference in her life, this manipulation. Was it going to go on, this arranging her life for her? It wasn't getting better, it was worse.

"But here was a young man who had no regard for her family, no reverence for any of them, someone she must have seen as a free spirit, independent, dashing, bold. Someone like herself, or like she could be if she too was free.

"Whose idea was it? His or hers? His, I think. But perhaps it would never have got off the ground if he hadn't kissed the gunner's daughter. And afterwards he said, 'All that could be *ours*. The house, the acres, the money.'

"It was a simple enough plan and would be simple enough to do. Provided he was a good shot and he was, he was a very good shot. He hadn't a gun and that was a stumbling block. For him, being without a gun was always a stumbling block. It was as if his right arm wasn't complete without a gun in the hand on the end of it. Did they perhaps discuss the possibility of there being a shotgun or a rifle at Tancred? Had old Harvey ever shot birds on the land? Would Davina have allowed that?"

Burden waited a while. Then, when Wexford looked up, said, "What happened when they got back here?"

"I don't think *they* did get back here. Daisy did with her family. She went back to school and perhaps it seemed to her like a dream, a wicked day-dream that now would never become real. But one day he turned up. He got in touch with her and they arranged to meet, here, in the stables, where she had her own place. No one saw him, no one came here but Daisy. How about it then? When were they going to do it?

"I don't think Daisy knew whether her grandmother had made a will or not. If there was a will and Naomi and Harvey were dead, she would certainly be the sole beneficiary. If there wasn't a will, Davina's niece Louise Merritt might get some of it. Louise Merritt died in February and I don't think it was a coincidence that they waited until after she was dead to carry out their plan.

"Before that, some months before, probably, in the autumn, he encountered Andy Griffin in the wood. How it came about I don't know, how many meetings they had before the proposition was put, but Andy offered to sell him a gun and the offer was accepted.

"He changed the barrel, he knew all about that. He'd brought the tools with him." Wexford explained how he had found the advertisement in the Heights town guide. "The gunsmith's name was Coram Clark. I knew I'd come across that name somewhere before, but I couldn't remember where. All I knew was that it was someone's name and someone connected with the case. It came back to me at last. Right at the start of things, the day after the murders, when the press were up here.

"There was a reporter on the local paper asked a question at the press conference. He hung about outside waiting for me afterwards. He was very cocky, very self-assured, a very young man, no more than a boy, dark, good-looking. He'd been at school with Daisy, he volunteered that information, and then he told me his name. He was talking about what he intended to call himself professionally, he hadn't made up his mind.

"He has now. I saw it on a by-line in the *Courier*. He's calling himself Jason Coram, but his full name is Jason Sherwin Coram Sebright."

"Sebright had also told me, apropos of nothing in particular, that his mother was American, that he visited his mother in the United States. It was still a long shot.

"He told me that at the funeral. He sat next to me. Later on, he went about interviewing mourners, in a manner which he proudly told me was his US TV technique. He came here to get an exclusive interview out of Daisy the day after the prowler came round the house. I met him coming out and he told me all about it. He was going to call his piece 'The Masked Intruder,' and perhaps he was, for all I know.

"A handsome dark young man Ishbel Macsamphire had seen her with in Edinburgh. That description might equally have fitted John Gabbitas, but Gabbitas is an Englishman with parents in Norfolk.

"Jason Sebright had just left school. He was eighteen, soon to be nineteen. In September he entered the journalism training scheme with a job on the *Courier*. He might easily have gone to Edinburgh at the same time as Daisy was there. I waited until it was ten A.M. their time in Nevada and put through calls to Coram Clark the gunsmith's in the city of Heights. Coram Clark himself, called Coram Clark Junior, wasn't there but to be found, they told me, at their store in downtown Carson City. Eventually, I spoke to him. He was keen to help. American enthusiasm I find very refreshing. You don't get so much of that 'might have been' stuff over there. Had he a young relative called Jason Sebright in this country?

"He told me that he was familiar with the technique of

changing the barrel of a gun. He told me that the tools for performing such a task would not be bulky and could easily be brought into this country. The Customs wouldn't know what they were for. But he had no young relative called Jason in the United Kingdom or anywhere else, for that matter. His daughters, *née* Clark, were married. He has no sons. He was an only child and has no nephews. He had never heard of Jason Sherwin Coram Sebright.''

"I'm not surprised," Burden said, not very pleasantly. "It was about as far-fetched as you could get."

"Yes. Still, it paid off. Coram Clark had no young relatives in this country or anywhere else. But he gave me a lot of useful information. He said he ran a class in marksmanship at a local shooting range. He also sometimes had students from Heights University working for him, driving, working in the store, even in some cases doing gun-repair jobs. Students at American universities do quite frequently work their way through college.

"After I put the phone down I remembered something. An American university sweat-shirt with letters on it that had nearly faded or been washed out. But I was sure there had been a capital ST as well as a capital U.

"My friend Stephen Perkins of Myringham University was able to tell me what those letters stood for by the simple expedient of examining the CVs in the applications of prospective creative-writing students. Stylus University, California. They call everything a city over there and Stylus is pretty small for a city, but it has a police force and a police chief, Chief Peacock. It also has eight gunsmiths. Chief Peacock came back to me, he was even more helpful than Coram Clark, and he told me firstly that Stylus University had a military history course on its syllabus and secondly that one of the gunsmiths frequently employed university students to help out in the store on evenings and weekends. I phoned the gunsmiths, one after another. The fourth one I phoned remembered Thanny Hogarth very well. He had worked for him up to the end of his final semester last year. Not because he needed the money. His father was wealthy and making him a big allowance. He loved guns, he was fascinated by guns.

"Chief Peacock told me something else. Two years ago two students at Stylus were shot on campus, both men and with one thing in common. They had, successively, 'dated' the same girl. Their killer was never found."

The bicycle was resting up against the house wall.

"Interior Creators" were inside the house, restoring the dining-room. Their van was parked close up against the window Pemberton had broken. Today the fountain was not playing. In the limpid dark water the surviving red-headed fish swam round and round.

The three policemen stood by the pool. "The second time I went to his house," Wexford said, "I saw the tools among a lot of other stuff on a table. I didn't know what they were. I think I even saw a gun barrel, but who knows what a gun barrel is when it's not in a gun?"

Burden said suddenly, "Why didn't he marry her?"

"What?"

"Before the shootings, I mean. If she'd changed her mind about him he'd have got nothing. She'd only to say she didn't want him any more after what he'd done and he'd be out in the cold."

"She was under eighteen," Wexford said. "She'd have needed parental consent. Can you imagine Davina allowing Naomi to consent? Apart from that, you're an anachronism, Mike, you're out of your time. They're children of today and I daresay marriage didn't occur to them. Marriage? That was for the old people and the Virsons of this world.

"Besides, it sets you apart, this kind of thing, a massacre. Maybe they understood something, that they were marked, that no one else would do for them, they had only each other."

He went up to the house and was about to pull the sugar-stick rod when he saw that the door was slightly ajar, left that way no doubt by "Interior Creators." He hesitated, then walked in, Burden and Vine behind him.

They were in the *serre*, the two of them, so intent upon what they were doing that for a second they heard nothing. The two dark heads were close together. On the glass table were a pearl necklace, a gold bracelet and a couple of rings, one a ruby with diamond shoulders, the other set with pearls and sapphires.

Daisy was looking at her own finger, the third finger of her left hand, on which Thanny Hogarth had perhaps just placed his engagement ring, a great cluster of diamonds, nineteen thousand pounds' worth of diamonds.

She turned round. She stood up when she saw who it was and, with an involuntary gesture of the diamonded hand, swept all the jewellery onto the floor.